The
G
BRIDE

The G.I. BRIDE

EILEEN RAMSAY

ZAFFRE

First published in Great Britain in 2018 by
ZAFFRE PUBLISHING
80–81 Wimpole St, London W1G 9RE
www.zaffrebooks.co.uk

A CIP catalogue record for this book is
available from the British Library.

ISBN: 978–1–78576–243–7

Also available as an ebook

1 3 5 7 9 10 8 6 4 2

Typeset by IDSUK (Data Connection) Ltd
Printed and bound in Great Britain by Clays Ltd, Elcograf S.p.A.

Zaffre Publishing is an imprint of Bonnier Zaffre,
part of Bonnier Books UK
www.bonnierzaffre.co.uk
www.bonnierbooks.co.uk

*This novel is dedicated with respect to the
American air force personnel for whom
I babysat while I was a student in Edinburgh.
I learned so much and yes, had so much fun.
Thank you.*

Chapter 1

May 1941

Sighing with tiredness, April made her way up from the ward where she'd been working. It had been a long, long day at St Thomas' and she'd spent most of her time running backwards and forwards with bed pans and changing dressings. So many, many dressings on so many poor people who had been injured. Still, despite her weariness, she was buoyed by the ward sister's words to her as she left: 'Carry on the way you're going, Harvey, and by the time we're finished with you, you'll be able to run the hospital in an emergency singlehandedly!'

She wasn't sure about that, but after eighteen months of training, she felt like she was finally becoming a proper nurse, and goodness knew, she was now an expert at setting broken bones and stitching cuts.

She thought back to her first weeks in training. How different life was then. When she'd started, there had been no bombs and though the country had just declared war, life had been carrying on much as normal. No one then had any idea of how truly awful war would be in London.

'Got tomorrow off, love?' called Cyril, the hospital night watchman, startling her out of her gloomy thoughts as she passed him.

She summoned a smile. 'Now wouldn't that be lovely, Cyril. After a beautiful day like today, it looks like tomorrow might be a nice day for a picnic in the park . . . for those who have time to picnic.'

He laughed. 'That's not you nor me, lass. I hardly remember parks and picnics. I used to love listening to the brass bands when I was a lad, though. This damned war – pardon my language – has spoiled the parks; air raid shelters where roses used to bloom. I ask you!'

'There are still flowers, Cyril, and even duck ponds. And I read somewhere that some famous American bands plan to come – Hands Across the Sea or something like that. I'd best be off; I hate cycling in the dark, although there is a lovely moon tonight. See you tomorrow.'

'You take care, love. That moon is beautiful, but it's a bomber's moon and no mistake. Go as quickly as you can.'

April pushed open the main door and paused for a moment, taking in the glorious sight of the Houses of Parliament bathed in moonlight. But Cyril's words had sent a shiver down her spine. He was right, it was a bomber's moon. Beautiful and full and illuminating the streets in an ethereal silver glow. Her father would have noticed too, and he'd be standing at the window, anxiously awaiting her return. She knew he wouldn't budge until she was safe with him, even if the air raid siren went. Ever since her beloved mother had died when she was eight, it had just been the two of them, with no other family to call their own, and her father watched out for her safety almost too much. It had been a little suffocating when she was younger, but now, older and wiser at the grand old age of twenty, she understood, because if anything happened to either of them, they'd be all alone in the world, and the thought completely terrified her.

She hurried around to the bicycle stand. Only three were there; many nurses came in on special buses, but as she only lived a few miles away in Camberwell, she could cycle to the hospital easily. Still, even a couple of miles can seem like a very long way when your legs were as tired as hers, she thought grimly.

As she wheeled her bike to the gate, she looked up into the night sky, not looking for twinkling stars but for enemy aircraft. A perfect May night, dark blue sky, stars flung generously against the darkness and that beautiful moon. There were, of course, no street lights, but at least tonight she'd be able to see well enough. But so would the Germans. Hopefully they'd stay away for once. She crossed her fingers and set off.

Out of the gate she went, on to Walworth Road, heading for home. Head down, pedalling furiously, ears attuned to every sound: the purring of a luxury car, the aggressive rumble of yet another military vehicle, the startled screech as a lorry driver realised he was too far over and almost in the wrong lane.

'Be there soon, Dad,' April said to herself quietly. Then she yelped in fear as a van loomed up out of the darkness and almost brushed her aside. She waited where she was until it was quite some way away and then, her trembling stilled, began again to pedal. How her calves ached. She walked miles every day in the hospital, down long corridors, up one staircase and down another, back and forth between beds and sinks, but cycling, she decided, used different muscles – and each and every one was crying out for a rest. Never mind, not too far now, April, just one more push.

She was just turning into Croxted Road, when she heard it: the terrifying sound that made her blood run cold and goose pimples break out all over her body. Bombers.

Glancing up quickly, she could see the first group of enemy planes. She tried counting but lost her place as wave after wave of enemy aircraft moved in across the capital. Sobbing now, April increased her pace. Sweat was pouring into her eyes, and her breath was coming in fast pants. She recognised the signs of panic, she'd seen it often enough in the patients brought in after an air raid.

She wobbled and fell off her bike, landing on her knees on the road. 'Oh, go away and leave us in peace,' she cried, as she heard the first explosion and then another and yet another. And they were close. Flames began to illuminate the sky and the noise was deafening.

She stood up and looked around for her bicycle; she had to keep moving. In her panic, she couldn't see it, but as she looked around helplessly, another wave of enemy bombers arrived, and the world exploded around her.

Her bike forgotten, April ran desperately towards her street, barely noticing the falling glass and masonry. Then a massive explosion threw her to the ground and she lay, stunned, as all around her it seemed as if the world was disintegrating. She squinted through the dark and the dust, shivering. Despite the warmth of the night and the flames leaping all around her, she felt cold, so very cold. She looked up and spotted the remains of the green and white awning that usually hung above the greengrocer on

4

the corner. Now it flapped in the heat of the blaze. She watched it in a daze until it fell to the ground amongst the broken glass that had once so proudly proclaimed 'Charlie's Fruit Bowl'.

Dear God, no! That was *her* street. The street she'd grown up on, played with her friends in, and walked along with her dear mother, was on fire. She could see it. She could actually feel the heat, but she refused to believe it. The buzzing of the enemy aircraft overhead brought her back to her senses and she jumped to her feet.

'Daddy!' she screamed. She had to reach him. He would be at the window watching for her, as he was every night. Or would he have heard the planes and hurried to the Anderson shelter? Oh, please. For once let him have just thought of himself. But she knew he wouldn't. There was nothing on earth that would make her father take shelter if he thought his precious daughter was in danger. She was all he had left in the world.

'Oh, Daddy, please be safe. I'm coming.'

She began to run. Past Charlie's Fruit Bowl, past her friend Silvia's house, now gutted and on fire, on through the rubble and the falling bricks, when finally she heard the eerie, terrifying noise that Londoners had been hearing almost every night for the past few months – the air raid siren. Too late, she thought, far too late. The wailing went on and on until she felt she could bear it no longer.

She was heading straight for the flames that were sending sparks dancing against the blue-black sky. Soon she would be able to see the polished brass door knocker in the shape of a wily fox that Dad insisted was the envy of their neighbours, and in no time at all she would be inside and Dad would be saying, 'There's your slippers, love. I'll just pop into the kitchen and turn on the gas under the milk.'

A huge explosion, followed by another and yet another, made the whole street shake and houses tremble. All around her were falling bricks, exploding windows, collapsing walls, and she could see nothing for the great billowing clouds of dust and smoke. She had lost her sense of direction but blindly pushed forward, falling twice over what turned out to be a broken chimney pot and, a few steps further on, a large flower pot, a pot that had once been home to a rose-bush that grew the most beautifully scented pink roses from early May to late September. Mum's last rose.

She turned around blindly, her nostrils full of the smell of cordite and dust and the awful black smoke that enveloped her, making her choke. Where was her home? It wasn't where she had expected it to be. Instead, a large hole full of bricks seemed to have appeared and surely that green velvet was not one of the sitting-room curtains?

She stood still, so shocked that she couldn't move, couldn't think. Then she ran forward, dropped to her knees and began to pull the bricks away. Her father was here, he *must* be, buried under this rubble, and she would find him. She would!

The noise and the confusion around her faded away as she focused on just one thing: finding her father. He must be here. Just waiting for her to find him. She dug on, oblivious to the pain in her hands and the glass cutting into her knees and the tears pouring down her face, and muttering over and over again, 'Daddy! Hang on, Daddy!'

Suddenly, an arm caught her around the waist and tried to pull her back. 'Come on, love, get to a shelter. You'll get yourself killed.'

'Leave me alone! Get away from me! I have to find my father.' She pushed the man away with a strength borne of panic and desperation, then turned and kept digging. Suddenly, a sharp pain brought her back to her senses. She looked at her hand. In the red glow of the flames, she could see that it was covered in blood. No matter, she could tend to it later. Wiping it down her jacket, she carried on throwing bricks and blocks of rubble out of the way.

The arms came back again, stronger this time. 'I'm sorry, love, you've got to get out of here.' The voice was kind but firm. 'I'll look for your dad, don't you worry. If he's there, we'll find him. Now, get to the shelter.'

'I'll take her.' Another voice suddenly appeared. And April found herself being enveloped in warm arms. 'Come now, April, there's nothing you can do here. Let me get you to the shelter, and we'll come back just as soon as it's safe.'

She squinted at the man. It was Mr Cary, one of the local fire wardens. She struggled against him as he wrapped his arms around her and pulled her away. 'Get off me!' she screamed. 'Let me look!'

'April.' The voice was low and insistent. 'If your father is injured, he's going to need you to look after him. But at this rate, you'll get yourself killed. Come on, love, you need to get away from here. Let the firemen do their job.'

April collapsed, sobbing on his shoulder. 'I have to find him. Please, help me. What'll I do if he's dead? Where will I go?'

'Shh, girl. Time enough to worry about that. But first, you need to be safe.' The man lifted April and carried her unsteadily over the rubble. April opened her eyes and looked up. High in the night sky, the moon shone down on the hellish scene, mocking them all with its deceptive beauty. It was the moon's fault, she thought. If it wasn't for that huge, stupid moon, she'd be with her dad now, drinking her cocoa. If she could reach up and pull it out of the sky, she would.

Suddenly, her breath caught in her throat. She tried to breathe in, to take in the horrible, dusty air, but nothing came.

'Please, help . . .' she wheezed.

And still she could not draw in a breath. The world around her started to darken, the noise to fade, until it all disappeared.

∽∞∽

April woke with a start. She was lying on a bench with a scratchy grey blanket covering her legs. The light was dim, but she could hear voices and knew that she was not alone. She lay for a moment, wondering why she felt so terrible. Then it came crashing back. She sat up with a gasp.

'Daddy?'

A woman appeared at her side. It was Mrs O'Connor, who had lived in the house opposite for as long as April could remember. 'April, thank goodness you've come back to us. We're in the shelter. One of the wardens carried you in here. What on earth have you been doing to yourself, dear? Your hands are a mess.'

'Have they found him?'

Mrs O'Connor shook her head sadly. 'I'm so sorry, April, your house took a direct hit. And there's not much left of mine, neither. They're out there now, lookin' for survivors. But you best stay here with me for now, love. It's not safe and the all-clear hasn't sounded, though I've not heard a plane for a bit.'

'But if there's an air raid I should get to the hospital! They'll need all the staff there to help.' She sat up and swung her legs on to the floor. A wave of dizziness suddenly hit her as she tried to stand.

'No, love, they'll just have to manage without you tonight. You're in no fit state to treat anyone.'

April looked down and noticed that her hands were roughly bandaged. 'What happened to them?'

'Accordin' to the warden, you cut your hands trying to dig the rubble away. I've tried to clean them as best I can, but for now, this'll 'ave to do.'

April stared at the kindly woman. She couldn't take it in. Her father, their house, the memories of her mother; they were all she had left in the world. If she lost this, then what did she have? Overwhelmed, she started to shake.

'Oh, Mrs O'Connor, what will I do if he's gone? There's no one else. There's nothing left.' She sobbed violently in the woman's arms.

Mrs O'Connor wrapped the blanket around April's shoulders and tried to soothe her. 'There, there, my love. There's many in the same boat. We'll all manage one way or another. And you're not alone. All of us, we'll look out for each other, you hear. Worst comes to worst you can come stay with me sister in Sussex. That's where I'll be goin' soon as I can. Not many bombs dropping down that way. Lucky buggers.'

Suddenly another voice cut in. 'Ah, April, you're back with us. I've brought you some sweet tea. Now come on, girl, buck up. Tears won't get you anywhere.'

April looked up, startled at the brusque tone. It was Mrs Osborne, the vicar's wife. April turned her face away. She was the last woman she wanted to see right now.

Mrs O'Connor leaped to April's defence. 'Mrs Osborne, the girl's just lost 'er 'ome and maybe her father and has nowhere to go. I think she's entitled to a bit of cryin'.'

'Don't you worry, April, you can come and stay with me and the reverend till you're back on your feet. Our boy Theo's away doing his duty, though we've got our refugees . . . Did I tell you about them, Mrs O'Connor?'

'Only a few times, Mrs O. Such a kind and charitable lady you are.' April wasn't too far gone that she didn't notice the sarcasm in Mrs O'Connor's voice.

'Well, they do say charity begins at home. And there's room in our house for one more refugee with no home to call their own.'

At these words, April sobbed even harder.

'I think it might be better if you left her with me, Mrs O. Not sure you're helpin' much.'

'Rightio, I see you've got this one under control. What a treasure you are, Mrs O'Connor. But bring her round to the vicarage as soon as the all-clear's sounded, won't you? I'll take good care of her.'

'Bloody woman,' Mrs O'Connor cursed under her breath once she'd left. 'Sorry, love,' she said to April. 'But I've been cleanin' for her for nigh on ten years, and she 'asn't got a

10

charitable bone in her body. All for show, that one. And those poor refugees work hard for her charity, believe me.'

'I don't want to live with her. It's her fault that Theo left me for that girl.' Remembering the heartbreak of Theo's betrayal brought fresh tears to April's eyes. She'd been in love with him all her life, and she'd thought he loved her, but it turned out she was wrong. And Mrs Osborne had taken great delight in telling her all about it; she'd never thought April was good enough for her precious boy.

Mrs O'Connor snorted. 'If Theo had an ounce of gumption, he'd have stood up to his mum and gone with whichever girl he liked best.'

'Well, he clearly didn't want me enough. I won't live with that woman. I can't. And Dad might still be alive.' April started sobbing again.

'Shh, now, love. He might be, but you need to take what's offered right now. And Reverend Osborne is a fine gentleman. He'll make sure you're all right. And then, maybe, once the dust has settled, so to speak, you can look to your future again. Maybe go and stay with some other family.'

'I don't have any other family. Just me and Dad.'

'Come now, there must be someone. Maybe on your mum's side?'

April moved away from the older woman's comforting embrace. 'I don't know. I was only eight when she died and I don't remember much about any of them. They came from Cornwall, but we never visited after the funeral. Although my mum sometimes talked about her childhood and the adventures she had with her twin sister. But I'm not sure I ever met her and I never knew why. The search for her father hasn't finished yet.'

'There you go. Once you've got yourself together, and your poor hands are healed, then maybe you can go to Cornwall to look for her.'

'But what about my training? I can't not work. How will I live?'

'Think, love. They have hospitals in Cornwall, don't they? Get down there and find yourself another hospital, and sure as eggs is eggs, the rest will follow.'

∞

Over the next few weeks, April thought about Mrs O'Connor's words continually. The search for survivors had continued late into the night, and April herself had cycled to every nearby hospital in the days following the bombing, walking amongst the injured, desperately hoping to find her father. But with so many weeks passed now, April had come to accept he was gone.

Life with the Osbornes was proving trying. Although Reverend Osborne was incredibly kind, his work in the grieving and shattered parish meant he was rarely home. Mrs Osborne, however, was another matter entirely. Mrs O'Connor had been right about her charity being for show. She had two Belgian refugees living with her, and they worked from morning till night in the vicarage, trying to keep it to Mrs Osborne's impossible standards. Now Mrs O'Connor had left to live with her sister, there was even more work to do, as, according to Mrs Osborne, 'You can't find good help these days for love nor money,' and Madame Goossens and Madame Martens, two sisters who had fled Belgium with nothing but the clothes they stood up in, were run ragged by her constant demands.

April was able to avoid the worst of it as she worked such long hours. She also managed to avoid Mrs Osborne for the most part, claiming study or taking on extra shifts just so she wouldn't have to talk to her. One day, however, much to April's surprise, Mrs Osborne was waiting up for her when she got back from the hospital.

'Oh, April, you'll never guess what,' she gushed as soon as April walked into the living room.

'Hello, Mrs Osborne, is everything all right?'

'It's so much more than all right.' She brandished a letter in April's face. 'I've just had word that Theo will be coming home on leave in a month. Isn't that wonderful?'

April felt her stomach sink. 'Theo?' she said faintly.

'Yes. And I rushed over to speak to Charlotte to see if she knew anything about it, which of course she did.' Mrs Osborne giggled girlishly. 'Those two are *awfully* close.'

April smiled stiffly. What was there to say after all? She was glad Theo was well, but he had told her when he left that he wanted to be with Charlotte. The years of friendship that had started when they were just eight and ripened into love as they got older was merely a 'childish crush', according to him. But not for April. She had loved him with all her heart, and though the pain of the break-up had lessened slightly, she still missed their friendship terribly. She often wondered what she would do if he wanted her back, because although she still loved him, she wasn't sure she could ever really trust him again.

'So, I was wondering,' – Mrs Osborne's voice cut into her thoughts '– if you might enquire as to whether there is a room for you at the nurses' home so Theo can have his old room back while he's here. I think he might find it a little . . . unsettling . . . to have you in his room, don't you think?'

'Yes, of course. That's wonderful news. I'm sure he'll be happy to see you. I will speak to matron tomorrow, but rooms are scarce and . . .' April trailed off.

'Yes, well, you can stay here if you must, but do try.' April kept her expression carefully neutral, then turned and left the room without another word. What on earth was she going to do now?

∽

In her room – well, Theo's really – she threw herself on the bed and stared at the ceiling. On top of everything else, how could she cope with seeing Theo again? It was bad enough living with his mother, but to see him and Charlotte together and blissfully happy would be unbearable.

She thought back over the years. She couldn't really remember a time when Theo hadn't been part of her life. After her mother had died, April had found herself isolated at school as her friends found it difficult to know what to say. But not Theo. He made a point of including her in his games, bringing her home to tea when her house was empty, trying to make her laugh. April smiled as she remembered. They'd become a pair without even noticing. And though Theo was lively and funny when he was at school, only April knew his other side. The quieter, gentler side that was passionate about music and longed to play cello in an orchestra.

But for all his talents, he'd struggled with his school-work, whereas April found it easy. So she'd help him after school, and then listen while he played his cello for her. They had been sweet years, she thought, and Theo was wrong to say it had been a childhood crush. She knew he'd loved her as much as she'd loved him. But as they got older, Mrs Osborne suddenly didn't seem to like her being at the house any more, so they'd gone out instead, exploring London and finding secret places where they could share kisses. She touched her lips at the memory. She could still feel his soft lips on hers . . .

Stop it, April! You'll only make yourself feel worse. But she couldn't help it. The memories came crowding back. Memories of walks in the park, tea in the Lyon's Corner House, evenings at the picture house watching Fred Astaire and Ginger Rogers. She started humming to herself, 'Cheek By Cheek.'

'Oh, I have to stop this,' she said out loud. But then the memory of the night her heart broke came back to her suddenly. Theo had been due to leave for his army training in two days, but before he left, they were going to a church dance. She'd noticed that Theo had been getting more withdrawn recently, and they hadn't seen each other quite as often, but she'd put it down to him worrying about going to war and had tried to be as supportive as she could. She'd been looking forward to the dance for ages, a chance at last to spend time with Theo, but that night, instead of spending time with her, Theo had volunteered to play the piano, while Charlotte Miller, the bishop's daughter, sang. She'd tried to hide her jealousy, but it had been difficult. Charlotte was so pretty and had such a beautiful voice that she felt plain and shabby by comparison.

She'd been sipping her orange squash and talking to an old school friend when Mrs Osborne had come up to her. 'April, my dear. How lovely to see you. Did you come alone?'

'No, Mrs Osborne, Theo brought me.' As Mrs Osborne knew. April had tried very hard to hide it from Theo, but she had begun to dislike Mrs Osborne intensely.

'He's such a good boy. So lovely of him to still bring you even though he really wanted to bring Charlotte. Such a marvellous voice, don't you think? And she does voluntary work at the orphanage. Such a lovely, giving girl. It's no wonder my Theo is so smitten. Did you know, they spent all last Saturday working together at the soup kitchen? Anyway, I must get on. Do pass on my regards to your father.'

And just like that, she'd shattered all of April's dreams. Theo had told her he couldn't see her last weekend because he was helping his father, but it seemed he'd been lying. She'd looked at Charlotte with her jet-black hair, blue eyes and pale skin. It was no wonder he'd rather be with her. Not only was she beautiful, but she was talented *and* kind, and her father was a bishop, which made her good enough for Theo in Mrs Osborne's critical eyes. She'd stared at the two of them, noticing the secret smiles they exchanged as they played, and her heart had twisted in jealousy and anguish.

She'd said a hasty goodbye to her friend and rushed home in tears.

When Theo had come to see her the next morning, he'd refused to come in. Instead he stood awkwardly on the doorstep, looking at her with a belligerent expression. After the night before, when she'd cried herself to sleep, April had been in no mood to pander to him, so she'd stood with her arms folded and waited for him to speak.

'Why on earth did you rush off like that? You know I'm leaving tomorrow. The least you could have done was say goodbye.'

'I didn't feel well, that's all.'

'Really? You seemed all right to me.' His tone was petulant.

'Well, your mother told me a few things that made me feel a bit sick. According to her, you are besotted with Charlotte. So besotted in fact that you only took me to the dance out of duty, and you spent the whole day with her last weekend when you said you were busy with your father. And you have the cheek to be cross with me?' She stopped and looked away. She didn't want to cry in front of Theo.

Theo looked shocked. 'She shouldn't have said that.'

'Well, are you? Besotted with Charlotte? Have you been stringing me along all this time?'

Theo looked down at the ground; a guilty child who'd been found out. 'April . . . You know I love you . . . but I think I love you more as a friend than anything else.' He looked up again, his eyes sad. 'I wanted to tell you, but there never seemed to be a good moment. I never intended for my feelings towards Charlotte to grow, but when Mother suggested that perhaps I could accompany her when she sang in church, and then she started inviting her to lunch after the service, and we'd help at the orphanage . . . well, I suppose . . .'

'What do you suppose, Theo?' April was surprised her voice was so steady.

'April, I think you're wonderful. Look at you, you're so beautiful and you're caring. I really admire that you're going to be a nurse. And we've hardly been apart since we were eight. I don't know any more whether what I feel for you is more a childish crush or a proper grown-up love.

17

And Charlotte . . . Well, it's different with her. Do you understand what I mean?'

April's heart was breaking, but she stood her ground. 'No, Theo, not really.'

Theo took a deep breath, then looked at her with sincere brown eyes, dark hair swept back from his high forehead. April tried not to notice how handsome he was.

'April, now that there's a war on, I think it's only fair that you don't wait for me. I might not come back, and I'd hate to think of you waiting for me when . . .' He stopped again. 'There's no easy way of saying this, but what I mean is, I don't think you should wait for me because I . . . I've asked Charlotte to . . .'

April had gasped. The pain had been almost physical, and for a moment she couldn't breathe.

Theo had wrapped his arms around her tightly. 'I'm so sorry,' he whispered into her hair. 'I will always love you, April. You are my first love.' He pulled back to look into her eyes and wiped a tear from her cheek with his thumb. 'Will you still write to me?'

April had shaken her head. 'I think you should go, Theo. If this is how you've been feeling, you should have told me sooner.'

'I know, but I just couldn't bear to hurt you. But Mother said it was only fair to tell you before I went away.'

'You talked about this with your *mother*! So was this your decision or hers?'

He'd looked at her regretfully. 'I'm sorry, I know I've upset you, but I'm a grown man and I make my own decisions.' He'd pulled her into his arms once more. 'I think I'll always love you, April. But I think she's right.

We've grown up now, and I've changed. Stay safe and take care of yourself. I'll understand if you feel you can't write to me.'

April sighed, trying to shake the memories away. She didn't think she could bear to see Theo and Charlotte together, so she needed to leave this house. She thought about what Mrs O'Connor had said about going to Cornwall. It was time. Her father was gone and she couldn't stay in this limbo forever. She would speak to matron and see if there was any way she could transfer to a hospital there. Even if she didn't find any of her family, anything was better than staying where she was with the constant reminder of happier times all around her.

'What do you think, Dad?' she whispered. 'Is it a good idea?'

There was no reply, of course there wasn't, but her mind was made up. It was time to leave her memories behind once and for all.

∞

The next day, April went to work with her heart even heavier than usual. But, as she did every day, she tried to push aside her grief and focus on helping the patients. Entering the women's ward where she was working that week, she went straight over to Alice, one of her favourite patients. Alice had broken both her legs in an air raid and was stuck in traction, and as she and April were around the same age, they'd struck up a quiet friendship.

'Good morning, Alice, how are you this morning?'

'I can't complain, nurse. And me mum and sister will be in at visiting time. I can't wait to see them.'

'How lovely. I'm looking forward to meeting them.'

But that afternoon, when Alice's mother and sister had arrived, full of hugs and kisses and concern, she wondered, If I were in hospital, who would visit me?

All of a sudden, the black cloud of loneliness that seemed to follow April wherever she went enveloped her and she rushed away. Taking refuge in a supply cupboard, she sobbed out her heartbreak.

'Oh, pull yourself together, April,' she said to herself firmly. 'You're no use to anyone like this.' Wiping her eyes on her apron, she straightened her shoulders, grabbed a bandage – so it wouldn't look like she'd been hiding – and strode back into the ward, hoping that Sister Bartlett, who was not the most sympathetic woman, wouldn't notice her red eyes. But no such luck.

The sister saw her the moment she entered the ward. 'Nurse Harvey, a word, if you please.'

April walked reluctantly to the nurses' station. 'I know you have lost your father and your home, Nurse Harvey,' Sister Bartlett said in a hushed voice. 'But look at some of our patients, the people you are supposed to be helping, and thank your lucky stars you're beside the bed and not in it. Now, do something useful like getting a bed pan to Mrs Latimer over in the corner. She's been asking for at least half an hour and if you don't hop to it soon, you'll be cleaning up the mess, I can promise you, *and* washing the sheets.'

'Yes, sister. I'm sorry.' April was mortified and determined to keep her mind on nursing until she was off duty.

Matron, who had been passing, gave Sister Bartlett a disapproving stare as she bustled past, then she turned to April. 'When you've seen to Mrs Latimer, please come and see me in my office, Nurse Harvey. Don't worry, my dear,' she said, noting the alarmed look on April's face. 'I just want to have a word to see how you're getting on. Try not to mind Sister Bartlett, she doesn't mean to be harsh but she's dealing with tragedy of her own, I'm afraid. Her son is missing in action.'

April sped away to do as she was told. Poor Sister Bartlett. She must try to remember she was not the only one to have suffered tragedy; everyone was coping with loss. Sister Bartlett might have been harsh, but she was right. She just had to keep her mind focused on helping where she could. They would not win this war by wallowing in self-pity.

A few moments later, she knocked on matron's door, steeling herself for a telling off. But also aware that this was the chance she'd needed to talk about moving to Cornwall.

'Come.' matron's voice always sounded formidable, and, trying to remember her kindness, April tentatively opened the door.

'Ah, Nurse Harvey. Take a seat and tell me how you are getting on.'

April sat, twisting her hands nervously together. 'I'm all right, thank you, matron.'

Matron stared at her over her glasses, a speculative look on her face. 'Are you sure, Nurse Harvey? Because I can quite understand if you are not, and if that means you need to take a little bit of time off to recover your spirits, then we should try to accommodate you. There is no point in having a nurse on duty who bursts into tears at the drop of a hat.'

April looked down at her lap in shame, trying to hide the tears that had once again welled up in her eyes.

'No, matron, I'd prefer to keep working. And anyway, I have nowhere else to go . . .'

'Where are you staying at the moment?'

'I'm staying with the vicar and his wife, but I feel I'm imposing . . .' She looked up at matron. 'Would it be possible to find a room for me at the nurses' home?'

Matron shook her head. 'There's so little space since the home was bombed, as you know. I'm afraid it sounds like you have a perfectly good place, and there's no need for you to take up room in the home. Do you not find it to your liking?'

'Oh no.' April knew she could not discuss her reasons for disliking Mrs Osborne. 'The Osbornes are terribly kind, and I've known them for many years.'

'Well, then, nurse, all I can suggest is that you keep yourself together on the wards. Think only of the people who need you and depend on you. Allow yourself to fall apart when you are at home alone, and then slowly and carefully put yourself together again. We are here when you need us.'

'Yes, matron. Thank you. But . . .' She stopped.

'Yes, nurse? Is there something else?'

April took a deep breath. 'Matron, I was wondering whether it would be possible to finish my training at another hospital?'

Matron looked surprised. 'Well, I suppose it would. But we'd be very sorry to lose you. You are proving to be a most excellent and capable nurse. But why? Do you have family elsewhere?'

'No . . . Well, yes, sort of. My mother was from Cornwall, and I would dearly love to go there and see if I have any family left there.'

'And where in Cornwall was she from?'

April searched her memory for the answer. 'I think she was from somewhere near Truro, matron.'

'I see. And you definitely would like to leave us?'

'Oh no, not at all. But . . .' She stopped, unsure what to say.

'No need to say any more, April. I understand perfectly. I was left orphaned by the Great War and wouldn't have known what to do with myself if it hadn't been for my aunts and uncles. Let me make enquiries, and I will let you know.'

Chapter 2

November 1941

April was making her way to the hospital cloakroom early one morning after a long night shift when she was stopped by matron.

'Good news, Nurse Harvey. It's all arranged. Your transfer to the Royal Cornwall Infirmary is confirmed and you can leave within the next two weeks.'

April, who over the past few months had found herself sinking ever deeper into despair, looked up in surprise.

'Really, matron? I can leave soon?'

'Yes, I've sent my reference to the matron there – and let me tell you it is glowing; I have been so impressed with your fortitude and your professionalism during this trying time – and she is expecting you at the beginning of December. They will sort out accommodation for you, and let you know on arrival. Now, nurse, you have one week left to work here, then a week to get down to Cornwall and settle in before reporting for duty. How does that sound?'

'Oh, it sounds wonderful. Thank you so much.'

'Are we that bad, eh, Nurse Harvey, that you can't wait to leave us?' Matron's eyes glinted with humour, but even so, April flushed with guilt.

'Oh, I didn't mean . . .'

Matron laughed. 'It's all right, I know what you meant. Now, off with you, nurse, and get some sleep. You have a busy time ahead.'

'Thank you, matron.'

∽

April fairly flew home on her bicycle that morning, all her tiredness forgotten. Maybe once she left this place that reminded her so much of her father and her happy times with Theo, she would stop having the terrible nightmares that forced her awake night after night. Always the same dream: her house burning, her father's terrified face at the window, and all around the sound of the air-raid siren wailing. She shook her head, determined not to think of that now. Instead she thought of how wonderful it would be to tell Mrs Osborne she was leaving. The relationship between them had become even frostier since Theo's visit in August, and she hoped that this news might lighten the atmosphere until she left.

When she got back, she was pleased to see that both the reverend and Mrs Osborne were in the kitchen having breakfast.

'Good morning, Reverend Osborne, Mrs Osborne. I have some news. I'm pleased to say that matron has just told me that I have a position at the Royal Cornwall Infirmary, starting in two weeks, so I will be leaving you at last.'

Mrs Osborne looked up from her tea and toast. 'Well, that is good news. Isn't it, Theodore?'

The reverend smiled at April, looking so like Theo, April had to look away. 'We shall be very sorry to lose you,

April. It's been an absolute pleasure to have you with us, hasn't it, Bella?'

Mrs Osborne said nothing, merely inclined her head.

'And I know Theo loved having you here when he was home. Always nice to have another young person about, don't you think?'

April thought back to the awkward week she had spent when Theo was home, and most particularly to the bewildering last evening. Theo had not minded at all that she was sleeping in his bedroom but even so, she had taken on as many extra shifts at the hospital as she could manage to try to avoid him. But on that last evening, they had found themselves alone together sitting on the sofa in front of the fire talking.

'April, I've been wanting to say since I came home how sorry I am about what happened before I went away.'

April had looked at him in discomfort. This was the last thing she wanted to be reminded of when Theo was sitting there, looking so handsome and relaxed. He still made her heart beat faster every time he walked in a room, and this past week, having him in the same house had been torture. She'd so longed to recapture their previous easy relationship. To laugh and talk with him as they'd once done. And yes, she admitted, she longed to kiss him again too. She'd realised then, with a sinking heart, that she still loved him. Maybe she always would.

She swallowed. 'Never mind all that, Theo. The most important thing is that you're safe for now, and home. I hope that you and Charlotte will be very happy together.'

'That's just it, April. Being home and seeing you every day has made me think. Charlotte is wonderful, of course, but sometimes I find myself remembering how it was, just you and me, and the fun we used to have. We've known each other almost all our lives, and I think you probably know me better than anyone else.' He took her hand and looked into her eyes. 'And I think I know you better than anyone too. I miss that. I miss our closeness and how comfortable we were together. How we could sit together and not need to say a word because, well, we just fit, somehow.'

'But last time we spoke, you said I was just a childhood crush. What's changed?'

'I suppose *I* have. Being away from home, fighting . . . thinking about you every single day. Not Charlotte, always you. And this might be my last chance to tell you how sorry I am for hurting you, and how I think I was wrong.'

April shook her head. 'You hurt me so badly, Theo. This last year has been the worst of my life. I lost you and then I lost Dad, and I'm not sure I can trust you again. I can't take any more loss, Theo, so please don't say things you might not mean.'

'I would never want to hurt you, April. You are far too precious to me. All I know is that I miss you. Sometimes I wish . . .' He stopped and looked at her wistfully.

April stared back. She didn't want to hope, and she didn't want to have her heart broken again by this man who seemed unable to make up his mind between two girls.

'I wish I'd never met Charlotte. I think I got confused,' he whispered. 'I understand if you can't trust me straightaway. All I ask is that you write to me. Who knows what the future holds, or whether we even have a future. I still . . . well, what I'm trying to say is that I still love you.'

'Theo, I . . .' April had spent enough time getting over her heartbreak and now she was dealing with the grief of her father's death. The thought that Theo might still love her made her heart leap, but also made her fearful. She wasn't sure she could take any more heartache. 'You must know, my feelings haven't changed, and it's true: life is short. Goodness knows, I see enough grief and heartache in my job. I will write to you. But please, Theo, don't play with my feelings. If this is friendship, then so be it, but don't make me love you again.'

'That's all I ask, my darling. And rest assured, my feelings for you go way beyond friendship.' He leaned over and kissed her tenderly on the lips. April drew back in surprise. 'Sorry. I couldn't help myself. You look so lovely with your golden hair shining in the firelight. Say you didn't mind.'

Unable to resist him, April leaned forward. 'I didn't mind, Theo,' she whispered. And this time she kissed him back. He pulled her closer and though she enjoyed the contact, she was also aware that something had changed. Once, when he'd kissed her, her heart would be singing; this time, though, at the back of her mind was the uneasy feeling that something wasn't quite right. She couldn't help but doubt his feelings for her and she wasn't sure she would ever be able to love him in the same way again.

Theo drew back and stroked her cheek. 'Darling April. I knew I could count on you. You are my shelter from the stormy blast.' He grinned. 'What a thing to say! You can tell I'm a vicar's son! But you know what I mean. With you, I feel I can truly be myself.'

Before she could reply, a sudden 'Excuse me' had them jumping apart guiltily. Mrs Osborne was standing in the doorway.

'I think it's time you were in bed, April, don't you? You have an early start in the morning, and I'd like to spend these last few hours alone with my son.'

April jumped up. 'Yes, of course. Good night, Theo. I don't think I'll see you before I leave in the morning, but I will write to you. Good night, Mrs Osborne.'

And she'd left. But ever since that night, Mrs Osborne, when she'd talked to her at all, had spoken only about Charlotte and her accomplishments. April had done her very best never to be caught alone with her. The thought of leaving this difficult atmosphere made April feel lighter than she had in months. And who knows, she thought, in a few week's time I might have some family of my very own.

She was brought back from her thoughts by Reverend Osborne. 'Now, April, is there anything you need for your new life? I know the Women's Voluntary Service has provided you with some clothes, and that lovely warm winter coat, but is there anything else?'

'Thank you, reverend, but I think I have sufficient. You can only wear one set of clothes at a time, and the WVS has been so generous. I could never have afforded to buy enough clothes with my coupons.'

'Very well, my dear. I must get on, but we will have a special farewell supper for you, shall we not, Bella?'

'Yes, I'm sure the Belgians can rustle something up. Though, on the rations we have, it won't be that special, I'm afraid.'

'That would be lovely.' April forced a smile. Although, she thought sourly, if I was Charlotte, I bet Mrs Osborne would have managed to find a little something special.

Oh stop it, April, she said to herself. You sound like a very bitter woman.

Chapter 3

December 1941

Two weeks later, after a long and arduous train journey in a freezing and cramped carriage that had included a hold-up of several hours due to sheep on the line, April arrived in Truro.

As she walked out of the station, she looked around, hoping to recognise something. But nothing looked familiar. Feeling a little lost and very lonely, April asked the station master how to get to the hospital. He directed her to the correct bus, and she was soon on her way, her stomach fluttering with nerves. Would she make some friends here? Would she be happy? But most importantly, would she find anyone at all who belonged to her?

By the time she got off at the hospital, April felt sick. St Thomas' was an impressive building, but so was this one. Right on the crest of the hill, the hospital was an imposing four-storey brick structure, with a wide flight of steps leading up to the door. As with every building she'd seen recently, thousands of sandbags were stacked high against its walls to protect it from possible bombing raids. She paused at the bottom of the steps and took a long breath, squared her shoulders and walked in, trying to look like she knew where she was going.

Once inside, April was comforted by the familiarity of the scene. A large staircase in front of her clearly led up to the wards, and nurses in their smart blue uniform dresses with white aprons and hats were rushing backwards and forwards, while white-coated doctors strode purposefully up the stairs, or disappeared down the long corridors that ran off the hallway.

She spotted a nurse rushing towards the door with her coat on. As she was on her way out, April decided that she might have time to stop and help her.

'Excuse me,' she said. The nurse, who had a cheerful, freckled face and beautiful deep red hair, stopped and looked at her enquiringly.

'I'm looking for the matron. I'm due to start work here soon, and I need to know where I'm to live.'

'Oh, hello there.' To April's relief, the nurse seemed very friendly. 'If you'll be starting work here, then I expect we'll get to know each other. We're one big family here. I'm Eunice, by the way, newly qualified, and working on the surgical ward with that dragon Sister Mulholland.' She suddenly looked a little embarrassed. 'Sorry, sometimes my mouth runs away with me. They're all nice here, honestly. Just some are nicer than others.'

Her voice had a soft Cornish burr, and April thought she could listen to it all day.

'Anyway, up the stairs, top floor, third door on the right. Matron runs things from a little cubbyhole up there. Although she might not be there at the moment as we're so busy. Good luck! Maybe I'll see you around soon.' And she disappeared out of the door.

Heartened by the friendly welcome, April followed Eunice's instructions and soon found herself outside a door with the name Matron Clark written on a card and stuck to it. She knocked tentatively.

'Come,' a voice ordered from the other side of the door. She sounded just like the matron at St Thomas', which, despite the stern tone, put her at ease. Perhaps, when you become a matron, they teach you how to speak in a matronly manner, she thought with a smile.

Opening the door, she poked her head inside. A small, round, bespectacled woman was sitting at a desk piled with papers.

'Good afternoon, matron. I'm Nurse April Harvey. I believe you've been expecting me.'

'Ah, Nurse Harvey, you are a very welcome sight. Trainee or not, your trauma experience will be a bonus to us, and your matron's references are glowing. We're very happy to have you join us. Now . . .' – she shuffled through some papers on her desk – 'Ah, here we are. I'm afraid we couldn't fit you into the nurses' home, as we've had a bit of an influx recently, and we're still quite a small hospital compared to St Thomas', but we've managed to find you lodgings with a Mrs Teague, who lives just down the hill in Truro. She's lodged several of our nurses and I've not had one complaint yet. Here's the address. It's easy to find, just walk down Infirmary Hill and take the second road on the right – then follow the road and it will bring you to Daniel Road.'

'Thank you, matron.'

Matron looked up and smiled kindly. 'I understand you've had a bit of a difficult time recently, but not to worry, we all look after each other here, and though the hours are long and the work is hard, I hope you will be happy. I've assigned you to the surgical ward starting on the eighth of December – next Monday. Your first shift will be from six a.m. sharp until six thirty. How does that sound? Any experience with surgical before?'

'A bit, matron.'

'Excellent. Get yourself off to Mrs Teague's, and we'll see you next Monday. Good day, nurse.'

'Thank you, matron. I hope I'll be an asset to you.'

Matron nodded briskly, and April rose and hurried from the room. The surgical ward. She was pleased, because that meant she might be able to get to know that friendly nurse Eunice a little better. It was a shame she wasn't able to live in the nurses' home with the other girls, but never mind. Anywhere was better than living with Mrs Osborne.

Walking down the stairs, April stopped a porter and asked for directions to Mrs Teague's house. 'Is it far?' she asked hopefully.

'Not far, my lovely. Twenty minutes up, and fifteen down, that's what I reckon. And as you'll be walking down, you'll be there in a jiffy. New, are you? Mrs Teague lodging you, is she?'

'Yes, I've just arrived from London.'

The porter sucked on his teeth. 'That's a bad business up there. Not to say we haven't had our share down here, but . . .' He looked at her sympathetically, noticing the dark circles under her eyes. 'You look all in. Get down the hill. Mrs Teague will look after you. She's a friendly sort.'

The porter was correct, and a scant fifteen minutes later, she found herself knocking on the door of a pretty white house with two windows on either side of a blue door. A tall, thin woman, who April estimated to be in her fifties or sixties, with grey hair pulled back in a loose bun, answered the door. April stared at her nonplussed. For some reason, she'd been expecting a small, plump woman who looked more like the matron. Then Mrs Teague smiled warmly, and her face transformed.

'April Harvey, is it? Come on in, my lovely, you must be exhausted after your journey. I've got supper on the go – a nice vegetable soup and home-made bread – and there's a small fire in the sitting room. Not much, mind, as there's hardly any coal, but I manage somehow.'

Slightly taken aback at the woman's garrulousness, April walked in.

'That's it, lovely. Let me get your coat. Now, go and sit down. I'll pop your case in your room and then we can get to know each other.'

April entered a small, crowded living room. There were two armchairs covered in a flowery fabric positioned on either side of the fire. Opposite it was a settee, covered in the same fabric. All the furniture had lace antimacassars on the arms, and a similar lace cloth protecting the back. The effect was a little eye-watering compared to Mrs Osborne's restrained décor, and her father's rather masculine taste. But it felt homely. There were knick-knacks on the mantelpiece above the fire, with a gleaming carriage clock sitting proudly in the centre. The walls were covered with paintings. To her untrained eye they looked like they were from India. The table between the settee and the fire had a lace doily in the centre, with a vase of flowers sitting on top of it.

Mrs Teague bustled in. 'Here's a cup of tea for you, April. And some scones that I baked just today to welcome you. I'm always happy to lodge the nurses. Since my Isaac died, I get lonely without company. Now, first things first, let's get the business out of the way. If you give me your ration book, I will do all the shopping and cooking for the both of us. But I'm afraid I hate doing laundry, so I'll change your sheets every other week, but any other washing you'll have to do yourself, if you don't mind. Meals are eaten in the kitchen, and I will make sure there's something for you when you get home. I like to do something special on a Sunday, so if you're here, we eat in the dining room. I like to invite people if I have enough food. Me and Mrs Beetie next door take it in turns. But now you're here, perhaps you'd like to bring friends back for lunch once in a while? I do like to have young people round my table.' Mrs Teague stopped suddenly. 'Oh, hark at me, going on at you, and you looking like you could sleep for a week. Go on then, drink your tea then come to the kitchen when you're ready and have something to eat. Then it's off to bed with you, I think. Plenty of time to talk in the morning.'

April was bewildered by the talkative woman. She couldn't have asked for a warmer welcome, but all the same, the thought of food then bed sounded wonderful. She only hoped she didn't dream tonight. Sometimes she woke screaming, and she was worried she'd wake Mrs Teague. Mrs Osborne used to complain about the disturbance, but April couldn't imagine the friendly Mrs Teague being quite so cruel. She walked into the kitchen, which was painted white and had a range cooker and a small table by the window that looked out on to the garden. It was dark now, but April wondered whether the vegetables Mrs Teague was using in her soup had come from there, or if she was still able to grow flowers.

'Just in time, lovely. Sit down and get that inside you. Carrots, potatoes and cabbage – all from the garden,' she said proudly, unwittingly answering April's question. 'The bread's warm. No butter, mind, but it's not too dry if you dip it in the soup.'

April sat and began to eat. 'Oh, this is delicious, Mrs Teague. I can't imagine how you've made it so tasty.'

Mrs Teague laughed. 'Oh, I have my ways. My Isaac used to say I was a wizard in the kitchen. It was one of the things he loved best about me.' She smiled sadly, then shook her head. 'Now I'm just happy to cook for anyone who'll join me.'

As she ate, Mrs Teague asked her about her journey down. When she explained about the sheep and the cold, Mrs Teague tutted. 'Oh, blast this war. Nothing is simple any more. I'm just glad Isaac didn't live to see this. After what he experienced in the last one, this would have broken his heart . . .'

Mrs Teague looked close to tears, and April put her hand on hers. 'Please don't upset yourself.'

'I'm sorry, April, I do get upset when I think too much about the war. I read the papers and listen to the radio, and seems to me the only way we'll win is if the Americans join us. Still, if anyone can persuade them, Churchill can.' She jumped up and started to clear the dishes away.

'Can I help you, Mrs Teague?'

'Oh, bless you, no. Let me show you to your room so you can get to bed. We'll talk more in the morning.'

Relieved, April followed her landlady up the stairs into a pretty, feminine bedroom. The bed was covered with a flowered bedspread, and a writing desk was pushed up against the window. In one corner, there was yet another flowered armchair – Mrs Teague seemed to like flowers maybe a little too much – that matched those in the sitting room, and against the opposite wall a wardrobe and a chest of drawers. It all looked so clean and welcoming that April nearly cried with relief. This looked like a place she could really find sanctuary in.

'There you go, April. I'll wish you good night. Bathroom's just down the corridor. You stay in bed as long as you like tomorrow. You'll need your strength for when you start work.' And with that, Mrs Teague left the room, closing the door quietly behind her.

April flopped down on to the bed. She was so tired she wasn't sure she had the energy to change into her nightgown. She lay for a few minutes staring at the ceiling and thinking about her day and everything that had happened. There was something about this place that felt familiar. Not just this house, but as if the very atmosphere was one she knew. Was this because she'd been here before? Or were her mother's Cornish roots so strong that just being in the place she had lived was enough. She shook her head. She was being fanciful. It was probably the way people spoke. They sounded just like her mother. She'd always called April 'my lovely' too.

With that comforting thought, April drifted to sleep, still wearing the tatty old skirt and jumper that had been given to her by the WVS.

Chapter 4

'April! April, whatever is the matter?'

April opened her eyes in shock, her body racked with sobs and her face wet with tears. The remnants of her dream were still with her as she stared into Mrs Teague's concerned face.

'Oh! Oh no! I'm so sorry, Mrs Teague. Did I wake you?'

'Never mind that, dear. Seems like you've had a nasty dream. Let me get you some cocoa, and you can tell me all about it.'

April sat up. 'Oh no. Please don't bother. I'm so sorry. I often have bad dreams, I'm used to it, so please go back to bed. I'll be fine.'

'As if I can leave anyone in the state you're in. And you just a young girl and under my care. No, lie back down, I'll be back in just a moment.'

April lay back with a sob of distress. It had been over six months, and still the dreams would not go. Her father's anxious face at the window, the wail of the sirens, the explosions, the flames, and the green velvet curtains flapping around the gaping hole where her father had been standing. It was driving her mad. And now Mrs Teague would probably want her to move out. She pulled the covers up over her head, wishing everything would just go away. Oh, this awful war! When would it all stop?

She heard Mrs Teague come back in and the bed sagged as she sat down on the edge.

'Drink your cocoa, lovely, and if it helps, you can tell me all about it.'

April pulled the covers down and looked at the kindly woman's face. Her blue eyes were soft and her tone was sympathetic. But what could she say?

'There's nothing to tell, Mrs Teague. I dream about the night my father died in an air raid again and again. I'm sorry, I don't always scream. Mrs Osborne, who I used to live with, used to get cross at being woken up.'

'She never did! The nasty old biddy! I'd give her a piece of my mind if I ever saw her. I'm guessing that you've not had much comforting after a nightmare before.'

April shook her head. 'No, I suppose I haven't. You are kind, Mrs Teague. Thank you. But I think you've been disturbed enough tonight. I'll be fine.'

The older woman looked at her searchingly, then said, 'Very well, April. But you must understand that I will never be cross with you for having nightmares. Me and Isaac never had any children of our own, so I care for others' children where I can. And while you're my lodger, pet, I will do the same for you. Have no fear.'

April almost cried at these kind words, and she smiled tremulously. 'Thank you. That is possibly the loveliest thing anyone's said to me for a long while.'

Mrs Teague patted her hand. 'Right. Now you know not to fear, I hope you can sleep well. I'll see you in the morning, dear.' She left, shutting the door gently behind her.

∽

When April woke the next morning, she was feeling much better, and remembering Mrs Teague's kindness during the night made her feel less alone than she had in months. She hoped that the woman hadn't had second thoughts during the night and decided she might be too much trouble as a lodger. She washed and dressed in some old woollen slacks the WVS had given her and a woollen jumper that had definitely seen better days, but it was warm and comfortable and April didn't anticipate going out much that day.

She crept quietly into the kitchen where Mrs Teague was standing at the stove stirring a pot of porridge. She jumped when she heard April pull a chair out.

'Bless me, you gave me a fright! How are you feeling, lovely? Better, are you?'

'Much better. Thank you for being so kind last night.'

'Pish, anyone would do the same. Here's some porridge for you. Get it down you, and if you like, later, I'd be happy to show you the way to Truro.'

'Would you mind very much if I just stayed here today? I'd like to unpack and I have some letters to write.'

Mrs Teague patted her hand. 'You do that, then. Sounds sensible to me. Rest and resuscitation, isn't that what they say?'

April smiled. 'I think it's recuperation.'

'Tsk, I am a silly old fool sometimes. You carry on, April. I've got some shopping to do in Truro so I'll see you at lunch, dear.'

April ate her porridge then went back to her room and unpacked. She didn't really have anything to do at all, but she felt so tired and bewildered that the thought of venturing out today had felt too much. She sat down at her desk and wrote a letter to the Osbornes to let them know she'd arrived safely. Not that Mrs Osborne would care one way or another, but it would be impolite not to contact them at all, and her father had been very strict about manners and the correct way to behave.

By the time she heard Mrs Teague return, she'd written three letters – one to Mrs O'Connor to let her know she'd moved, one to the Osbornes and, finally, she wrote to Theo, giving him her new address. She kept it quite brief and to the point as she still wasn't sure about her feelings towards him any more.

That night, after a very leisurely day and some more of Mrs Teague's glorious cooking, April was finally starting to feel more relaxed. Her landlady really did seem like a lovely woman who was so interested in everything April had to say. The signs were good, April thought later as she lay in bed, that this had been the right move for her. Smiling to herself, she drifted off into what she hoped would be a peaceful sleep.

~∞~

'April! Wake up. It's just Mrs Teague here, no need to fret.'

April opened her eyes, suddenly aware that her blankets were on the floor, the sheet was twisted around her and the pillow was soaking wet.

'Oh no! Not again. I'm so sorry, Mrs Teague.'

'Hush, my girl. It's fine. You sounded so terrified and so heartbroken, I had to wake you. Was it the same dream?'

April nodded.

Mrs Teague's eyes were kind and full of concern. 'I'll make you something hot, my love. Hold on there.'

When she returned with a mug of cocoa, she sat on the side of the bed. 'Do you want to tell me about it?'

April shook her head. 'It's like I said last night. The air raid.'

Mrs Teague nodded sympathetically. 'And who's Theo? Did he die too?'

April was startled. 'Did I call his name? Oh. He's an old friend. I was staying with his parents before I came here.'

'Ah. Is he your sweetheart?'

April looked away. 'Not any more.' She felt tears well again and dashed them away impatiently.

'Why don't you tell me all about it? You know the old saying – a problem shared and all that.'

April shook her head, but the tears kept coming. Mrs Teague stroked her hair back from her face. 'There now, it's all right. Tell your old landlady all about it, and maybe you'll feel better.'

It had been so long since April had been able to confide in anyone and Mrs Teague's presence was so comforting that she gave in and told her everything. From her father's death, to Mrs Osborne and Theo, and Theo's last visit. And finally, she spoke of her hopes of finding anyone who might be related to her.

'You poor child. What a time you've had, and all alone in the world. Well, don't you worry any more. I have nothing but time, and I can help you in your search. It can't be too difficult, can it, now? Do you know where your mother's buried? That's where we should start.'

'Yes, I think it's in a place called St Merryn.'

'Oh, I know St Merryn. It's not so far on the bus. How about I take you up there one day so you can pay your respects? I know the church and old Mrs V up there knows everyone's business. If anyone knows where your mum's sister is, it'll be Mrs V.'

April's heart lifted. 'Really? You'd do that with me?'

'Of course I will. Now snuggle down for what's left of the night and we'll talk more in the morning.'

Mrs Teague was just closing the bedroom door when April asked tentatively, 'Mrs Teague, would it be all right if we went tomorrow?'

'I think that's a very good idea. Go there before you start working and you don't have so much time. Good night, my dear.'

∞

The next morning, April dressed and went down to the kitchen to find her landlady at her usual spot by the stove. This time, she seemed to be concocting some sort of stew. Whatever it was, it smelled wonderful. April smiled at the sight and reflected that she didn't think she'd ever met anyone quite as kind.

Mrs Teague turned. 'Ah, there you are, dear. How are you feeling this morning?'

'Much better, thank you, Mrs Teague. And I just wanted to say how sorry I am for waking you last night, and thank you for being so kind to me.'

'Nonsense, child. I was just happy to be there. Now, get this tea down you, and I'll make you some toast, will that do you? No butter, I'm afraid, and only dripping for the toast, is that all right with you?'

April sat down. 'That sounds perfect. Thank you.'

'And do you still want to go up to St Merryn? Or have you changed your mind?'

'I would like to go. Thank you. But if it's not convenient for you I can make my own way if you give me directions.'

Mrs Teague tutted. 'I said I'd come, didn't I? Anyway, it'll be nice to have a little journey.'

April smiled in response. She couldn't wait to see her mother's grave, and maybe, just maybe, the woman at the church could help her find some of her family.

∞

Gazing out of the window, April watched the beautiful Cornish countryside roll past. Mrs Teague, thankfully, had bumped into an acquaintance and was busy chatting to her, so April was able to sit quietly and think about her mother. Had she gazed at this very sight when she was younger? Maybe she'd even visited the hospital. April liked the idea of treading where her mother once had; it gave her a warm feeling of belonging.

When they finally got off at St Merryn, April drew in a deep breath and looked around her. How wonderful, she thought. My mother belonged in this village, belonged in Cornwall, and therefore I belong too.

In her mind she had painted what she now realised was a chocolate-box picture of a quaint English village, but St Merryn was no more than a long straggly line of houses

46

with a larger building that was probably a hotel in the middle. She refused to be disappointed, though, and looked up in expectation at the church, only a few hundred yards along the road. The massive stone tower loomed over the village and the moors, visible from every direction as it climbed up towards the grey December sky. Almost as if she had stepped along the road every Sunday of her life, she hurried to the ancient stone wall that encircled the church and graveyard, opened the old gate and stood for a moment gazing up at the church tower. Her first thought was not of her roots but of how enormous the church was for such a small community.

The church door was open, and with Mrs Teague trailing silently in her wake, she went inside. A feeling of peace washed over her as she walked down the long aisle, looking around her at the rows of wooden pews, the embroidered kneelers, and, at the front of the church, the beautiful stained-glass window depicting a Madonna and child. She stared at. Was it a sign? She shook her head. She was letting her emotions take over, something that, as a nurse, she had been taught never to do. She walked back to the door and stood at the entrance for a moment, noticing the houses visible over the stone wall that surrounded the church. They were large with generous gardens – one of them was probably the vicarage. If she couldn't find her mother's grave, she would knock and see if the vicar was in. Perhaps he would let her look at the church records so she could verify she was in the right place. But first, she was anxious to search the graveyard. It was large and full of gravestones – some older than others. If she looked at only the relatively new ones, that should save her some time.

Mrs Teague came and stood beside her. April jumped slightly. She'd been so wrapped up in her thoughts that she'd almost forgotten the older woman was with her.

'How about we split up to look for your mother's grave?' she said gently. 'That way we have a better chance of finding it quickly.'

April nodded. 'That sounds like a very good idea. I'll go this way' – she pointed to the left – 'and if either of us finds it, we will give a shout.'

Mrs Teague set off, then stopped suddenly. 'What was your mother's name?'

'Oh, it was Mellyn Harvey née Rowe.'

'Right, I'll get on.' Mrs Teague turned right on the neat pebble path that wound around the perimeter of the church while April walked in the opposite direction. Some of the stones seemed as ancient as the surrounding wall and a few showed signs of having fallen and been replaced, but the large area of grass was neat and tidy, and she could tell that the graves were carefully tended. Not a vase or flower was in the wrong place. Someone worked with love here and April was glad. At least she knew her mother's grave was well looked after.

She shivered as the wind blew into the churchyard, and paused for a moment, looking out over the vast expanse of moor. In her mind she pictured her mother as she remembered her: beautiful with long, golden hair and blue eyes, just like her own. She'd been small, April remembered, but strong. And in her memory, her mother was always smiling. April felt tears well up in her eyes and shook her head; she needed to focus on the task in hand.

She became more methodical and returned to the gate, turned right and looked at every stone as she passed it. Teagues, Dashells, Hammetts, Landreys and other Cornish names aplenty but no Harveys or Rowes. April kept walking and reading. 'Dearly beloved wife of' and 'dearly beloved husband of' – the litany of the dead continued, and then suddenly she saw a fairly modern stone standing against the boundary wall, facing the entrance to the venerable building. A discoloured marble vase, which held two fresh sprigs of holly, sat on the ledge at the bottom of the stone. April kneeled down before it, her heart beating wildly, and read the inscription.

In loving memory of Mellyn Rowe Harvey, dearly beloved wife of Edward, mother of April, daughter of Eleanor and Frank, and sister of Hilda. Born 7 October 1900 and departed this life on 9 June 1928.

Her eyes were so clouded by tears that April could read no more. She remained on her knees, unaware of the dampness seeping through the material of her slacks, repeating the words: Eleanor, Frank, Hilda. *Her family.* Could they still be alive? Perhaps it was Hilda who had left the holly on the grave? And if not her, who?

She stood up and looked around. She could see Mrs Teague still searching the gravestones nearby. 'Mrs Teague, I've found it!'

Mrs Teague rushed over, strands of grey hair that had blown loose from her bun whipping around her face and her blue eyes sparkling with excitement.

They both stood for a moment, gazing down at the simple stone. Then April said, 'Do you recognise those names? And do you think someone from my family might have left the holly?'

'No, I'm afraid I don't, lovely. And maybe someone who knew your mum did leave the flowers, but old Mrs Vellanoweth, who looks after the churchyard and lives in that small house over there, might know. She's lived here all her life, so she'll have known your mother, I'll lay my life on it.' She gestured across the road at a little house with a blue gate.

'Do you think she'll mind if we knock on her door and ask her?'

'Bless you, no. Isolde loves a gossip and a bit of company. Come on, I'll introduce you.'

They walked across the road and entered the little blue gate. The door was painted the same bright blue as the gate, and April held her breath, praying that this strangely named woman would be in.

She needn't have worried. Almost immediately, she heard footsteps approaching the door, before it was flung open by a small old woman with snow white hair hanging in a plait over one shoulder. April noticed that although her face was lined, her eyes had a youthful sparkle.

'Why, if it isn't Doris Teague. What are you doing here? It's been a while since you've been up this way. At the village fete, wasn't it? You baked a lovely cake for the raffle, if I recall. Come in, come in and have a cup of tea, if you've got a moment?'

'Hello, Isolde, I've brought my young friend April to see you as she's looking for any relations of her mother. Do you remember Mellyn Rowe, by any chance?'

'Mellyn Rowe . . .' Mrs Vellanoweth's brow furrowed as she thought for a few long moments. 'Yes, of course—' She stopped abruptly as she looked at April for the first time. 'Bless my soul! If I hadn't laid holly on Mellyn's grave myself just yesterday, I'd say she's standing right in front of me now.'

April couldn't contain her excitement. 'Oh, you knew my mother! How wonderful. Would you be able to tell me anything about my family?'

Mrs Vellanoweth's expression clouded for a moment, then she smiled again. 'Of course, as long as you'll come in out of the cold and have a cuppa, and I'll answer anything you care to ask as best I can. Come through to the kitchen, do.'

April and Mrs Teague followed the old woman into her cosy, overcrowded sitting room that was lit by a window that looked out on to the church. 'I'll just go and pop the kettle on, then I'm all yours,' she said to April.

She soon returned with a tray on which stood a teapot decorated with flowers, and matching cups, saucers and a milk jug. 'I'm afraid there's no sugar today – haven't had a chance to get my rations. But still. It's wet and it's warm, and what more do you need on a grey day like today, eh?'

She busied herself pouring out the tea, then handed around the cups, before finally – April felt the whole process had taken far too long – she settled back on her chair with a sigh.

'Right, now, April, what would you like to know?'

'I just wondered whether you knew the Rowes? My mother moved to London and that's where I've been until now, and apart from coming to her funeral here, we never came again. But I don't remember any family being there, and yet the gravestone has her parents' and sister's names. Do you know where they might be?'

Mrs Vellanoweth took a sip of tea and sat quietly. 'So dreadful,' she said. 'What happened to that family. But then, it was happening to everyone all over the country at the time.' She shook her head. 'Such terrible, terrible times. And now, here we are, doing it all again. I just can't understand it.' She sighed sadly, all sparkle gone from her eyes.

Mrs Teague sat forward and put a hand on her arm in sympathy. 'There, Isolde, try not to upset yourself. It is terrible for us old folks who've gone through all of this before. The war to end all wars, they said . . . They lied, Isolde, they flat out lied, and now our young folk are having to pay the price we thought we'd already paid.'

April watched the two older women quietly, her stomach sinking. It seemed it was bad news. Did she really want to hear? To let go of her hope of finding any of her family? She couldn't wait any longer to find out, so she interrupted them.

'Mrs Vellanoweth? Please don't worry about giving me bad news. I'm more than used to it, and I'd rather know than not.'

'Of course, child, of course you would. Such lovely girls, Mellyn and Hilda. Peas in a pod, they were, and never apart.' She sighed again. 'Anyway, your grandfather was the postman – everyone knew Frank. Salt of the earth. And your grandmother did a bit of sewing in the village and helped in the shop. Oh, your mum and aunt used to wear the most beautiful dresses. She was clever, your grandma. But then, after the war, the flu came and . . .'

She paused and took a sip of tea. 'Oh, your poor mother, she did all she could. Nursed her family until she nearly dropped dead herself of exhaustion. But there was nothing to be done. Her mother, father and sister all died within a week of each other.'

April's eyes filled with tears. Her poor mother. And she'd never breathed a word of her tragedy to her. But then, she'd only been a child, so of course she wouldn't have wanted to tell her such a horrible story. But her father must have known. Why had he never said? As her mother's gentle face came into her mind, the tears started to fall. How she must have suffered. No wonder she had never spoken of it, she probably just wanted to put it all behind her.

'Was there no other family?'

'It seems not. Your poor mum was so brave. Buried them all and kept her chin up and her back straight the whole time.' Mrs Vellanoweth shook her head. 'Everyone rallied round to help, of course, but she needed to leave, see? The memories were too painful. Anyway, not long after that, the doctor helped Mellyn find a position in London working in a department store and she left. And, until you and your dad came to bury the poor soul, I heard not another word about her. And now here you are. As beautiful as ever your mother and aunt were with your golden hair and blue eyes. Oh, the lads in the town went mad for the Rowe twins, I can tell you.' She sniffed and held out her hand to April, who was sobbing openly.

April took it. 'Surely there must be someone? Anyone? Perhaps cousins?'

She shook her head sadly. 'No, my dear. I'm so sorry. No grandparents, aunts or uncles for the Rowes. This village was their family, but so many young men died in the war, and then others in the flu, that the community almost died too. And now, once again, most of the young men have gone to war. Oh, I don't know what's to become of us all, but it's never been the same here since the flu. Never.'

April didn't know what to think. She'd come all this way to find her family – anyone at all that she was linked to – but now she knew for sure she was all alone. No one in this world would know or care whether she lived or died. Why had she come all this way? At least in London she had friends. But here, it was just her, facing the future without support or love. This must have been how her mother felt when she'd left Cornwall. Her heart broke at the thought and she burst into violent sobs.

Mrs Teague quickly rose and put her arm around her shoulder. 'Oh April. Hush now.'

April just shook her head.

'Come now, everything will be all right. Listen, you might not have found any family, but here you are anyway, a Cornish girl with roots in this very land, so you have to remember that you're not alone, because in Cornwall we look after our own.'

April continued to sob, and Mrs Teague gently brought her head to her shoulder and stroked her back comfortingly. 'There, you let it all out, and maybe you'll feel better.'

Mrs Vellanoweth was sitting in the chair, ringing her hands with distress. 'I'm so sorry, dear. Really I am. I never meant to upset you so.'

April looked up at her through tear-streaked eyes. 'No, Mrs Vellanoweth, this is not your fault. I wanted to know and you have been so kind. I'm sorry, it's just . . . oh, my poor mother. And now what's to become of me? There's no one left at all.'

'You will build your own family, my dear.' Mrs Teague stroked her hair. 'Just as your mother did. Didn't she go to London with not a friend in the world? And yet she found your father and had her own little girl to love and care for. There, you see. From the ashes she rose again. Just as you shall, my dear. Because you have your mother's spirit running through you.'

April tried to smile. 'I hope so, Mrs Teague. But I feel cast adrift. There's nothing to keep me from floating away and no one to care if I do.'

'Oh, now. Of course there is. What about me? I'd surely notice if you floated away.' She gave a little laugh. 'And you'll soon make lots of lovely new friends at the hospital.'

April sniffed. 'You're right. I know you're right, and I'm sorry for being such a watering pot.' She fished in her pocket for a handkerchief, and blew her nose and wiped her eyes before taking a deep breath. 'Right, we should be getting back,' she said with false cheer. 'But before I do go, Mrs Vellanoweth, do you know where my mother lived? I think I'd like to see it.'

'Why, of course. They lived above the post office, like all postmasters do. Go out of the church, turn right and you'll see it soon enough at the crossroads.'

∞

'Are you sure this is a good idea, April?' Mrs Teague said as they made their way along the street. 'You're so upset, and this might make it worse.'

55

'No, I think I'd like to see it. At least I'll be able to picture my mother there in happier times. And it will add to my memories of her. I have so few, you see.'

'All right, if you're sure. I packed us a thermos of tea and some sandwiches to keep us going. So even though it's not exactly picnic weather, maybe we can find somewhere sheltered to eat.'

April didn't think she could swallow a morsel, but she didn't want to upset Mrs Teague, who had been so incredibly kind and helpful. 'How clever of you to think of it. That would be lovely.'

They wandered down the street and soon enough came to the two-storey building that stood at the crossroads of the village, with the words 'St Merryn Post Office' written over the door. April stopped and looked at it, her breath catching in her throat. It looked so familiar, but surely that was only because she'd come here when she was a child.

She tried to picture it as it might have been when her mother lived here. She imagined two little blonde girls, dressed in white dresses with blue pinafores and little black ankle boots running out of the door giggling with their arms linked. They looked so pretty and happy in her mind, and even though she knew it was just her imagination, the vision was comforting.

Smiling to herself, she looked around to find Mrs Teague standing there with a bemused expression on her face. 'April? Is everything quite all right?'

'I was just picturing my mother and my aunt as little girls. I know it's silly, but I swear I almost saw them coming out of the door.'

Mrs Teague patted her arm. 'Well, if they looked anything like you, I bet they were pretty little things.'

April laughed. 'They were, as it happens. From what I remember, my mother was very beautiful. But then, don't all children think their mother is the most beautiful woman in the world?' She sighed and tried to keep the tears from her eyes. She'd cried enough for one day, and she wanted to hang on to the happiness she felt as she pictured the girls. 'You know, Mrs Teague, it's funny, but the house looks familiar. Maybe I saw it when we came to the funeral, or maybe ... Oh, ignore me. Just the emotion of the day, I expect. Come on, you look freezing. We should get going before you turn into a block of ice.'

On the way back to Truro, Mrs Teague left April to her thoughts, for which she was grateful. She had so longed to find her family, but now she understood that she really was alone in the world. She needed to pull herself together and move forward, just like her mother had. And she'd make a start by doing everything she could to make friends at the hospital. What had that friendly nurse said to her the other day? 'We're all one big family here.'

That's it. And now I'm part of that family too. And that's a lot more than many people have, so I will try to find happiness. For my parents' sake.

Chapter 5

Bright and early the following Monday morning, April set off down the avenue of detached old stone houses, wrapped up warmly in her old shabby coat and thick-soled, fur-lined boots on her feet. Across her shoulder was an old leather satchel, lent to her by Mrs Teague, which contained her uniform, a hat – carefully packed so as not to squash it – and her white ward shoes. Mrs Teague had offered to lend her a bicycle, and though this would be useful, today she wanted to walk, so she'd left earlier than she'd normally have to – no matron would tolerate tardiness, new nurse or not.

All the houses on the street were similar – detached with an attic and a basement coal cellar. Like houses all over Britain, the steps leading up to the front door had once boasted a wrought-iron railing but all that was left now was a small knob of iron on the far side of each step, proof that the householders had sacrificed the beautiful iron work to aid the war effort.

She turned left and, seeing the enormous bulk of the hospital buildings above her, she quickened her pace. She walked in through the gates, which were open to admit vehicles, and stared up at the imposing building, with the sandbags piled high against it.

I hope those sandbags are never needed, April thought to herself, remembering the many bombing raids that St Thomas' had suffered.

Walking along the wide pavement leading to the hospital, she wondered how many cleaners and how many hours it took to clean that number of windows. She stopped to stare across the view of Truro. It was still dark, but by the light of the moon, she could make out the cathedral spire reaching high into the star-lit sky. She took a deep breath. This was it, the start of her new beginning. And she was going to make the most of it.

∞

Near the splendid conglomeration of other hospital buildings, including the airy nurses' hostel, she bumped into the red-headed nurse she'd seen. It looked like she, too, was about to start duty, and April's heart lifted at the thought.

She hurried after her. 'Hello, it's Eunice, isn't it?'

The nurse looked around. For a moment, April thought she wouldn't recognise her, then Eunice's face brightened. 'Oh, hello. I saw you the other day, didn't I?'

'Yes, I'm April Harvey. I'm just starting today to finish my training. Matron told me I'd be on the surgical ward, and I think that's the ward you said you worked on.'

'Oh, yes, that's me. I've just qualified, so no doubt sister will have me showing you the ropes today. Follow me, I'll show you where to change and leave your coat, then I think there's just time to grab a quick cup of tea before we start. I'm due to meet Bess in the cafeteria – she qualified at the same time as me – so you can meet her too.'

Grateful to have a guide, April hurried along beside her, and as soon as they'd changed, Eunice helped her pin on her hat. She laughed as it slid off April's hair.

'Your hair is so smooth and shiny, it won't stay.' She put in another pin. 'There. Neat as you like. Goodness, I love the colour. I wish my hair was golden like yours, instead of this horrible red.'

'But your hair is so vibrant. Lots of people have my colour hair but I've never seen such a beautiful deep red on anyone before.'

Eunice snorted. 'You should try living with it. And with these freckles, the Cornish sun plays havoc with my skin. I spend the entire summer looking like I've been boiled. Come on, or we won't have time for that tea.'

They hustled to the cafeteria, which was bustling with life as nurses and doctors took the chance to have a quick bite to eat and a cup of tea before they started their long days.

Eunice paused in the doorway, looking around. 'There she is. Bess!'

April saw a dark-haired girl sitting at a table chatting to another nurse. Even though she wasn't wearing any make-up – which was strictly prohibited for nurses on duty – something about the jaunty way she wore her hat, and how her dark hair curled around her face, made her look very glamorous. The other nurse was equally glamorous, although, April thought, Mrs Osborne would probably describe her as 'blowsy'. Her uniform looked a little too tight, from what April could see, and her hair was dyed a strange orange colour. They looked up when Eunice called and the dark-haired nurse waved. Feeling slightly intimidated, April followed Eunice to the table.

'This is April, Bess. She's still doing her qualification and starts today.'

Bess gave April an appraising stare, her eyes scanning her from head to toe. Her expression was cool and April wondered whether her hat really was on straight.

Finally, she held out a slim hand. 'Pleased to meet you, April. I do like your hair. Is it real or do you bleach it?'

April put her hand up to her hair self-consciously. 'No, it's all my own.' She laughed, feeling uncomfortable.

'Hmm, well, I knew someone with hair just that colour once and hers definitely wasn't real.'

'Oh, hush now, Bess, you're just jealous,' the other nurse said. 'Anyway, nothing wrong with dying your hair.' She patted her orange curls complacently.

Bess snorted. 'If you say so, Nancy.'

Nancy merely smiled at her, oblivious to the insult.

'And this,' Eunice said, 'is Nancy, who's nearly qualified.'

In contrast to Bess, Nancy gave her a warm smile, which made April feel guilty for her thoughts earlier.

'So tell us what you've been up to,' Eunice said to both of them as they sat down.

Bess suddenly looked animated. 'I met the most delicious man on Friday who took me to the pictures. Stanley, his name is. He's in the air force – stationed up near St Merryn. Officer, he is.'

Eunice sniffed. 'Another pilot, Bess? Is that a good idea?'

Bess gave her a filthy look. 'Yes, another pilot. This time it'll be different. It *is* different.'

April gazed between them, wondering what that was all about, but she didn't feel she could ask just yet.

Eunice looked sceptical, then turned to April. 'Bess and Nancy are man mad, as you'll soon see.'

Bess looked annoyed. 'Well, it's all right for you, you've got a man, but us single girls need to keep a look out. Speaking of which, have you heard from Norm recently?'

Eunice sighed. 'No, still no letter. Oh, I do worry about him.' She looked at April. 'My fiancé, Norm, is in the navy, and I have no idea where he is. And after everything that happened at the weekend, all those poor sailors dead at Pearl Harbor, I'm even more worried.'

April couldn't blame her for being worried. She and Mrs Teague had listened to the terrible news on Sunday in disbelief. Mrs Teague, who April was coming to realise wore her heart on her sleeve, had been in tears.

'Oh . . . all those lovely boys! It doesn't bear thinking of. Two thousand . . .' She'd sat sobbing while April had made her a cup of tea and tried to comfort her.

'Try not to worry,' April said to Eunice now. 'His ship wouldn't have been at Pearl Harbor, would it? It's the poor Americans that suffered yesterday. Anyway, it sounds like they'll join the war now, doesn't it? And that's a good thing. Gives us more of a fighting chance.' April wasn't sure her words would be of any comfort.

'Them Yanks won't stand for it, all those ships and men,' agreed Bess. 'Bet they start bombing Japan.'

'How will that help us?' asked Eunice. 'We need some help here. Our hospitals are full to bursting with injured servicemen and more arriving every day. Which reminds me. Bess, are you still thinking of nursing in the field?'

Bess stood up. 'Thinking about it. I want to make my gran proud. She's the only member of my family I even care about. She lost her hubby and her only son in the last war. Nancy's thinking about it an' all, aren't you, Nance?'

'Oh yes. I want to do my bit, and help all those poor wounded soldiers, but my mum's not keen. She wants me home. Says she can't bear to have her only daughter away as well as her son. So, I don't know. What about you, April?'

'Well, I don't have family to worry about but I need to qualify first before I can think of doing that.'

'Course you do.' Bess smiled at her for the first time. 'Anyway, word is that if the Americans join the war, we're going to have lots of lovely G.I.s coming over here. I hear they're ever so smart, and rich, and I bet every one of them is utterly gorgeous!'

Eunice rolled her eyes. 'Oh, for goodness sake, Bess, give it a rest with your talk of men. Every man you meet is always completely divine and crazy about you. Sure, you'd probably say the same about my Norm.'

Bess looked indignant. 'What sort of a girl do you think I am, Eunice Granger? As if *I* would ever steal another woman's man.'

'Of course you wouldn't, I was just joking. Anyway, come on, girls, we've got to get on or sister will have our guts for garters.'

∽

When April and Eunice arrived at the men's surgical ward, Sister Mulholland looked at April over her glasses. 'Matron told me you'd be coming. And very grateful we are for the extra pair of hands, even if they are inexperienced.'

April couldn't help feeling a little annoyed at that. 'I've done eighteen months training, sister. I've worked on surgical, maternity, children's and I've had lots of experience with trauma due to all the air raids.'

'Hmm, well, hopefully we won't need to use too much of that experience, nurse. Anyway, matron wants you to start on Florence Ward today, looking after some of our more elderly patients. One of the nurses is off sick. Nurse Granger, take her down and then get back here quick as you can.'

'Yes, sister.' Eunice beckoned for April to follow her. 'Don't mind her, her bark is worse than her bite,' she said, as she led her down the endless corridors. 'We'll be having our break at the same time, April, so come down to the cafeteria and let me know how you get on.'

By the time they reached Florence Ward, the doctor's round was in full swing. The ward, like most of the others she'd glanced in as they'd sped down the numerous corridors, was light and airy – a nice change from St Thomas' underground wards – with single iron bedsteads well-spaced down each side. A chair and a bedside table was beside each bed, while down the middle of the long room there were tables on which sat potted plants, magazines and books, neatly arranged.

Sister Turnbull greeted her at the nurses' station. 'Nurse Harvey?' She glanced at her watch. 'You are five minutes late. I'll let it pass today as it's your first day, but rest assured if you're late again, you'll be sent to the laundry for the rest of the day.'

April gulped. 'Sorry, sister.'

'Dr Spence is just beginning his rounds. Accompany him, if you please.'

April turned to see a pleasant-faced, middle-aged man wearing a white coat. He had thick, black-rimmed spectacles perched on the end of his nose.

'Come on, nurse,' he said cheerfully. 'We need to see a couple of the new admissions.'

He walked swiftly to a bed, where a very grumpy-looking elderly woman was lying.

'Good morning, Mrs Black. I hear you've not been able to eat recently, is that right? Pull the curtains, if you please, Nurse Harvey.'

April hurried to do as she was told, then watched as Dr Spence thoroughly examined the woman.

'You've lost a lot of weight since I last saw you, Mrs Black. What seems to be the problem?'

'I'm just not hungry these days. I think it's part and parcel of getting old.'

'Hmm, I think you need to let *me* be the judge of that.' He turned to April. 'Get the patient some porridge and a cup of tea, nurse. If she doesn't swallow anything, call me and we'll put her on a drip immediately.'

'Yes, doctor.'

'Attached a drip before, nurse?' he asked.

April shook her head. 'Only watched, doctor.'

He laughed. 'Have a look at the back of her hands. You should find a good vein there, but let's hope she's able to swallow.' Then he hurried away to check on the next patient.

Mrs Black did not eat her porridge and neither could she swallow the tea. In fact, she refused to even put the spoon to her lips.

'Are you listenin' to me, nurse? I'm not hungry. And forcing that slop down my throat ain't goin' to help.'

'But, Mrs Black, surely you'd rather eat than have a drip?'

'Hmph. If you think you can drip food down my throat, then you've got another think coming.'

April hid her smile. 'No, Mrs Black, a drip is when we put a needle in your vein and feed liquid straight into your blood, to stop you being so dehydrated.'

Mrs Black looked horrified. 'Over my dead body.'

'Come on, now, you want to get better, don't you?'

The old woman put her head back wearily. 'Well, if it's that or eat, I suppose I'll try this drip thing,' she said reluctantly.

'Come on, then, let's get you comfortable.' April plumped the pillows behind her back. 'Right, please let me see your hands, Mrs Black.'

The old woman pushed her hands behind her back like a naughty child; clearly she'd lied about being willing to try the drip.

Dr Spence returned and stood at the foot of the bed. 'How was the porridge this morning, Mrs Black?'

'As good as ever it is,' she answered grumpily.

'So you've not had any, then?'

April shook her head.

'Tell-tale,' she growled at her.

'Well, don't say I didn't warn you. Come on, then, give me your arm.' He held his hand out expectantly, and reluctantly Mrs Black pulled her arm from beneath the covers. Gently but firmly he pulled it towards him. 'What a lovely vein, nurse.' He explained what he was going to do and April held the free hand, noting the paper-thin wrinkled and mottled skin, and watched the doctor's actions with interest.

'You'll see, Mrs Black. You're going to feel much better soon,' she told her.

'Then you let him stick a great big needle in your hand, see how you like it. Ow! That hurt, doctor. If this is how it's going to be, then just let me die in peace.'

Dr Spence ignored her and continued attaching the drip. 'There,' he said at last. 'Don't let her out of bed today, nurse – bedpans only. If she's a little better tomorrow she can walk to the lavatory but her drip goes with her.'

For the rest of the morning, April was kept busy moving from bed to bed. All the patients were elderly and some needed very delicate handling. By the time she was due her break, Sister Turnbull gave her an approving nod.

'Not bad, Harvey. Seems you'll be useful to me after all.'

April smiled briefly, though inside she was seething at the patronising tone, and hurried to meet Eunice, who was already sitting at the table with a cup of tea, looking disconsolate.

'Is everything all right?' she asked her.

'Yes, fine, it's just I'm so hungry and look what they're advertising for lunch – chopped raw cabbage and Marmite sandwiches.' She pulled a face.

'Oh well. I'm so hungry I no longer care what I eat. Although I can't stand Marmite.'

'I'll have yours then,' said another voice.

'Bess,' Eunice said. 'Good to see you. How was your morning?'

'So so. Sister's on my back because I called in sick for night shift last week.'

'Did you? You never said you were ill.'

'Well . . .' Bess started to whisper. 'You remember I told you about the pilot? I wasn't feeling so good after our late night and thought it best not to come in feeling like that.'

Eunice gave her a disapproving look. 'Bess Walker! Are you telling me that you weren't sick, just a bit tired? Honestly, how could you be so irresponsible? Just because you're qualified doesn't mean they can't get rid of you, you know. And then where would you be?'

Bess tossed her head. 'Honestly, Eunice, you can be such a stick-in-the-mud. And I was ill. Up all night, I was, with a gippy tummy, and you can't pass that sort of thing on to the patients.'

April remained silent through this exchange. She thought it highly unlikely that there had been anything wrong with Bess at all that day. The girl was clearly man mad. She tried not to be too judgemental, though. This was Eunice's friend, and she didn't want to fall out with anyone. After all, this was her new family, and no family was perfect.

Chapter 6

May 1942

The following months sped by quickly for April as she settled into her new home. She'd spent a quiet Christmas with Mrs Teague, opting to work on Christmas Day, to try to banish any dark thoughts of previous years with her father. Mrs Teague had taken special care of her at Christmas, and April had reflected how she seemed more like a kindly aunt than a landlady, and it was clear that Mrs Teague took great delight in looking after her orphaned lodger.

Gradually, April found that with Mrs Teague's gentle care, and busy days at the hospital, she was having fewer and fewer nightmares, until one morning she woke to realise that she'd not dreamed at all for more than a week. It had been a year since the terrible night that had changed her life, and now she wondered if, finally, she was getting over her grief. There were still times when she yearned to see her father, to have him rather than Mrs Teague waiting for her, but the pain was not as sharp, and the dark cloud that had enveloped her in the months after the air raid seemed to have lifted.

As for work, the absence of nightly bombings, and the fact that April wasn't looking after terribly wounded and shocked patients, made her love her work even more – laundry duty and sanitary-towel-making notwithstanding.

And her happy mood meant that she was becoming a great favourite with doctors and patients alike – or so Eunice said, although Bess was quick to put her in her place.

'It's just 'cos you're a new face, April. A change is as good as a rest, so they say, so don't go getting too uppity.'

April had felt a little crestfallen at this, but then, Bess never shied away from speaking her mind, so she tried not to take offence.

As Eunice had promised, the hospital was small enough that soon she felt she knew most of the people who worked there, and on the whole, the nurses were friendly. She particularly liked Mattie Hargan, a qualified nurse in her mid-twenties, whose husband had been killed and who was now left bringing up their three-year-old daughter Angela by herself. And, of course, wherever Bess was, Nancy was sure to follow. Nancy was as man mad as Bess, but she had a warm heart, and April had never heard her say a bad word about anyone. Even when Bess was being especially catty, Nancy kept her good humour. For the first time since her father had died, April felt as if she truly belonged.

One warm May morning, April was sitting having her usual quick cup of tea in the cafeteria before she started her shift, chatting to Eunice, when Bess rushed up to them, full of news.

'You'll never guess, you two!'

'What are you talking about?'

'Guess what I saw, not fifteen minutes ago on the main road?'

'A fox,' said Eunice, who had a very dry sense of humour.

'I won't tell you if you don't take this seriously and then you'll be the only people in Truro who won't know.'

Eunice and April looked at each other. 'What could be more exciting than a fox?' asked Eunice sarcastically.

Bess laughed triumphantly. 'Yanks,' she shouted and then, aware of where she was, she lowered her voice. 'You do know there are thousands of them coming to Britain now? And at last some of them are in Cornwall. I saw them – rich, good-looking, in a truck and a . . . jeep, I think he said.'

'Who said?'

'The Yank, the officer – he was absolutely *gorgeous*. Think James Stewart in a green uniform, just as tall but broader and with short, dark hair.'

'Well, I do wish you'd taken a little time to look at him, Bess,' said Eunice sarcastically, 'if he even exists.'

'They all do. He asked me for directions to Pencalenick House.'

'Pencalenick House? Isn't that where they took some of the injured soldiers from Dunkirk? I don't think it's being used as a hospital any more, so why would they want to go there?'

'I don't know, do I? But that's what he asked for.'

'How many were there?'

'Don't know. Quite a lot in the truck and two in the little open car.'

'It's a jeep,' said Eunice. 'I've seen them in American films. Heavens, run for it. We're late!'

It was late afternoon before they had time to talk again about the American soldiers. April was sitting with Mattie and Bess, finishing a well-earned cup of tea and eating a quick, and rather stale, cheese sandwich.

'Ladies, salvation is nigh. The Yanks are finally here in Cornwall.' Dr Blacklaw, one of the younger doctors in the hospital, came across to them. Apparently, he'd seen them on the road to Trebah that morning.

'Did you speak to them?' Bess was eager to hear everything she could about these dashing soldiers.

'No, they were just beeping and waving at anyone around. Seemed rowdy to me. God knows what they can do to help us win the war.'

'Don't be ridiculous!' Bess was indignant. 'Just because they like a bit of fun doesn't mean they're not brave.'

Dr Blacklaw held up his hands. 'Sorry, Bess,' he said in mock fear. 'Didn't know you were so well acquainted with them.'

'I'm not.' Bess tossed her head. 'But I intend to be. Me and Nancy are going to go to Truro next day off to see if we can do anything to help them settle in, aren't we, Nance?'

'If you like, Bess. Got to make our allies feel welcome, don't we?' She winked.

Dr Blacklaw laughed. 'Well, I can think of no one better than you two to do just that,' he said as he went to spread his news further.

Nancy laughed with him, but Bess was fuming. 'Bloody cheek. What did he mean by that?'

'Oh, Bess, can't you take a joke?'

'Not when he's implying nasty things about me. Anyway, I'm only interested in one American. The one I saw this morning.' She shivered. 'Ooh, if I can only find him again, I'd make him very welcome. I think I'm in love.'

'Again,' groaned April and Mattie together.

72

'No need to be like that. This time I'm serious. No other man will do.'

'Well, I hope you see him again, Bess. I can't wait to meet this paragon.'

'You'll be laughing on the other side of your face, Mattie Hargan, when I finally do find him and work my charm.'

'And I'll be happy to admit my mistake. Now come on, you two, let's get back.'

∞

In the next few weeks everyone who lived in Truro saw the arrival of the first groups of American personnel. Their great vehicles with the steering wheel on the wrong side, huge white stars on the fluttering canvas, filled with smiling, waving men in unfamiliar green uniforms, roared through the towns, along the narrow country lanes and then seemed to disappear.

One morning, April was running some errands in town for Mrs Teague, who was, so she said, 'feeling a bit blue'. April was used to Mrs Teague's moods by now, and she knew that she took all the terrible news they'd been hearing about the war to heart. The night before, they'd listened to the news of the bombing of a hospital ship by the Luftwaffe in Alexandria and Mrs Teague had wept bitterly. She kept demanding that April promise not to do field nursing.

'Mrs Teague, I have no intention of doing that. Anyway, I'm still not qualified so they wouldn't have me yet.'

April's first stop was the butcher, where, as usual, there was a long queue of women waiting patiently to pick up their rations. April took up position beside a young woman who was clearly pregnant.

'Mornin,' she said to April.

April smiled in return.

'Aren't you Mrs Teague's nurse that she's always going on about? It's all "April this" and "April that". I'm Mrs Dashell, by the way.'

'Oh goodness, does she? I am sorry. Yes, I'm April. I'm just picking up her groceries for her.'

The other woman smiled. 'Well, I'm happy to meet you at last. Listen, what do you think about all these American soldiers? Are you treating any at the hospital?'

'No, I keep hearing about them, but I haven't seen any yet.'

'Well, my dad says that they're setting up tents all over the place, and there'll be even more here soon. He says they send in ordinary G.I.s to do all the hard work like fencing, roads and setting up tents. Then the officers come in and live like kings.'

'Sounds like my old man's stories of the last war,' said a sour-looking older woman standing in front of Mrs Dashell. 'And anyway, where have they been for the past two years while we've been dodging bombs?' She snorted. 'Safe at home feasting on beef, that's where.'

'Still, they're here now, and they're going to help us.'

'Huh. They took their time.'

'Don't forget they've already been helping us, what with sending food and all kinds of goods for years, and getting their ships and their men sunk doing it. My Peter was telling me all about it last time he was home.' Mrs Dashell rubbed her stomach dreamily, as if remembering a happy time.

74

'All I can say is no Yank is coming anywhere near my daughter. They're soldiers, too far from home and with too much money. I've heard some terrible stories from my sister in London.'

By this time, the older woman had reached the front of the queue and Mr Hughes, the butcher, had overheard the conversation.

'You talking about the Yanks? There's a load of them up in the woods by Pencalenick House. Was up there with the wife the other Sunday and there were fences with signs saying "Restricted Area. No entry". I mean, whose country is it?'

'Perhaps the owners wanted to keep out the Americans, not the locals,' said Mrs Dashell.

'No, we heard music, that jazz. I don't think many of the locals would have been playing jazz, do you?'

'Jazz?' said April, interested despite herself.

'Yes, and we could see some tents, large ones, and huge piles of wood and even metal strips. And then an American voice said, "Please move away from the fence, sir, madam. This is a restricted area." He was polite, I'll give him that, so we moved. But I'll tell you one other thing: the polite soldier was coloured.' He shook his head. 'Never seen a coloured man before 'cept in the films. Still, no different from the rest of us, I imagine.'

∽

April told Mrs Teague about the conversation over their supper of cottage pie.

'Good heavens.' Mrs Teague put down her fork in astonishment. 'Do you mean to say they're all just camping out like vagabonds?'

'I have no idea. Bess is constantly going on about some handsome officer she met, and I doubt he's camping. She's completely obsessed with the lot of them, though.'

'Hmm. "The friendly invasion", the papers are calling it. But why aren't they abroad fighting next to our soldiers? Are they expecting to find Nazis hiding on the beach? I just can't understand any of it, really, I can't. But we must trust in Churchill and Mr Roosevelt – funny old name, that is – as I suppose they know what they're doing.'

April smiled. Mrs Teague did make her laugh sometimes. Every day, she found herself growing more and more fond of her. 'I'm sure they do. And everyone is saying that with the help of the Americans we can win this war. Who knows? Maybe it will all be over by this time next year.'

'Oh, I do hope so. I didn't tell you, but the reason I'm so blue today, April, dear, apart from all the terrible news, is that I saw Mrs Green in town yesterday, and oh, it broke my heart. Her boy, Alfred, has been killed in action. He used to deliver the papers and I always gave him sweets on a Saturday. Such a lovely boy.' As always, when Mrs Teague thought about soldiers being killed, silent tears started to make their way down her cheeks.

April went and sat on the edge of her chair and put an arm around her. 'It's so dreadful, Mrs Teague, I know. Let me get you a little tot of brandy, what do you say? I know you have some stashed away for emergencies. Or would you prefer some cocoa?'

'You are a dear girl, April. I'm so glad you came to live with me. Just a small brandy. And then I will take myself off to bed for a nap.'

'How about on my day off next week, we go into town, and maybe we can have tea and cake in the Bluebell. Cheer you up a bit. What do you say?"

'Wonderful, April, I would love that.'

'That's settled then. I'll just go and get your brandy, and let you rest.'

◦◦◦

Over the next couple of days, April still hadn't seen an American soldier. Then, one morning, on her way to the hospital, she heard a loud roar and beeping behind her, and jumped back quickly as an American truck sped by. The men whistled and waved at her as they passed, and April couldn't help blushing and smiling back.

She told the others about it as soon as she saw them. 'I wonder where they were going?' she said.

'Well, I might have some idea,' said a smug Bess.

Mattie glanced at Bess disbelievingly. 'You going to tell us you're engaged to one of them already, Bess?' She rolled her eyes.

Bess bristled. 'No, but I am going to tell you that I had dinner with the handsome officer I told you about the other day. You know, the one that looks a bit like Jimmy Stewart.'

'Oh, did you now?' Mattie clearly didn't believe her, having heard far too many of Bess's exaggerated stories before.

'I did, as it happens. I was just walking down the street, and he stopped and asked if there was anywhere he could get some food. Given he looked rich and far too sophisticated for the Bluebell, I suggested he try the Royal. And he only asked me to join him!'

'Oh, how exciting!' April was still trying her hardest to keep on the right side of Bess, though sometimes she wasn't sure why she bothered.

'It was, and we drank French champagne and ate lobster.'

'Ha! I believe the lobster, plenty of that around here, but champagne? From a total stranger?'

'Believe what you want. You're just jealous.'

'So what was this incredible officer's name, then?'

'His name's odd. Crawford something. I called him Crawfie.' Bess smiled slyly. 'He definitely seemed to like it.'

'So, when are you seeing him again?'

Bess started to look a little less confident. 'Well, he's very busy, you know. But he's stationed up at Pencalenick House, so I could probably cycle up there one day to visit him. I told him he could find me at the hospital, so I'm sure I'll be seeing him again very soon.'

'Oh, yes, it definitely sounds like he can't wait to see you again. Why, he's no doubt in the hospital right this moment looking for his beautiful princess.' Mattie laughed so hard at her own joke that tears came to her eyes.

Bess looked at her with dislike, then scraped her chair back and stormed off.

Eunice, who had just come over, looked at Mattie and April in bemusement.

'What's eating her?'

'Oh, ignore her,' said Mattie airily. 'She's just having one of her fantasies and got cross 'cos I didn't believe her. Anyway, I have to get on. Mum's been looking after Angela all night, and I need to take over.' She gave a tired smile, all traces of laughter gone now.

When she'd gone, April turned to Eunice. 'Poor Mattie, it must be so hard with her husband dead and bringing up her little girl on her own. I wish I could help. Perhaps I'll offer to babysit for her when I can.'

'Yes, she's very brave. I'm sure she'd love to have you babysit, though she doesn't go out much. Not since poor Paul died. He was in the navy too, you know . . .' Eunice's eyes clouded over.

'Still no news?' April put her hand over Eunice's in sympathy.

'No. I don't even know where his ship is. Oh, April, I've written him so many letters, and for all I know they're just thrown on a great pile of other letters meant for service-men who have died. And on top of all that, I've not heard from my brother and father for months. Mum's going spare. I'm really worried about her, living all alone.'

'Don't you think if something had happened to his ship, you'd definitely know? Word always gets through one way or another. So don't invite worry until it knocks on your door, as my father used to say.'

Eunice sighed. 'I know you're right. Anyway, what about you? Have you heard from that soldier you mentioned? Theo, wasn't it?'

In fact, April had written several letters to Theo, as he'd asked, but had heard nothing back. She wasn't sure whether this was because they hadn't arrived – the post was slow, and she had no idea where he was – or because he hadn't written. She hoped it was the former. But despite what he'd said to her, April couldn't help thinking that Charlotte had probably received lots of letters. She'd never been a jealous type, but he'd destroyed her trust in him, and she was no longer sure what to think. If she'd been on better terms with his mother, she would have written and asked her if she'd heard from him, but she wondered whether Mrs Osborne would even reply to her.

These thoughts made her feel guilty. She should be happy to support any soldier, and whatever had happened in the past was of no consequence in the face of the terrible danger he was in.

April glanced at the watch pinned to her chest. 'I'll tell you all about it another day, but now I better go or sister will have me in the laundry all day.'

As she bustled away, she realised how all their conversations seemed to end with one or all of them rushing off to do something else. One day, maybe they could all have lunch, or spend more time with each other rather than snatching moments in the cafeteria.

Oh, well, that was nursing for you, she supposed. Then again, that was war. Nobody's time was their own any more; they were all pulling together to try to end this beastly conflict.

Chapter 7

The following week, April and Mrs Teague made an early start for the promised outing to town. Mrs Teague had suddenly developed a need to buy some new curtain fabric for the sitting room. April thought her curtains were fine as they were, but Mrs Teague was adamant, and April understood she needed another project to keep herself busy.

'To tell the truth, April,' Mrs Teague said as they walked down to the town, 'I never really liked those curtains; Isaac's aunt gave them to us as an anniversary gift, and I never had the heart to tell him I found them too gloomy.'

April refrained from asking her why she had kept curtains she disliked once she was alone. Instead she said, 'Just think what fun we'll have choosing new ones.'

But if April thought she was exhausted after a long shift at the hospital, shopping for curtains with Mrs Teague put exhaustion into a new category. It soon became apparent that if Mrs Teague wanted new curtains, she would either have to refashion the ones she had, or wait until rationing had ended, and who knew when that might be? But even so, they visited every shop they could find and examined every bolt of material that could be hauled out. None of it was suitable, and it was unlikely there'd be enough even if she had liked it. After almost three hours, April finally said that she would die if she did not have a cup of tea immediately.

The Bluebell was always packed in the mornings and at lunchtime, but by the afternoon one could usually find a comfortable seat at a table set with china cups, saucers and plates, all decorated with dancing bluebells. When they got there, however, they found almost every table had at least two men wearing green uniforms sitting at it.

'Are they Americans, April?' Mrs Teague whispered.

One of the men sitting at a table nearby had clearly overheard her. 'Yes, ma'am, we are,' said a very tall, young soldier with red hair. He stood up and pointed to the chairs around the table. 'There's room right here if you'd care to join us. I'm Red Cooper and this is Phil Taylor.'

April looked quickly at Mrs Teague and then around the room. If they wanted a cup of tea, then they would have to share a table. Perhaps they should just go home.

Mrs Teague, who had been bursting with curiosity about the American soldiers for weeks, hastily spoke before April could decline the invitation.

'How kind of you. Thank you. I'm Mrs Teague, and this is April Harvey. She's a nurse, you know.' She laughed girlishly, and April cringed. 'How silly I am – how could you know? But now you do. And Red, you say? Goodness, how strange. I suppose that's a bit like Ginger Rogers being called Ginger . . . But you're a man, obviously, so not the same.' She giggled again, while April wondered what on earth to do with her.

Red grinned broadly at her. 'I never thought of that, Mrs Teague. But you're right, Red is not my real name. I was christened plain and boring old John, but I prefer Red.'

'Mrs Teague . . .' began April.

'Oh hush, April. Then I shall call you Red too, if you don't mind.'

'I should be honoured, Mrs T. Do you mind if I call you Mrs T? A terrible American habit of shortening everything.'

'Oh, I like it very much. Do you know, I have never met an American before? I'll sit over there' – Mrs Teague pointed to the empty chair beside Red – 'and April, why don't you sit here where you have a lovely view of the comings and goings.' She pointed at the seat next to Phil, the quiet soldier who, to be fair, would find it hard to get a word in edgeways with her landlady around.

Once they were settled, April examined Red. He must be well over six foot, she considered, and with his bright red hair, he'd always be easy to spot.

'Now, Red, I've been so curious to meet all you young men. So much talked about, but so seldom seen. Do you know, when my Isaac was alive we used to go to see all the cowboy pictures; I *always* wanted to go to Texas and meet a real cowboy, or to California to see them making a film, but we never managed it.'

''Fraid we can't get you to California till this war is over, but before the war, I worked on my daddy's ranch.'

'Oh, a *ranch*! Just like a real cowboy. And do you have lots of horses?'

'Well, it wouldn't be a proper ranch without horses. I love horses. Riding them, rearing them, you name it, I love it.'

'He's a genuine cowboy,' said Phil, finally managing to get a word in, and stressing each syllable in genuine. 'If we could find a horse, Red would give us a show.'

Mrs Teague clapped her hands together with excitement. 'A real cowboy? Can you use a lasso?'

Red smiled. 'There's always something needs ketching on a farm. Next time I'm in town I'll bring a lasso and I'll teach you.'

Mrs Teague looked extremely startled. 'Good gracious, Red, I couldn't possibly ask you to do that.'

'But you didn't ask, I offered,' said Red with a smile that lit up his face.

While they all drank their tea, April watched in amusement as Red and Mrs Teague chatted as if they'd always known each other, and by the time everyone was ready to leave half an hour later, Mrs Teague knew all about Red's parents, grandmother, brothers and sisters, and the ranch they lived on. If she wasn't mistaken, she'd even caught him telling Mrs Teague about his sweetheart back home.

Finally, Red looked at his watch. 'C'mon, Phil, time to go. When we're in town we'll be here or in that pub that has the big fireplace, ladies.' Red took Mrs Teague's hand and kissed it. Mrs Teague blushed with delight. 'It's been a real pleasure to meet you, Mrs T. You remind me a lot of my grandma. I bet you two would get on like a house on fire.'

'Well, it's been an equal pleasure meeting you, Red. Oh, and wait, there have been all sorts of things in the paper about making our American friends welcome in our homes, so I would like to extend an open invitation to you and any of your friends to pop by for a cup of tea if you ever want to. I can't promise there'll be much food, but there'll always be a welcome.' Mrs Teague scrabbled in her bag to find a pen and paper, then scribbled her address and handed it to Red. He took it solemnly.

'I would surely love to do that, Mrs Teague. Thank you.' Then he saluted them both briefly and left with his friend.

Mrs Teague sat back with a happy smile on her face. 'Oh, how lovely. I will look forward to seeing that Red again. A cowboy? Gosh, who'd have thought I'd have a cowboy come to tea.'

April thought it unlikely that Red would ever turn up for tea, but said nothing. The two really had seemed to hit it off, though, and she knew Mrs Teague couldn't help collecting young people to mother.

April put her hand on hers and gave it an affectionate squeeze. 'Mrs Teague, you are quite one of the loveliest and warmest people I have ever met.'

'Pshaw.' Mrs Teague blushed again. 'I'm just trying to do my duty. There's little enough that an old woman like me can do, after all.'

April got up to pay the bill, but was startled when the waitress said, 'No need for that, love. One of the Yanks paid it. Looks like you're in with a chance there.' She raised her eyebrows disapprovingly and turned away.

April stared after her in mortification. She wasn't sure how to take this unexpected turn of events. Mrs Teague, of course, was in raptures about 'what lovely boys' the G.I.s were, with 'such beautiful manners'. But April felt uncomfortable. Then again, maybe she was just being over-sensitive.

At the hospital the next day, she told Eunice and Bess what had happened. 'I was so embarrassed. You don't think they meant anything by it, do you?'

Bess snorted. 'Honestly, April, what's the matter with you? Sounds like a very nice gesture to me. Were they handsome?'

'But a complete stranger paying for me and that woman on the till said I was "in with a chance". I was mortified!'

'A cup of tea, April,' said Eunice. 'They're in a foreign country; they're unsure of themselves and probably they're lonely. The only one I've seen so far looks as if he hasn't started shaving yet.'

'Well, the ones we met will be fine if Mrs Teague has anything to do with it. She's invited them all round for tea when they have a moment. One of them is a cowboy. Mrs Teague thought she'd died and gone to heaven. She's seen every cowboy film ever made, apparently, and reeled off names by the dozen on our way home . . .' April giggled as she remembered Mrs Teague's almost childlike delight the day before.

Bess interrupted her. 'Mrs Teague, a cowgirl? I'd buy a ticket to see that. And the cowboy? What's he like?'

'Very well-mannered and kind.'

'What does he *look* like? Come on, April, the important stuff.'

'I suppose he's good-looking in a cowboyish sort of way. Tall – he had to bend himself in half to get down far enough to shake hands with Mrs Teague – broad shoulders, slim, red hair. Not deep red like yours, Eunice, but quite bright. His nose looks as if it's been broken, but cowboys are always being thrown off their horses, aren't they?'

'Hmm, I wouldn't mind someone like that throwing a lasso over me.' Bess winked. 'Anyway, that's nothing. The other evening, I was cycling back to my nan's from work and a US Army truck stopped beside me and they absolutely insisted on driving me back. Ooh, and they were handsome. Well, apart from the one who offered to drive me home. Buck teeth.' She grimaced. 'They mentioned that they would be having a dance soon, and insisted I had to come so they could all dance with me.' She smirked at them. 'So it looks like I can take my pick. Lucky me, eh?'

'Are you out of your mind? Several G.I.s? How many is several?'

Bess gave the question some thought. 'Four, maybe five, and they were perfect gentlemen.'

'And what were they doing out at night? Drinking, probably.'

'A girl doesn't like to ask, Eunice. Anyway, they'd been at some beach exercising; at least they said they were on an exercise, if that's the same thing.'

'No, it's not,' said April. 'Theo used to talk about exercise and it meant they were practising something, like creeping up on the enemy without being discovered.'

Eunice did not give in easily. 'I'm sorry, Bess, but you were very silly to get into a vehicle with a bunch of soldiers. Don't you know what could have happened?'

Bess looked at her as if she could not believe her ears. ''Course I know. Believe it or not, I'm a qualified nurse. Anyway, they're coming into town on Sunday afternoon and I'm going to meet them. They haven't been to a British pub yet.'

'And you didn't tell them they won't get into one on a Sunday?'

'Oh Lord. I completely forgot. One of them, Spike something or other, read me a list of instructions every serviceman was given. All about manners, really. Don't insult the English, they're your hosts and it would be impolite, especially don't insult the king or queen, and besides' – she adopted what she thought was an American accent – 'it's *real* stupid to insult one of your oldest allies – things like that, but nothing about licensing laws.'

'Should you be meeting a group of men on your own in the pub?' Eunice was still very disapproving, much to Bess's annoyance.

'I won't be on my own. Nancy is coming with me.'

'But what about your boyfriend? The dashing officer who looks like Jimmy Stewart?' April couldn't help asking.

Bess looked evasive. 'Doesn't mean I can't have a drink with other people, does it? And I've already invited him for a drink. Cycled up to Pencalenick House the other day.'

'So, did you talk to him?' asked Eunice.

'The guards at the gate told me to leave a message and they'd get it to him. Honestly, you'd have thought I was a German soldier, the way they looked at me! Still, once he's seen the message, I expect he'll turn up here.'

April and Eunice looked at each other, but wisely said nothing. It never did any good to tease Bess, she always took it the wrong way.

Just then they heard an alert for an Emergency Room physician, put down their cups of unfinished tea and hurried back to their stations. April, who was assigned to post-op that week, hoped that whoever the patient was, they could be saved.

When she got to the ward, the sister greeted her. 'Good, glad to have you back, Nurse Harvey. Seems a young American serviceman has overturned his truck and is very seriously injured, poor thing. Doesn't look old enough to be driving, let alone serving as a soldier.' She shook her head sadly. 'You've had a lot of trauma training, so I want you to look after him when he gets out of theatre.'

'Yes, of course, sister.' April wasn't looking forward to the task, and she hoped the soldier wasn't one of the ones she'd met the day before.

Sadly, though, a short time later, the sister came to tell her that the boy had died on the operating table. April tried hard to keep the tears from falling. She was a nurse, and death was ever-present in a hospital, especially during wartime, but even so, she found it hard to keep her emotions in check when tragedy occurred.

When April got home that night, she found that the news had spread through the town already. Mrs Beetie was sitting in the kitchen with an inevitably tearful Mrs Teague.

'Oh, April, it wasn't Red, was it?'

'No, Mrs Teague, it wasn't anyone we met. But it's still so sad.'

'Come on, Doris, how many times have I told you not to take on so. You have to stop feeling like you have to care for every young person in the town. And now we have all these young soldiers here, I can see you're only going to get worse.'

Mrs Teague sighed. 'I know, but they are so young, Celia. I can't help feeling responsible for them somehow.'

'There, now, let me get you another cup of tea and then I must get off. Mr B hasn't had his tea yet, unless he's shifted himself to get his own.' She rolled her eyes, knowing full well that he wouldn't have even thought of it.

The town was quiet that weekend. Not one American soldier appeared.

Chapter 8

One day towards the end of June, when April came down for her afternoon break, she noticed a crowd of people gathered around the noticeboard in the cafeteria, all chattering excitedly.

'What's all the fuss about?' she asked Jean Gray, a nurse she didn't know that well.

'Look!' She pointed to a large piece of paper pinned to the board. 'The Americans are having a dance and we're all invited! Apparently, they're going to construct a dance floor in the woods outside Bodmin and lay on transport for all of us. Oh, how fabulous! I haven't been to a dance for ages.'

'Goodness! In the woods? Well, that sounds fun.'

'Telling me. I just hope I can go.'

There was so much noise that two of the sisters came over to disperse the crowd and chivvy them all back to work.

'The world is at war and they're putting in a dance floor.' Sister Turnbull gave a disdainful sniff.

'I think it's a splendid idea,' said Sister Smith, the nicest of all the sisters at the hospital. 'Life is so uncertain for everyone at the moment, and those young soldiers are so far from home that if their colonel thinks a little time spent dancing is good for morale . . . Well, let me tell you, if they can find someone old enough to dance with me, we'll all go.'

'Well, I suppose we should go, then.' Bess had appeared at April's shoulder. 'We should do everything to make them feel welcome, just as Sister Smith says.'

'You'll only be going if I say you're not on duty, Nurse Walker.' Sister Turnbull wasn't fooled by Bess's mock reluctance. 'And that goes for all of you. Don't make any plans until the duty rosters have been drawn up. Now come along. Just because the Americans have nothing better to do than hold dances doesn't mean you can stop work.' And with another sniff, she turned and walked briskly away.

∽

For a few days after the invitation was posted, tea breaks were filled with happy chatter about what to wear.

'It's sometimes hard to believe there's a war on,' said Eunice, 'with all this talk of dances. Anyone who can get into my taffeta skirt is welcome to borrow it.'

'But won't you be going?' April asked.

'No, I'm happy to work. I'm not sure how my Norm would feel about me jitterbugging with every American soldier in Cornwall.'

Bess laughed. 'Honestly, Eunice, you're not married yet, and it's only a dance.'

'Even so, I'd hate to do anything to upset him while he's fighting for us all. No, my taffeta is up for grabs, girls. First come first served.'

Nancy perked up at that. 'Can I borrow it, Eunice?'

'Course you can. I'll bring it in tomorrow.'

April considered Nancy's statuesque form, and Eunice's slim, almost boyish figure, but didn't say anything. Nancy loved her clothes to be tight, but she hoped she wouldn't rip it.

Bess looked over at April. 'What about your Theo?' April wished Bess didn't know about Theo, but she'd been sitting with her and Eunice when they were talking about him one day.

'He's not my Theo. We are friends and he would tell me to go to the dance and have fun, and I will if I can find something to wear. Otherwise, it's a skirt and blouse – marginally better than wearing my uniform.'

'Doesn't matter what you wear, April,' said Nancy. 'You always look gorgeous, doesn't she, Bess? Wish I could say the same. Takes me hours to look my best.'

Bess swept April with a long, hard look. 'I suppose she does, if you like the innocent, girlish look,' she said witheringly.

April blushed, feeling suddenly very frumpy even though they were all in uniform.

'Anyway,' Bess continued, 'in the spirit of Eunice's generosity, I have a spare pair of nylons if anyone wants to borrow them.'

'Have you?' Nancy looked entranced. 'You never said. Where did you get them from?'

Bess tapped the side of her nose. 'I might have mentioned a handsome officer I met once or twice, girls, do you remember?'

'What? The one you keep saying will turn up here, but somehow he never does?' Eunice said sceptically.

'You're not here all the time, Eunice Granger. But what say we all meet up to go and look for something new to wear? Anyone else off on Saturday?'

'Oh, yes, let's all meet up!' Nancy was almost bouncing with excitement. Can we get tea at the Bluebell as well?'

Bess rolled her eyes. 'If you insist.'

'I'll be there, even though I don't need to buy anything for the dance. I'll be going to St Agnes that afternoon to stay with Mum for the night, as she's been feeling blue about not hearing from Dad and George, but I can come in the morning. What about you, April?'

'Oh yes, it'll be fun. Though I probably can't buy anything.'

'Good, that's arranged. See you then, everybody!' Bess called as she left.

∽

The day of the shopping expedition dawned bright and warm, and before she left, April went out into the garden where Mrs Teague was weeding the vegetable patch.

'We're going to have a bumper crop of lettuce if this gorgeous weather continues,' she said. 'I can't remember when we last had such a long stretch of good weather.'

'I know. The hospital has been roasting. Makes the patients very grumpy. Anyway, I'm just off to meet the girls, Mrs Teague, to see if we can get anything for the dance. Do you want anything from town?'

'Wonderful. So glad you girls are getting some time to relax together. You work too hard, if you ask me.' She looked at April, who was wearing one of only two summer dresses she possessed. 'And you should get yourself a new frock, April Harvey. That one looks like it's about to fall apart. You can't wear that to the dance.'

April looked down at herself. Mrs Teague had a point. The cotton shirt dress was faded and what had once been a pretty blue, flowered material now looked very worn. She thought of the dresses she used to own. All gone now.

'You're right,' she said ruefully. 'But I'm not sure it's worth spending the money on a new dress just yet. I can make do with what I've got.'

'You'll be wanting to look pretty in case some handsome G.I. comes and whisks you off your feet. Maybe that lovely Red will be at the dance.' Mrs Teague gave her a sly grin.

'Honestly! Don't you go letting your thoughts stray in *that* direction! That's the last thing I need. I'll leave all that to Nancy and Bess.'

'Oh, April, I completely forgot, talking of young men. You were in so late last night and I was so tired I didn't tell you about your letter. It's on the mantelpiece. I think it's from your soldier friend, Theo.'

April's heart leapt. 'Gosh, at last! I'll go and get it. Bye for now!'

April rushed to get the letter, stuffed it in her pocket, then darted out the front door. She'd gone just a few steps when she heard Mrs Teague calling her from the doorstep.

'Do bring your friends home for tea, April. I'd be *so* happy to see them.'

April smiled to herself. If Mrs Teague could invite the whole of Truro to tea she would. She wondered if Red would ever turn up. She hoped so. In just that one brief meeting, Mrs Teague had taken him to her heart and was still talking about him. If she ever saw him again, she would make sure to shepherd him back to Daniel Road if it was the last thing she did.

The girls had arranged to meet at the cathedral, and April and Eunice arrived there simultaneously, but Nancy and Bess were nowhere to be seen.

'Hmph. They've probably met some unbelievably handsome Americans and we won't see them at all,' Eunice said scathingly.

'No, here they are, look.'

She watched as Bess and Nancy, looking incredibly glamorous and a little overdressed, strutted towards them. Bess was wearing a beautiful white, slim-skirted dress that was cinched in at the waist with a slim black patent belt. On her feet were a pair of high, wedged sandals. Her dark curly hair was in a Victory roll at the sides, with the curls flowing down her back.

Nancy was looking equally glamorous, in a pair of beige slacks that showed all her curves. She wore a blouse tucked in tightly, with the buttons undone just a little too low. She also wore wedge sandals similar to Bess's. Her hair, which she'd now dyed black, was clipped at the sides and hung to her shoulders. Both girls had painted their lips the same vivid scarlet.

'Good grief!' Eunice was staring at the pair. 'Have I missed something? Are they going to the dance now?'

They looked beautiful, thought April glumly, suddenly feeling plain and unsophisticated in her hand-me-down dress. She'd thought Eunice looked nice in her green shirt-waister, but these two were really turning heads – although she could see some very disapproving looks being thrown their way as well.

'Hello, girls.' Bess came to a stop in front of them and did a little twirl. 'What do you think? Reckon we'll catch anyone's eye today?'

'Hmm. Well, you've certainly caught the eye of that man over there.' Eunice gestured across the road.

Bess looked over eagerly, only to see an old man, wearing a flat cap, who'd been cleaning a shop window. He now stood, cloth in hand, water dripping down on to his shoes, and a cigarette practically falling out of his open mouth.

She tossed her head at him and looked away. 'Well, I hope this isn't how you're going to be for the whole day, Eunice. I just want a bit of fun.'

'Me too.' Nancy was standing with her hand on her hip, posing for anyone who cared to look.

'Anyone would think you were going to a night at the Savoy, not just trailing around the market in Truro and having a cup of tea. Admit it, the minute you see a handsome man you're going to be off, aren't you?'

'Course not. We're here to spend time with our pals, and that's what we're going to do. But you never know who you might meet. Tell you what, let's pop into the Bluebell now for a quick cuppa before we go to the market. What do you say? I'll treat you all. I might even throw in a bun if you're lucky.' Bess winked and sashayed away, the others trailing in her wake.

∞

The Bluebell was full, as usual, but luckily one table became free just as they walked in so they rushed over to sit at it. April saw that Nancy and Bess were flicking their eyes around the room, hoping, no doubt, to see some G.I.s, but there were only the usual locals here this morning. Once seated at the table, the waitress, who had been so disapproving of April when Red had paid her bill, came over, looking unimpressed at the sight of the girls.

'Don't know who you're expecting to meet, but just so you know, there's not been any Yanks in for a while, so no point getting all dressed up, eh, girls?'

'I don't know what you're talking about, Kath. Me and the girls just want a bit of tea before we look round the shops. If that's not too much trouble.' Nancy smiled at her winningly.

Kath flounced away and Nancy leaned over the table and whispered conspiratorially, 'She never did like me. Used to be two years above me at school and bossed us all around something rotten. But she really hated me, and I never knew why.' Nancy looked a little mournful at that, and April patted her hand.

'She was just jealous 'cos everyone likes you, Nance, that's all.'

Nancy brightened. 'Do you think so?'

'Never mind all that,' Bess said impatiently. 'What's the news? Anything from Norm yet, Eunice?'

'Oh, yes.' Eunice's answer was surprisingly muted. 'I got a letter yesterday. He's safe, he's well, and he misses me.'

'Well, that's good, isn't it? You've been moaning for ages about not having a letter, so why the glum face? Didn't he tell you he loved you?'

Eunice sighed. 'No. It's not his way. Norm is a man who keeps his feelings to himself. It's more a case of showing than saying. But that's all right. We understand each other . . .' She trailed off. 'It would be nice to have him write it once in a while, though. Still, it was lovely to hear from him. On top of that, Mum's heard from George and Dad as well. Things are looking up.' She grinned around at them.

'Oh, that reminds me.' April dug in her pocket. 'I got a letter too. There must have been a big delivery or something, so all the letters are arriving at once.'

'Ooh! Who's that from, April? Is it from your sweetheart, Theo?' Nancy looked at April eagerly.

'He's not my sweetheart, how many times do I have to tell you all?'

'Come on, you said you loved him last time you spoke about him. If that's not a sweetheart, I don't know what is.'

'Well, I do love him. As a friend. After the way he threw me over, I don't think I can trust him again.' April was not willing to discuss her complicated feelings for Theo further than that.

Bess reached across the table and snatched the letter from her hand. 'Let's have a read, and see just how *friendly* he is, shall we, girls?'

'Hey! That's private.'

'Oh, don't be such a bore. If he really is just your friend, it can't be that interesting.'

April was mortified. He might not be her sweetheart, but even so, she didn't want anyone else reading her letters.

Eunice came to her defence. 'Come on, Bess, give it back. You're not being fair.'

Bess sighed. 'You're such a spoilsport. I'll give it back on the condition you read it to us.'

'Let me see what's in it first.' April took the letter, her cheeks flaming, anger making her hands shake.

She scanned the single page quickly.

Dear April,

Thank you for writing to me. You can't imagine how your letters cheer me. I don't get many. Mother writes regularly, of course, but otherwise, there's only you. I'm glad you love Cornwall, and that you found out what happened to your family. But very sorry that it was bad news. How I wish I had been with you to soften that blow, my darling. But Mrs Teague sounds nice and it comforts me to know you are in good hands.

I can't tell you much about where I am, but it's pretty boring. I miss you and I miss my cello. Some of the boys get together and we sing sometimes, just to pass the time, but it's not the same. I wish I could play for you now, like I used to. Do you remember?

I've been thinking a lot about you and our last evening together – there's not much to do here but think, apart from the endless exercises, of course. Anyway, what I want to say is that I'm sorry. I realise how I behaved was not right, and if I confused you and hurt you, it was never my intention. I suppose I was confused too. And didn't know how to behave.

I keep remembering our kiss that last night. How very special it was. How much hope it gave me that we can get back to the way we were. Until my mother ruined it. She does have a habit of doing that, doesn't she? I am keeping you in my heart, April. And begging for your forgiveness. I know now that I was wrong to treat you the way I did.

100

I don't expect you to wait for me – why should you after what I did? – but I want you to know that I will wait for you. And I hope that when this war is over, you will find it in your heart to forgive me, and maybe return my love again.

All my love,

Theo

The words started to blur as she read. She thought about how he'd looked that last evening, his face lit by the fire, his eyes tender. But alongside that memory was the one when he told her that she was just a childhood crush.

Oh, Theo, she thought, I don't know if I can ever trust you enough to love you as I used to. She wiped her eyes and looked up, suddenly aware of the expectant silence around her.

'Well?' Bess was clearly impatient. 'Why the tears? Has he thrown you over again?'

'No, I'm not reading this out. It's private.'

'Ooh, does he *love* you?' Bess made kissing noises with her mouth.

Just then the door opened, saving April from answering as a couple of very tall, very smartly dressed G.I.s walked in. The four looked with interest at the men. Though she'd heard many people mention it, these were the first coloured soldiers April had seen.

Kath looked up, and then around the restaurant. 'I'm sorry, gentlemen, but I think you may have to come back later. As you can see there are no tables.'

Just then Nancy stood up and called loudly across the crowded room, 'That's no problem, Kath. We'd be happy to have these fine soldiers sit with us, wouldn't we, girls?'

She flicked her hair prettily and looked around at the others. Bess and April nodded in agreement.

April was very aware that the whole tearoom had fallen silent and everyone was looking at them. She glanced around. It was true all the tables were taken, but there were enough seats for them at other tables, and everyone was used to sharing. She felt both embarrassed and angry on the G.I.s' behalf. She'd heard that the American soldiers were strictly separated into coloured and white areas, but she didn't really understand why. And she assumed that Kath was taking her lead from the other G.I.s. It seemed rude to her. She felt a flash of warmth towards Nancy. Even though her actions were probably motivated more by how handsome the men were than anything else, she was glad she'd spoken up.

The men looked between Kath and Nancy uncertainly.

Bess smiled invitingly at the men. 'After all, we have been told to make our allies welcome. Isn't that right, Kath?' She glared pointedly at the waitress, who gave her a withering look in return.

April decided it was time she waded in as well. 'Oh, please do join us.' She glanced at Eunice, who had remained silent throughout all of this, which was strange; she was usually the first to try to right an injustice. But to her surprise, Eunice was sitting stock still, staring at the shorter of the two soldiers – although he was still around six feet tall as far as April could tell – with a very strange expression on her face. On top of which, her face looked flushed.

April gave her a gentle kick under the table, which brought Eunice back to earth with a start. She glanced quickly at her, then back at the soldiers. 'Yes, of course, please come and sit down,' she said a little faintly.

April noticed that the soldier Eunice had been staring at was returning her intent look as they walked over to the table with broad smiles on their faces. Did they know each other, she wondered? Eunice had never mentioned it, which was odd.

'You are most kind, ladies, but we have orders not to cause trouble,' one of them said quietly.

'No trouble at all, boys,' Bess said, trying to sound seductive, but really, sounding a bit ridiculous.

The taller G.I. took off his hat and sat down. 'I'm Homer, ma'am,' he said to Nancy. 'And this is A.J. We're very happy to make your acquaintance.'

'Gosh how tall you both are.' Nancy giggled girlishly. 'Where on earth can they fit two such strapping men? I'm sure there's not a bed in Cornwall that would be long enough.'

A.J. laughed. 'We brought our own beds over. Anyway, they're just camp beds, and yes, our feet hang off the end. Especially Homer's here. And his feet are so big that when he's lying on his stomach, his toes hit the floor.'

Everyone laughed.

'Golly.' Nancy batted her eyes at Homer. 'I can't imagine feet can be that big. And as a nurse, I've seen a lot of feet.'

Homer grinned at her while April watched in fascination. So this was how flirting was done. She'd never managed to do it, and she'd probably be too embarrassed, but Nancy really was good at it.

'So where are you stationed?' Bess asked A.J.

'We're up near Pencalenick House, ma'am. Although we don't sleep in the house itself, obviously, we have our own camp in the woods.'

Bess sat forward, looking suddenly eager. 'Oh, I've been there. I know one of the officers stationed there. Crawford something. Do you know him? He's a *very* good friend of mine.'

A.J. raised his eyebrows at this. He didn't look convinced. 'I do know him, ma'am. And a very fine officer he is.'

'Could you give him a message for me? He's so terribly busy that obviously he's not had a minute to write a letter to me. Even though I've been sending some to him.'

A.J. looked a little uncertain. 'Well, I guess so,' he drawled. 'But he's not there at the moment, so I don't know when he'd be able to answer you.'

'Oh, that's all right. I completely understand. When you see him, could you tell him that Bess – from the Royal – would like to see him again? And he can find me at the hospital or the nurses' home. I did tell him, but he must have forgotten, being so busy and everything.'

'I'll be sure to tell him if I see him, but like I said, our camp is separate from theirs, and I don't go over there much.' A.J. looked over at Eunice then. 'Hello, ma'am, I haven't met you, but I saw you at church last Sunday, didn't I? At St Agnes? No way could I forget that pretty hair.' AJ raised his hand to her head, almost as if he was going to touch it.

Eunice blushed. 'Um . . . yes. Um, I saw you singing there. You have a beautiful voice.'

April could not believe that her usually confident and chatty friend seemed so shy. Could it be . . . ? No. She was being unkind, Eunice would never betray Norm, but A.J. certainly was handsome with his smooth, dark skin, close-cropped hair and large brown eyes.

Eager to be included in the conversation, Bess interjected, 'Oh, Eunice mentioned something about that to me the other day. She said she'd never heard such beautiful voices, didn't you, Eunice?'

A.J. laughed. 'Well, I'm not sure about that' – he looked back at Eunice – 'but I'm glad you enjoyed the singing. Will I see you in church again sometime? I'd surely like that. I don't get to go as often as I'd like, but I will try if you're there.'

Eunice was silent for a moment, then she got up quickly. 'I don't think I'll be able to go for a while. Anyway, I must get on. So nice to meet you A.J., Homer. Goodbye.'

A.J. looked after her as she hurried to the door, bemused. Homer and Nancy, who were wrapped up in their own conversation, didn't seem to notice, but Bess stared after Eunice with a speculative look on her face. She turned to A.J.

'Poor Eunice has to see her mother who's not well. How about you and me, and maybe Nancy and Homer, take a walk around the town?' She looked at April. 'You're welcome to join us, but the numbers are a bit uneven and I wouldn't want you to feel like a third wheel. Or actually a fifth.' She giggled at her own joke.

April stared at her, furious. What had got into Bess? One moment she was talking about this Crawford, the next she was inviting a complete stranger to go walking with her. And then there was the way she'd been about her letter.

April pushed back her chair. 'No, I have to get back to Mrs Teague. You won't mind sorting out the bill, will you,

Bess? You did promise after all.' She smiled at her sweetly then turned to the G.I.s. 'Lovely to meet you both, gentlemen.'

Keeping her head high, she walked out of the café and stormed down the street, fuming. Her whole day had been ruined by that nasty cat, Bess, and she'd had enough. From now on, she would be polite when she saw her, but that was it. Over the past months, Bess had been getting increasingly cruel towards her, and she had no idea why. She'd tried everything to become friends with her, but not any more. She would stay out of her way from now on.

Chapter 9

April wandered down the road and was surprised to see Eunice sitting on the steps of the cathedral. She ran towards her.

'Eunice! What happened to you in there? I was worried about you. I didn't think you were seeing your mother till later.'

Eunice looked up. 'I just needed to get away. Anyway, what are you doing here? Where are the others?'

April plopped down on the step beside her and told her what Bess had said. Eunice shook her head. 'Try not to mind Bess, April. She's had a bad time of it in the past, she's told me a little of it, and it's not nice. I think she gets very insecure, and for some reason she feels she's in competition with you.'

'But why? I'm not even qualified yet, I never go out with her. I just don't understand, Eunice. And if she's so crazy about this Crawford, why is she then making googly eyes at another man?'

'She wants everyone to love her, that's why.'

'Except me,' April said ruefully.

'Except you,' Eunice agreed.

'Anyway, enough of all that, what was your problem with A.J.? He seems ever so nice, and he's very handsome, don't you think?'

Eunice looked away. 'I suppose. If you like that sort of thing.'

'Well, Bess and Nancy definitely do. Look, there they are now, coming out of the café. Good grief that man is tall. Nancy must be half the size of Homer.'

Eunice looked over and snorted. 'I might have guessed it. Bess is all over A.J. I know I said she's insecure, but sometimes I wonder whether she's just plain mean.'

'You know, Eunice, that is exactly what I think. But why are you so upset about Bess being with A.J.?' She looked at her friend carefully. 'You find him attractive, don't you?'

'Of course I don't. I'm in love with Norm, remember?'

'But surely that doesn't mean you can't find other people attractive? When Theo took me to see *Top Hat* one time, I thought Fred Astaire was completely dreamy.'

Eunice laughed. 'It's hardly the same thing, is it? It's not as if you'll ever meet him. And anyway, I've always thought Fred Astaire looks a bit like a tortoise.'

'Eunice Granger! How can you say such a thing?'

Eunice grinned, then sighed. 'But if I'm truthful, yes,' she said quietly. 'I do think A.J. is attractive, and even though I've only ever seen him once, I've been thinking about him. What sort of girl does that make me? Poor Norm out there on the sea somewhere, in fear of his life, and here's me, admiring another man.' She put her face in her hands.

April put her arm around her friend's shoulder. 'This all sounds like nonsense, Eunice. Have you walked out with him? Gone to the pictures with him? Tried to see him? No, you haven't. You have nothing to feel guilty about. Anyway, now the other two have gone off, looks like it's just you and me. I'm not in the mood for looking round the shops now. There's nothing to buy anyway. Tell you what, why don't you come back to Mrs Teague's for lunch? She'd be delighted to see you.'

'Yes, I'd like that. Mrs Teague's food is so delicious, and it'll make a nice change from the hospital muck.'

They were just walking down the cathedral steps when April spotted a familiar redhead crossing the road. 'Hang on, Eunice, I think that's Red. The G.I. I told you about that we met the other week.' She rushed up to him.

'Red? Is that you?'

Red turned around and looked down. 'Hey, it's you. How are you? And how is your lovely friend, Mrs T?'

'Oh, she speaks of you often. She hasn't forgotten your promise to show her how to use a lasso. And she was so sorry to hear about the soldier who died. I hope he wasn't a friend of yours.'

'No, I didn't know him. But it shook us all up. Brought it all home to us.'

'Well, Mrs Teague was very keen to invite you round to lunch or tea when you're free.'

'That's mighty nice of her. I would love to have a real British tea.'

'I know it's a bit short notice, but we're just on our way back there now. Why don't you come too, if you have time? It'll make her day.'

'As it happens, I am free. I've got the afternoon off and was just taking a stroll around.'

'Let's go, then. She's going to be *so* excited to see you. Oh, by the way, this is my friend Eunice, who works at the hospital with me.'

Red tipped his cap. 'Pleasure, ma'am. Looks like you and me have something in common.' He grinned and gestured to Eunice's head.

'Looks like it. But anyone who's tried to call me Red hasn't lived long enough to do it again.' They all laughed and April was relieved to see that Eunice seemed to have shaken off her mood.

'By the way, Red, are you going to this dance near Bodmin? All the hospital has been invited, and it would be wonderful to see a friendly face there.'

'I'll be there. Maybe you can save me a dance.'

'I most definitely will. Although I don't know too much about some of those American dances.'

'Then it'll be fun to teach you, if I manage to get a look in. I have a feeling you'll be surrounded by so many soldiers, I'll have to beat my way through to get to you.'

April laughed and smacked him on the arm. 'Don't be ridiculous. There'll be lots of girls there. I might say the same about you. The nurses are going to love you.'

'Well, a man can hope, can't he?' He grinned and linked his arms companionably through the two of theirs.

Once at the house, April led them into the sitting room, where Mrs Teague was sewing and listening to the wireless. She jumped up in delight the minute she saw them.

'Ooooh, my goodness, Red, I am so happy to see you, my love. Come in, come in. I've got cold meat pasties for lunch, along with lettuce and tomatoes from the garden. I'm sure if I cook a few potatoes, we can make it all stretch.'

'Mrs T, don't you worry about feeding me. I get plenty up at the camp.'

'Nonsense, my dear. No one comes to my house and doesn't eat. And wonderful to see you too, Eunice.'

Later, as they sat at Mrs Teague's dining-room table and feasted on the delicious meat pasties, Mrs Teague battered Red with questions, which he answered with good humour.

'Red, dear, I don't understand. Sometimes the town is full of all you young men, but at others, there's not a sight of one of you. It's as if you've never been here. Where on earth do you go?'

'Highly classified information, Mrs T.' Red tapped his nose. 'Let's just say that we are not always the relaxed and happy band you see, and we are working hard to help you Brits win this war. So try not to worry. I reckon everything's going to turn out just fine if the US Army have anything to do with it.'

'Bless you, dear. Of course you are. I forget sometimes that you have work to do. You're all so brave coming over here to fight with us. Aren't they, April?'

April smiled. 'Yes, of course they are. We're very grateful to you all.'

They sat for some time longer, chatting easily, almost like a real family having lunch together, April thought with a smile. But eventually, Red got up to leave.

'Well, Mrs T, I can't thank you enough. And next time, I will bring my lasso and some supplies. But now, I've got to get back. This has been a real pleasure, ma'am.'

'Nonsense, Red. It was our pleasure, wasn't it, April? Just as it was a pleasure to have you with us, too, Eunice.'

Mrs Teague rose from the table and went to retrieve Red's cap. She handed it to him and stretched up on tiptoe to kiss his cheek. Red tipped his hat gallantly and left.

'Oh, what a lovely man, don't you think, April? Just the sort of man any mother would be happy to meet if their daughter brought him home.'

April sighed in resignation. 'Yes, I'm sure, Mrs Teague, but please don't be thinking in that direction for me. I am not looking for a boyfriend. Certainly not one who will leave and go back to his home thousands of miles away.'

'Oh, of course, dear. Well, all I can say is any girl would be lucky to walk out with a gentleman like Red, don't you think, Eunice? Though I know you've got your Norm.'

Eunice gave April a mischievous look, then said, 'I couldn't agree more, Mrs Teague. And do you think that our April is perhaps protesting too much? I think Red is perfect for her.'

Mrs Teague beamed at the two of them, while April gave Eunice an 'I'll kill you' look. 'I think you need to go, don't you, Eunice?'

Eunice laughed. 'I do, so I'll say goodbye. Thank you so much for the lunch. I wish you worked in the hospital kitchens. We'd all be a lot happier.'

Mrs Teague flapped her hand at her. 'Get on with you. You do say the silliest things, Eunice.'

'Yes, doesn't she,' said April pointedly.

Eunice left laughing, and April was glad she'd been able to cheer her up. All in all, considering how badly the day had started, it had ended beautifully. Suddenly, the reason for the bad start came back to her. The letter! She must reply to Theo before she became too busy.

But what to say? The year since she'd seen him had brought so much change for her, she wasn't sure she still felt the same for him. She sat at her desk for a little while, sucking the end of her pen. Then finally, she wrote:

Dear Theo,

It was lovely to hear from you and sorry life is so boring wherever you are. But that's better than the alternative, isn't it? I'd rather think of you bored and safe than the other way around.

Life here is very busy, and I really do love Cornwall. I think I feel more comfortable here than I ever did in London. Which is strange, considering I grew up there. And, of course, I had you, my dear friend, as a companion. But then, I suppose, war changes everything.

I'm going to a dance at one of the American bases that have sprung up around here in a couple of weeks. They've invited all the hospital staff. I hope it'll be fun. The last dance I went to was with you . . .

Anyway, Theo, it's late and I must get to bed. Stay safe always. I'll be thinking of you.

Love, April

She considered the letter for a moment, wondering whether it was mean to mention the dance when she'd first found out about Charlotte. She sighed and put the letter in an envelope. Was it really only a year ago when they'd shared that tender kiss? Now, after being in Cornwall for

113

eight months, she realised how much she'd changed. She was no longer the besotted girl she'd been that night of the dance, nor the sad, grief-stricken girl of just a year ago. She may still grieve for her father, but she'd found a home and a makeshift family of her own, and she'd discovered just how strong she could be.

Chapter 10

April managed to avoid Bess for most of the week. But her luck ran out one afternoon when the ward was unusually quiet, so Sister Turnbull sent April to make some nappies and sanitary towels. It was boring work, but if there were several nurses, it was a good opportunity to have a chat. On this occasion, though, April was surprised to see both Bess and Nancy. As qualified nurses, they usually didn't get assigned such a tedious and unskilled task.

'Oh, what are you two doing here?' she asked.

Bess gave her a cool stare, but didn't answer. Nancy was more garrulous. 'I'm in trouble with matron for being late for duty on Saturday. It was only a couple of hours! As for Bess, apparently she didn't turn up again. Won't tell me why, though.'

'Oh dear. What happened?'

Nancy smiled slyly. 'Well, between you and me, I was having such a good time with Homer that I forgot the time. He is absolutely dreamy, don't you think? So big and powerful. I'm going to see him again next time we can both get away. I can't wait.'

'What about you and A.J., Bess? Will you be seeing him again?' April looked at Bess expectantly.

Bess sniffed. 'That's none of your business. What about you? I saw you walk off arm in arm with that red-headed G.I. Anything *you* want to tell us?'

Even though there was nothing to feel guilty about, April blushed. 'That's the cowboy me and Mrs Teague met at the Bluebell. She's been talking about him so much that when I saw him in the street, I asked him to come back for lunch.'

Bess raised her eyebrows. 'Really? Not five minutes after reading a letter from your sweetheart, you're off with another man. You're no better than the rest of us.'

'Theo is *not* my sweetheart. Anyway, I only asked him back for Mrs Teague's sake. It's hardly as bad as what you did.'

Bess looked enraged. 'What do you mean?'

April sighed. 'All I mean is that you seem to put seeing men and having a good time over your work.'

'Oh really? That's a bit rich, coming from someone who just picked up some man off the street and took him home.'

'I told you, Red isn't just some stranger. In fact, maybe you should meet him. He's ever so nice, and I bet you two would really get on.'

'I don't need your cast-offs, April. I'm doing just fine, and I don't like what you're implying. All I'm doing is being friendly, and you seem to think I'm some sort of slut. Yet, when you're friendly, it's fine. I'm a bit sick of your holier-than-thou attitude to everything, to be honest.'

April was beginning to feel exasperated, and she put down the roll of cotton she was cutting out. 'Oh, for goodness sake, Bess, what is your problem with me? And when have I been holier than thou?'

Nancy, ever the peace-maker, weighed in. 'Bess, I think you are being a bit unfair. April did know him already. And, April, we are both dedicated nurses. Missing one duty isn't exactly the crime of the century.'

Luckily, before things could get any more heated, Sister Mulholland came into the room. 'Nurse Walker. I need you immediately. One of your patients is asking for you.'

Bess threw down the cotton and got up noisily from the table. 'Coming, sister.' She turned to April and whispered, 'You think you're so much better than the rest of us, April, don't you? Well, did you hear that? A patient is asking for *me*. I'm better than you think I am, and I'd thank you not to talk to me again until you change your attitude.' With that she flounced out.

April turned to Nancy with a bewildered look. 'I never thought I was better than her. Why does she hate me so much, Nancy?'

Nancy sighed. 'Between you and me, things weren't quite so fun for Bess that day, and you know how sensitive she can be. Anyway, that night, I don't know what happened to her, because me and Homer went our own way, and A.J. left, so I have no idea what she did. She'd been asking and asking A.J. to take her to the camp so she could find that Crawford fellow, but he wouldn't. I think she might have gone up there by herself again to see if she could find him. I think she's gone a bit crazy over that fellow, to be honest. And it's not . . .' Nancy paused, then shook her head. 'Anyway, don't worry about it. She'll get over it, when she's had a chance to calm down.'

April wasn't quite so sure. It felt like things between her and Bess had reached the point of no return and she dreaded the night of the dance. If Bess had her way she would make things very awkward for her.

∽

Despite these fears, though, to April's relief, when the convoy of army trucks arrived to pick up the nurses, the excitement of the occasion seemed to have mellowed Bess, and in the truck on the way over she'd nudged April.

'Listen, I'm sorry about the other day. Nancy and Eunice say I'm too rough on you, and I think they're right. What do you say we put our differences behind us and start again? I know I can be a bit moody sometimes, but just ignore me when I am. Everyone else does.'

April looked at her uncertainly. 'You really were horrible, Bess. I don't know why you seem to dislike me so much.'

'Oh, I don't, April, I like you very much. I can just be a bit of a cow sometimes.' She held her hand out. 'What do you say? Friends again?' She smiled at her and April, though she didn't entirely trust her, was happy to call a truce, if only for tonight.

She returned her smile and shook her hand. 'Of course, friends. Always.'

'Good. But let's get one thing straight, and this goes for all you girls. If my officer is there, he's mine, all right? Hands off.'

'Oh, shut up, Bess,' one of the others said. 'I swear this man doesn't even exist.'

'Well, he doesn't to you, Jean Gray, understand?'

'All right, all right. He's all yours, I promise.' She rolled her eyes. 'Anyway, I reckon there'll be enough men to go round so there's no need to worry; we won't steal your mythical man.'

When they arrived, April was astonished at how many people there were. The soldiers had done a very thorough job of rounding up any unattached woman who lived in or near Truro or Bodmin. And, as rumour had had it, the dance floor was in a tent. It was the biggest tent April had ever seen and, despite the fact it was khaki, it glittered with coloured lights that had been strung around the entrance and across the ceiling. Inside, tables had been set up around a dance floor and at the back of the tent a large trestle table had been set with bottles of drink, while to the side, musicians were playing the songs she'd been hearing on the radio.

April gasped as she walked in. 'Oh, it's beautiful. Like a magical cave in the forest.'

Very soon the nurses found themselves sitting at a large round table with several G.I.s.

One of them offered April a bottle of something he called Coca Cola. She looked at it suspiciously.

'It's perfectly harmless, ma'am, and surprisingly refreshing. But if you'd care for something a little stronger I can top it up with a little rum.' He held up a hip flask that he'd dug out of his pocket.

'Rum?'

'Does wonders for cola.'

April laughed. 'I better not. Don't want to fall over.'

He shrugged and added a generous slug to his own drink before turning to Jean, who was sitting on the other side of him.

April turned to Bess. 'So, is he here?'

Bess had been anxiously scanning the people in the tent. 'I haven't seen him yet. He's probably too high-ranking to come to this sort of thing.'

'What about Homer, Nancy? Is he here?'

'Oh, I wish he was, but he's not allowed. This is for white soldiers only – can you believe that? Apparently, the coloured soldiers will have a dance another time. Seems unfair to me. Still, plenty of nice boys here, don't you think?' She winked, and April couldn't help laughing. She really was incorrigible.

'Well, Red is here somewhere. So if you see a tall red-head, point him in my direction, won't you?'

'Ooh, April. I thought you weren't interested.' Bess gave her a sly look.

'I'm not. But he's lovely so I'd like to introduce you all.'

The talking stopped for a moment as the band started to play. One after another well-known hit tunes were played, both American and British. 'Falling In Love With Love' was followed by 'Roll Out The Barrel', which was followed by 'Three Little Fishes', and then by a later hit, 'Chatanooga Choo Choo'. And so the music went on and the girls never left the dance floor, because as each song finished, another soldier would appear, introduce himself and away they would go again. It was wild and it was exuberant but it was also exhausting. Finally, April and Bess returned to their table accompanied by some of their new partners, each carrying a chair – a clear hint, decided April, that they intended to stay.

A fanfare from the band announced the arrival of a large table laden with food, the appetising aromas making everyone in the tent hungry.

To the girls, who had been living with food rationing, the selection was quite amazing. There were strange sausages, which were called hot dogs, and hamburgers, which had never been near ham but were made with real beef. There were unrecognisable side dishes with mouth-watering smells that turned out to be delicious varieties of salads. And on each table was a packet of chewing gum, some American cigarettes and a bottle of Coca Cola. Looking at the food, April felt guilty, but one of the soldiers relieved her mind.

'It's all shipped in from Stateside, part of our war effort.'

Just then, a voice whispered in her ear, 'Boo!'

She turned in surprise and then exclaimed in delight, 'Red! I've been looking out for you but couldn't see you.'

'Well, now that's because, just as I predicted, I couldn't get close for the men surrounding you.'

'Come and eat with us, won't you? You can meet my friends Bess, Nancy and Jean.'

'I'll see you there.'

When Red joined them at the table, he brought some friends with him. The conversation flowed easily, and Bess seemed charmed by Red. April smiled to herself; maybe now she would forget her obsession with that invisible officer.

Finally, after more dancing, it was time to leave. But when April looked around there was no sign of Bess and she wasn't on the dance floor.

'Maybe she went to powder her nose,' suggested Jean. 'If we wait here, she'll be back.'

Twenty minutes later, Bess had still not returned.

Red stood up. 'Maybe she took a wrong turn. It's a big camp. Why don't we go look.'

April, who was now getting worried, stood up and followed Red. They'd just checked the toilets when they heard a woman's strained voice.

'No, I said no,' she said, and then a man's much deeper tone: 'You know you said yes, honey.'

'That was Bess's voice,' began April, but Red was already gone.

Like a bullet from a gun, he raced across the compound, jumped a fence and disappeared. April raced after him. She heard shouts and blows and Bess's voice. She was in tears. April struggled with the fence but managed to get over it, and a moment later Bess was sobbing in her arms.

'It's all right, Bess, you're safe.' April was unsure what to ask but she was Bess's friend and a nurse. 'Did he hurt you . . . in any way?'

'Yes . . . no,' sobbed Bess. 'Oh April, I feel so stupid. He seemed ever so nice. He asked me if I'd ever played night baseball and of course I hadn't, but I knew Americans played baseball so I went with him. We kissed a few times and it was nice, but then . . . it wasn't fun any more and he wouldn't let go.' She continued sobbing. 'I'm so stupid.'

'Hey, Bess, of course you're not. You're not the one who did anything wrong.'

'He seemed to think I was asking for it.' Bess sniffed and wiped her nose on her sleeve.

'He's a nasty idiot. And he's the one who's asking for it!' she said fiercely.

'Really? You don't think this is my fault?'

'Of course it isn't.'

'No one else is going to think that,' she wailed.

Suddenly, Red was back. 'Do you want to charge him, Miss Bess?'

Bess started to cry again but between her sobs they could hear a vehement: 'No. I need to go home.'

'I'll walk you both back to the dance hall and no, Bess, you don't need to go in. I'll sign out a jeep and drive you home. Will you come with me, April?'

∞

Less than fifteen minutes later they were driving out of the camp gates. The journey was very quiet. No one spoke but occasionally there would be a slight sob from Bess. Once in the town Red asked for directions and, since Bess was too upset, April directed him to the nurses' home.

By the time they reached it, Bess was calm and able to thank both April and Red for their help. 'I don't want any trouble over my stupidity and I don't want people talking about me; if my nan got to hear she would be so distressed.'

'There'll be no talk, Bess, and your baseball player won't get out of line again. Trust me.'

Bess looked at Red as if he was a knight come to rescue her. Which in a way he was. No doubt Bess would be telling everyone how 'gorgeous' he was in the morning. At least this time, the man deserved the title. Red really was a very special man.

Chapter 11

August 1942

Over the next few weeks, people could talk of nothing else but the dance. Bess kept quiet and when April tried to talk to her she brushed her off. Clearly, she wanted to forget the entire incident, so April didn't push it. In any case, she was kept too busy to worry about much except work, eat, sleep and study.

Then one evening, she was hurrying out of the hospital on her way home, when she caught a flash of a white cap disappearing around the side of the hospital. Curious, as no one tended to go that way, she followed, and as she turned the corner she stopped abruptly. Was that . . . ? Surely not. She moved a little closer and saw she'd been right. Eunice was leaning up against the sandbags with a tall, dark man bending over her. It looked like they were kissing!

Oh, Eunice, she thought, shaking her head. She'd assumed that Eunice had put her attraction to A.J. behind her, as she'd not said a word about it since that day in Truro. But it appeared she hadn't. Well, A.J. seemed like a lovely man, and she wasn't going to judge her friend. But she was worried that no matter what happened, someone was going to end up with a broken heart. Perhaps the best thing to do was pretend she'd never seen them. She turned and hurried quickly away.

Seeing A.J. made her wonder how Homer and Red were getting on. Red had sent Mrs Teague a thank-you card after the lunch and said that he would be away for a few weeks. She prayed he was safe. There had been reports of bombs being dropped in Cornwall throughout June and July, and she hoped desperately that this wasn't the start of a concerted effort by the Luftwaffe to target the US camps.

She shook her head. She wouldn't think about it. It only brought back the nightmare memories of the night her father died, and she'd come so far since then. She mustn't let herself sink back into despair.

To calm her fears, she stopped to admire the view from the hill over Truro. The light was just beginning to fade, and the setting sun over the moors bathed everything in a soft pink glow. This really was the most beautiful place she had ever been, she thought. Despite everything, when she looked at a view like this, she felt like the luckiest girl alive.

The following day, April was hurrying to the cafeteria for her break. She'd been hard at work since 8 a.m. and she hadn't managed to have a bite to eat since then. Six hours on, she was starving. The first person she saw was Eunice and she wondered whether to say anything about what she'd seen the night before. She didn't have the appearance of a woman in love. In fact, she looked troubled, and her eyes were red. Had she been crying?

'Eunice, are you all right?' April asked. 'You don't look too well.'

Eunice glanced around at her with a frown. 'I'm absolutely fine. In fact, never better. I had another letter from Norm waiting for me last night, and it seems he might be coming home on leave soon.'

'That's wonderful news, Eunice. You must be so excited to see him. When will he be here?'

'In a month or so. It'll be so strange. I haven't seen him for over a year and things are so different now . . .' Eunice trailed off and shook her head. She looked miserable, but April wisely held her peace. If she wanted to talk to her about A.J., then no doubt she would do so in her own time.

'Oh, I'm sure it will be fine,' she said soothingly. 'Anyway, look at that, vegetable soup for lunch. Let's hope the soup has something other than cabbage in it for a change.'

They walked together to the table and sat down. April took a mouthful of soup. 'Ugh, as I suspected, more cabbage than anything else. Oh wait, can this be a potato? Such luxury.' She hoped her light tone would cheer Eunice, but she didn't seem to be listening. 'Ah, well, at least the bread's nice. But don't ask me what it's made of. Porridge oats and seeds as far as I can tell.'

When Eunice still didn't answer, April sighed. 'Eunice, is something troubling you? You know you can talk to me if there is.'

Eunice smiled at her briefly. 'I know, thank you. I suppose I'm just feeling a bit confused. Anyway, let's talk about something else.'

They were heading for the door at the end of their break when Eunice grabbed April's arm. 'Cripes, will you look at him? The man talking to Dr Spence. He looks a bit like Jimmy Stewart . . .' Eunice paused. 'Hey, do you think that's Bess's famous G.I. officer? Looks like today might be her lucky day! Maybe now she'll stop being so difficult.'

April said nothing. She was transfixed. She'd never seen anyone quite like him. He was tall and broad, and his green jacket fit snugly across his shoulders. He was wearing a hat, so she couldn't see what colour his hair was, but she guessed it was dark as his skin looked tanned. They'd have to walk past him to get out of the cafeteria, and she suddenly felt nervous.

As they skirted the two men, Dr Spence stopped her. 'Ah, Nurse Harvey, I wonder if you could help Major Dunbar. He's looking for matron, and I have to be on my way. Could you show him to her office?' He nodded at the major and left swiftly.

Eunice nudged her and whispered, 'Lucky you! But if that is Bess's major, you better watch out!' And she, too, left. April watched her go, wishing Dr Spence had asked Eunice to take him instead of her.

Steeling herself, she looked at Major Dunbar properly for the first time. Her heart thumped. She was right, he had dark hair and the greenest eyes with the thickest lashes she'd ever seen.

Lord, save me, she thought. She wondered if this was how Eunice had felt when she'd seen A.J. for the first time.

'Pleasure to meet you, Nurse Harvey. Please, call me Crawford. We Americans prefer a more informal approach.' He looked into her eyes and held out his hand. She took it, and found her hand enveloped in his large, rough one. She shivered.

'Pleasure to meet you too, major.' He raised his eyebrows. 'Crawford,' she corrected herself. 'If you'll follow me, I'll take you to matron.'

She turned around and rushed towards the stairs. 'It's on the fourth floor, so quite a climb.'

'Oh, I think these old legs can manage it,' he drawled, easily keeping pace beside her and giving her a heart-stopping grin. 'So, Nurse Harvey, do you have a name? I can't believe your parents called you "Nurse".'

'My name's April.'

'Ah, beautiful. My favourite month. Have you been in Cornwall long?'

'No, I'm quite new to Cornwall.' She was pleased that her voice didn't shake as she spoke. Honestly, what was wrong with her? This had never happened with anyone before. But it felt very much like the major was flirting with her and it made her nervous.

'Well, that makes two of us. Say, maybe we could explore some places together.'

She looked at him in surprise. Was he asking her out when they'd only just met? 'Umm, I'm not sure, Major Dunbar,' she said, using his title deliberately to put him in his place. 'I'm quite busy . . .' she said.

'Pardon me, ma'am, I didn't mean to be forward. My intentions were purely friendly. And please, like I said, call me Crawford.'

Realising they'd stopped in the corridor, she glanced at her watch. 'We better hurry. There'll be dire consequences if I'm late back to the ward.'

They were walking towards the final flight of stairs when April stopped, her stomach sinking. Bess was coming out of

128

one of the wards. When she saw the major, her face broke into a huge smile.

'Why, major, you are a very elusive man. Have you come to see me? How kind of April to bring you to me.' She gave April a sweet smile, but her eyes were shooting daggers.

The major looked surprised. 'Uh . . . well, hello there. April was just showing me the way to matron's office. But it sure is nice to see you too. Maybe we'll catch up some-time.' He tipped his cap at her and continued on.

April threw Bess a quick glance. She looked absolutely furious. Crikey, I'll pay for this, she thought.

Rushing to matron's door, she knocked and was relieved to hear the customary 'Come' from inside.

'I'll leave you here, major. Very nice to meet you.'

'It's Crawford, April. And likewise. I hope we see each other again very soon. Say, I'll be here till late, got a few things to discuss with matron about helping each other out, so what time do you get off? Maybe I can walk you home?'

'Oh, I expect you'll be long gone by the time I've fin-ished, major. Lovely to meet you, though.' She rushed away, head down, anxious to get away from him as soon as possible. Getting to the top of the stairs, she jumped as she heard a low, venomous whisper.

'I should have known *you* couldn't be trusted, April Harvey. I heard you arranging to meet *my* man.'

April sighed. 'I did no such thing, Bess. If you were listening, you'll know *he* asked *me*, and I didn't accept. So you can keep your nasty insinuations to yourself.' April swept past her, very aware of Bess's footsteps running behind her.

'Well, just make sure you don't see him again. Remember what I said at the dance. He's mine, so hands off. And if I see you with him again, you'll regret it.'

April stopped to let her pass. Clearly, their brief truce had come to an end. And she hadn't done anything wrong! She didn't plan on being anywhere near the major again, he unsettled her far too much, but Bess's words made her change her mind. Who on earth did she think she was, telling her who she could and couldn't see? Well, if April did see the gorgeous Major Dunbar later, she'd make a point of saying hello to him.

She marched down the stairs, determined not to let Bess intimidate her. But was it really anger that was making her heart beat faster?

❧

April felt jumpy for the rest of the afternoon. What if the major was waiting for her when she left? She shook her head. Of course he wouldn't be. But what if he was? the little voice kept asking her. Would she really risk Bess's wrath and let him walk her home? As far as she could tell, the major didn't seem to recognise Bess, which meant either Bess had exaggerated their acquaintance or the major liked to string girls along and then drop them. April pictured his smile, the way it crinkled the corners of his beautiful eyes. He looked so sincere and trustworthy; surely it was Bess who was telling lies?

As the time to leave drew nearer, April kept glancing at her watch. Finally, Sister Turnbull called to her, 'Nurse Harvey, I don't know what's got into you today, but seeing as it's quiet, go down to the cafeteria and get everyone a cup of tea. Maybe when you get back, you can keep your mind on the job for the rest of your shift.'

April flushed. Had she been that obvious? She must try to do better.

She was just getting the tea when a sultry voice surprised her.

'Got a minute to have a cup of tea with me, ma'am?'

She jumped and looked up into Major Dunbar's smiling face. Her stomach flipped. 'Um, I'm afraid not, major. I'm just getting tea for sister and the other nurses.'

'Well, perhaps I can help you carry it up?'

'I don't think she'll be very happy if I bring an American soldier back with me. She's already cross with me.'

'I can't imagine you making anyone cross, April.' He grinned cheekily at her. 'But if you insist, I'll wait for you here. Surely you must be due off soon?'

'Not for an hour or so, so you don't have to wait around for me.'

'I know, but I hoped to see you again. I'm a good guy, April, I promise you.'

'You're a very persistent man, major . . . Crawford.' She couldn't help smiling. After all, what girl wouldn't be flattered that a man like this would want to see her again?

'Uh huh. I kept thinking of your pretty blue eyes all afternoon, and I said to myself, "Crawford, you'll kick yourself if you don't at least give yourself the chance to persuade that lovely nurse to come out with you".'

'But . . . but you've only met me once. We've hardly spoken.'

'Exactly. And I wanted to put that right.'

April looked away, flustered. She had no idea how to handle this at all. But as she floundered around for something to say, the roar of aircraft overhead echoed around the room. She looked up in alarm.

'To stations!' a commanding voice shouted. 'Everyone go!'

Tea forgotten, and heart beating fast, April rushed out of the cafeteria towards her ward, Major Dunbar by her side.

'You best get to safety, major. I need to get back to the ward to help move the patients,' she panted as she ran.

'Don't be ridiculous. I'm a soldier, I can help.'

'Ambulatory patients first,' called a staff nurse as April pushed her way through the crowd rushing up the staircase.

As the roar of the plane got closer, April fought back the memories that were starting to crowd in on her. 'Keep going, April, this is not the same. Just do what needs to be done.' But despite her reassuring words to herself, April's vision was darkening. Stopping for a moment, she bent over and took deep breaths. 'It'll all be fine, just keep going,' she whispered to herself.

'April.' She felt a hand on her arm. 'Are you OK?'

The voice brought her back to the present and she stood up, her vision clearing, but her breath was still coming in short, sharp pants.

'Nurse Harvey!' April jumped at the sound of her name being shouted. 'Get over here this instant, the patients need you. This is no time for rest.'

The harsh tone was just what she needed, and she continued running up the stairs and rushed into the ward, the comforting bulk of Major Dunbar beside her.

'Where have you been? I need you to get Mrs Black out of bed. Immediately.'

'Sorry, sister,' she said. 'I was overwhelmed for a moment.'

'Yes, well, if you could keep the panic attack until after the patients have been moved, I'd be most grateful. Now chop chop, no time to waste.'

Doing her best to ignore the terrible noise of the aircraft roaring overhead, April worked tirelessly with the other staff and Major Dunbar as they rushed to get the patients to safety. She had just delivered an elderly patient to the shelter and was halfway back up the staircase when there was a loud crash and the window on the nearest landing blew in, sending a deluge of glass in several directions. She felt the sharpest of cuts on her legs and stumbled, thrusting her hands out to save herself from falling. One hand buried itself up to the wrist in a deep pile of the tiniest of pieces. Suddenly something heavy fell on her back.

'Oh God, oh God, please let me get out of this. I have to keep my head.'

But it was too late. Suddenly she was back in Camberwell, the green curtains flapping, her father's face at the window, the flames sending sparks into the dark sky. 'I'm coming, Daddy! Hold on, I'll get you out!' she shouted, then the world went dark.

Chapter 12

She didn't know how long she lay there, but slowly her senses returned.

'Hey, hey.' A deep, soothing voice in her ear sounded. 'April, come back to me, honey. You're with me, your friendly G.I. Now let me check you're not hurt.'

She blinked and moved her head to the side, opening her eyes. Major Dunbar's handsome face stared down at her. It was smudged with dirt, but his expression was soft and reassuring.

'Can you move, April?'

She moved her legs, and then her arms. 'Yes, I think so. I'm all right.'

'Good girl. Now, I'm going to help you to your feet and get you out of here, OK?'

'Out of here? No! No, we have to go back. There are others still here.'

'OK, OK, honey. I'll help you. Don't get distressed. Come on, on the count of three. One. Two. Three.'

April felt herself being lifted to her feet. She blinked slightly to clear her vision. Around her she could see people rushing here and there. It was organised chaos, but she was amazed at how calm everyone was. Moving purposefully with only one aim: to save as many people as possible.

'I'm fine, major. I'm so sorry. Now come on, let's get back to it.'

Suddenly, she heard again the too-familiar sound of low-flying aircraft.

Oh, dear God, that sound, that frightful sound ... where was her father? No! She was not in London, this was Cornwall, and she was a nurse with patients depending on her. She would not let the memories defeat her.

'I am a nurse,' she said plainly, as she forced herself upright.

'That's right, honey. You're a nurse and I'm a soldier. Just think of the good we can do if we work as a team. Come on, now.'

Just then, above the wail of the aircraft, she heard the piercing scream of a child. She focused on the sound. Yes, there it was again. But where? She hadn't seen a child up there earlier.

Suddenly, an unfamiliar male voice sounded close by. 'Take shelter! They're coming back!' April felt her hand being grabbed, but she shook it free and ran, almost stumbling, back up the staircase.

'Let me go, there's a child up there. Can't you hear it?'

Oh, God, a child alone in this nightmare, I have to get to them.

A massive explosion shook the building and acrid smoke streamed in. April was knocked off her feet, and for a moment lay stunned, her ears ringing, unsure where she had landed or what had just happened. She opened her eyes; she could see nothing and smell nothing but cordite and dust. Staggering to her feet, she stumbled blindly forward, hands out in front of her. She tripped over something and fell again.

Another explosion rocked everything near her and April screamed as debris fell all around her. Once again she felt something heavy on her back, and she tried to fight it off.

'Stay still, darlin'. We just need to let the dust settle, then I promise we will look for the child.'

She realised that the weight on her back was Major Dunbar lying across her, shielding her from the worst of the falling masonry. She whimpered, trying to fight off the terrible memories.

'Hey, it's OK. I'll keep you safe.' To her surprise, she found the warmth of him on her back and the soothing tone of his voice comforted her, and slowly her trembling eased.

'It's just . . . oh, I have to find that child. To be alone in an air raid, I know what that's like . . .' She stopped.

'Shh, now. You're not alone this time. We'll get them out safe and sound.'

They lay there for a while, as screams and shouts echoed around them. Finally, Major Dunbar whispered, 'OK, I think we can get up now. I'm going to get off you real slow. Are you injured?'

April wriggled her fingers and toes. Although her legs felt sore, she didn't think she'd broken anything.

'No, I'm all right. Let's go.'

'I'm going to need you to think about where he might be. I don't know the hospital like you do, so you'll have to be the guide.'

They stood up slowly, and April blinked through the dust and the chaos. 'The cries were coming from up there,' she said, pointing at the staircase. It seemed to be intact, so she was hopeful they could find him. 'Come on.'

Gingerly they began to climb the stairs. A nurse came running down. In the fading light coming through the broken windows, April could see the gleam of red hair.

'Eunice! Thank goodness you're OK. Is everyone out?'

Eunice's eyes were wild, but her voice was calm. 'Yes, I think we got everyone out from up there. The south wing's been hit, though. I saw from the window. I'm going there now to see if I can help. Where are you going? There's no one there.'

'I heard a child, Eunice, I'm sure of it. I'm going to check.'

'No, everyone's out. Best come back down. It's not safe.'

'Don't worry, nurse. I'll go up with her. You go see what you can do to help elsewhere. I'll take care of her.'

Eunice nodded, clearly too distracted to argue further, and hurried down the stairs.

'OK, April, lead on.'

They reached the top of the stairs and turned into the corridor. Evening was drawing in and the light was fading.

'The floor's a minefield so be real careful, there's glass everywhere. Don't you have an auxiliary power system?'

'We do, or perhaps did; obviously it's not working. But don't worry, I know my way around even in the dark.'

They stepped through the first doorway they came to – there was no door now, and April could see it had been blown to the far wall of the ward. Treading carefully over the fallen trollies and tables, April tried to move a bedside table and chair that lay in her way, entangled together.

'Let me do that.'

She ignored him and, once again, tried to separate the pieces of furniture. She failed.

'I'll push them out of the way.'

Crawford lifted the entangled furniture and carried it across the ward, where he added it to a pile that had formed naturally during the attack. 'How about you be the brains and I'll be the brawn?' Then he raised his voice. 'Hello? Is anyone here?' There was no answer. 'I don't think the little one's here. Let's try the next one.'

She nodded and, carefully stepping back into the corridor, they made their way towards the door of Dover Ward. This time, the door was intact, and she leaned against it, listening intently, but all was quiet. She pushed but nothing happened.

'Allow me, ma'am. It'll be like the other one, possibly a piece of ward furniture rammed up against it.'

April stepped back and the American leaned his right shoulder against the door and pushed with all his strength. Eventually they heard the excruciating sound of metal being scraped across the floor and, very slowly at first, then with a speed that almost made him fall into the room, it opened, propelling both of them into the badly damaged room. Crawford caught April's arm and managed to stop her from falling to the ground.

'Thank you,' she said breathlessly.

They stood together, breathing heavily and looking around. As with most of the building, the windows had been blown out, and the setting sun shone through, lighting up the devastation. The long, rectangular ward looked as if a giant had picked it up and shaken it, letting all the pieces fall where they might. Some of the beds were seriously damaged, mattresses were ripped and the stuffing was lying like dirty snow all over the floor. The wooden bedside tables had suffered most: doors had been pulled off, drawers were lying upside down on the floor, emptied of all contents – books, newspapers, hair brushes, even money. The once comfortable bedside chairs, recently bought for visitors, were ripped and damaged beyond repair.

April started across the room, but Crawford caught her arm once more.

'No, ma'am, wait here. I'll look.'

She pulled her arm free. 'Don't be ridiculous. We'll go together,' she said forcefully.

'How about if I call hello? Your strength will be needed when we find him. Let's stay real quiet for a minute and listen.'

They stood and listened but, apart from the constant tinkling of falling glass and the far away shouts of people, they heard nothing.

'Hello, anyone there?'

Nothing.

April stumbled on, twice almost falling over objects on the floor.

'Nurse, you need to conserve your strength for the patient. Excuse me.' And to her surprise he lifted her as if she were a child and walked carefully on, calling 'hello' every few steps.

'What was that?' April asked. They stood quietly and listened. Was that a faint cry? 'Hello, anyone there?' she called desperately. 'Put me down.' She pushed at Crawford's chest, then reluctantly added, 'Please.'

Gently, he put April on her feet and she decided not to notice that he was still supporting her.

'One, two, three,' he said, and together they shouted, 'Hello, is anyone there?'

They held their breath and were rewarded by a faint squeak.

'Was that a voice?' April whispered hopefully.

'You call this time, April. If someone's there, your voice will be more reassuring.'

'Hello, is anyone there?' called April again, although she thought that if she were lost and hurt, it would be the American's voice she would find most reassuring.

Suddenly they heard it. A faint, high-pitched cry. 'Mummy?'

'Oh, thank God,' said April. 'It's coming from over there.' She pointed to a mountain of mattresses, pillows, bits of bedside tables and chairs thrown against the wall. Almost everything that was in the ward seemed to be in the pile of wreckage. How was it possible that he was still alive under all of that? 'Oh, I wish I knew his name.'

'I'll have to move this stuff,' Crawford said. 'Hey, buddy, we're coming to get you. OK?'

Again, there was a tiny sound.

'I'll help,' April said. 'I'm stronger than I look.' She winced as she reached for a chair and hoped Crawford hadn't noticed. But he had.

'Hey, careful there. We don't know what we'll find, so let me move everything, then hopefully we'll clear enough space for you to crawl into. If . . . when we find him, it'll be you he needs.'

'All right.' April conceded defeat. He was a lot stronger than she was, and she didn't want to jeopardise the operation.

April watched as he disentangled chairs and bedside tables, which he moved into the empty space near her. She winced, not from pain but from fear as she saw him attempt to lift an iron bed that had been tossed upside down by the blast and now had the wheels of a second bed and several mattresses entangled with it.

'Hey, buddy, am I close?' he called. 'I'm kinda big to get under here but I know you'll be helping me. Can you say hi?'

'Mummy.'

'Even better. Now, I'm also kinda dirty, bet you are too, and so we won't be scared when we see each other. Ouch. Would you believe I almost put my foot in a drawer? Stupid or what? Who puts their drawers on the floor – not my mom.'

A sound like the smallest of laughs brought a flood of relief, and April let out the breath she hadn't realised she was holding. Surely the child couldn't be too badly injured if he had the energy to laugh.

'OK. I see the problem.' Crawford had managed to lift a mattress away, and she could see that a bed had been tipped over and was leaning lengthwise against the wall, leaving a space big enough for a child to sit behind. The problem was that there was another bed entangled with the one against the wall, and it looked too difficult for one man to lift them both.

'Hang on, Crawford. Let me crawl through this space. Hopefully I can get to him, then you'd better go and see if you can find help. I think it'll take more than one person to lift those beds.'

The American looked uncertain. 'What if something falls on you?'

'For goodness sake! There's no time for that sort of thinking. And so help me, if you stop me, I'll try and lift the bed by myself.' From his expression she was almost sure that no one had ever argued with him. 'Or we could try together.'

Crawford strained against the tangled beds, trying to move them. 'No, you're right. Can you fit through there?'

April moved to the tiny space at the end of the bed and peered through. It was dark, but she could just make out a small scrunched-up figure.

'Hello there. It's April here. Can you see me? Me and Crawford are going to help you get out, but he needs another big, strong soldier to help him, unless you can crawl towards me?'

'No! I want Mummy!' he cried.

'All right, we'll find her. But how about I come and sit with you and we can sing some songs while we wait?'

'Where's my mummy?'

April's heart lurched. She hoped she was safe in the hospital somewhere. It would be too awful to get him out and find his mother had been killed. 'She's waiting for you downstairs. Now, do you think this big fat nurse can squeeze in?'

The boy laughed. 'You don't look that big.'

'Well, let's see, shall we?'

April squeezed through the space. She felt her dress catch on something, and then there was a ripping sound.

'Oh my goodness, sounds like my dress has torn. Deary me, matron won't be happy with me. Unless you promise to tell her it wasn't my fault. Will you do that for me?'

There was no answer.

'What's your name, sweetheart?'

'Stevie.'

'Do you have any brothers and sisters, Stevie?' April knew that talking was the best way to calm him down so she kept up her chatter as she crawled slowly and carefully behind the bed, throwing out bits and pieces of rubbish that littered the way. Finally, she was there, and she could see him.

'I'm in, Crawford. Go and get help.'

'I won't be a moment, April, hang on in there.'

She heard his footsteps crunching through the debris as he went to the door and she put a comforting arm around the little boy, who hid his face in her shoulder and started to sob in earnest.

'Don't you worry, Stevie, we'll be out in a jiffy. Tell you what, let's sing a song. What's your very favourite song?'

There was silence for a moment, then she heard a whispered, 'Teddy Bear.'

'Oh, that's my very favourite as well. Shall we sing together?'

Soon the two of them were singing away, from 'Teddy Bear's Picnic' to 'The Laughing Policeman'. Finally, as they were singing 'Who's Afraid of the Big Bad Wolf?', she heard voices.

'Hey, A.J., sounds like there's a little piggy in there who thinks he isn't scared of the wolf. Shall we see if we can huff and puff and blow this house down?'

'I sure would like to catch myself a little piggy,' said a deep voice that April recognised.

'A.J.? Is that you?' April was delighted. 'It's April here. Eunice's friend. We met in the Bluebell. Is Homer here? He could probably shift this pile of beds with one hand.'

'Well I never! April. Wish I could say it was good to see you, but I can't see much of you from here. Just hang on and we'll have you out in a moment.'

She heard the two men grunting with effort as they began to move the piles of debris blocking the bed. Then there came an ear-damaging screech as metal pieces rubbed against one another. The pile was moving.

Chapter 13

April gasped and prayed the whole thing wouldn't collapse on top of them. Stevie whimpered against her, so she started to sing again. But this time he was too scared to join in.

'Not long now, Stevie,' she whispered. 'Soon you'll be with your mummy and she will be so happy to see you.'

'OK, we're ready to move the bed, April.' Crawford's voice sounded very close.

'Well, hurry up, will you? Me and Stevie are a bit bored in here, aren't we, Stevie?'

She was rewarded with a 'Hurry! Hurry!' from Stevie. Now that they were nearly free, he was starting to recover his spirits.

'Ready, A.J. On the count of three. One, two, three, lift. Two steps to your right. One, two.' The bedstead trapping them against the wall finally started to move and, suddenly it was gone, and April and Stevie sat blinking up at them.

'Well, what do we have here? Looks like there are two piggies hiding in the house. Hello, buddy, it sure is good to see you. Hey, A.J., look at this. Have we got a prize for the dirtiest face, like maybe a chocolate bar? I thought I was dirty and you're awful dirty too. But Stevie here has to win the prize for the dirtiest face I've ever seen.'

'Of course, there's chocolate.'

Stevie's eyes went round with surprise when he looked at A.J., who was possibly not only the tallest, but also the darkest man he'd ever seen. 'Chocolate,' he said commandingly.

'You bet there's chocolate.' A.J. grinned at the boy. 'Ever heard of a Hershey Bar?'

'No.'

'It's from America and it's like your very, very favourite chocolate but better.'

'Honest?'

'Absolutely.' A.J. bent down and scooped Stevie up. Stevie giggled delightedly as A.J. walked towards a chair and sat down with him on his lap. 'Now, sir, let's see if you can find it. I'll give you a clue. It's in my jacket.'

April watched as Stevie, so recently terrified, grinned and started patting A.J.'s chest, looking for the promised chocolate. She smiled in relief; apart from a bit of shock, he appeared completely unhurt. She stood up, but a wave of dizziness hit her, and she leaned against the wall.

'Sit down, April. You look about ready to collapse. And your legs are bleeding. Come on, sit right here.' Crawford sat her on a mattress on the floor. Resisting the temptation to lie down, April put her head between her knees. Crawford sat down next to her. 'Hey, it's all fine now. Come on, let's get you out of here and have a doctor check you over.'

She raised her head and smiled at him. 'I'm fine. The doctor will sort it out once we've reunited this young man with his mother, I just felt a little shaky there for a moment. Thank you so much, Crawford. I couldn't have done this without you.'

'Sure you could. I just did the heavy lifting. Anyone with muscle would have done. Just my lucky day that I was the one who was here.'

She looked over to where Stevie, who could not be more than five or six, was nestled comfortably in A.J.'s arms, eating his promised bar of chocolate.

'Goodness, young man, you look mighty comfortable.'

Stevie grinned, chocolate smeared around his mouth. April hadn't thought his face could get any dirtier. Still, she doubted his mother would care.

'We should go and find your mother, Stevie.'

'Come on, tiger.' A.J. stood up. 'How would you like to ride on my shoulders and I'll take you to look for your mommy? If you're way up there it'll be easier to spot her.'

The boy looked delighted at the prospect, and A.J. hoisted him easily up on to his shoulders.

'Careful, there,' April said nervously. 'He looks like he could fall at any moment.'

The G.I. laughed. 'No way. I am the biggest bear in the wood. Tell the nurse not to be such a scaredy cat.'

The little boy laughed delightedly. 'Not be scared, nurse.'

The four made their way carefully out of the ward and down the stairs, Stevie holding on to A.J.'s head and shouting, 'Gee up, horsey.' The power generator had kicked in, so although it was dim, at least it was light enough to see where they were putting their feet. The destruction was heart-breaking. Everywhere she looked, April could see broken glass, bricks and the inevitable dust. She had no idea how they would get the hospital back up and running again, and she prayed that no one had been killed.

Finally, they made it downstairs and into the cafeteria, which seemed relatively undamaged. It had been set up as a temporary first-aid area, and, though everyone was calm, there was an undercurrent of delayed shock and lingering terror, and April saw several people sitting, staring into space, oblivious to the activity around them.

As soon as they entered, a cry went up, and a woman came rushing over. 'Stevie! Oh, thank God! I've been beside myself! Where did you get to?'

At the sight of his mother, the little boy seemed to remember what had happened and began to cry. A.J. lifted him down gently and placed him in his mother's arms.

'The nurse and the major here found this little man hiding behind a bed. He seems perfectly fine, so don't worry.'

'Oh, I don't know how I can ever thank you. Stevie, did you say thank you to the nice gentleman?'

'The nurse sang songs and he gave me chocolate,' Stevie said, pointing at April and then A.J.

Laughing and crying, Stevie's mother looked at them tearfully. 'I don't know what to say. Just thank you. We lost his dad last year, and I don't think I could carry on if I lost the little one too.'

April smiled tiredly at the woman. 'I'm just glad you're both safe. Now I really must go and see if I can help.'

'Not so fast.' Crawford put a hand on her shoulder. 'First you need to get those cuts on your legs and hands checked. Then we'll see.'

She huffed in annoyance, but really, she didn't have the energy to argue, and she was glad of Crawford's support as he practically carried her over to the nearest doctor. It was Dr Stafford, the paediatrics specialist, and next to him stood Eunice, holding a basin of water as the doctor tended to a cut on somebody's face.

'Oh thank God!' Eunice cried when she saw April. She put down the water and hurried over. 'Here, April, sit down. Thank you so much, major. I've been so worried.'

'Is everybody safe? Bess? Nancy?' April asked anxiously.

'We managed to get most people to safety, thank God, but there are several people unaccounted for, including Sister Williams and Rachel Harris. Bess and Nancy have gone with some of the patients who have been moved to the nurses' home, and we've got ambulances taking patients to various safe places around Truro. The main worry is fire, at the moment, so we're trying to get everyone to safety as quickly as possible.'

'Sister Williams and Rachel? Oh no.' April rested her head on the table and wept. She hadn't known either well, but they were part of the hospital family, and their loss was unimaginable.

'Come on now, nurse, no time for tears.' Dr Stafford patted her shoulder awkwardly. 'Give me a few minutes for a quick check-up of the little lad, and then I'll see to you. Major Dunbar, thank you and your associates very much. We are all incredibly grateful.'

'Well, if it hadn't been for Nurse Harvey here and her sharp ears, we never would have found little Stevie. She's been magnificent.'

April raised her head and gave him a watery smile. 'As have you, major. I would never have been able to rescue him without you.'

'It really was my pleasure.' He took her hand and smiled deep into her eyes. In the grey of his face, his eyes looked startlingly green, and his teeth very white. Even in such desperate circumstances, April's stomach did a little flip.

'Now, I'll leave you in the doctor's capable hands. I need to see if there are any other of my men around. I had no idea that A.J. was here, so I better see who else is. But wait here for me, April. I'll take you and anyone else home that I can fit in the jeep.'

April glanced at Eunice at those words and noticed a deep flush rise up her friend's face. Once they had a moment to talk, she decided she was going to find out what on earth was going on.

Chapter 14

By midnight, the cafeteria was almost empty. Most people had been evacuated and Eunice had gone to help at the nurses' home, where so many of the patients had been taken. There'd be little sleep for anyone that night.

April had wanted to help, but the doctor had given her strict instructions to rest. Her injuries weren't serious, but she was very shaky, so she hadn't demurred. She sat in the cafeteria waiting for Crawford to take her home and thought about the stories of bravery and near-misses that she'd heard. The children's ward had been badly damaged, and yet even so, almost everyone had escaped, thank goodness. But it was the girl who manned the switchboard who seemed to have had the luckiest escape. When the bomb had exploded, tons of masonry had fallen around her, and yet rescuers had managed to pull her out of a window with nothing more than a few cuts and bruises.

April lay her head on the table, and before she knew it, she was asleep. She was shaken awake by a gentle hand on her shoulder.

'April, honey, sorry to be so long, but it's time to take you home.'

She blinked sleepily and smiled at Crawford. Considering they'd only just met, she felt as if she'd known him for years, and the sound of his voice made her feel secure.

She got up, swaying slightly, and Crawford put his arm around her protectively. 'Lucky I had a full tank of petrol today. I've been ferrying people backwards and forwards all night. You're my last trip.' He grinned to her. 'I've always liked to save the best till last. Come on, honey, you look all in. Tell me where you live and we'll be there in a jiffy – as you Brits say.'

April leaned her head on his shoulder and allowed him to guide her out into the night. In the moonlight, she could make out the ruins of the south wing, still smouldering after fire had swept through it, and it brought tears to her eyes.

'How are we ever going to be able to treat people tomorrow?' she asked in despair.

'It'll be back up and running in no time. I'll make sure to send some of my men down to help, and I know everyone in Truro will pitch in. But for now, you need to sleep. Who do you live with?' Crawford hoisted her up into the passenger seat of the jeep.

'Oh my goodness! Poor Mrs Teague will be beside herself. I should have got word to her before now. She does worry about me. She's my landlady. Oh, she'll adore you, Crawford. Hopefully having you bring me home will help take her mind off the tragedy.'

'Well, if she looks after you so well, I reckon I'll adore her too.' Crawford started the engine and they drove slowly out of the hospital gates.

∞

The house at Daniel Road was dark when they arrived. But then, she supposed, Mrs Teague would be too scared to show even a chink of light after the horrendous events of the night. Crawford helped her down and kept his arm around her as they walked up the path.

As soon as they knocked on the door, it was thrown open, and Mrs Teague, holding an old oil lamp and wearing a dressing gown and slippers, stood in the doorway. Her face was streaked with tears, but when she saw April she put the lamp down, pulled her into the house and enveloped her in a warm embrace. Crawford followed behind and carefully shut the door.

'Oh, oh, April! I've been so worried. I was sure you'd been injured or worse. Mrs Beetie told me to stop being such a worry wart and that all the nurses would be far too busy to come home, but oh . . .' She broke into sobs, and April found herself comforting her, rather than the other way around.

'Hello, ma'am. Mrs Teague, I'm very happy to tell you that April has suffered no serious injury. In fact, she's a heroine. You should be very proud of her.'

At the sound of the smooth, deep voice, Mrs Teague stopped crying and glanced up in surprise. For a moment her eyes widened. 'My goodness me. Where are my manners? Thank you so much for bringing my April home. Can I get you some cocoa, or some tea?'

Crawford smiled, and April was amused to see Mrs Teague blush and flutter her eyelashes. 'I would like nothing more, but perhaps another time. April's all in, and she needs to be put to bed with a warm drink. Can I leave her in your expert care? I need to get back to base and wash up too.'

'Don't you worry about young April. I'll be taking very good care of her. In fact, I won't let her out of my sight ever again. Honestly, the fright you gave me, April.' She stood back and looked at April. 'Oh, my lovely, you need a good clean up, and what's happened to your dress? And your poor legs. Damn Hitler.' Her voice broke for a moment as more tears threatened. Then she gathered herself. 'Come on, let's get you clean and into bed. Thank you so much . . .'

'Major Dunbar, ma'am.'

'You have my eternal gratitude, major. Maybe you'd like to come for lunch or tea one day soon?'

'I would like nothing more. Now, I best go.' He touched April's cheek briefly. 'See you soon, Nurse Harvey. It's been real nice meeting you, despite everything.' He opened the door and disappeared into the night.

April watched him go, a feeling of loss rising within her. Without him by her side, she suddenly felt vulnerable and afraid again.

'Oh my, what an absolutely *charming* young man,' Mrs Teague said breathlessly. She, too, was staring at the front door, a bemused expression on her face. Then she put her arm around April. 'Come on, my lovely, let's get you washed and into bed. Now, can you manage the stairs on your own? I'll just go and put some milk on for cocoa, and I'll be up in a moment.'

April climbed the stairs wearily and went into the bathroom. She stared at her face in the mirror. Her eyes were haunted, her face smudged with dirt and her hair was grey with dust. In short, she looked as terrible as she felt.

Could a man like Crawford really want to see her again? She pictured him as he'd looked downstairs: his uniform jacket torn at the arm, his tie askew, his face as dirty as hers and his eyes dark with fatigue, and comforted herself with the fact that neither of them looked their best. Who would, after the night they'd had? She could scarcely believe it herself. But she wouldn't think of the horrors of the night. Tomorrow would be time enough when the clean-up began. She'd make sure to get to the hospital as early as possible, but for now, she had to get to sleep.

She washed her face and hands, then trailed back to the bedroom and changed into her nightclothes. Mrs Teague arrived with a steaming cup of cocoa and sat on the bed beside her.

'I have never been so glad to see anyone walk through my door before, April. Now drink your cocoa and get to sleep. Tomorrow you can tell me what happened at the hospital and I want to know all about that handsome major who brought you home.'

Smiling sleepily, April did as she was told, but her night was disturbed by terrible nightmares. She was vaguely aware of a comforting presence next to her, whispering soothing words and stroking her hair, but she never managed to fully wake up.

When she woke just as the first light of dawn was appearing behind the black-out curtain, she saw, to her surprise, that Mrs Teague was curled up in the armchair with a blanket over her, fast asleep. April felt her heart flood with warmth. The dear, dear woman had stayed with her all night to try to keep her nightmares at bay.

She tiptoed over to her. 'Mrs Teague.' She touched her gently on the shoulder. 'Why don't you go back to bed now? I'm fine. But thank you for being so wonderful.'

Mrs Teague stirred slowly and blinked at her. 'Is it morning already?' She got up and walked towards the window, peering behind the curtain. 'It's true what they say, isn't it, April? The darkest hour is just before dawn. But look at it now. The sun is already starting to shine, and you'd never know such horror even existed in the world.' She shook her head sadly. 'I am tired, lovely. So if you're sure you'll be all right, I'll go and try to catch forty winks in my own bed.'

April kissed her gently on the cheek. 'I'll be fine. You sleep well. I'll bring you a cup of tea before I go to the hospital.'

'Must you go today? I think you should stay and rest.'

'No, it's all hands on deck. We need to get the hospital back on its feet. We can't let them beat us.'

'No, of course not. When I've had a bit of a rest, I'll ask around the neighbours and if we pool our rations, I reckon we can get some sort of food production line to keep you workers going. Who knows? I might even be able to make some buns.' She smiled in anticipation. Just the thought of feeding people cheered her up.

'That sounds marvellous, Mrs Teague.' She couldn't resist giving the woman a warm hug. She wasn't sure she'd ever met anyone with a heart as big as her landlady's.

∽

Over the next few days the staff worked tirelessly to get the hospital back up and running. Fourteen people had been killed altogether in the raid on Truro and the town was in shock, yet still they pulled together to make sure the hospital could start treating people again. Just four days after the raid, they had managed to open fifty beds. April would hardly have believed it was possible.

Crawford had been as good as his word, and amongst the staff and emergency services, several G.I.s joined in to help. Most of the men were coloured soldiers and all of them were welcomed with open arms. In fact, as the day wore on, many of the locals were questioning the strange attitude of the white G.I.s to their coloured colleagues that they'd witnessed again and again around the town. Why on earth were they kept so separate? As far as they were concerned, anyone who was there to help was welcome, and by the end of the first day, everyone was firm friends.

As promised, Mrs Teague marshalled her neighbours and friends together, and they managed to set up a bit of a production line of food. Based in Mrs Teague's kitchen, she oversaw the making of sandwiches, pies, cakes and, with the aid of the grocery delivery van, she parcelled it all up and sent it to the hospital. Someone else donated a couple of huge urns, in which tea was brewed and kept warm on primus stoves. The Americans, too, donated food, and they had some of their army cooks producing food for everyone on one of the army camp's stoves. Luckily the weather remained fine, and the workers were able to picnic on the lawn of the hospital when they took their breaks. If it wasn't for the fact that people, including children, had lost their lives, the atmosphere might almost have been festive. Instead, everyone worked with a grim efficiency; there was no way that the people of Truro would be defeated by the Luftwaffe, and their determination and willingness to help was humbling to watch.

April didn't see Bess or Eunice on the first day; apparently they were busy looking after patients at the nurses' home. However, she, Nancy and Mattie were there and the three of them worked side by side with other hospital staff, sweeping up glass and debris and clearing rubbish from the destroyed wards.

Finally, hot and sweaty, they were told to get some refreshments. After lining up at the trestle table for sandwiches and tea, they searched around for somewhere to sit.

Nancy gave a little cry. 'There's Homer! Come on, girls, let's go and join them.'

April looked to where Nancy was pointing and saw A.J. was with him, along with several others. A.J. and Homer rose to greet them as they approached. Homer looked very happy to see Nancy, and the two were soon sitting side by side, engrossed in each other.

April smiled and sat down beside A.J. 'What happened to you last night? I didn't see you after we delivered Stevie back to his mother.'

'Miss April.' A.J. greeted her with a wide smile. 'I sure am glad to see you. And looking a mite cleaner than you were last night. But are you certain you should be here?' He glanced down at her legs that were covered with a pair of dark slacks. 'Your legs looked pretty bad last night.'

'Just superficial wounds. I'm fine. So where did you get to? And why were you here in the first place? Crawford said he was surprised to see you.'

A.J. looked a little shifty. 'Oh, I was just visiting someone.'

'Really? Who? One of the nurses?' April watched him carefully, wondering if she should push it any further.

'Doesn't matter now. What matters is you're OK. And I spent the night with Major Dunbar, helping to move the patients. He took me back to base before coming to get you. I've known the major a long time, and you sure made an impression on the guy. And he's not a man who impresses easily.'

April blushed and looked away. 'Yes, well . . . Anyway, this is Mattie, who's also a nurse.' She decided she wouldn't mention Eunice; it was better she spoke to her friend first.

She and Mattie were soon happily chatting with A.J. and his friends, whom he introduced as Junior, Marvin and Spencer. Americans had the strangest names, April thought. She learned, much to her surprise, that A.J. and Crawford came from the same town, and in fact had grown up on Crawford's parents' plantation. She filed the fact that Crawford's family owned a plantation away for consideration later. But she couldn't help the small stab of disappointment at the news that his parents were so wealthy. Clearly he was much too far above her. She shook her head. Listen to her, she'd really only met the man once, and though circumstances had thrown them together in the strangest way, it didn't mean that anything would come of it.

Later, as the light faded, A.J. insisted on driving April and Mattie home. Nancy was staying at the nurses' home, so Homer offered to walk her back. They really were quite sweet together, and though Nancy had always been as man mad as Bess, she seemed genuinely taken with the gentle giant. April smiled at the sight of them walking off together.

'Goodness, do you think she'll be all right with him, April?' Mattie was staring anxiously at them as they walked away.

'Homer may be as big as a mountain, but he's as gentle as a kitten.' A.J. had overheard her comment. 'And he's become mighty fond of your friend. Don't you worry about her.'

'Of course I'm not. And thank you for offering to take me home. My mother-in-law is looking after Angela so I better hurry. Poor little thing was terrified last night when the bombs dropped. She kept asking if I was dead. I nearly didn't come this morning because she was in such a state.' Mattie looked upset at the memory.

'Don't forget my offer of babysitting if you want to go out and can't ask your parents.'

'Thank you, April, but I don't like to leave her if I don't have to. Anyway, from what A.J. was saying about your major, seems like your free time might be taken up very soon.' She gave April an arch look. 'You better be careful, though, April. Before the raid yesterday, Bess was going on and on about how you were trying to steal her man. She said you'd asked him out even though you knew she was walking out with him.'

'What?' April was outraged. 'How could she tell such lies? I did no such thing. Anyway, the major didn't even seem to remember her name when we bumped into her. And he was the one who asked to walk *me* home and I refused.' She sighed. 'I thought after the dance Bess and I had sorted out our differences, but it seems she still hates me and I just don't understand why.'

Mattie looked at her. 'Don't you? I think I have quite a good idea. Bess hates it when someone else is more attractive than her.'

April blushed. 'That's such nonsense. I'm no better or worse than her.'

A.J., who'd apparently been listening to their conversation, broke in. 'I don't like to gossip, but I think your friend is right, April. That girl seems to have developed a powerful crush on the major. Kept asking me about him when I was with her that afternoon. She wouldn't be the first. But he's a good guy, so don't listen to her. I don't like to speak ill of anyone, but wouldn't surprise me if she tries to cause mischief for you.'

April sighed. 'I can't imagine why. I probably won't ever see him again, so she's got nothing to worry about. Come on, I need to get home to wash and change.'

A.J. said nothing, but she noticed him and Mattie exchanging a sceptical look.

❦

Once they'd dropped off Mattie, A.J. drove April to Mrs Teague's. She was too tired to talk and her legs were throbbing so they drove in silence.

The door opened as soon as the jeep pulled up, and Mrs Teague stood on the doorstep with a big smile on her face. 'April! How was everything? I hope the food arrived safely. And who is this young man? You must come in and have some tea.'

'This is A.J. He helped me and the major rescue little Stevie yesterday.'

'Oh, how *wonderful*. I've been longing to thank you. Come in, come in. I still have a little bit of cake left, which I kept back for your return, April. You both look like you could use a cold drink.'

A.J. smiled and accepted the invitation. They walked through to the kitchen, which was still strewn with food and debris – evidence of Mrs Teague's valiant attempts to feed every person working at the hospital.

'Looks like you've been working harder than we have, ma'am.' A.J. looked around in amusement.

'It's been such fun. I do love to cook. Now sit and tell me everything about your day.'

For the next fifteen minutes, A.J. charmed Mrs Teague with tales of the day, and of April's bravery the night before, which made April blush. Then he finally rose.

'I best go. I'll be back at the hospital tomorrow, though, and so will the others. Do you want me to pass any messages to anyone? It's no trouble, I'll be passing that way.' He looked at April meaningfully.

'Umm, no. No, thank you.' She paused a moment, then said, 'But perhaps you'd like *me* to pass a message for *you*?'

A.J. looked away, and she was sure that if he wasn't so dark-skinned, she'd have seen a blush rising up his cheeks. He cleared his throat. 'I can't think who I'd pass a message to but thank you anyway. Good night, ladies.'

April walked him to the door.

'Come back again soon, A.J. You and your friends are welcome any time,' Mrs Teague called after them.

A.J. laughed. 'Is she always so friendly?' he asked April.

'Oh yes. And once you've gone, she'll be going on and on about what a lovely boy you are. She'd adopt the lot of you if she could.'

'Did she mean it then? Not many white folks back home would invite us into their house.'

'She'll be heartbroken if you don't. So please do come again. Perhaps I'll ask Eunice to come too.'

A.J. didn't say anything, just smiled briefly and left.

❧

Inevitably, Mrs Teague was in ecstasy over the day she'd had and A.J.'s visit. But her main interest was in Crawford Dunbar and she was disappointed to learn that April hadn't seen him.

'Don't you worry, my lovely. Soon enough he'll be haunting my doorstep, you mark my words. Beautiful girl like you and a handsome man like him belong together. I have a feel for these things, you know.'

April rolled her eyes. 'Only the other week you'd paired me off with Red.'

'Red? Don't be silly. Don't get me wrong, he is a lovely boy, but not right for you. Oh no, nothing less than a hand-some major will do for my April.'

April couldn't help laughing. 'If you say "lovely boy" one more time, Mrs Teague, I think I might scream. And stop talking such nonsense. Anyway, he's the officer Bess has been going on about forever, and she's already been spreading nasty rumours about me, so I think my life will be a lot easier if I don't see him again.'

'Pshaw, and what would he want with a girl like Bess? Not that she doesn't have her good qualities – she's a nurse, after all – but she's not you, April Harvey. You're special, you are.'

'Thank you, Mrs Teague. I think you're pretty special too. Now, I better clean myself up before supper. I smell like a navvy.'

Chapter 15

A week after the air raid, April finally had her first shift of proper nursing. The hospital wasn't fully functioning, far from it, but the nurses were now taking it in turns to help clear up, and today April had been looking after the children, some of whom had been severely traumatised by the air raid. But they had all been greatly cheered by the donation of teddy bears and games from the US Army. April suspected that Crawford was behind the gesture, and she secretly wondered why, if he could take the time to arrange this, that he didn't have the time to contact her. Clearly he didn't want to. Well, so be it. Her life was busy enough without any complications.

'Hello, lovely,' Mrs Teague called from the kitchen when she got home. 'There's a letter for you on the mantelpiece.'

Heart thumping with excitement, April rushed into the sitting room. But as soon as she saw the envelope, she knew immediately it was from Theo. She was annoyed at how disappointed she felt. Taking the letter back to the kitchen, she sat down at the table and read it while Mrs Teague busied herself at the stove.

Dear April,

I hope all is well with you. I am writing this from a hospital bed in Egypt. I was wounded in battle and now lie here waiting to be sent home. The nurses are wonderful, of course, but how I wish I had my own dear nurse to look after me. Hopefully, I will be home soon. Looks like the war is over for me. I count myself lucky that I can say that. So many of my comrades can't. Oh, April, I knew war was brutal, I'd seen what was happening in London, but it's only when you're lying injured under a blazing hot sun that you really understand. And finally, I think I know what's truly important in life. I thank God every day that I will soon be home and I hope that I will see your dear face once again. It is all I think about.

I will write to let you know when I get back.

With all my love,

Theo

April gasped.

Mrs Teague turned from the stove. 'Is everything all right, my dear?'

'Theo's been injured. It sounds serious because he's being sent home and he doesn't think he'll be fit enough to go back. Oh, poor Theo and his poor parents. I feel terrible. There's me mooning over the major, when Theo is lying injured in a hospital bed. What sort of girl does that make me?'

'Poor boy. But why do you feel bad? It's not your fault that he's injured. And from what you told me, you'd made no promises to each other. If anything, he's the one who let you down. So if he thinks to use his injury to get you back by his side, then he's not a man you want to have any more to do with, my dear. Of course you must write, and maybe you can see him again – he is a childhood friend, after all – but he's not your responsibility and you don't owe him your love.'

April wiped her eyes. 'Don't I? We were such friends, Mrs Teague. He's a part of my life as much as a brother might have been.'

'Exactly, April. Like a brother. Now dry your eyes, you've done nothing wrong.'

'Yes, you're right. I'm being silly. But poor Theo. I suppose I felt so guilty because . . .' She shook her head.

'Because what, lovely?'

'Oh, I'm being stupid. But I feel guilty that I'm so disappointed the letter wasn't from the major.'

'I expect there's a very good reason for that. Because if he said he'd be in touch, then he will. He has honest eyes. I know you think I'm a silly old woman sometimes, April, but I'm not often wrong about people. You've learned a thing or two about people by the time you get to my age.'

'I never think you're silly, Mrs Teague. Warm, affectionate and kind, yes. But never silly.'

Mrs Teague tutted. 'Get away with you, or you'll have me weeping. Go and get changed and I'll dish up this cheese and potato pie. I've even managed to put a bit of bacon in there. That'll cheer you up.'

Once they were sitting down, eating the delicious pie, Mrs Teague asked about Bess. 'Has that young woman been saying any more nasty things about you, April?'

'No, I've not had any trouble.' In fact, April had seen nothing of Bess since their bad-tempered encounter on the stairs before the air raid. According to Eunice, she had been granted compassionate leave as her grandmother's house had been damaged in the bombing and she needed help. It had made April realise how little she knew of Bess's life. She remembered Eunice had said she'd had a hard time, and she hoped things weren't too difficult for her.

She hadn't felt able to broach the subject of A.J. with Eunice either. On the second day after the bombing, Eunice had joined the clean-up party, but though A.J. was there, April noticed that she avoided him. He'd tried to talk to her, but Eunice had made an excuse and walked away. A.J. had looked baffled and hurt, but when he'd seen April watching him, he'd quickly hidden his expression, shrugged and turned his attention to the job in hand. As far as she knew, he'd not tried to speak to her again.

Eunice had seemed so sad and tired when she'd spoken to her later, that April hadn't had the heart to berate her. Instead she'd carried on as normal, and the chance to talk had not come again.

On the other hand, Nancy and Homer's relationship seemed to be going from strength to strength, and they didn't seem to care who knew it. Homer was such an imposing figure that it was hard to miss the two of them and their kissing and giggling. April had felt almost jealous, but at the same time she was glad to see them so happy. Nancy, for all her flightiness, deserved a man like Homer to love her. And it seemed he really did.

∽

Bess returned nearly two weeks after the bombing, and though April tried to avoid her, they bumped into each other as April was rushing along the corridor. Bess stood in front of her so April had no choice but to stop.

'Glad to see you're up and about, April. From the way people were talking, you'd have thought that you were at death's door. Some of us manage to carry on regardless. Anyway, I hear the major hasn't been around. *Shame*. But don't worry, he's fine. Thought you might like to know.' She smiled sweetly and walked off, leaving April staring after her.

She knew she shouldn't let Bess get to her, but her words had hurt. She shouldn't be surprised, though. After all, he'd known Bess first. It was time to put all thoughts of Crawford out of her head.

The following day, April was in the children's ward, sponging down a little girl whose fever was causing some concern. The poor child had been wounded in the air raid and the deep cut in her side had become infected. Suddenly there was a commotion at the door. She looked up and was surprised to see an enormous bouquet of flowers taking up most of the door space.

Who would send a small child flowers? she wondered.

She carried on with her work until Sister Smith interrupted her. 'Nurse Harvey, you have an unscheduled visitor but just this once I'll allow it. Nurse Simpson will take over.'

April smiled at the other nurse, who was relatively new, and handed her the sponge. 'Here you go, Rose. She gets a bit fretful sometimes, but I've found singing to her helps.'

The flowers had moved closer and her heart gave a thump as she realised the man holding them was Crawford.

'*Crawford*?' she whispered to herself, delighted at the sight of him. Then she remembered Bess's words. She hurried towards him. 'My goodness, I've never seen such an enormous bunch of flowers, but I think you're in the wrong ward, major. Bess is working in Florence Ward today. It's just opened again so if you go back to the hallway, turn right, it's the third door on your left.' She turned and walked back to her small patient.

'April? Hey, I came to see you.'

'Nurse Harvey!' Sister Smith's voice was unusually harsh. She was by far the nicest of all the nursing sisters. 'I believe I gave you permission to leave the ward. Kindly do so.'

Flushing, April nodded and walked towards the door, aware that Crawford was following her. Once outside he caught up with her.

'Would you like to get a cup of tea or something, April?'

She turned and looked at him, furious with herself at feeling so happy to see him. 'Like I said, major, Bess is in Florence Ward. If you like, you can take a seat in the cafeteria and I'll let her know you're here.'

'What are you talking about? I didn't come to see Bess. Why would I? I came to see *you*.' He thrust the flowers at her. 'I got these for you. The prettiest flowers I could find for the prettiest girl I've ever seen.'

Sighing, she took them from him and instinctively buried her nose in them. They were beautiful and smelled divine. 'Thank you, major, I appreciate it. But now, I really must get back to work.'

'Are you mad at me? I'm real sorry I haven't been able to be in touch, but I've been in the middle of nowhere – not a post box in sight. Then I figured I'd be back before a letter could be delivered, so decided to wait. But I promise you, I haven't been able to get you off my mind for these whole two weeks.'

'Well, if that's the case, major, how come you managed to contact Bess, yet somehow it was too difficult to send me a message?' She cringed inwardly. She hadn't meant to reveal her hurt and disappointment.

'What are you talking about? I haven't seen or talked to Bess more than twice in my life.'

'Oh really? She kindly let me know yesterday that you were fine. Sounds like you're lying, major. And I can't imagine why. You don't owe me anything.'

'No, but I thought we shared a pretty special connection, and I wanted to see you again. Seems I was wrong about that.' He searched her face, but seeing no encouragement from her, he sighed. 'I apologise, ma'am, for bothering you. Seems I may have got the wrong idea.' He saluted and began walking away.

She stared after him in consternation. She so desperately wanted to call after him. After all, Bess had lied to her before, and had spread nasty rumours about her. A.J.'s words came back to her. 'He's a good guy.' She knew that, didn't she? Hadn't he protected her and cared for her during the air raid? Surely, if she should believe anyone, it was Crawford.

'Crawford! Wait!'

He stopped and turned, looking hopeful.

'I'm sorry. I'm being ungrateful. Thank you for the flowers. Truly. I suppose I was just disappointed when Bess told me you were fine and I jumped to all the wrong conclusions. Would you still like to have tea?'

Crawford's face broke into a heart-stopping grin. 'No need to apologise. Seems Nurse Bess is a bit of a trouble-maker. And I'd like nothing more than to have tea with you. Even though I hate tea.'

'Hate tea?' April laughed. 'How on earth have you survived this long in England?'

'It's a struggle, that's for sure. Luckily the US Army keep us supplied with plenty of coffee. Thank the lord. Only place you can find a decent cup of coffee in England is on an American base.'

April's heart was singing as they walked down to the cafeteria together. She must remember to take anything Bess said with a pinch of salt. Crawford really did seem happy to see her. She hugged the flowers tighter to her.

Once seated, April with a cup of tea, Crawford with a glass of squash, he said, 'How have you been since I last saw you? I hated leaving you like that, knowing what you'd been through, but I could see your landlady takes good care of you, so I figured you'd be OK. And how are your poor legs?'

'I'm all healed. And it's thanks to you shielding me that my injuries weren't worse. I don't think I thanked you properly.'

He waved her apology away, then took her hand. 'That night . . .' He stopped. 'That night, when we were lying on the floor and everything was falling around us, you started screaming for your dad, talking about being in an air raid. What happened, April? I've been so worried that all the horrible memories you seemed to be living through again would be resurrected. I've seen it before in soldiers. How are you, really?'

April looked away, embarrassed. 'Oh, it's nothing. Just bad memories. Before I came to Cornwall, I was living in London and I saw my father killed in an air raid. Well, I saw the street destroyed. I suppose it's haunted me since.'

'Ah, my poor girl. I wish I could take those memories away from you.' His voice was so sincere that April had to fight back the tears. Sympathy always seemed to make her weepy. Seeing her reaction, he changed the subject. 'I really would love to get to know you a little better. That night was crazy, dangerous and scary. But I can't regret it happened, because it brought you to me. So the reason I came here in person, apart from to apologise, was to say, I'm able to get away most evenings this week, and I wondered if perhaps we could . . . ?' He stopped and raised his eyebrows.

'Oh, yes please. I'd love that. I'm free on Thursday evening.' April couldn't help the words bursting from her. Oh dear, did she sound too eager?

She needn't have worried. Crawford laughed with delight. 'OK, then. So how about I pick you up at, say, seven thirty?'

'That sounds perfect. But be warned, as soon as she sees you, Mrs Teague will be making all sorts of assumptions. Please don't be alarmed.'

'I won't be alarmed at all. I hope you'll be making the same assumptions. I know I am.'

'Really?' April blushed. 'We've only known each other for a day.'

'It's enough for me. For now.' He looked deep into her eyes, and his expression was so intense that April felt her stomach swoop. 'Now, I better let you get back to work. I know how fierce these ward sisters can be and I don't want you getting in trouble because of me. Until Thursday,

April.' She stood up with him, and he kissed her cheek. 'Catch you later.' He grinned boyishly and left.

April glanced around the room, suddenly embarrassed. While they'd been together, she had completely forgotten that they were in the cafeteria, but now she saw that people were staring at her. Flushing, she picked up the flowers and was about to leave, when one of the staring faces came into focus.

Bess.

Hoping to leave before she got to her, April quickly scooted towards the door. She'd provided too much entertainment for the staff already today and the last thing she wanted was to cause another scene. But Bess was too quick for her.

'How could you, April?' Bess caught her at the door. 'You can't say you didn't know I was walking out with the American major. I told you and Eunice right here in this cafeteria, didn't I? And I saw you both before the raid, didn't I? And told you again. You are a nasty, man-stealing cow!' The last word was almost shouted in her face.

April wanted the floor to open up and swallow her right there, but she couldn't let accusations like that, made in front of so many of her colleagues, go unchallenged.

Keeping her voice low, she hissed, 'For goodness sake, keep your voice down. Do you want everyone to know your business?

'No, I just want everyone to know what a lying, two-faced bitch you are. They all think you're little Miss Perfect. "Oh, isn't April brave, she saved a little boy."' Bess put on a high-pitched sing-song voice. 'Well, any one of us would have done the same; there's nothing special about you.'

'But I haven't done anything wrong. Crawford told me he'd never walked out with you.'

'What? You think taking a girl to dinner isn't walking out?'

'Calm down, Bess. It was weeks ago, and it was only once. Anyway, all I did was help the major in an emergency.'

'Oh, are you sure that's all?' Bess sneered. 'From where I was standing you looked very cosy. In fact, I'd say you looked very . . . intimate. And isn't it strange how you ended up together that night. He'd probably been coming to see me that day, yet you thrust yourself forward and somehow managed to fall into his arms. How terribly convenient.'

April felt sick. Was that really how people thought of her? Suddenly she doubted everything. Maybe Bess was telling the truth and he had been coming to see her. Then she shook her head. Of course he hadn't been. Just before the raid, he'd been waiting outside for her, hadn't he? But whatever the truth, she was embarrassed by the scene and desperate to calm Bess down.

'Look, I'm really sorry that you feel that way, but I promise that's not how it was at all. If you really were walking out with him, then I wouldn't go near him with a barge pole, but when we saw you on the stairs, he didn't seem to remember who you were.' She saw Bess's face had gone red with fury. Oh dear, she really wasn't handling this well at all. 'Here, Bess, have some flowers. The bouquet is far too big, and I doubt Mrs Teague has enough vases.' April knew she'd been tactless the minute the words came out of her mouth, and she closed her eyes briefly. Oh, lord, now she'd made things a million times worse.

'I don't want your flowers,' snapped Bess. 'I know your game, April. You want him for yourself, don't you? I've been telling you about him for ages, and it's not right that you'd try to steal the man I love. I've met girls like you before. Everyone thinks butter wouldn't melt, but underneath you're nasty and jealous and hate seeing other people happy. Well, you won't get away with it this time. You're going to regret you ever set eyes on my man, that I promise you.' And with that, Bess stomped away.

April heard a few titters and looked around. Everyone seemed to have heard, and though some were laughing, others clearly believed what Bess said and sent her filthy looks. Face flaming, April rushed away.

Chapter 16

As April left the hospital that evening, carrying her huge bouquet of flowers, she heard a voice call, 'Hey, April, wait for me. I want to talk to you.'

April stopped reluctantly; she really didn't want to talk to anyone. She just wanted to go home and pretend the day had never happened. If it hadn't been for Bess, she would have been on cloud nine right now and looking forward to her dinner with Crawford. As it was, she felt sick at heart, and embarrassed that people seemed to think so badly of her.

Eunice quickly caught up and, grabbing hold of her arm, she pulled her towards the gate. 'I heard about what happened with Bess today. Good heavens, did the major give you those?' Eunice bent over to sniff the flowers. 'Mmm. No wonder Bess is in such a snit! She's always jealous of other people's good fortune. Jean saw the whole thing. She said before Bess arrived you and the major had been sitting together talking as if no one else in the world existed. What on earth is going on? You're not going to let Bess put you off, are you?'

'No, of course not. I'm just mortified. Do you think there's any truth in what she was saying? Do you think Crawford is lying to me? He just doesn't seem the type.

Not that I really know him that well, but . . . well, when you've been in such a life-or-death situation with someone, maybe you get fooled into thinking you know that person better than you do.'

Eunice snorted. 'I couldn't say, only having met him briefly. But you know how insecure Bess is. And she's so jealous of you. Anyway, I'm really not in a position to talk about love.'

April felt terrible. Caught up as she had been in her own personal drama, she'd forgotten all about Eunice and A.J. She needed to tread carefully, though.

'Isn't Norm due back on leave soon? Are you looking forward to it?'

Eunice was silent; she'd stopped walking and stood by the hedge bordering the hospital grounds, plucking the leaves and tearing them into shreds. Finally, she said, 'Yes. We're expecting him in a few weeks. My mum and his mum have organised a party and everything.'

'Well, that sounds nice.'

Eunice looked up with a tortured expression. 'Once, I would have been beside myself, but recently . . . I've been questioning my feelings. I mean, I've known Norm all my life. Everyone's always wanted us to be together . . .'

'But you don't?'

Eunice shook her head miserably. 'April, if I tell you something, do you promise never to breathe a word to anyone?'

'Of course I promise. You know you can trust me.'

'And do you promise not to think badly of me?'

April decided to put her out of her misery. 'Is it A.J.?'

'How on earth did you know?'

'I saw you kissing one day. And I guessed that he'd been at the hospital the day of the bombing to see you. I've also seen how he looks at you.' She put her arm around Eunice's shoulder. 'Do you want to tell me what happened?'

Eunice began hesitantly. 'It was after we'd seen them at the Bluebell. I was on a late the next day so stayed with mum and we went to church in the morning. I was secretly hoping he'd be there. And he was. Oh, April, you should hear him sing. I've never heard anything like it. And his face just transforms . . . Anyway, after the service the vicar was talking to the men and inviting them to tea, and A.J. said hello to me when we passed, so of course me and Mum had to go as well, the vicar insisted.'

April nodded encouragingly. She knew all about tea with the vicar. Briefly, Theo came into her mind, but she pushed the thought of him away.

'Afterwards, I had to come back to the hospital and A.J. offered to take me. I thought he meant with his friends, but it turned out they'd brought two vehicles, so they all piled in one, leaving A.J. and me alone. He told me later he'd arranged it. I should have been angry, but I wasn't; I was excited.'

'Does A.J. know about Norm?'

Eunice started to cry. 'No! I haven't told him. I just didn't know how, and I didn't want him to stop seeing me. Oh, I've made such a huge mess of it. But I like him so much. I've never felt like this before and now . . .' She looked embarrassed, but then clearly decided to finish her tale. 'Well, let's just say, there's no way I can marry Norm.'

'Well, of course you can't. You don't love him enough and it wouldn't be fair on any of you if you went ahead with it.'

'No, you don't understand what I'm saying.' She cleared her throat. 'A.J. and me . . . we . . . well, kissing him is like nothing I've ever experienced before, and we were on the moors one day, and the sun was shining and it was so beautiful, and so was he . . .' She flushed a deep red.

April looked at her in bewilderment. Then she suddenly realised. 'Oh! Oh, Eunice. What will you do?'

'It was wonderful, April. It was the most beautiful experience of my life.' Then she collapsed on April's shoulder, sobbing. 'Oh, what will I do? I think I love him. I really, really love him! But Norm is expecting to marry me, the neighbours are all muttering about coloured people, and A.J. says that if we stay together he'll never be allowed to take me home because in America, a coloured man and a white woman aren't allowed to marry. I want to marry him, I honestly do! But if we marry then he'll never be able to go back home,' she wailed.

'Has he asked you?'

Eunice sniffed and lifted her head from April's shoulder. 'Yes. After . . . you know . . . he said we should marry and that he loved me. He didn't care about anything else, all he cared about was me. Isn't that the most wonderful thing you've ever heard?' She hiccupped.

April wrapped her friend in a comforting hug. 'Oh, it is, Eunice, it really is! You love him, he loves you. Yes, you have obstacles, but in a while everything will become clear. But you must tell Norm when he comes home, otherwise it's just not fair.'

'My mother will kill me!'

'Of course she won't. She loves you.'

'My dad will definitely kill me!'

April laughed. 'Now you're just being stupid. Your parents love you and doesn't that mean they'll support you?' But even as she said these words, she knew it wasn't true. She didn't know Mrs Granger well, but from what she had seen she was a woman who liked things just so; she wouldn't be happy with Eunice for upsetting everyone else's carefully ordered plans. And how would she feel about A.J. being coloured? It shouldn't matter, but she feared it might.

'Do you really think so?' Eunice's face was full of hope.

'Of course I do. Now, dry your eyes and get back to your room before anyone sees you like this. And, Eunice, it's amazing, don't you think? You're in love! And he's a wonderful man. How lucky you are.'

Eunice beamed, her entire face lighting up. 'You're right. I'm the luckiest girl alive to have a man like that fall for me. And together we will overcome everything. Thank you, April, you've given me hope. Now, I must go. And don't you mind Bess. You go out with that gorgeous man. A.J. says they're friends, which is odd. The white soldiers don't mix with the coloured ones at all. They're not even allowed in the pub at the same time. I find it all quite ludicrous. But that just shows what fabulous men they are, don't you think? Your major and my A.J. And maybe, once everything is sorted, you, me, A.J. and the major can have a double date – that's what it's called in America, apparently. I know because Homer said me and

181

A.J. should double date with him and Nancy.' She giggled at the thought. 'Anyway, I've got to fly.' She gave April a quick kiss on the cheek then dashed off towards the nurses' home.

April walked on, deep in thought. She was genuinely pleased for Eunice, but she was worried, too. She'd been positive for her friend, but she wasn't convinced that everything would work out for them. She sighed. It seemed love was never simple. Just look at her and Theo. Once, she would have given anything to receive the sort of letters he'd been writing. Now, they just made her feel sick with guilt.

Chapter 17

When she got home, Mrs Teague was at her usual place in the kitchen.

'Dinner's ready, April,' she called. 'I've made rabbit stew. Come in, sit yourself down and tell me all about your day.'

April came in, carrying the flowers. 'Do you have any vases, Mrs Teague?'

Mrs Teague turned from the stove and her eyes widened. 'Good heavens! Who on earth . . . ? Oh, the major.' She smiled broadly. 'Didn't I tell you he'd be in touch? You need to have more faith, my girl. I don't think I've got enough vases, but I'm sure I can find a few jugs and jars to put them in.'

Soon, they'd managed to find enough receptacles to hold all the flowers, and the house looked like a flower shop. Mrs Teague clasped her hands in delight.

'Oh, I can't remember seeing so many beautiful flowers in the house. Apart from the time my Isaac bought up a whole flower shop on my birthday once. He could be a romantic old devil when he wanted to be.' She sighed sadly. 'Hark at me, going on about my old love, when you have a brand new one to tell me all about. Sit down, I'll dish up the food, then I want to hear everything.'

'It's been quite a day. And not just because the major brought me these flowers.'

Once they were tucking into the stew, April told her everything from Crawford's invitation, the argument with Bess and her conversation with Eunice. It was funny how she'd come to view Mrs Teague as a confidante; she never felt she had to hide anything from her.

'Well, my dear, you really have had an eventful day. As if every day isn't eventful enough. But, you know, life is like that; every part has both sadness and happiness in it.' She sighed. 'Like poor Eunice. On the one hand, she's had word that her fiancé is safe, on the other, she's fallen in love with someone else. Oh dear, Mrs Granger won't like it. All you can do is help her and support her in the days to come. It'll be a rocky road for that young couple, if I'm not mistaken. Not least because of his colour, but also, he'll be seen as the culprit in all this – stealing a local's girl. Well, we shall see how it unfolds, I'm sure. But let's talk about your young man. Dinner on Thursday. How marvellous. But what will you wear? And where will you go?'

'Luckily I don't have many clothes, so that decision will be easy. The red cotton skirt and my white blouse are the smartest clothes I have. And I think Crawford has a place in mind.'

'A cotton skirt?' Mrs Teague sounded outraged. 'For dinner with an American officer? I don't think so, my girl. It's time you got yourself a pretty frock.'

'But I've got no time to buy anything before Thursday, I'm on duty every day.'

'Luckily for you, your old landlady has a few ideas. Now, it just so happens that I went into town today with

184

Mrs Beetie, and you know I've been saying for a while that you need to get yourself a new frock. Well, and don't be cross, April, but you work so hard, and after all the horror of the air raid and your bravery, I wanted to get you something. So, I put five shillings down on a party frock. I'm sure if I go and buy it tomorrow and you don't like it I can take it back, but it's perfect for you.'

'Mrs Teague, no!' April was so touched that she'd done this for her, but she couldn't accept such an expensive gift.

'Oh hush. You wait till you see it; you won't be able to resist. It's pale green, buttons neck to waist in the back with a narrow belt, has little sleeves, and, believe it or not, a full skirt, mid-calf.'

'I do like green,' said April.

'Here's the best bit, my lovely. Don't know how the designer got away with it but there's a lemon appliqué flower just below the neckline and another one, slightly larger, at the hem. It was made for you, April.'

'Yes, I suppose that would be lovely. Did you check the size?'

'Not exactly but it looked as wide as your uniform and a little longer. Anyway, tomorrow's Wednesday, let me get it for you and you can try it on. You want to look your best for your major, don't you?'

April laughed. 'You are dreadful, Mrs Teague. But thank you, I would like to see it. But did you see anything else that might be suitable?'

'Well, for thirty shillings there was a long-sleeved, grey shirtwaist dress with large, shiny black buttons fastening it from collar to hem.'

'Oh, that sounds perfect.'

Mrs Teague snorted. 'Lovely for an office or a school teacher.'

'I think shirtwaist dresses are elegant. You have two yourself.'

'And I'm an elderly woman who's not going to a posh dinner with a dreamboat of a young man.'

April laughed. 'Dreamboat? Mrs Teague, where did you pick up a word like that?'

'No idea, but he is lovely in lots of ways, isn't he? And the swirly dress is only a few shillings more and I'm almost sure she'll take something off if you can pay all at once.'

'Oh, all right. You've persuaded me, but rather than you buying it and having to take it back if I don't like it, why don't I meet you at the shop during my break tomorrow? We get a couple of hours, though I hardly ever take it all, so I can get to town and back in time. What do you say? Then I can pay for it myself.'

'Good idea, but as to who's buying, we'll see. Now, let's have a cup of tea in the sitting room and listen to the wireless for a bit before we go to bed.'

The two women sat companionably in the front room, listening to the news on the wireless. They were becoming familiar with the names Rommel, El Alamein and Monty, and the words 'Let us go forward together', which featured on a poster of the prime minister surrounded by tanks and fighter planes. April had just started to say that she thought there should be ships somewhere on the poster when they heard the words, 'Coloured American servicemen'.

They listened in horror as the newsreader told of a fight that had taken place in a pub somewhere in the north of England, when some of the local drinkers had objected to white girls dancing with coloured American servicemen, several of whom had been attacked on the walk back to their base.

'Oh, turn it off, April. How can people behave like that? We've had men of colour from all parts of the Commonwealth fighting with our men, being injured and dying with them. Dogs and cats don't worry about the colour of another animal. Are we less intelligent than animals? As if it's not bad enough that the whole world is fighting each other, but now we're fighting our friends too? Oh, poor Eunice and A.J. I hope people are kinder to them.'

The very same thought had occurred to April, and she felt sick with fear for her friends. Please God, if they did get married, she hoped people would be more accepting of them.

She went over and hugged Mrs Teague. 'Why don't you go off to bed, and I'll bring up some cocoa.'

'Thank you, I think I will. You don't think this would happen to Eunice and A.J., do you? Look how well everyone's been getting on at the hospital these last weeks. We know how to behave in Truro, don't we?'

'Yes, we do. You go off to bed now.' April bent down and kissed Mrs Teague's cheek.

But when she got into bed herself, April was kept awake long into the night worrying about her friends and wondering what the future held for all of them.

Chapter 18

The following day, instead of eating lunch, April hurried into town to meet Mrs Teague to try on the dress. The assistant had put it aside, so brought it out for April to try, and once she had it on, she had to admit it did look beautiful.

'Well, April? How does it look?' Mrs Teague said impatiently through the curtain. April stepped out to show her.

'Oh my!' Mrs Teague put her hand to her chest. 'Don't you look a picture. Now turn round, dear, and let me fasten it.'

April felt like Cinderella. She was sure she'd never owned anything so lovely in her life. She tentatively touched the appliqué.

'I like it very much. Is it terribly expensive?' she asked the shop assistant.

'I was going to ask for two guineas but I'll say two pounds.'

'April, I told you not to worry about that. I have the money right here, and I can think of nothing I'd rather spend it on.'

April thought quickly. She didn't have enough money quite yet, but if she paid a bit a week, it wouldn't take her long to pay her landlady back. 'All right. I'll have it. But I'm going to pay you back.'

'Nonsense. Now go and get changed while I pay.'

'You've made the right decision,' the assistant said. 'He'll fall in love with you all over again.'

April blushed and Mrs Teague laughed with delight. 'He will, won't he? Such a beauty you are, lovely.'

Once the purchase was completed, Mrs Teague insisted she had to rush back home. 'I've got gardening and cooking and washing, my love, so I better go. I'll take the dress with me, save you carrying it.'

They were crossing the street when Mrs Teague caught her arm. 'Look, dear, isn't that Red with that young troublemaker, Bess?'

April looked across in surprise; she hadn't realised that Bess and Red had kept in touch after the dance.

'Well, bless my soul. They look very cosy, don't you think? The cheek of it, after she's given you such a hard time about the major. I'm going over to say hello.'

'No, Mrs Teague, I don't think . . .'

But it was too late. Mrs Teague, looking tall and a little fierce, was sailing towards them at speed. There was nothing April could do but trail nervously behind her.

'Is that you, Red? How wonderful. It's been weeks since we saw you. When did you get back, my dear?'

Red looked up and a broad smile crossed his face. 'Why, Mrs T and April. I've not been back long, and you were going to be my very next call. What have you been up to?'

'We've just been to the shops and got April the most perfect dress for a very special occasion. She looks such a picture in it. Oh, I'm happy to see you back safe and sound. Aren't we, April?'

April, who was aware that Bess hadn't moved, merely smiled and nodded.

'A special occasion, eh? That sounds mighty intriguing.'

'Well, if you come round, we can tell you all about it. Oh, do come, Red. Maybe at the weekend, if you can. We've missed seeing you, haven't we, April?'

Bess interjected at that. 'Oh yes, April misses a lot of men, don't you?' she sneered.

Mrs Teague looked at her in annoyance, while Red glanced between the two young women in confusion.

'I was sorry to hear about the hospital, April. But I heard all about you saving that little boy with Major Dunbar. Yes sir, everyone was talking about it.'

'Oh, she was brave, Red.'

'Oh yes, she was very brave.' Bess's voice dripped with sarcasm.

Feeling too embarrassed to stay, April ignored her and said, 'Well, everyone, I need to get back. Red, hopefully we'll see you soon. I'll see you later, Mrs Teague. And you, too, no doubt, Bess.'

'Yes, don't you worry, April. You'll see me very soon,' Bess said nastily.

April hurried away, feeling furious that Bess once again had ruined a perfectly good day.

Suddenly a voice sounded behind her. 'Isn't one man enough for you?'

Some other shoppers, hearing the raised voice, stopped to look at them.

'Oh, for goodness sake, Bess. You know very well that Red and Mrs Teague are good friends.'

'Actually, Red told me a very different story about what happened at Mrs Teague's. How you kept throwing yourself at him, and how embarrassed he was. Can't say I'm surprised. You seem to throw yourself at pretty much anyone.' Bess whirled around and stomped back to the bench, where she could see Mrs Teague and Red were deep in conversation, happily oblivious to the drama going on around them.

April marched back to the hospital and arrived, pink and breathless.

'What chased you, April?' asked Sister Turnbull. 'Unlike you to come to work puffing and panting.'

'Sorry, sister, met a friend and chatted.'

'Well, gather yourself, I need you to look after a very sick young woman. She's in the bed with the curtains drawn. Poor Mrs Dashell went into sudden labour after hearing that her husband had been killed. I'm afraid we lost the baby, and she's not at all well after losing so much blood, and we just don't have enough blood to give her a transfusion – not after the bombing. She needs a gentle hand, nurse, and I've seen how caring you are with some of our more traumatised patients.'

'Of course, sister. I'll be right there.' With a sinking heart, April made her way to Mrs Dashell's bed. The name was familiar, but she couldn't place it. When she stepped through the curtains, the memory came back. She'd spoken to her in the queue for the butcher. April remembered how she'd stroked her stomach dreamily when she'd talked about her husband's last leave.

She sat down beside her. 'How are you feeling, Mrs Dashell?' she asked gently.

Sister had followed her and whispered quietly in her ear. 'I'm afraid she probably won't answer. She hasn't spoken since she was brought in last night.'

April looked at the once animated and happy face, now pale and stained with tears. She was lying on her back, staring at the ceiling with tears running intermittently down her cheeks. It was no wonder, thought April sadly.

'Do you remember we met a few weeks ago? Queuing at the butcher. We talked about the G.I.s, remember? I think you know my landlady, Mrs Teague . . .' April continued to talk as she gently sponged the young woman down.

'Water.' She scarcely heard the word, the voice was so low. April felt a bit of hope. If she started to speak, then maybe she would come back to them.

She held the cool glass to the woman's lips. 'There you are, lovely cold water. Doctor will be here directly and you'll soon feel better.'

The woman's lips began to move again, and April bent closer to hear. 'I want to go, nurse. I can't live without them. They're waiting, see, my Pete and our baby. They need me with them.' The last two words were breathed rather than spoken. The young woman's eyes closed and a beatific smile softened the pained face and the low voice stilled.

April called to Sister Turnbull, who came hurrying over. She took one look at the woman in the bed and went to get the doctor, while April sat and held her hand.

'Don't leave us, Mrs Dashell. There can still be hope if you just hold on. There are others who love you too. Please don't go.'

But she was unresponsive, and soon, the slow rise and fall of her chest ceased altogether. April had seen death before in many of its aspects – dying patients wracked with pain, exhausted patients whose thin lips still moved in prayer – but this one felt like none of the others. Three people gone just at the start of their lives together. Tears trickled down her cheeks. She couldn't make sense of it. Just two days before, Mrs Dashell had been a hopeful mother looking forward to the birth of her baby and the return of her husband. But they'd both been snatched from her. Little wonder she didn't want to face life.

April bowed her head, wanting to say a prayer, but found she couldn't find the words. She felt that she had failed her somehow, even though there was nothing she could have done.

Warm tears started to slide down her cheeks and she brushed them away. Were Mrs Dashell's husband and baby really waiting for her? How she hoped it was true. She wanted to believe there was a greater force somewhere, but in the face of the constant tragedy besetting the world, she was finding it harder and harder to believe.

'What in blazes are you doing, nurse?' The voice was loud and very angry.

She could only tell the truth. 'Praying, doctor.'

'Get out of my sight.' The doctor whisked the curtain around the bed, shutting out April, who was not quite sure what to do.

Sister Turnbull was there. 'Come now, it's always hard when you lose someone so young who should have recovered,' she said gently. 'Come along. I watched you care for your patient and you did nothing wrong. You are in no way to blame for her death. The doctor will agree but it doesn't get any easier, you know. You care very much for your patients, nurse, and yes, you must have compassion but you have to make yourself strong enough to deal with all aspects of this work you've chosen or you're in the wrong job.'

Dealing with death, April supposed sister meant. She thought of all the losses she'd endured: her father, the countless casualties she'd seen at St Thomas', all the people killed in the air raid recently, her mother, who lost her family so tragically. Then she thought of Theo lying injured in a hospital in Egypt. Would he survive? Oh, God, it was unbearable when she thought too much about it.

'Chin up, nurse.' Sister interrupted her sad thoughts. 'Take five minutes and stand outside looking at the moor. That should make you feel better – small but stronger.'

April removed her cap and apron, and walked as quickly as she could to the nearest door. Once outside she went down the main driveway and walked on to the grass verge. She raised her eyes and stood looking over the town, at the fields and moorland stretching out for miles. The almost ever-present wind blew a cocktail of scents to her: woodsmoke from a nearby farmhouse and the mixed scents of moorland plants and grasses. April smiled sadly. Sister had been right, gazing at the view did make her feel small, but also reassured her that there was still good in the world.

She stretched and sighed. 'Go in peace, Mrs Dashell,' she whispered into the wind. A gentle breeze touched her face, as if telling her that all would be well.

Chapter 19

April was tearstained and depressed when she got back home that evening.

'Oh, my dear, I hope you're not still upset about that Bess?'

'No, of course not. I've decided that there's nothing I can do about how she feels about me. It's Mrs Dashell. I think you knew her. I met her once in the butcher. Do you remember her?'

'Why, of course I do. Dear woman. She's so excited about her baby. It must be due any day.' She stopped as she saw the expression on April's face. 'Oh no. Please don't tell me she's passed.'

April burst into tears and between sobs told her the sad story. It wasn't long before Mrs Teague was crying too. Eventually, when their tears had subsided, they sat together at the kitchen table holding hands.

April sighed. 'I just want it to stop. I'm so tired of the tragedy and the bad news.'

'I know, April. It seems like there's no justice in the world at the moment. But come on, now. We should eat something, and then maybe you should try on your dress.'

'Yes, all right. It might help me take my mind off everything. Did you speak to Red for long after we left?'

'We had a lovely chat. The dear boy has told his mother all about me, and she's writing to me, apparently. Isn't that exciting? A letter from America. Who'd have thought? And he says they're showing a cowboy film at the church hall soon and he's offered to take me! Maybe I need a new frock too! Now get upstairs and show me what you'll be wearing. We can't sit grieving all night.'

April smiled tiredly. She was excited to try her dress, and especially to see Crawford, but right now, nothing seemed very important. But for Mrs Teague's sake, she went and put the dress on.

'Oh, my dear, you look so pretty. But your shoes! How can you wear those clompy great things with such a beautiful dress!'

April looked at her serviceable black lace-ups ruefully. 'These are my best shoes!'

'Wait there, dear, I have just the thing.' She returned with a box from which she took a pair of gold lamé shoes. They were definitely not the latest fashion but they were beautiful, with a small heel and a gold strap that fastened around the ankle with a little button. Having been seldom worn they were in perfect condition.

'My Isaac had these made for me in India. I was a bit of a flapper in my day. I think they'll fit you perfectly.'

'Thank you. I'll take the best care of them, I promise. I've never worn such beautiful shoes.'

'Now that's settled, I think it's time for bed. You need a good sleep so you're fresh for your major tomorrow. What time do you start?

'I'm on six till six tomorrow. Crawford's coming to get me at seven thirty.' Despite the emotion of the day, April felt herself getting excited all over again.

'Get your head down, then, lovely. And I'll see you in the morning bright and early.'

∞

Her shift couldn't go fast enough the following day. All she could think about was her evening with Crawford. But although she was excited, she was also worried. What if they couldn't find anything to talk about? Or she bored him? They'd known each other for such a short time, what did she know about him really? Or he her?

She saw Eunice briefly when they passed in the corridor, but as they were on different shifts, they could share only a hurried word. Eunice looked preoccupied and tired.

'Are you all right?' April asked.

Eunice's eyes filled with tears. 'I can't talk now, but are you on duty on Sunday?'

April shook her head.

'Would you be able to come to church with me and Mum in St Agnes and have lunch with us? I'd so love to speak to you.'

'Of course I can. Do you want to meet at the bus stop?'

'No, let's cycle. It'll take about forty-five minutes, but it's a beautiful ride. I'll explain everything on the way.'

Finally, it was time for her to leave and she rushed home, arriving breathless and hot.

'I've run you a bath, love. There was just enough water. Hop to it and get ready. Oh, I'm almost as excited as you are!'

April had a quick and glorious bath, leaving the water in so Mrs Teague could use it later. Then she attempted to put her hair up, but failed miserably – it was always so slippery – so decided to just clip it on one side with a little jewelled clip, leaving it to fall loose about her shoulders. She pinched her cheeks and used the tiny stub of lipstick that she had, and finally she put on the dress.

Just as she stepped into her gold shoes, there was a knock at the front door. April checked her watch. Right on time. She gave her hair a last brush, then made her way nervously downstairs.

Mrs Teague and Crawford were standing at the bottom, Mrs Teague looking as proud as if her daughter was coming down in her wedding dress.

'Doesn't she look lovely, major?'

Crawford was staring at her, an appreciative look on his face. 'She sure does, Mrs Teague. Like I told her before: the prettiest girl I've ever seen.'

April blushed, suddenly feeling shy. But when she saw him smile at her, his beautiful green eyes crinkling at the corners, his face suffused with warmth, she felt herself relax. It really did feel as if she'd always known him. Feeling bold, she went to him and kissed him on the cheek.

Crawford looked into her eyes. 'You really do look beautiful, April. I'm the luckiest man in Cornwall tonight. Hell, scratch that. The luckiest man in the whole wide world.'

Mrs Teague beamed at them. 'Go on, you two. Get out of my sight. And have a wonderful time.'

Laughing, Crawford caught April's hand and pulled her towards the door. 'We will, and I'll bring her home safe and sound, I promise.'

Once in the jeep that Crawford had commandeered for the evening – a perk of the job, he called it – he said, 'I thought we could have dinner at the officers' mess at the base. What do you say?'

'Where are you based again?'

'We're at Pencalenick House.'

'Gosh. Is it very grand?'

'I'm sure it was once. But not with all us soldiers tramping through it.'

When they reached the gates of the house, Crawford showed his pass to the guards, and they were let through. The house looked beautiful in the pink twilight, half covered with ivy, with an imposing Victorian portico. April looked at it, slightly intimidated by its size and grandeur.

Crawford took April's elbow. 'Come on, honey, don't be alarmed. It's just a house.' He guided her through the entrance, where yet more soldiers saluted them. In the hall, April could see what Crawford had meant. Once, she was sure, it had been beautiful, with a black-and-white tiled floor and paintings on the wood-panelled walls, but now, there were bare patches where the paintings had hung, some of the floor tiles were cracked and the carpet on the grand staircase leading to the upper levels was threadbare and ragged. Several corridors ran off the hall, and she could see that every door along the hallway had a soldier stationed outside.

April stared wide-eyed. 'Good heavens, Crawford, are the crown jewels being kept here, or something? Why all the guards?'

Crawford grinned. 'That I can't tell you. Let's just say plans are afoot. Now come on, I'm starved and I want to show you off.'

The original dining room had been retained as the officer's mess and looked better kept and smarter than the hall, but even so, evidence of the privations of war was everywhere, in the worn furniture and tatty carpet. Still, the tables gleamed and the atmosphere felt friendly. Several of the officers stood to shake Crawford's hand, and much to her embarrassment, Crawford introduced her as the nurse who had saved the boy at the hospital. She kept shaking her head and saying she couldn't have done it without Crawford, but the men ignored her, complimenting her on her bravery.

Finally they were seated, and a corporal came to tell them that there would be steak accompanied by mashed potatoes and vegetables. It sounded delicious to April, but then Crawford asked him to bring a bottle of wine.

April was surprised. 'I've never had wine before. My father didn't drink, and apart from communion, it's not something anyone ever had in Camberwell. Mrs Teague certainly never has any.'

'Well, I'm delighted to introduce you to your very first bottle.' He poured a glass of rich, red liquid, and when both their glasses were full, he tapped his glass to hers.

'To you, April. And to getting to know each other.' He smiled straight into her eyes.

April smiled back. 'To us, Crawford. And thank you very much for inviting me.'

Over the excellent dinner, April finally got to know the man behind the movie-star looks. Crawford entertained her with stories about his home and his family – his father owned a plantation in North Carolina, while his mother filled their house with rescued animals – and how he had come to know A.J., who had apparently grown up on the plantation where his father worked with the horses.

She asked then about the attitude of the white soldiers to their coloured comrades, and Crawford looked grave for a moment. 'I wish I could understand it better. Let's just say it has its roots way, way back. Our country even fought a civil war over it, but attitudes haven't changed in the hundred years since. But who knows? Maybe this war will change things. Something good has to come out of this carnage, don't you think? But I've been talking about myself for too long. I want to hear all about you.'

So April told him about her mother and father. 'You know about the air raid, of course – you saw my embarrassing reaction to the bombs.' She looked down.

Crawford took her hand. 'There is nothing to be embarrassed about. It's entirely normal, honey, and you shouldn't be ashamed. What happened after that?'

April told him about the Osbornes, and how she had left London in the hope of finding her family. But she left out all the other reasons she had wanted to get away, and didn't mention Theo. She didn't want him to think badly of her for having dinner with him, when Theo was lying injured thousands of miles away. Still, she felt guilty, and feared Crawford would see her in a different light if he knew.

After she'd finished telling him about her visit to her mother's grave, Crawford shook his head sadly. 'There seems no end to the damage we humans inflict on each other. I'm sorry you didn't find any family. I can't imagine being without mine. The Dunbar clan is pretty huge. Perhaps . . .' He paused and looked at her meaningfully.

'I probably shouldn't say this yet, but perhaps one day I could take you there, and you could look on my family as your own.'

April stared at him in surprise. What was he saying? They'd only just met, and he was talking about introducing her to his family? The thought made her feel dizzy. Was it possible, she wondered, to feel so strongly about someone so soon after meeting? She thought back to how she'd felt with Theo. Because she'd grown up with him, it was hard to say, but she knew her feelings hadn't been as intense. She'd never felt so completely wrapped up in Theo that the rest of the world disappeared. She'd loved his company and they'd spent many happy hours together, but the way she felt with Crawford – as if her blood was zinging through her veins – was new to her.

'I'd like that, Crawford,' she whispered. 'I think I'd like that very much.'

He grinned at her, and the moment passed as they went on to talk about other things, laughing about some of her more recalcitrant patients, and his life as a lawyer before the war.

As they were leaving, a man wearing a smart dark uniform jacket passed them at the door. They exchanged salutes.

'Major Dunbar, who do we have here? I hope you weren't thinking of leaving before you introduced me to this lovely lady.'

'Colonel Rivers, sir, may I introduce you to April Harvey, the young nurse you've heard so much about.'

The colonel took April's hand and raised it to his lips. 'It's a real pleasure, ma'am.' April smiled uncertainly.

'Major Dunbar, I hope you'll be bringing Miss Harvey to the Thanksgiving dinner in November?'

'I fully intend to, if she'll agree.' He looked at April questioningly.

April's heart lifted. He wanted to see her again! Tonight had been one of the most magical of her life, and nothing short of an air raid would keep her from seeing him again.

'Well, if that's an invitation, then I accept.' She smiled with delight.

'Good, then I'll look forward to getting to know you better then.' The colonel winked at her and walked away.

'Your commanding officer?'

'Yup. And I was going to ask you to the dinner anyway, April. It's not for a while, but it'll be a real treat.'

'I'd love to come. And you can tell me all about what Thanksgiving actually is on the way home.' She couldn't help the yawn that escaped her lips. 'But I better be going. I'm on early again tomorrow and Mrs Teague will be waiting.'

'Your carriage awaits, ma'am.' Crawford bowed and gestured to the door, making April laugh.

Conversation flowed easily as they drove back to Mrs Teague's cottage. Crawford stopped and got out to open April's door. He helped her out and kept hold of her hand as they stood by the gate.

'It has truly been the most wonderful evening, and I hope we can do it again very soon.' Crawford stroked her cheek. 'I feel like I've known you forever, April Harvey. And though we met only a few weeks ago, I hope I *will* know you forever.'

'Do you mean that?' Everything was moving so fast that April suddenly felt uncertain. Could he be playing with her?

Maybe there was a girl back home, someone his mother approved of, and he was just using her to pass the time.

'Every word. Trust me; I've never felt like this before. Do you trust me, April?'

His voice was so tender and his eyes so sincere, that April found her doubts disappearing. 'Yes, I think I do.'

'Enough to let me kiss you?'

He did not wait for an answer but put his arms around her, pulled her close to him and bent his head and kissed her, at first a mere soft meeting of lips and then, as she raised her arms and wound them around his neck, the kiss became more fierce and his hold stronger.

'Wow,' he said when he finally drew back. 'That is definitely the best kiss I've ever had. And you are a lady in a million. I don't think I ever want to let you go.'

'Then don't,' she whispered, pulling his head down and kissing him again. Finally, reluctantly, she drew back. 'I must go. Can I see you again soon?'

'You can count on it. How about Sunday?'

April thought for a moment. She had a day off on Sunday, but she was seeing Eunice and she couldn't let her down. 'I'm going to church in St Agnes on Sunday with my friend Eunice,' she said sadly.

'How about I come too? Maybe I can take you both to lunch. I'd love to meet her properly.'

'Let me ask her.'

'I could drive you both there. I'm sure I can get a vehicle, and I don't mind going to church with you.'

'Like I've told you before, you certainly are persistent, major. I'll speak to her and get a message to you.'

He leaned his forehead against hers. 'I just know what I want, darlin'. But if you really need to see your friend alone, how about later? I could come round here and we could go for a walk?'

'How about this? You come and meet us in St Agnes after church – there's only one, you can't miss it. Eunice has some things she needs to talk to me about, and that will give us a chance to talk. Then you can take us to lunch and drive us home?'

'I'll be there.' He kissed her, lightly this time, then jogged back to the jeep. Waving his hand out of the window, he drove off into the night.

April stared after him. Her lips were tingling, and she lightly stroked her mouth. That kiss had been nothing like the kisses she'd shared with Theo. Those had been pleasant, and she'd enjoyed them, but Crawford made her whole body tingle and her skin come out in goose bumps. Really, she knew nothing of love, it seemed. But it looked like she was about to learn. Humming softly to herself, she entered the house.

Chapter 20

The next morning, despite the early hour, a very relaxed April was awake before Mrs Teague. She put the kettle on and began to set the table for breakfast, listening all the time for sounds from her landlady's bedroom. Mrs Teague prided herself on being the first to rise every morning, no matter what time she started work, and tea was always ready when April came into the kitchen.

She was just pouring the tea into a pretty china cup decorated with the ubiquitous flowers, when Mrs Teague, in her dressing gown and with her hair still in curlers, hurried into the kitchen.

'I'm so sorry, April. I don't know what . . .' she began and then she looked at April and at the cup in her hand. 'Is that for me? Oh, I'm sorry,' she said again. 'I don't know why I overslept.'

'You were tired. Here, sit down and have your tea. I'm perfectly capable of making toast, you know.' April patted her landlady in an attempt to make her feel better. 'What's wrong, Mrs Teague? Are you ill? Is that why you overslept?'

She was surprised to see a blush rise up Mrs Teague's cheeks. 'Well . . . you know I watch out for you every evening if you're due home before midnight, and, well, I was so eager to see you after your dinner, that I stayed up even later than normal, and when I heard the car, I watched from the window.'

'So you saw me come home?' Now April was feeling a little embarrassed.

'I closed my eyes when he kissed you, honestly I did. But, oh, what a handsome man! If I was thirty years younger, I'd be giving you a run for your money, I can tell you.'

April laughed. 'Then I shall have to keep you away from him – already he thinks you're wonderful, and I'm not sure I could match up to you in his eyes.'

Mrs Teague giggled and waved her away. 'What nonsense you speak. Anyway, if I were younger my heart would belong to Red, you know. I got a letter from his mother yesterday. Such a lovely letter full of American news. And she invited me to come and stay when the war is over.'

'How marvellous. You must go if you can.'

'Tsk. An old woman like me travelling all that way.' She looked into the distance. 'But then . . . it would be wonderful to see a real ranch. Maybe Red could teach me to ride, if my old bones could take it. Ah well, we'll see. First this beastly war has to finish. And please God all our lovely new friends get through it safely.'

The thought of anything happening to Crawford dampened April's mood slightly, and made her think of Theo. Her heart sank and she felt guilty again. While she'd been kissing Crawford, poor Theo was lying injured somewhere, thinking of her. Maybe she should write and tell him not to hope that they could be together again. But the thought of him receiving such a letter when he wasn't well made her feel terrible. No, she would take some leave and visit him when he returned, but she wasn't looking forward to it, because she would have to be honest and she hated to hurt him.

∽

Over the next couple of days, April couldn't get Theo's face out of her mind, so finally, on Saturday night after a long day at the hospital, she decided she had to write to him. She didn't want anything to ruin her day with Crawford on Sunday, so she needed her conscience to be clear. It took her several attempts, but finally, she had something she was relatively happy with.

My dearest Theo,

I was shocked to hear that you'd been injured, but so relieved to know that you will be home soon. Of course I will visit you. You are one of the last connections to my childhood, and so very dear to me. I hope that by now you have returned home safely and if so, I am sure your mother is looking after you well and that you will soon be back on your feet and playing your cello once again.

I think of you often, Theo, and I pray for your recovery. I am enjoying life in Cornwall still, and Mrs Teague takes care of me so well. It's strange, you know, having a woman take care of me. I'm not used to it, but I find I like it very much.

I'm not sure if you heard but the hospital was bombed the other week. It brought back such terrible memories. I'd managed to forget the sheer terror of an air raid, but it was only one night and it made me realise how lucky I am to be in this relatively peaceful place. I hope you, too, find your peace.

Write to me when you are back, and I will do my very best to get up to London to see you.

Love from April

April reread the letter. Was it too affectionate? Not affectionate enough? Oh, she didn't know. On the one hand she didn't want to hurt him, but on the other, she didn't want him to have any expectations of her. This would have to do. Addressing the envelope to the vicarage, she rushed out to the post box. She needed to post it straightaway, before she tried to rewrite it yet again.

∞

April opened her eyes on Sunday morning, feeling tired and a little unhappy. What was wrong with her? She was going to the beautiful village of St Agnes with Eunice today, and Crawford was going to meet them there. The thought of seeing him again lifted her spirits briefly. He'd sent a note to the hospital the day before.

Looking forward to seeing the most beautiful girl in the world tomorrow. I've missed you these past two days. I hope you've missed me too.

She smiled as she remembered, but the feeling of melancholy remained. Had she dreamed last night? She hadn't had a nightmare, as those left her sweaty and crying, and that wasn't how she felt this morning. She lay quietly for a moment, searching her memory. Theo. She had dreamed of Theo. He was trying to get to her, but just as he reached his hand out to her, he'd slipped back again.

'Oh Theo, I hope you're safe,' she whispered to herself. 'And I hope you find another girl to love very soon.'

Leaping out of bed in an effort to chase away her gloomy thoughts, she ran to the window and stared out. It was a beautiful early September morning and Mrs Teague was in the garden tending to her vegetable plot. Goodness, it must be late. But when she looked at her watch she saw it was only eight. She just had time to get ready, have breakfast and cycle to Truro, where she was meeting Eunice. She washed and dressed hurriedly, then ran to the kitchen.

'Good morning, Mrs Teague. Why didn't you call me? I'm running a bit late.'

'You needed the rest, April. All this running around and working so hard. I was getting the last of the tomatoes in. Aren't they beautiful? I'm going to make a nice salad for my guests today. Maybe you and Crawford can join us when you get back?'

'Don't worry about feeding us. Crawford says he's going to take us to lunch, so I'll probably be stuffed. I haven't eaten so well in years. Two meals out in the same week! I haven't had two meals out in the same year before!'

'You deserve it, dear. I've got some porridge for you here, and a little bit of honey from Mr Morcambe's hives. Delicious, it is.'

April ate her porridge at double speed before leaping up from the table, grabbing her old blue cardigan and throwing it around her shoulders. As she was going to church, she'd chosen to wear her red skirt and white blouse, and she thrust her feet into her sandals.

'I'll be off then. See you later. Who have you got coming to lunch today?'

'Oh, just the usual people – Mrs Beetie and her husband, and then Mr Morcambe from next door. His wife's had to go and visit her sister, who's not well, so I said I'd cook for him.'

'Well, have a lovely time. See you later.'

She ran out and collected Mrs Teague's old bike from its place next to the house, then whizzed down the hill into Truro, where Eunice was waiting for her by the cathedral.

She looked tired and strained, and April's stomach sank. Clearly nothing had been resolved for her friend, and she wondered what had happened.

'There you are. I was worried you weren't coming.'

'Sorry I'm late, I overslept. Come on, let's go.'

They cycled off and April felt her mood lighten as the beauty of a sunny Cornwall day washed over her. The moors were bright green in the distance, and as they drew closer to St Agnes, she could hear the sea. Finally, after close to an hour of cycling, Eunice stopped at the top of a cliff overlooking the sea. April slowed and dismounted beside her.

'We've still got some time before church starts. Would you mind if we talked for a moment?' Eunice paused and looked out across the ocean. The sky was a bright blue, and the sunlight made it look as if it was covered with tiny diamonds. Seagulls flew overhead, cawing loudly. Far below, the beach was deserted – out of bounds to everyone now.

'We used to walk down there, me and Norm,' Eunice said reflectively. 'Before the war. Norm was going to take over his father's hardware shop – did I tell you how clever he is at mending things? If it's broken, Norm can fix it.

And we were going to have two boys and two girls. Jack, David, Iris and Rose. He chose the boys' names and I chose the girls' names.' She sighed. 'It would have been a good life, you know, April. Before this bloody war ripped it all away from us.'

'Does this mean you've decided to marry him after all?'

Eunice shook her head. 'It's too late for that now.'

'Have you spoken to your mother?'

'How can I? She's so excited about the wedding, although we haven't even set a date. She's talking about us getting a special licence and marrying while Norm's on leave. She says there's no way of knowing what might happen so we should "seize the day". Those were her very words.'

'You need to tell her, Eunice. Have you told A.J. about Norm yet?'

Eunice's eyes filled with tears. 'No. He'll hate me. I haven't seen him since before we spoke anyway. He sent me the most beautiful letter.' She thrust a piece of paper at April.

'Are you sure you want me to read this?'

Eunice nodded, then walked away slightly.

Dear Eunice,

Words can't describe how honoured I feel at the precious gift you have given me. Not just those moments we shared on the moors – moments that have burned into my heart – but also the gift of your love. Just the thought of it warms me like the North Carolina sun. When you told me you loved me, I felt I was the luckiest guy to walk this earth. I felt taller than Homer, and a hundred times as wide. Before I came here, I didn't realise what it was to be respected and loved by anyone but my family. Yet you say you do. I keep pinching myself to make sure I'm not dreaming.

My beautiful girl, with hair like fire and a face dusted with angel's kisses, how I wish we had the time for me to kiss every one. But as we don't, I want you to know that I love you, my fire-girl. I love every little bit of you. You've hit me like a train at full speed, and my head is spinning. What I said that day about us getting married — I meant it. I would live anywhere with you. Life will be hard, maybe, but we can do anything if we face it together. And I can think of nothing I want more than facing my future with you by my side.

So, what I'm doing in my clumsy way is asking you again to marry me. We might not be able to live together for a while, and I don't know what the future holds, or even how this war will end. But whether I have just a short time, or whether I will live to be an old man, I know I want to spend every moment I have left with you.

So, what do you say? Will you have this soldier, who knows nothing much, other than that he loves you, and will do forever?

Yours always,

A.J.

April looked up from the letter at Eunice, who was still gazing out over the ocean. She felt the tears that she had been holding back since she woke start to fall. Such beautiful, heartfelt words. How could she not risk everything for a man who felt like this? And yet . . . so many obstacles, so much disappointment and heartache lay between her and this man's love.

She walked over to her friend and put an arm around her shoulders. 'I've always liked A.J. He's so sweet-natured and charming. But I never realised what a sensitive, romantic soul he has. Oh, Eunice, what are you going to do?'

Eunice wiped her eyes. 'I'm going to break his heart. And mine.' Her face crumpled, but she held the tears back. 'If we marry, not only will he lose his family, but I will lose mine. My mother won't speak to me again. She's already made some remarks about seeing me talking to A.J. She suspects, I'm sure.'

'But he's right, surely? If you face this together, then it won't be as bad as if you're alone. Can you imagine a whole life without A.J.?'

'How can you say something so cruel, April?'

'But that's what you're suggesting! You are throwing away a man who loves you for your mother? Does it really have to be a choice? You haven't even spoken to her, so how do you know?'

'But what about Norm?'

April didn't say anything. She didn't know Norm, so her sympathies lay entirely with A.J., but, she reflected, if Eunice was feeling even half the guilt she did about Theo, then she did understand.

'I just think you need to take the risk. Surely it's worth it?'

'And if it's not? I have nothing. No family, no husband, just me and . . .' Eunice shut her eyes. 'I'm late.'

April looked at her watch. 'No, we still have a few minutes, we don't have to hurry.'

214

'For God's sake, April, you're a nurse, surely you can't be that stupid!'

Understanding dawned. 'Oh, Eunice.' She had no idea what she could say that would make this better. 'How late?'

'Nearly three weeks, but I'm never late. Ever.'

'Well, then, that settles it. You have to marry A.J., and from the sounds of it, that's not such a bad thing. He'll probably be delighted.'

'Will he? Suddenly he's saddled with a baby and he can't go home? Or even take his child to meet his family? And it's all my fault.'

'Not entirely your fault, is it, Eunice? Sounds like he was pretty happy about the whole thing.' April knew her attempt at levity would fall on deaf ears, and she was right.

'You think this is funny?'

'No, of course not. All I'm saying is you can't blame yourself entirely. And you can't deal with this problem alone. You need to tell A.J., and then you need to marry him.'

'I can't.'

'What do you mean, you can't?'

'I just can't.'

'Well, one thing's for sure, you can't marry Norm now, can you?'

Eunice didn't say anything, just turned and got back on her bike and cycled away.

Hurrying to catch up, the two rode in silence, free-wheeling down the hill, until they reached the pretty little medieval church set right in the heart of the village. They left their bikes against the wall and walked through the lychgate. The organ was already playing, and as they entered, April could see that they were just in time. A woman sitting in the middle of the church turned her head. She was wearing a smart grey suit and a black hat. She waved at the two of them. April recognised the rather severe figure of Mrs Granger. She was tall, like Eunice, but unlike Eunice, every bone seemed to stick out. Her face was narrow and her lips were thin, set under a long, narrow nose. She had bright blue eyes, and though she smiled at them both warmly, April could tell that Mrs Granger was probably fierce when she was cross. She shuddered. Sometimes, she thought, it was probably easier to live without any family expectations weighing you down. She thought again of Theo and his mother, and began to understand, at last, how he must have felt when he decided to go with the girl his mother preferred. It was funny, really, she reflected, how her and Eunice's lives seemed to be mirroring each other's. Both with feelings of guilt over old loves, both suffering because of a mother's expectations. The difference being she was an outsider like A.J. No ties to bind her, no one to watch her. No one to care who she married or where she lived.

She stopped. Self-pitying thoughts like these were of no use to anyone. She had Mrs Teague, Eunice, the hospital, and now, maybe, she had Crawford. She should be counting her blessings. She gave Eunice's hand a reassuring squeeze as they walked down the aisle towards her mother.

As the congregation sang the first hymn, 'Onward Christian Soldiers', there was a thump as the church door opened and shut. She turned around and was surprised to see Homer, A.J. and several other G.I.s entering. She looked at Eunice, who was keeping her face resolutely forward. Mrs Granger, however, was looking behind her, her lips pursed with disapproval.

She knew A.J. would be here today, April thought to herself. Is that why Eunice wanted her to come? So April would distract her mother while Eunice spoke to A.J.? She nudged Eunice and gave her a hard stare. Eunice glanced at her briefly then turned back, her face blank.

Suddenly, the church was filled with the most beautiful deep, rich voices. It was as if the ancient walls were vibrating with the sound and the rest of the congregation's voices rose in response, trying – and failing – to compete. At the front, standing by the altar, the vicar was smiling broadly.

April continued to sing with the rest of them, but inside she felt a terrible foreboding. How on earth was this day going to end? She hoped Crawford got here soon; perhaps he could head off the confrontation she felt was coming.

Chapter 21

After the service, April was desperate to get outside and see if Crawford had arrived, but Mrs Granger was whispering fiercely into Eunice's ear. April decided to leave them to it and walked swiftly up the aisle.

A.J. was standing outside with his friends. 'April.' He smiled broadly at her.

'Hello, A.J. I didn't expect to see you here today.'

'Well, I like to come. We have a service at the base, but this little church is so pretty, we ain't got anything like it at home. Plus, it's far enough from Truro to mean we can come without worrying about bumping into anyone.'

April knew he was referring to white American soldiers.

'It is gorgeous, isn't it?' She paused. 'Did you know Eunice was going to be here?'

A.J. shifted his feet and looked uncomfortable. 'Not exactly. But I know this is her church, so I hoped.'

April sighed. 'Well, I hope you haven't had a wasted journey because she's with her mother, and I'm not sure she approves of you.'

'I gotta take that chance. I'm leaving for exercise soon and don't know how long we'll be gone. I might not see her for a while.'

'I'll see if I can distract Mrs Granger. Hopefully Crawford will be here soon because he'd be best at doing that job.'

A.J.'s face lit up. 'He's earning? Well, now that is good news. I haven't seen him for a while.'

There was the sound of a car's engine in the street. Given how quiet the village was, and the fact that no one was allowed to drive for pleasure any more, the chances were this was Crawford. Only the Americans seemed to have enough petrol to drive anywhere.

Sure enough, she soon saw him walking through the lychgate, his tall, broad figure looking devastatingly smart in his green uniform, the brass buttons gleaming on the jacket and his white shirt and tie providing a contrast with his tanned face. His side cap was perched on his head at a jaunty angle. How he managed to make it look so stylish she would never know, but Crawford seemed to carry everything off with panache. April felt her stomach swoop as she watched him, transfixed for a moment, before she gathered herself and rushed over to him.

'Crawford! I am so glad to see you.'

'Hey! Now that's a very nice welcome. I've missed you too.' He picked her up and twirled her around.

'Stop it,' April chided, hitting him on the shoulder. People had gathered at the church door and she could see them looking at her. Eunice was watching with a strange expression on her face. 'A.J.'s here,' she said.

Crawford smiled. 'A.J.? Where?' He walked away, but she caught his arm. 'I don't have time to explain, but we are going to need to speak to that tall lady in the grey suit, so A.J. can speak to Eunice. Do you think you can work your magic?'

Understanding dawned in his beautiful eyes. 'So that's why he keeps coming here.' He sighed and looked troubled. 'This could be a difficult situation, April. But I'll help any way I can.'

'Good. Now come on.'

She pulled him towards Eunice and Mrs Granger. 'Mrs Granger, may I introduce my friend, Major Dunbar. He, along with A.J. over there, helped rescue that little boy at the hospital.'

Mrs Granger flicked her gaze over to A.J. dismissively, then turned her attention to Crawford. Inevitably, as soon as Crawford smiled at her, the icy veneer melted.

'How delightful to meet you,' she said. 'Tell me, what unit are you with and where are you based? I didn't know my daughter knew such high-ranking officers.'

While April kept half an ear on Crawford charming Mrs Granger, she watched Eunice melt quickly away and disappear around the side of the church. Not long after she'd left, A.J. followed. She prayed no one else had noticed.

All too soon, Mrs Granger said, 'Now, major, I must be off. I'm having lunch with my friend and I just need to say goodbye to my daughter.' She looked around expectantly. Then she looked over to where Homer and the other soldiers were talking to the vicar. April saw the moment Mrs Granger realised A.J. wasn't there, as her previous warm expression suddenly disappeared and the ice returned.

April slipped away quickly, following the route she'd seen Eunice take. Sure enough, she saw them standing in the corner, half hidden from view. A.J.'s arms were around her, and Eunice's face was buried in his chest.

April hurried over. 'Eunice, your mother is looking for you.'

'Yes, of course.' She gave A.J. a meaningful look. 'Goodbye, A.J. Stay safe, won't you?'

He looked devastated, but even so, he gently brushed the hair from her face. 'I'll write to you.'

She shook her head. 'No, please don't.' Then she rushed away.

April didn't know what to say, so she took A.J.'s arm and gently led him around to the other side of the building, to give Mrs Granger time to leave.

Her plan worked, and when they returned to the front of the church, Eunice was standing beside Crawford in silence. April looked for Homer and the others, but they'd clearly left already. She wondered how they'd got here.

'Well, it looks like it's just us four. And I promised April I would take her and Eunice out to lunch. And, A.J., seeing as you're still here and the others have cycled off, why don't you join us? I see a hotel across the street – we could go there.'

A.J. shifted. 'I'd like nothing better, but . . .' He looked at Eunice, who did not look back at him. 'I'm not sure that's a good idea right now,' he said quietly.

Eunice collected herself. 'No, A.J., please come. You haven't seen your friend for a while, and I'd like to get to know him too.'

'It's not just that, Eunice . . . I might not be welcome. Especially not with you, Crawford.'

'Not welcome? But I thought you said this was far enough out of the way not to have restrictions?' April was

221

fuming at the injustice of this. Why couldn't A.J. feel free to go wherever he pleased, just like everyone else?

'You just never know who might be watching, and I don't want to get Crawford in trouble.'

'I'm a big boy, you don't need to watch out for me. Now come on, let's go.'

Chapter 22

They left the church and crossed the road. Eunice looked around warily to make sure her mother really had left. When it seemed she was nowhere in sight, she scurried across the road and disappeared into the hotel.

A.J. stared after her sadly. Crawford clapped him on the back. 'Come on, it'll be fine.'

When the three of them entered, Eunice was standing rigidly by the bar. As a woman on her own, she was the object of some fascination. The hotel bar was quiet as it was a little out of Truro and off the beaten path. The St Agnes Hotel was not a common haunt for the American soldiers.

The barman stared at A.J. and Crawford as they walked towards him. 'Listen, fellows, I don't want no trouble here. I've heard what happens when white and coloured soldiers come together, and I think it's best you go elsewhere.'

Crawford smiled winningly at him. 'There'll be no trouble from us, sir. Me and my friend just want to buy a nice lunch for our girls. We're all friends here.'

The barman looked between them and raised his eyebrows. Finally, he nodded and indicated they should sit.

'Just rabbit stew or fish on the menu today, so if you want something fancy you'll have to go elsewhere. Ain't got the meat to do a proper roast today.'

'Sounds perfect. Ladies?'

They sat at a round table near the back of the dining room of the hotel. Eunice and A.J. were quiet, so April decided that she'd have to wade in.

'So, A.J., is this what you Americans call a double date?'

A.J. smiled briefly. 'It's only a date if the couples are dating each other. Looks like you and Crawford are, but me and Eunice, well, it seems we're not dating. Not any more. I'm not sure we ever were.'

Eunice looked across at him. 'A.J., kindly keep our personal business to yourself.'

'Don't worry, Eunice, nothing will go any further,' April reassured her friend.

'Look, I'm sorry,' Eunice said, pushing her chair back from the table, 'I'm afraid I don't have much appetite. I'm not feeling too well, and think I'll just go back to the nurses' home. You'll be OK getting back without me, April?'

'I'll come with you if you're not feeling well, Eunice.'

'No.' She held her hand up. 'I'd rather go by myself.' And she left swiftly.

A.J. got up. 'Don't worry, I'll see her safely home.' He rose and followed her out.

'Well . . .' Crawford looked a little bemused. 'I can't say I'm sorry it's just the two of us, but this has been a mighty strange meeting.'

April stared after them in concern. 'Would you mind if we went back to Mrs Teague's, Crawford? I know it's not what you were expecting, but I've lost my appetite too, and I think Mrs Teague's lunch might be a little tastier than anything we can get here.'

'Of course we can. Come on, I reckon I can fit that bike in the jeep, and we'll be on our way.'

∞

They drove back to Truro in silence. April was thankful that Crawford didn't ask about A.J. and Eunice, though she guessed he was curious.

When they got back, Mrs Teague's lunch was in full flow. Mr and Mrs Beetie and Mr Morcambe were seated at the table, the remains of a toad-in-the-hole in front of them.

Mrs Teague jumped up when she saw them. 'Why, April and Major Dunbar. How marvellous. You're in luck, I have a little food left over. Have you eaten?'

'I'm not that hungry, but I bet Crawford is. I'm afraid we didn't get lunch after all.'

'Sit down then, major, and I'll get you some. Oh, how exciting. A major!' She rushed from the room, while Mrs Beetie stared at Crawford in fascination.

'Is this your young man, April? He doesn't look injured to me.'

'I hope I am April's young man. Although I'm not sure why you thought I was injured.'

April looked at her curiously. 'Whatever gave you that idea?'

'Oh, but Doris said your young man had been badly injured, April.'

April blushed. She was talking about Theo.

Crawford looked at in confusion. 'No, ma'am, as you can see, I'm all in one piece. Maybe she has another young man stashed away somewhere.'

'Don't be silly, Crawford.' April laughed uneasily. She felt as if she was lying, even though she wasn't. She was saved by Mrs Teague bringing in plates of food and rearranging the dining-room table, and the moment passed.

Despite the rocky start, they had a wonderful afternoon. Mrs Teague regaled them all with tales of her time in India with Isaac, while Mr Morcambe told them about his time as a pilot with the Royal Flying Corps during the first war. He seemed such an unassuming man, with his pipe and his glasses perched at the end of his nose, and April reflected that looks could be deceiving, and she should always remember to try to look beneath the surface. In particular, she thought about Bess and her unreasonable behaviour. Perhaps there was a reason for it that went beyond jealousy? And when Theo had left her to go out with a girl his mother approved of, that too only made sense now, as she saw Eunice's struggles with her mother, and how it was tearing her apart.

She noticed how Crawford listened attentively to every person at the table, smiling and encouraging them to talk, and felt her heart swell. He was such a . . . such a *gentleman* in the true sense of the word. He was courteous and kind to everyone. And yet it seemed she was the one he wanted to be with. Could she believe it?

She hadn't been aware that she was staring at him until he raised his eyes from Mr Beetie and smiled at her. Her heart flipped and she stood suddenly.

'I hope you don't mind, Mrs Teague, but Crawford needs to get back soon, and he promised he'd take me for a walk around the golf course, didn't you?' She looked at him meaningfully.

'So I did, but I was having so much fun with you lovely people I almost forgot. Mrs Teague . . .' He raised her hand to his lips. 'As always, a pleasure. And the food was delicious.' He repeated the gesture with Mrs Beetie, who nearly fainted with delight, then he shook hands with both men. Finally, he took April's arm and guided her out of the room.

He laughed as they left the house. 'You, Nurse Harvey, are not just a pretty face. Not to say I wasn't having fun, but it feels like I've hardly had two moments alone with you.'

They strolled to the golf course, where Crawford pointed out the assault course that the Americans were building. 'Our soldiers need to be fit for what's to come, so this seemed like a good idea.'

'What *is* to come? No one says anything, and we're all curious about what all of you are doing here.'

'I'm too far down the line to be in the senior staff's confidence, April. I just pass on their orders. All I know is it'll take time, and it'll be big. And it'll win us the war.'

'I pray to God it does. I'm not sure how much more people can take of it.'

'People can take it. What choice do they have? Now, enough war talk, let's do something much more fun.'

They had pulled into the golf course and were skirting along the edge of what had once been the green before it had been dug up to make way for the assault course.

Crawford stopped and turned April towards him. 'You know, April, we've known each other for around four weeks, give or take, and during that time we've been bombed, we've rescued a boy, we've had one tea, one dinner, one lunch, and yet I feel as if I've known you so much longer.' He put his hand to her face. 'As if I've known you for a lifetime,' he whispered.

April put her hand on his. 'I feel the same, Crawford. I feel dizzy at the thought of seeing you and bereft when you're gone.'

'What I want to say as well, April, is that you can tell me anything.'

She looked at him, puzzled. 'There's not much to tell. I think I've told you the sad story of my life so far. Why?'

'At lunch, when Mrs Beetie mentioned an injured sweetheart, it made me wonder if there was someone else?'

April hesitated. She should tell him. But what was there to say? That she had loved someone else, and he had loved her, but stopped. And just as she was getting over him, he'd started loving her again, throwing her into confusion and guilt. How did that make her look? But she couldn't lie either.

'That is just an old friend of mine. You remember the Osbornes, who I stayed with? Their son. We were at school together. He's been injured and is being sent home soon. He's not my sweetheart.'

Crawford smiled. 'Well, thank God for that. I was worried there. I thought I was going to have to fight a wounded soldier for you, and you know, a Southern gentleman never fights anyone weaker than him.'

April stood on tiptoe and pressed her lips to his. 'You don't have to fight anyone for me, major. I'm free as a bird, and happy to be at your disposal.'

He kissed her back fiercely, pulling her in tightly to his body. April wound her hands around his neck, stroking her fingers through his hair. Their tongues met and she felt a jolt of pleasure run through her.

Crawford groaned, then pulled back. 'April, honey, let's walk. If this ever goes further, it won't be outside on the golf course where anyone could pass by.'

April reddened. What on earth had got into her? She straightened her skirt and looked away shyly.

'Hey.' He caught April's chin and forced her to look up at him. 'Don't ever feel ashamed of how we feel together, OK?'

She stared into his eyes for a long moment, searching for any hint of insincerity and finding none. She nodded, then leaned her head against his chest, listening to the strong beat of his heart. He kissed the top of her head, then caught her hand.

'Come on, let's walk and you can tell me more about this old friend of yours and what you got up to in your childhood.'

April gulped uncomfortably. 'We didn't get up to anything! What made you think that? I was a good girl, and he went out with the bishop's daughter.' Well, that wasn't a lie. But, she supposed, she was lying by omission, which was just as bad.

Crawford laughed. 'I meant whether you climbed trees or got into trouble at school. Did he pull your hair in class? Put frogs in your schoolbag? Come on, I want some details here.'

Breathing a sigh of relief, April laughed. 'Yes, as a matter of fact he did pull my hair. And he tripped me up in the playground and I cut my knees. To be fair, he was sorry about that. I got my own back, though, as I put my jam sandwich on his chair and he sat on it. He had to go around school for the rest of the day with a great big splodge on his backside.' She giggled at the memory. 'He never tripped me up again.'

'Seems boys and girls are the same the world over. I believe there were similar goings on at my school, but of course I never took part in any of it.'

April looked at him quickly and caught his smirk. 'Why, Crawford Dunbar, you great big liar! I bet you were the scourge of the girls.'

'Not me, ma'am. My mom taught me to treat all girls with the greatest respect. Except, of course, the girls I liked. Those I used to worry like a coyote chasing cattle. Maude Thomas, she was a particular favourite of mine. Long black hair, brown eyes, creamy skin . . .'

April hit him on the arm. 'Hey, are you trying to make me jealous?'

'Don't you worry. I prefer girls with golden hair and blue eyes these days. And I definitely prefer them to be over ten years old. Anyway, poor Maude ended up in the creek.' He chuckled. 'Dad was so mad, I couldn't sit down for a week.'

'Goodness, my father never hit me. He was the gentlest of men.'

'Ahh, but then I bet you never gave him cause. Tell me about him.'

'He was lovely, but a man of few words. I don't have a lot of memories of my mother, but I do know she loved to tell me stories, and she was always singing. Once she was gone, the silence was hard. Poor Dad, he did his best, bringing me up on his own. And once I started nursing, he was so proud. And he'd wait at the window for me, ready to heat the milk for cocoa. That's what I see, you know, in my nightmares. My dad's face at the window, the house in flames, and he's calling to me.' She shuddered.

Crawford didn't say anything, he just put his arms around her. It felt wonderful having strong arms holding her again after so long without anyone. She felt safe, secure. As if she'd come home at last.

'You don't have to be alone any more. We have each other now.'

'Do we?'

He kissed her nose. 'We do.' He changed the subject. 'Now, tell me what all that was about at church with A.J. and Eunice.'

April sighed. 'I can't say much without betraying confidence. But they're in love.'

'I gathered. But it's not straightforward.'

'No, it's far from straightforward. I wish I could help, but there's nothing I can do. I'll help Eunice as much as I can, but A.J. will need a friend too. Will you watch out for him?'

'I always do, honey. As much as I can. But he's a grown man, and proud. I doubt he'd ask for help even if he needed it.'

'No, I don't suppose he would. Anyway, let's get back. I'm on early again tomorrow, so I need to get myself together.'

They wandered back in companionable silence, holding hands. When they got to Mrs Teague's, April was surprised to find Red sitting on one of the flowery armchairs with a cup of tea and a plate of cake.

'Red! What are you doing here?'

'Just visiting my gal.' He grinned at her. 'Making sure she still wanted to come see a cowboy film with me.' He stopped when he saw Crawford, stood and saluted smartly. 'Major.'

April felt Crawford stiffen beside her. 'Did you, now?'

'I think he means Mrs Teague. Don't you, Red?'

'Yup. Thought she'd like an outing.'

There was an awkward silence, which was broken when Mrs Teague came back into the room. 'Did you have a good walk, you two? And look who's here. Red popped by to bring me some presents. Oh, you'll never guess, April, he brought ham! What a treat. And some coffee.' She wrinkled her nose. 'Although, I think that's for him rather than us. And, even better, he brought some nylons – a pair each!' She beamed at them all. 'I shall wear mine to watch the cowboy film. Do you want to come, April?'

She glanced at Crawford uncertainly. He had a grim set to his mouth, which annoyed her. He didn't think Red had come to see her, did he? Well, she could see whoever she liked; they'd only known each other a few weeks.

'When are you going? If I'm free, I'd love to come.'

'Perhaps I can take you, April.' Crawford did not look happy at all.

'Yes, we could all go. How about that?'

Red was looking uncomfortable, but he smiled at them all. 'That sounds like fun. Well, Mrs T, April, I need to be on my way. I'll see you in a few weeks.' Mrs Teague followed him to the door.

Once they'd gone, Crawford looked at April. 'So, why is Red going to take you to the cinema?'

'He's not, he's taking Mrs Teague, like I said.'

'I asked you if you had a sweetheart and you said no. Yet now there seems to be two other guys in your life, and I suddenly find I don't know what to believe.'

'For goodness sake. Red and Mrs Teague have formed a special bond, so he visits. As for Theo, I told you about him already. I didn't expect you to be the jealous type.'

'I'm not.'

She raised an eyebrow at him.

'Hell, April, what am I meant to think? Mrs Beetie mentions an injured sweetheart, and not long after I find Red here talking about taking you to the cinema. I know we've only been out a couple of times, but you're not just a casual date to me. I thought it was something more.'

April softened. 'It's not casual for me either. There's no one else in my life, I promise. You have to trust me, though. I'm not used to having anyone tell me who I can and can't see.'

For a moment, Crawford looked like he was going to argue, then his shoulders dropped and he sighed. 'I'm sorry. You're right. I'm being an idiot. Of course you'd have had a life before me. I don't know why I got so wound up. I'm not normally like this, I promise. You make me feel things I never have before.' He took hold of her hand and kissed it. 'Forgive me?'

'As long as you never jump to conclusions again. You make me feel things too, Crawford. Things I have never experienced before. Is it possible after so little time?'

Crawford leaned down and kissed her lips. 'I wouldn't have believed it, but it seems it is. So, you and Red . . . ?'

She stroked his cheek. 'You have nothing to worry about on that score, I promise you. In fact, I think he and Bess might be getting together.'

'Hey! First you, now Bess. Seems Red is trying to steal all my women.'

'Why you!' April laughed. 'Don't tell me you and Bess really did walk out?'

'Honestly, I met her maybe twice. Second time, she very kindly showed me and another guy where there was a good local place to eat and, heck, I couldn't leave her standing on the street. I invited her to join us for dinner.'

'What? It wasn't just you?'

'No, I was with a friend.'

'And champagne from Paris?'

'Champagne? Afraid not. They were fresh out.'

'That's all right, then. Though she tells a very different tale. According to her it was an intimate dinner for two.'

Crawford put his hand over his heart. 'Absolutely not. And anyway, this belongs to you, April. No one else.' Though his tone was light, his eyes were serious.

April copied his gesture. 'And this belongs to you.'

'You mean that?'

'I do.'

He kissed her again. 'It's all I want from you,' he whispered.

Mrs Teague bustled back in. 'Why, look at you two lovebirds.'

They moved apart and Crawford smiled at her. 'I need to get going, but do you mind if me and April crash your date at the movies? That is, if I can make it.'

'Oh, please do come, major.' Mrs Teague's cheeks were flushed with pleasure.

'I'll do my best. In the meantime, you look after my girl.'

April walked him to the door, where Crawford pulled her into a warm embrace and kissed her again.

'Is there a chance you won't be able to make it?' she asked.

'I should have said sooner, but I've got to go away again mid-week, but should be back soon. But hey,' he said when he saw her downcast expression, 'I'll write to you every single day.'

'Goodness, every day? You don't have to. One letter is more than enough.'

'But I want to. I can't have you forgetting me while I'm gone.' He stroked her cheek.

'There's no chance of that,' she whispered.

'See you later, darlin'. I'll be counting the days.' He bent down and kissed her again, swiftly this time, before turning and jogging down the path.

April watched from the door until the car was out of sight, then, pressing her fingers to her lips as if to hold on to the sensation of his kiss, she sighed and went back inside.

Chapter 23

April kept an eye out for Eunice at the hospital over the next couple of days. She was desperate to find out what had happened when she'd left with A.J. She hoped that somehow Eunice had found the courage to tell him about the baby, and even about Norm.

When she couldn't find her by the second day, she started to worry. Had something terrible happened? Looking around, she spotted matron and hurried over to her.

'Excuse me, matron, but I wonder if you know where Nurse Granger is today?'

'Oh, I'm surprised you didn't hear, Harvey. Poor Nurse Granger had to go home to look after her mother. They got a telegram on Sunday.' Matron looked grave. 'Her father, I'm afraid, is missing in action.'

April gasped. On top of everything else, this would devastate her. Poor Eunice. Poor Mrs Granger. She pictured the older woman as she'd been just a few days before, unaware that tragedy was about to descend. Enjoying church, having lunch with her friend . . . before suddenly everything was turned upside down. She remembered her own journey home that fateful night. Everything had seemed just as it should, and then it was taken away from her in the blink of an eye.

Forgetting that she had not eaten, April hurried back to her ward, her mind now full of the tragedy that had hit her friend's family. She needed to see how they were. After her shift ended, she would cycle over to St Agnes and check that they were all right.

During the afternoon, she tried to clear everything from her mind as she went from bed to bed, checking notes, smiling, encouraging, changing dressings, reading letters, chatting to her patients, pouring water or juice when requested, going over the treatment options if questions were asked that she was qualified to answer. At last the end of her shift arrived, and she hurried back to Mrs Teague's to collect the bike.

It was a warm September afternoon, so April knew that she could cycle to St Agnes, stay for a little while and be back before it got too dark. Rushing through the door, she explained what had happened to Mrs Teague.

'Oh, that poor girl. You get off there and give her some comfort, my love. But have something quick to eat before you go. I've found a recipe for a new macaroni dish in my magazine. Tinned tomatoes, cheese, the macaroni, an onion, some parsley, seasoning and a little marge. Plus John brought some tinned peas along with everything else the other day.'

'John?'

'Red, but his mother calls him John, and seeing as I feel like I'm his wartime mother, I should call him that too, shouldn't I?'

Despite everything, April laughed. 'You are funny. I don't think he minds what you call him. But I don't think there's time. I'm hoping to get there and back before it gets too dark.'

'Give my love to Mrs Granger, won't you, dear?' She shook her head sadly. 'Such terrible things happening. The papers say lots of American soldiers are going to North Africa. Why would they be in Africa? Isn't it all desert up there? Look at today's paper. All those strange names I've never heard any of. Oh, I do hope Red doesn't have to go to any of these places.'

April hugged her. 'Try not to think of it. He's here for now, so just enjoy this time. I'll tell Mrs Granger you're thinking of her.'

∞

Eunice opened the door when she knocked. She looked dreadful. Her eyes were red-rimmed and her freckles stood out in stark contrast to the paper-white paleness of her face.

'April! I didn't expect to see you. Come in.'

April gave her friend a hug. 'You poor, poor thing. Of course I came. How are you?'

They went through to the sitting room, where Eunice sat on an armchair and put her head in her hands.

'It was terrible. Dad's missing somewhere in Crete, apparently. I don't even know where that is! I got the message when I got back to the nurses' home yesterday, and A.J. came back with me. Mother was in such a state and seeing A.J. made it worse. She told him to leave and never come back. Said I'd been complaining about him pestering me, and if he turned up at the church again, she'd make sure everyone knew the sort of man he was. Poor

238

A.J. looked devastated,' Eunice sobbed. 'And now she's hardly talking to me. And worse, she's acting as if Dad will be home. She refuses to believe that he might have been killed.'

'Oh, Eunice. Does she know, then, about you and A.J.?' April wondered how much more her friend could bear. She was worried about what the stress would do to the baby, but she kept that thought to herself.

Eunice nodded. 'She guessed that something was going on the other day, so when A.J. brought me home, her suspicions were confirmed. And now this has happened and she keeps flying off the handle at me. Shouting about me bringing shame on the family. Telling me to wait until Dad gets home, he'll make sure A.J. gets what's coming to him.'

Just then, Mrs Granger came into the room, looking ten years older than she had just a couple of days before.

'Mrs Granger, I'm so sorry to hear your terrible news. If there's anything I can do, please just let me know.'

She nodded. 'He's not dead, you know, April. I'd know if he was, wouldn't I? Sometime soon, my Albert will be back. I'll make us some tea, shall I?' She left the room.

While she was gone, April sat on the sofa with her arm around her friend, while Eunice sobbed into her shoulder.

'Do you see what I mean?' Eunice raised her head and sniffed. 'She's behaving as if he's just a bit lost and will turn up any time soon.'

'Perhaps it's the only way she can cope. And there is still hope, Eunice, so try not to think the worst until you have to.'

Eunice nodded and sighed. 'I suppose you're right.' She sat back and closed her eyes. 'I just wish I could be as certain as she is. But instead, I just keep fearing the worst.'

April murmured some soothing words, but she knew there was nothing she could say that would make her feel better, so she stopped talking and held her friend's hand, praying silently that Eunice would have the strength to get through the next few weeks. With everything that was going on in her life, it wasn't going to be easy.

When Mrs Granger returned, she set the tray on the table and poured each of them a cup of tea. April noticed she didn't look at her daughter at all.

'Thank you for coming, dear,' she said once the tea was poured. 'Though, as I said, I'm sure all will be well. Anyway, there's no time for all this grieving. We've got Norm coming soon, and I'd like to have a little celebration. Goodness knows what Mr Granger would think if I went off into hysterics just because he's missing.'

April shifted uncomfortably in her chair. She had no idea what on earth she could say to that. And the mention of Norm had set Eunice crying again. She decided to humour Mrs Granger.

'You're right. There's always hope. You're very brave to stay so positive.'

Mrs Granger nodded then looked at Eunice, her expression hardening. 'That's enough, Eunice. Anyone would think it was Norm that was missing. Oh no, come to think of it, you wouldn't shed a tear for him, would you? Considering the way you leaped on someone new the minute he turned his back.'

'Please don't, Mother'

'Look at the way you're carrying on when your father's not even dead. I think you're grieving more about not seeing that darky fellow again. You better get your priorities straight before Norm gets back.'

'How can you say such things?'

'Anyway, maybe it would be just as well if your father was dead, considering the shame you're bringing on this household.'

'Mother . . .' Eunice's voice was defeated, as if she'd heard it all before. Which, April thought, she probably had.

'Your father will be furious when he gets back. No daughter of his is going to marry some foreigner, I can tell you that. Now stop your snivelling. I can't stand the noise.'

April was shocked at Mrs Granger's words. She found it hard to believe she could be so insensitive to her daughter's grief. But then she noticed that, as Mrs Granger lifted her cup to her mouth, her hand was shaking so badly, the tea spilled down her dress, causing her to jump up with a cry of frustration and leave the room. Suddenly, despite the way she'd just spoken to her friend, April's heart went out to her. Eunice had always said that her mother was a woman of strong conviction, who did not like anything upsetting her plans. Now she was facing the possibility that her husband was dead, and the bright future she'd envisioned for her daughter seemed to be slipping away as well. And it was all out of her control.

Eunice hiccupped as she tried to hold back her tears. 'I don't think she wants me here, so I'm going to come back to work tomorrow; staying here is driving me mad. The neighbours said they'd make sure she was all right, and to be honest, I think the sight of me upsets her.'

'It's good to keep busy and focus on other things. But hard. And, Eunice, about all the other stuff:' – she gestured to Eunice's stomach – 'you really only have one choice. You have to tell A.J. and Norm. You know that, don't you?'

Eunice bent her head and nodded. 'I just can't face it right now, though.'

'But when Norm comes back you're going to have to.'

'Please, not now, April.'

April squeezed her friend's hand. 'All right. But remember, I'm here for you, no matter what. One way or another things will work out eventually. Now I better go.'

Eunice held on to April's hand as she rose from the sofa. 'Thank you. For coming, I mean. I can't tell you how much it means to have someone on my side.'

April nodded and went to the hall to get her coat. She heard Mrs Granger moving about in the kitchen and popped her head around the door to say goodbye.

'April, before you go, there is something you can do for me. You're a good friend of Eunice's, so perhaps she'll listen to you. I know she's been running around with that . . . that *man*, and I'm disgusted with her. She's an engaged woman and needs to face up to her responsibilities. She needs to get rid of that other fellow before poor Norm catches wind of anything. Talk to her for me, will you?'

April didn't know what on earth she could say, so simply nodded.

'Thank you. I knew I could rely on you; I've always thought you were a good, steady girl. Not like that Bess. I'm sure it's her influence that's led Eunice off the rails. Now, I've just spoken with Terence next door and he says he'll take you back to Truro. The bike will fit in the van. He's got deliveries to make and he's happy to help.'

'That would be lovely, thank you.' April was relieved. The thought of cycling back made her weak with fatigue.

Just then a horn tooted outside. 'There he is now. Off you go and remember what I said.'

Terence was a portly, middle-aged man with a cigarette dangling from his lips, and after telling him where she lived and thanking him for the lift, the two drove in silence for a few minutes.

Suddenly Terence broke the silence. 'Bad business, that. At the Grangers.'

Assuming he meant the fact that Mr Granger was missing, April murmured an agreement.

'Saw that darky turn up at the house the other day with Eunice. And her engaged to Norm. We don't see many people of colour here and that's how we like it. A very nice neighbourhood, this, no riff-raff around here. I have to say he seemed nice enough, but Eunice's dad wouldn't allow it. Wouldn't like it at all. He's definitely a stick-to-your-own-kind sort of chap.'

April felt her cheeks flush with anger. 'I assume you mean A.J. Timpson? He's a friend of ours. And because he was with us on Sunday, and he's a gentleman, he didn't want Eunice cycling over on her own when she was so distressed.' She hated the way this man was talking. She'd rather cycle back than listen to him. 'Anyway, I prefer to believe that Mr Granger would have got to know him before he judged him.'

'No, lass, he couldn't even tolerate the English. A bad year for the Grangers, this, and the last thing they want is their daughter getting a reputation. Expect you've got some Yank boyfriend too. They're all over the place. Sick of them, I am.'

'We have made many American friends since they arrived. My landlady often has young American visitors, including A.J. She mothers them a bit and it's good for her and them.'

'As long as they don't get too friendly. Elderly, is she?'

'She's not young but she enjoys young company.'

'Hmph. Just tell her to watch herself, that's all. Can't be too careful these days.'

April didn't say any more, instead she gazed sightlessly out of the window. She'd known things were difficult for Eunice, but suddenly she understood just how isolated she might be once people realised she was pregnant, and who the father was. No wonder she was in such turmoil. It would have been bad enough without having to contend with her mother and the attitude of the neighbours. She wondered, if the worst came to the worst, whether Eunice could stay at Mrs Teague's. She wouldn't be allowed to live at the nurses' home once they realised she was pregnant, and her mother probably wouldn't want to help either. It was a lot to ask, but given Mrs Teague's need to mother, and her complete lack of prejudice or judgement, she was certain she would be happy to help.

Terence's voice broke into her thoughts. 'Here we are, m'dear.'

She forced herself to smile at him. 'Thank you for the lift.'

'Mind how you go now, love,' he said, then drove off, tooting his horn and waving a hand out of the window.

After saying a quick good night to Mrs Teague, April went straight up to bed. But despite her exhaustion, it was a long time until she was able to sleep. Thoughts of her friend kept going around and around in her head, but with no possible solution to offer, her mind conjured up Theo's face. She needed to talk to both Theo and Crawford, because if Eunice's situation had taught her anything, it was that you needed to confront your problems before they became too large. The last thing she wanted was for anything to jeopardise her relationship with Crawford.

∞

Work was especially busy the next day, but April was cheered to see Eunice when she went to the cafeteria. She was less thrilled to see Bess, but seeing as the girls were sitting together, along with Nancy, she had little choice but to talk to her.

When she sat down, Bess was telling the other two about Red and how he was going to take her to the picture house.

'Oh, Red was at Mrs Teague's the other night and said he was taking her. Is he taking you both then?'

'He was at *your* house? Why the—'

'No, he wasn't asking me, he was asking my landlady.'

'I think you must be mistaken. He'll be taking me.'

'I don't think ...' Seeing Bess's expression, she decided to say no more. Things were awkward enough as it was and Red could sort out his own mess. She also thought it wise not to mention that she might be going with Crawford. She looked at Eunice. 'How are you today, love?'

'Glad to be back, to be honest.' Eunice smiled wanly but didn't seem inclined to talk much. So April turned to Nancy.

'What about you? Will you and Homer be going to see the film?' She realised her mistake the minute the words were out of her mouth. 'Sorry. That was insensitive of me. I expect Homer's not allowed to go, is he?'

'No. Anyway, I'm working that night. They're showing the film for the coloured soldiers the next night, so I'll be going then. Honestly, if we women are fine with it, I can't understand why the men can't all mix together.'

Eunice snorted. 'It's not just the men. Some of the women are just as bad.'

Nancy sighed. 'I know. Lucky for me my mother doesn't care. Anyway, got to love you and leave you.'

Eunice looked at her watch. 'Yes, me too. See you later.'

After they'd left, Bess caught April's arm and hissed at her, 'If you think I believe that rubbish about Red going to see Mrs Teague, then you must think I'm stupid. Bet Crawford doesn't know about it either, does he? Think it's time someone told him what sort of girl you *really* are.'

'Actually, Crawford was with me at the time, so if you think you can spread nasty little lies about me, it's you who needs to think again.' She pushed her chair back from the table and stormed off, wishing she could understand why Bess hated her so much. From what Crawford had told her, Bess had lied about them having any sort of relationship at all, and she was heartily sick of the girl.

A couple of hours later April managed to grab a quick word with Eunice in the changing room just before she left. 'When's Norm back?'

Eunice looked away. 'I'm not sure. Next week, I think.'

'And will you be seeing A.J. before then?'

Eunice looked shifty.

'You will, won't you?'

'I have to see him. Just one more time. Because once I tell him the truth, he'll never want to see me again.'

'Even if you tell him *everything*, I don't think A.J.'s the sort to turn away from his responsibilities.'

'And do you think that's what I want? To be a responsibility? How can he ever love me again after I've told him the truth? How can I keep him here under duress because I'm going to have a baby? What sort of life do you think we'll lead? If our relationship was ever going to work then we have to be completely committed to each other. Instead, he'll just resent me for keeping him away from his family.'

'But *you'll* be his family. You and the baby.'

'For God's sake. How can you be so naïve? You think we can all have things nice and easy like you and Crawford. You have everything to gain and nothing to lose by being with him. Whereas I . . . I'll lose everything. His love, my family, my friends, the respect of the people I've grown up with . . . You could never understand, so please, just leave me alone and let me deal with this my own way.'

Tears sprang into April's eyes at her friend's harsh words. But she was right. What did she know about family ties? Apart from her father, she'd never been connected to anyone. The closest she'd come was Theo, and that didn't really count. Because if she'd truly loved him, she would not have fallen for Crawford.

'You're right,' she said quietly. 'I don't know much about what you're going through. But I do know you need to give A.J. the chance to prove himself. At least then, if it doesn't work out, you won't spend your life tortured by "what ifs". I need to go now, but let me know if you need me.'

'April . . .' Eunice's tone was imploring. 'I'm sorry.'

April merely nodded then walked away. Eunice was right: she needed to let her deal with this in her own way. All she could do was be there if it went wrong.

Chapter 24

The days until the much-anticipated film night were difficult for April. She felt weighed down by Eunice's troubles and Bess's antagonism, and so she took to taking her breaks away from the hospital in an attempt to avoid all confrontations. If it hadn't been for the fact that Crawford had kept his promise of writing every day, she would have been thoroughly miserable.

The first one had arrived the day after she saw him. She'd torn the envelope open joyfully and smiled as she read:

> My darling April,
> It is nine seventeen a.m. and it is two hundred and sixteen hours and forty-three minutes until I see you again. But it may as well be two hundred and sixteen years, the way I feel.
> You have captured my heart completely.
> Crawford.

She wrote back immediately.

Dear Crawford,

It is now eight forty-five p.m. and it is one thousand, six hundred and twenty minutes since I last saw you. Every one of those minutes has been filled with thoughts of you.

Is this what falling in love feels like?

Yours,

April

Crawford's notes continued to arrive all week, each detailing the number of hours until they saw one other again. Then, the day before she was due to see him, she received two letters. One, inevitably, was from Crawford, and she tore it open eagerly.

Dear April,

Finally, the time is nearly upon us. I've been counting the hours, sweetheart, in case you hadn't noticed.

The bad news is that after tomorrow, I'm going to have to go away again. For longer this time. We'll all be on exercise, Red included. But I'll be back in plenty of time for Thanksgiving. Will you come to the dinner with me? You promised, remember?

I'll be over at six to pick you and Mrs Teague up. Red will meet us at the hall.

I'm writing this at lunchtime, and by my calculation there are only twenty-eight hours and thirty-three minutes left.

Until then, my darling.

Crawford xx

April couldn't help it, she sniffed the paper to see if it smelled of Crawford. It didn't. But the kisses by his name spoke volumes. She kissed the page and hugged the letter to her chest. With Crawford by her side, she was sure that she would be able to face anything.

Her happiness dimmed slightly, however, when she saw the other letter was from Theo. With everything that had been happening, she'd pushed thoughts of him to the back of her mind. She opened it with some trepidation.

Dear April,

I will be on my way next week and all being well – provided we don't get torpedoed! – I should be back in England three weeks after that. I'm not yet well enough to go home, so I will be taken to a hospital. Hopefully it will be close to my parents. I can't wait to be home. The thought of seeing you is one of the only things that is keeping me going.

Pray for me, sweet girl. And, God willing, I will see you soon.

Much love,
Theo

Anxiety and guilt fizzed through her. How on earth would she tell Theo that her feelings had changed? She wondered how she would feel about Theo now if she hadn't met Crawford. She shook her head. No, she would feel the same, because she'd already been uncertain when they had kissed by the fire so long ago. Could it really only have been last year? She still loved him, he was her oldest friend, but compared to the love she felt for Crawford, it was an insipid, insubstantial feeling. She hoped he would understand, but the thought of hurting him, especially when he was injured, made her feel sick. She decided she would talk to matron about getting leave in a few weeks' time, so she could go to London and talk to him. It was the only way, and she had promised to come.

∽

The next evening at six, April was standing by the window anxiously scanning the street for any sign of Crawford. Mrs Teague stood beside her. Her excitement at the prospect of watching the film was almost as much as April's was at the thought of seeing Crawford again. When the jeep appeared, April ran to the door, threw it open and dashed down the path. Crawford had just got out of the car when April barrelled into him, throwing her arms around him and burying her nose in his neck, sniffing the distinctive, woody scent of him.

He laughed with delight and hugged her back. 'Oh, thank God! I swear, April, this has been the longest few days of my life. Did you get my notes?'

'Yes! Did you not get mine? And how did you manage to get a letter delivered every single day?'

He tapped his nose. 'I cheated slightly. Made friends with Mrs Jones in the post office and left them all there for delivery. And I got yours today when I got back. And I think the answer to your question is yes, this *is* what falling in love feels like.'

She drew back to look into his eyes. His were green and intense. 'You, Crawford Dunbar, are not only devious, but you are also completely wonderful.'

'I hope that means I get a little kiss as a reward.'

'That was never in doubt.' She pressed a kiss on his lips, and he pulled her closer to him. For a moment, everything else was forgotten, until she heard Mrs Teague.

'April, my dear, it's raining and you'll need your coat. Goodness gracious, major, you've turned that girl's head to mush! Now, come on, I don't want to be late.'

∽

When they arrived at the hall, Red was standing outside waiting for them. April was less pleased to notice that Bess was also with him, hanging on to his arm possessively.

As soon as Crawford opened Mrs Teague's door, she was out of the car and rushing up to Red. 'Red! My dear, isn't this exciting?' Her smile dimmed slightly when she looked at Bess. 'And Bess. Nice to see you again.'

Bess smiled at her. 'Hello, Mrs Teague, I hope you don't mind me joining you. When Red said you were all coming, I simply couldn't resist.' She looked at April and Crawford, and her eyes hardened. 'Hello, Crawford, I am happy to see you again. It's been a while – we should really catch up some time.'

Crawford smiled absently. 'Well, hello. It's Bess, isn't it?'

Bess's smile faltered at this, then she laughed insincerely. 'Of course it is Bess. Who did you think it was? Anyway, come on everyone, let's go inside.'

Crawford raised his eyebrows at April, then turned to go inside with the others. Bess, meanwhile, was staring across the street, her eyes wide with surprise. She turned to April and caught her arm.

'April,' she hissed. 'Look!'

April glanced in the direction that Bess was indicating. Walking away from them down the street was a tall G.I. and a shorter, red-haired woman. Their hands were linked and their heads bent towards each other. April's heart stopped. Eunice and A.J.

'Is that . . . ? Well, she's a sly one, isn't she? But why isn't she with Norm?' Bess looked over at April. 'Did *you* know about this?'

April didn't say anything, but Bess drew her own conclusions.

'You did, didn't you? How come she told you and not me?'

'She didn't tell me, I found out. Is Norm back yet?'

'Don't think so. Sure it's tomorrow. At least, Eunice isn't coming to work for the next couple of days, and she says that's why.'

'Oh dear. I hope no one else spots them.'

Bess looked around quickly, checking to see if anyone else had noticed. Suddenly, her face paled. 'Oh gawd!'

April turned and saw a tall, thin man wearing the uniform of a Royal Navy petty officer walking down the street. He was smoking a cigarette and his gaze was fixed firmly on the couple in front of him.

'It's Norm,' Bess whispered. 'He must have arrived early. Looks like he's on the way to the nurses' home. Quick, we've got to do something. I'll go and speak to him, you go and warn Eunice.' She gave her a shove.

April didn't need asking twice as she sped towards Eunice and A.J. As she reached them, she glanced back. True to her word, Bess was talking to Norm and had somehow managed to turn him so he was no longer facing in their direction.

April grabbed Eunice's arm. Eunice jumped and turned around in surprise. '

April! What's wrong? I didn't know you were here.'

'Eunice, you need to get back to the nurses' home as soon as possible.' She looked at her meaningfully, indicating up the road with her head.

Eunice looked in the direction she was indicating. 'What are you . . . ?' Suddenly she stilled, then looked back at April, her eyes full of panic.

A.J., oblivious, gave April a warm smile. 'Hey, April. I forgot the film. I'm hoping to go tomorrow, if Eunice will come with me is on tonight. Does this mean that Crawford is here?' Suddenly his face clouded. 'And a whole load of other soldiers, I bet. Eunice, honey, we better move on. Let's go to The Swan.'

Eunice snapped out of her paralysis. 'Actually, A.J., I'm really sorry, but Bess needs me back at the nurses' home. I really need to go. I'm so sorry.' Before he could say anything, she rushed off, practically running up the road.

'Eunice? What about tomorrow?' A.J. called after her, then turned to April. 'What the hell is going on?' He glanced up the road and saw Bess, and suddenly his eyes turned hard. 'She lied. Bess is right here. It seems whenever it looks like things are going OK, she disappears on me. Darn it. I love that girl, yet she keeps pushing me away.' He turned to follow Eunice, but April caught his arm.

'A.J., I think you should leave her be for now.'

'Leave her be? That girl is twisting me in knots. One minute she says she loves me and the next she's running away. It's breaking my heart, and I'm not sure I can take much more.'

She glanced over to the hall and saw Crawford standing in the doorway, watching her with a puzzled expression. She gestured for him to join them, desperate for his support.

He hurried over and slapped A.J. on the back. 'A.J. Great to see you, buddy. I didn't know you were in town. Thought you lot had gone on exercise.'

'Nope, we leave day after tomorrow. I was just seeing my girl, but she's run out on me . . . again.' He looked in the direction that Eunice had gone, but she had disappeared.

Just then, Bess walked over, a smile plastered on her devious face.

'Hello, you three, look who I just bumped into. This is Norm, Eunice's *fiancé*.'

April shut her eyes in despair. This was not how A.J. should have found out. It was typical of Bess to stir trouble, she must have realised what was going on, but instead of keeping her mouth shut, she had to drop her bombshell and create more drama.

She smiled as best she could and held out her hand to Norm. 'Hello, Norm.'

Norm didn't even look at her. His furious gaze was fixed firmly on A.J., who was standing stock still, staring at him in astonishment.

Crawford nudged April and raised his eyebrows. She moved her head slightly, trying to indicate that he should leave with A.J. Luckily, Crawford was quick on the uptake, and he looked over at Norm.

'Great to meet you, Norm. Now, me and A.J. have to go. Sorry about the film, April, will you be all right?'

'Yes, you go. Me and Mrs Teague will be just fine.'

He nodded at her, then pulled a shell-shocked A.J. down the road in the direction of his jeep.

'So, Norm, Eunice said she wasn't expecting to see you till tomorrow. She'll be very surprised to see you today, won't she, April?' Bess began.

'So I gather.' Norm's tone was cold and before she could say anything else, he pushed past them and jogged off in the direction of the nurses' home.

Bess and April watched him go. 'Oh my good God! That's torn it. What the hell is going on with Eunice and A.J.?'

April shook her head. 'You'll need to ask her that. But I wonder if one of us shouldn't go and check she's ok? Norm won't get violent, will he?'

Bess looked worried. 'He's never been the violent type, as far as I know, but the way he looked . . . Me and my big mouth, I shouldn't have said anything, but I didn't realise it was so serious.' She came to a decision. 'I'm going after him. Can you explain to Red? He probably won't even notice anyway. See you later.'

For the first time in a long while, April felt some warmth towards Bess. The girl might not like her, but she definitely cared about Eunice, and if the situation got ugly, Bess was a much better person to help Eunice than she would be.

∞

There was nothing for April to do but go and explain the situation to Red and Mrs Teague, then she planned to make her way to the nurses' home to check that Eunice and Bess were all right. She had no desire to watch the film now, but she couldn't expect her landlady to leave, not after she'd been so excited.

The film hadn't started yet – although April could have sworn she'd been outside for hours – and she pushed through the crowd of people still waiting to take their seats. The hall had been set out as if for a concert, with rows and rows of chairs facing a huge screen. She spotted Red's distinctive hair towards the front of the hall and made her way towards them.

Mrs Teague looked up at her in delight as she sat down. 'Ooooh, isn't this exciting, April? Apparently the film is called *Stagecoach* and the actor is John Wayne. Stagecoach! Doesn't that just scream the Wild West to you! I can't wait.' Mrs Teague looked behind her. 'Where's the major?'

'He's had to leave, I'm afraid. I'll explain everything to you later. Red, can I ask you a huge favour? Me and Bess have to go and help Eunice. Would you mind very much looking after Mrs Teague and taking her home?'

Mrs Teague looked concerned. 'Don't worry about me, April. You go and do what has to be done. I can find my own way home. I'm quite old enough, you know.'

'I wouldn't hear of it, Mrs T. A gentleman never lets a lady walk home on her own. Of course I'll take you home. Is everything all right?'

'Yes, yes, it's fine. Eunice is just a bit upset. I'm so sorry. I hope it hasn't ruined your evening.'

'Of course not, lovely. You get on. I'll see you later.'

April left hastily and moved off in the direction of the nurses' home. It was a fifteen-minute walk from the centre of town, and she found herself running, desperately worried about what she would find there.

When she arrived, she ran straight up to Eunice's room and knocked on the door. 'Eunice? Are you all right?'

Bess answered the door. She looked strained. Behind her, she could see Eunice crumpled on the bed, sobbing into her pillow, but there was no sign of Norm.

'What happened?' she whispered to Bess. 'Where's Norm?'

Bess shook her head. 'It was awful. He was shouting at her about A.J. Saying he'd heard she'd been seen around town with a darky, but he hadn't believed it. Said he was going to show him what he thought of him, and then he ran off. Didn't even give her a chance to talk. I hadn't even realised that she and A.J . . .' Bess trailed off.

'I hope Crawford's taken him back to base. He'll be safe there. Can I come in and see how she is?'

'I think it's best if you just leave her with me. Go and enjoy your evening with Crawford.'

The last was said with a sneer, but April chose to ignore it. She knew how Bess felt about her, but she'd also always known that Bess genuinely liked Eunice – otherwise why would Eunice have stayed friends with her? Maybe that was why Bess hated April so much – she'd moved into their little group and, as Bess saw it, taken away Eunice, and Nancy too, to a certain extent. And then she'd taken Crawford – even if Crawford wasn't hers in the first place, in Bess's mind, it seemed he was.

'All right, I'll go. Take care of her, won't you?'

'What, you think I won't? I never thought this would happen when I opened my big mouth. I feel like it's my fault. Instead of telling *you*, she should have told *me* what was going on, then all this could have been avoided.' With that, Bess shut the door in April's face.

April shook her head. Typical Bess, blaming others for her own failings. Still, she knew she'd take good care of

259

Eunice, and having both of them hovering over her might be annoying for her friend.

Outside the nurses' home, April dithered. Should she go back into town to see if Crawford had gone to find her, or should she go back to Mrs Teague's? She decided it was more likely that he'd go to the hall first, so she returned and stood outside waiting. The film had started and she wasn't able to go in.

She'd been standing there for about fifteen minutes when she heard an engine. Crawford, at last. He parked the car, hopped out and walked up to her, his expression grim.

'Thank God you're here! What the hell was that all about? Do you mean to tell me that Eunice is engaged to someone else? Why didn't you tell me?'

'How could I? It wasn't my secret, and Eunice insisted she was going to tell A.J. before Norm got back.'

'Well, it looks like she didn't stick to her word.' Crawford was furious. 'What sort of a woman does that to a guy? A.J. is one of the most decent human beings I know, and right now he's crushed. What is it with you women? Leading men around by the nose then dropping them.'

'Hang on, this isn't my fault! I've been pleading with her to talk to him, but ... she was too scared, Crawford. Surely you can understand that?'

'The hell I can! She's been lying to him, April. God! What she's done to him – I've never seen him like that.'

'Crawford, please don't shout at me. It's not my fault.'

He sighed. 'I know, honey, I'm sorry. But I'm furious with her.'

'If you could only have seen the state she's been in . . .' She didn't carry on. There was no way she could betray Eunice's other secret. A.J. deserved to know about that first. 'I tried to persuade her, but she bit my head off and I've hardly spoken to her since.'

Crawford put his arm around her. 'Come on, I don't fancy the film now. In fact, I need a drink. Even if it is one of those disgusting English beers.'

'Where's A.J.? Did you take him back?'

'No, I was going to, but we saw Homer and a few of the guys, and A.J. wanted to join them. I think they're going to take him for a drink and I figure if anyone deserves to drown their sorrows, then it's him. So I left them and came to find you.'

They walked down the road a little way until they came to a pub. Walking in, April went to find a table while Crawford got the drinks. She looked around. Tonight was clearly a night when the white soldiers were barred, which meant she and Crawford would have to leave. She had just stood up when she realised a man was looming over her. She looked up. It was Homer, and for the first time since she'd met him, he was not smiling.

'Homer! Is A.J. with you? Is he all right?'

'What do you think? I need to see that girl and give her a piece of my mind.'

'Please try not to be angry with her. She's as heart-broken as A.J. I promise you, she loves him. Do you think you can tell him that? She just needs a bit of time to sort some things out.'

261

'Right. Like her fiancé? You think A.J. can ever be with her now when she's lied to him like this?'

'Please, Homer. Trust me. Eunice wants to be with A.J. She's been trying to keep everyone happy, and in the process has hurt everyone. Including herself.'

'My buddy is over in the corner crying into his beer. You think I'm exaggerating? You can go and see for yourself.' He shook his head. 'I think you better tell your friend that he's done with her.'

'Homer, please . . .' She put her hand out to stop him, but he ignored her and walked to the back of the pub.

Crawford came over just then with a couple of drinks.

'How did you manage that? I thought white soldiers wouldn't be allowed tonight.'

'Seems he liked my face. Though he said if I caused trouble he'd see it was rearranged.' Crawford grinned in amusement.

'Homer and A.J. are here.'

'What? I better go over.'

'No, I think you should leave them. Homer's furious.'

'A.J. is one of my best friends, of course I'm going over.'

As he walked away, there was a commotion at the door. April looked over to see four men wearing the familiar green uniform of the US Army. She noticed they also wore black armbands with the letters MP printed on in large white letters. Why were the military police here? There was no trouble. Unless it was because Crawford was here when he wasn't meant to be. She swallowed nervously as the men stormed through the bar, clearly looking for someone.

The barman shouted over to them. 'Oy! What are you doing in here? There's no trouble, so get out!'

He wasn't the only one disgruntled at the disturbance. Many of the locals had a healthy disregard for the American military police, and they considered them the main culprits behind some of the disturbances between the coloured and white soldiers.

A large, burly man wearing filthy overalls rose from his table and stood beside the bar, blocking the men from going any further into the saloon.

'You got a problem, officer?' he sneered.

'Step aside, sir, please. This has nothing to do with you.'

'Is that so? You're in *my* pub, in *my* town, in *my* country!' The man was yelling into his face now. 'I think it's *you* who needs to step aside.'

'Sir, I will ask you only once more, move out of the way or I will arrest you for obstructing the US Army in its duties.'

The man folded his meaty arms over his considerable midriff. 'Who are you looking for?'

Crawford moved towards the policeman. 'Sergeant, you may leave. There's no problem here.'

The man saluted. 'Sir, I have it on good authority that a Sergeant A.J. Timpson has been involved in a disturbance with a local man, and I'm here to arrest him.'

The big man stepped towards the policeman. 'I think you better listen to the officer. We all know A.J. and there's no way he'd be involved in anything like that. And if you don't leave now, me and my mates will help you. You don't arrest our friends in our pub. You understand?'

April was watching the scene wide-eyed, unsure whether to stay or go. Who could have told such a dreadful lie? She looked towards Crawford, who was still standing in front of the policemen.

'Sergeant, I am telling you to leave the premises. That is an order!'

'I'm sorry, sir. My duty is to arrest the soldier. If the charge proves to be false, we will release him.'

'A likely story. We've seen how you lot behave with the coloured soldiers. Listen, mate, you better leave now before things get ugly,' the burly man said.

April noticed the policeman's eyes flicker towards the door. She looked across and saw a tall man in Royal Navy uniform loitering there, watching proceedings.

It was Norm.

Chapter 25

Suddenly there was a shout behind her, and April turned to see the man in overalls punch the policeman squarely on the chin. He went down like a sack of potatoes, but was soon replaced by his colleague. As the pub erupted, she somehow managed to slip past the fighting men and hurried to the back of the room. The barman was standing at A.J.'s table, gesticulating towards the back. Homer and A.J. rose and left in the direction he was pointing. She hurried after them.

'A.J., Homer, wait!' she called. The men turned to look at her, but their expressions were not friendly. A.J.'s eyes looked red, but Homer simply looked furious.

'Leave us alone, will you? And tell your friend to leave us alone too.' He caught A.J.'s arm and hustled him down the street, away from the sounds of fighting emanating from the pub.

April leaned against the wall and sighed. How could an evening that had promised so much fun have turned so bad? She longed to go back in to find Crawford, but given the shouting she knew she was safer waiting where she was. She hoped he didn't get involved in the fight.

It wasn't long before Crawford burst out of the door. He was breathing heavily, and his uniform was askew, but he appeared unharmed.

'April! Thank God! Where did they go?'

'They went in that direction. They're not really going to arrest A.J., are they?'

'Not if I can help it. Who the hell would do that?'

'It was Norm. I saw him by the door.'

'Jesus H. Christ! As if that *woman* hasn't done enough harm! You better tell your friend to stay away from A.J. from now on, do you understand?'

April was furious. Why was he behaving as if this was her fault? 'I'm not one of your men that you can order about, Crawford, and none of this is my fault, so why don't you go and tell her yourself. I'm going home. You can do whatever you want.' She stomped off, hoping that Crawford would follow and apologise, but he didn't. Choked with tears and anger, she turned around and saw him walking in the direction of the hall, where his jeep was parked.

∽

Once she got home, April paced around the house, trying to calm down. She looked at her watch. Eight o'clock. It felt like a lifetime since they'd set off for the cinema, was it possible that this was the last time she'd see Crawford? He'd said he was falling in love with her, but from the way he'd blamed her for what had happened, it didn't feel like it. She wondered whether she should go to the nurses' home to see Eunice, but decided against it. Bess was with her, and she imagined that Eunice wouldn't be up to talking. Finally, at around ten thirty, Red returned with Mrs

Teague, who was chattering excitedly about the film, and offering Red a cup of tea. Red declined, although he sent April a curious look. April shook her head and shrugged, indicating she had nothing to say.

Once he'd gone, Mrs Teague turned to April. 'You look dreadful, my dear. I'm going to make us some tea and then I want you to tell me everything. And I mean everything, mind you.'

When she returned, the two settled in the sitting room and April, who was desperate to confide in someone, told her all that had happened. She even told her about Eunice's pregnancy, knowing it would go no further, and that Mrs Teague was in the best position to help, should Eunice need it.

When she'd finished the tale, Mrs Teague sat back with a gasp. 'Good heavens, what a muddle. Poor young A.J., he doesn't deserve this at all. But what on earth will Eunice do? Dear, dear, dear. Love can be so complicated, and I know Eunice didn't set out to cause so much trouble, but she has to face what's happened and do everything she can to win that young man back. Her baby deserves a father. And poor Norm. What a horrible thing to happen while you're off fighting and risking your life.' She shook her head sadly.

'I'm worried Mrs Granger will throw her out of the house once her pregnancy becomes obvious, and she won't be allowed to stay at the nurses' home after that . . .' April paused and looked at her landlady expectantly.

Mrs Teague looked back with a knowing expression on her face. 'I see. You want to ask me if she can stay here if she has nowhere else to go?'

'Can she?'

Her landlady sighed. 'It's a terrible situation, and I can't condone what she's done. You know that, don't you, April? She's behaved very badly to everyone. But it seems you know me well enough to understand that I can't see any child suffer. And her child will suffer if she can't sort this situation out. Poor little thing, none of this is the baby's fault.' She wiped her eyes, then sighed heavily. 'Very well, she may stay if she needs to, on the condition that she does her best to make amends to the people she's hurt. There's nothing she can do to make things better for Norm, but she can do her best to convince A.J. she loves him.'

April went over and hugged her. 'Thank you, thank you, you wonderful woman. I knew you wouldn't let me down.'

'And you, young lady, need to make sure that your major understands that you love him, and that it's not you he should be cross with.'

'I already more or less told him. And he said he loved me too, but maybe we spoke too soon if something like this can make him so angry with me. Maybe it's not meant to be.' Her heart broke a little at the thought. 'We've not known each other long, after all, so it's not surprising.'

'Nonsense. What does it matter how long you've known him? Three weeks after I met Isaac, I married him and we sailed to India. We were happy until the day he died. Thirty-two happy years. You've known Crawford longer than I knew Isaac before I married him. There's a war on, April. Soldiers die in wars. Stop wasting time.'

The words hit April like blows from a hammer. Of course she loved him, and she needed him to understand that before he went away.

Just then there was a knock at the door. April looked at the clock: it was nearly midnight. Who on earth could be calling at this time? She got up and peered around the black-out curtains. Crawford's jeep sat outside the house.

'It's Crawford!' she gasped.

'There, you see. I thought he'd come. Now go and make up with him, while I go to bed. I'm exhausted from all this excitement.' She disappeared upstairs without even waiting to see April's dashing suitor.

April hurried to the door and let in a grim-faced Crawford. She pulled him inside and led him to the sitting room, where they sat down on the sofa.

'What's happened? Is A.J. all right? He hasn't been arrested, has he?'

'No. I managed to catch up with Norm and, well, I persuaded him to drop the charges.'

'You didn't fight him, did you?'

'Of course not. Let's just say I can be very persuasive when I need to be. Don't forget I'm a lawyer. But listen . . .' Crawford rubbed his hands over his face wearily. 'It was unfair of me to shout at you, honey. And I respect that you didn't want to betray Eunice's confidence. But A.J.'s one of my oldest friends and I hate seeing him like this.'

April took his hand and put her head on his shoulder. ' And I'm sorry this happened and that you had to be involved.'

'Sweetheart, I can face anything, as long as I know we're OK. Are we? Do you forgive me?'

'Of course I do.' She kissed him then, a long, intense kiss that flooded her with warmth. Crawford returned it, then pulled back.

'There's just one thing I ask, and that's complete honesty. I need to know if there's anything bothering you, or if there are any little secrets like Eunice's hanging around in your past. I'd rather hear these things from you so we can talk about them, than from anyone else. I couldn't bear to be in the situation that A.J. finds himself in.'

'I promise you, there's no one. There never really has been. And what about you?'

'From the moment I saw you in your uniform with that cute little hat perched on your golden hair, there's been no room in my mind for anyone but you. Don't get me wrong, I have had girlfriends, one of them even writes to me. But she's married now, so it's purely friendship.'

'The only man who writes to me is Theo, and you know about him already.'

'So you're all mine.' He nuzzled her neck.

'Oh yes, I'm all yours, Crawford. For as long as you want me.'

His green eyes softened. 'Well, that's good to hear, April, because I plan on keeping you around for a very long time. I was thinking . . .' He paused and wrinkled his brow in thought. 'Would forever be long enough for you?'

April laughed. 'I'm not sure it is, Major Dunbar. But let's start with that and see how we go.'

'That sounds like a deal to me, Nurse Harvey. Now, I think we need a kiss to seal it.'

He lowered his head and kissed her deeply. They lay back on the sofa, and April felt one of his hands on her breast. No one had ever touched her there before and it felt wonderful. Her own hand wandered inside Crawford's jacket, and she slipped her fingers between the buttons of his shirt, stroking his bare chest. She could feel hair there, as well as smooth skin. Fascinated, she moved to undo the buttons, but Crawford's hand came up to stop her.

'I'd like nothing more than to keep going, but I've got an early start tomorrow, so I better go.'

April groaned. 'When will you be back?'

'We'll be gone a few weeks, so mid-November, I think. Don't forget, I'm expecting you to come with me to the Thanksgiving dinner.'

'I wouldn't miss it for the world. I'll write to you.'

'And I'll write to you, though I'm afraid it won't be every day this time.' He got up reluctantly and walked to the door. April followed him. They stood there for a long time, looking at one other. Finally, April stood up on tiptoe and kissed his cheek.

'I'll be counting the days.'

'As will I, my sweet girl. I love you, Nurse Harvey.'

'And I love you, Major Dunbar.'

Chapter 26

Over the next few days, gossip about Eunice, A.J. and Norm inevitably spread like wildfire around the hospital. Eunice had taken a leave of absence, and though April was desperate to see her friend to make sure she was all right, she was glad Eunice didn't have to hear some of the horrible things that were being said about her.

One morning, as she was sitting alone, having a cup of tea in the cafeteria, she heard voices talking in a hushed tone behind her.

'Apparently she's pregnant,' she heard the voice say. There was a collective gasp from the other girls at the table. 'Molly says she's heard her being sick in the mornings and only put two and two together when she heard about what happened with Norm. Wonder whose it is.'

April froze. Surely no one knew about that yet, did they? She glanced around. It was Jean Gray; she should have known. Jean loved to gossip and could never keep her nose out of anybody's business.

One of the other girls at the table joined in. 'Could be anyone's the way she seems to have been carrying on, but my money's on the darky.'

'Agreed,' said Jean. 'So let's wait and see what colour it is, eh, girls? Then we'll be able to narrow the field down. Ooh, she's a dark horse, that one. I never would have thought it of her. Nancy, maybe. Even Bess. But not Eunice. Just shows, you never can tell, doesn't it?'

Suddenly, the table went quiet. 'Do you want to repeat any of that, Jean?'

April looked around again and saw Nancy, her face purple with fury, towering over the other nurse. Jean paled but refused to be cowed.

'Not really, Nance. And you know I'm only speaking the truth. Let's face it, if anyone in this hospital was going to be pregnant by a darky it was going to be you.'

'His name is Homer, Jean. And I hope that one day I will be pregnant with his baby. And, for your information, though God knows you should be aware of this as you're meant to be a nurse, the baby will be lighter than the father, darker than the mother – a perfect mixture of both parents. Don't let me hear you saying one more word against Eunice, A.J. or any of the other coloured soldiers, or so help me, I won't be responsible for my actions.'

Jean scoffed. 'If you can't take it, then you know where the door is.'

Suddenly, Jean squealed in shock. Bess had crept up behind her and, grabbing her by the arm, lifted her out of the chair. 'You better get going, Jean. Can't have your sort clogging up our dining room with your filth. Go on, get out before I knock you out!' Bess looked around at the other nurses, who avoided her gaze. 'And that goes for the rest of you. If I hear one more word against my friends, then you'll regret it, do you hear me?'

'Who do you think you are, Bess? You can't talk to us like that!'

273

'I just have, haven't I? And I thought I told you to get out. Go on! Before I report you to matron.'

'I haven't done anything wrong!'

'Haven't you? You've sat here spreading lies and insulting our allies. Oh look, there's matron now. I might just go and have a word with her.'

Jean pulled her arm from Bess's grasp. 'It's all right, I'm going. But if you think the gossip will just go away 'cos you say so, you're going to be very disappointed.' Jean flounced off, followed closely by the other three nurses.

April came over. 'Are you two OK? I heard everything. Why can't they leave people alone?'

'She's not really pregnant, is she?' Nancy whispered.

'Course she isn't. I'd know if she was.' Bess looked over at April. 'Then again, I didn't know about A.J., but you did. So, do you know anything about this?'

April shook her head, desperately trying to hold eye contact. When Eunice's pregnancy was confirmed, she didn't want it to come from her. 'Well done for putting Jean in her place. It's good Eunice has you to stick up for her.'

Bess snorted. 'She's going to need more than us to live this one down. Folk aren't going to forgive her for dumping a local for a G.I. any time soon, especially not her mother. Poor Eunice. It's going to be a rocky road for her. Anyway, what about you, Nance? Have you seen Homer?'

The two chatted on, and April reflected on what Bess had said. It really was going to be hard, especially once everyone was aware of her pregnancy. If only she'd found the courage to tell the truth earlier, so much of this could have been avoided. But then, hadn't she shied away from telling Crawford the truth about Theo, and it wasn't half as serious as Eunice's secret? She should tell him the full story next time she saw him. She didn't want any misunderstandings to come between them.

∽

The weeks passed slowly for April, and she spent most of her time either at the hospital or studying for her final exams, which she was due to take just before Crawford got back. Although it was tiring, she found having to work so hard took her mind off how much she was missing him, and she fell into bed every night and was asleep before her head hit the pillow.

There was one bright spot, however. Since the night Norm had returned, Bess's attitude towards her had softened and the two had talked several times about the situation with Eunice. Apparently, Bess had gone over there, only to be turned away by Mrs Granger who, at least in part, blamed her for leading Eunice astray. When April mentioned her intention of going anyway, Bess told her not to as Eunice had asked that everyone stay away. Norm had apparently left the day after the fight in the pub, and now she needed time to come to terms with what had happened. Not just with Norm, but also with A.J. and her father. April felt as though she was abandoning her friend, but she respected her wishes and stayed away, contenting herself with sending a letter, offering to help in any way she could. She didn't receive a reply.

Then, two weeks after the film night, they were informed that Eunice had resigned. As far as April was concerned this could only mean one thing: Eunice's pregnancy had been revealed and she was not allowed to return.

She discussed the situation with Mrs Teague as they were listening to the wireless one evening. The news was full of the war in North Africa and the Pacific, none of it very good, and Mrs Teague was worrying about the G.I.s – and Red and A.J. in particular – despite the fact that she knew they were still somewhere in England.

'Bess says I should stay away, but I don't feel right about it. She loves nursing so much, I just can't imagine she'd give up all of a sudden. Although, being unmarried and pregnant probably means she's not allowed to work there any more. Should I go anyway, do you think?'

'You absolutely must, April. That poor girl needs friends right now, and though she's done wrong, she's suffering the consequences. Why don't you cycle down there on your next day off, dear? Make sure she's all right.'

∞

So a few days later, on a cold, blustery October morning, April wrapped up warmly and cycled over to Eunice's house. She was surprised to see her friend painting the front gate.

Hopping off the bike, she walked over. 'Eunice? What are you doing?'

Eunice looked up at her, her expression bleak. 'What does it look like?'

'All right, I can see you're painting the gate, but why?'

Putting her paint brush down, Eunice stood back. April gasped. Beneath the thin coat of white paint that had been applied, she could clearly see 'Darkies Go Home' scrawled across the gate. Fury welled within her.

'Who would do such a thing? And why?'

'Mother can't keep her mouth shut, that's why. It didn't take her long to figure it out once I was living here. I've been sick as anything. And now she's told everyone.' Eunice's voice ended on a sob, and April rushed to put her arms around her. 'Where have you been? I'd thought you'd have come to see me before now.'

'But Bess said . . .' April stopped. She should have known. Bess might like Eunice, but perhaps her hatred for April was stronger.

'Never mind, let's go in and you can tell me what's happened.'

Luckily Mrs Granger had gone shopping and so, over a pot of tea, the whole sorry story came out. It seemed that once she'd moved back, Mrs Granger had soon discovered her condition. She was insisting that if she wanted to stay living at home, then she must put the baby up for adoption. Then, the previous Sunday in church, she'd snapped when Eunice had had to rush behind a bush at the end of the service to be sick. Apparently, Mrs Granger had hurried after her and shouted at her.

'Oh April, it was all so embarrassing. Everyone knows now, so you see I had no choice but to resign. They'd have probably sacked me if I hadn't. And now all the neighbours just turn away when they see me, and . . . Mother says when father gets home he'll not want me here. She's still behaving as if he'll be back any minute.' She paused, wiping her eyes, then said more quietly, 'Now I know how A.J. and his friends feel every day of their lives. And I'm ashamed. Of all of us, to think we can treat people like outcasts when they've done nothing more than love someone else or been born a different colour.'

'Not everyone's like that. The men in the pub did everything to help A.J. get away when Norm tried to get him arrested that night.'

More tears came at that. 'Poor A.J. As if it wasn't bad enough that he'd just discovered I'd been lying to him. He must hate me so much.'

'What happened with Norm?'

Eunice shuddered. 'It was truly horrible. He came round and screamed at me. Then he cried. Asked me how I could betray him like that. I never meant to hurt him, I promise, April. I just didn't know what to do. He cut his leave short and left soon after. So now his mother's not talking to me *or* my mother. Something else she blames me for. What if something happens to him? I'll never forgive myself for this, April. Never. I wish I'd handled it all differently.'

'I know you do, love. Do you want to come and stay at Mrs Teague's for a bit? I know she'll be happy to have you, and it will give you a break from all these disapproving stares.'

'No, I've got to stick it out. I don't deserve to have a break. This is all my own fault. I should have written to Norm and told him. I should have told A.J. And now he's not talking to me either and he still doesn't know about the baby.'

'You need to write to him and tell him everything. He won't get it for a little while but do it today and then see what happens. And don't forget, Mrs Teague says you can stay any time. Now, are you healthy? You don't look too well, to be honest, and you need to start thinking about that little baby. Your baby needs you to be strong. Have you seen a doctor?'

'I can't see anyone, I'm too ashamed. I'm about three months gone now. Perhaps you can be my midwife.'

'But I'm not trained in that.'

'I know, but you're a nurse, aren't you? You can do the odd check-up, listen to its heart and things, can't you? Please, April. I can't bear the shame of seeing anyone else.'

'All right, of course I will.'

'Thank you! You don't know how miserable I've been thinking that even you had abandoned me.'

'I won't ever do that, I promise.' Privately, April decided it was time to have a stern word with Bess, but her stomach sank at the thought.

'You need to go. If you're here when Mother gets back, she'll only shout at you.'

'Yes, all right. Come any time. And write to me. Let me know how you are. I might have to go away in a bit, but only for a few days.' April explained about Theo, suddenly realising that she'd not told her friend about it before. She also mentioned her guilt at not feeling the same for him as he did for her.

'Poor Theo. You must tell him. Honesty is always best. Just look at me. I am what happens when you hide your head in the sand and don't confront your problems.'

April hugged her. 'I know. I will.'

'And tell Crawford too, won't you? You don't want him getting any wrong ideas.'

'Yes, I'll do that too. And try not to be too hard on yourself. You've made a mess of things, but you never acted out of malice.'

Tears sprung into Eunice's eyes again. 'I don't think I'll ever be able to put this right.'

'Course you will. You can mend a broken pot, can't you? It's never the same, and it's not perfect, but it can still work. There's always hope. And now you have a brand new life that needs you, so you can't hide away from any of this.'

'I promise I won't. I've learned my lesson. I'm going to be the best mother ever for this baby.' She stroked her stomach. 'Despite everything, I love this little mite. It's part of A.J., after all. And even if A.J. wants nothing to do with us – and I wouldn't blame him – I will spend my life protecting it. Mother wants me to get it adopted, but I won't. I'd rather live on the streets than ever do that.'

'It won't come to that. And you'll be a brilliant mother.' April kissed her friend's cheek and put her coat on. 'Take care, won't you. And don't forget, I'm here if you need me.'

April cycled away, her heart heavy. Despite her optimistic words, she couldn't see how this situation could end happily.

❧

Over the next week, rumours continued to circulate about Eunice, and the news of her pregnancy was now out. As a result, April avoided almost everyone and concentrated on her studies. She'd heard nothing from Crawford, which disappointed her, even though she hadn't really been expecting to. She did, however, write a letter to both Theo and the Osbornes, asking them to let her know when he was back so she could arrange some leave. She made a concerted effort to avoid Bess as well. She knew she needed to speak to her, but right now she just didn't have the appetite for a fight, so rather than have to tell her about visiting Eunice, she simply stayed out of her way.

∽

The day of her exam dawned, grey and rainy. Mrs Teague woke her with tea and toast in bed.

'You didn't have to do this,' April said in surprise.

'I know, lovely, but I want you to go into that exam relaxed and ready to do well.'

'Thank you, dear Mrs Teague. I don't know what I'd do without you.'

'You'd do very well without me, as you've shown. But now that you do have me, I want to make your life as easy as possible. Honestly, April, I've been happier having you living with me than any of my other lodgers. If I'd had a daughter, I would hope she'd be just like you.'

Tears sprang to April's eyes. 'And you, Mrs Teague, have been the mother I've been missing for so many years. Thank you for everything.'

'Tsk. Enough of this talk. No time for sentiment today. It's all business, so eat up then get yourself to the hospital. And think, soon the major will be back, and all will be right with the world again.'

April smiled at the thought. She'd missed Crawford so badly, she couldn't imagine how she'd managed before she met him.

Before long, she was standing outside the room where the exam was to be held with several others. No one said much, as they were all too nervous. But April found that once the exam began, her nerves disappeared, and by the end she felt pleased with how it had gone. She hoped she'd done well.

As they filed out of the room, April was surprised to see Bess waiting at the door.

'April, matron told me to come and get you. She wants you in her office right away. How did it go?'

'It was all right, but why does matron want me?'

'I have no idea. Better hurry, though.'

April sped off and found matron's door open, as if she was waiting for her. She knocked and poked her head into the office.

Matron looked up, her expression serious.

'Please do sit down, Nurse Harvey.' April did as she was asked, and matron looked at her over her glasses for a moment before continuing. 'I've received a telephone call from a Reverend Osborne. He's asked that you be allowed to call him back. As you know, I only allow personal calls in the gravest circumstances, and on this occasion, I think it's best you call right now.'

April gasped. 'Theo! Has something happened to Theo?'

'I really couldn't say. Call the switchboard and they'll put you through. I will leave you in privacy, my dear.'

April picked up the phone with a trembling hand. Oh, God! She felt terrible. Had he died on the way home? She'd just assumed he'd get home safely, but nothing was safe these days.

Automatically she held the receiver to her ear and spoke to the switchboard. When Mr Osborne's voice came, she whispered, 'Hello', then embarrassed herself by bursting into tears.

The vicar spoke gently and calmly. 'April, my dear, please don't cry. Theo's not dead.'

Relief washed over her, and she swallowed hard, trying to stop the tears. 'Oh, thank goodness. Then why . . . ?'

'He came home last week, but he's gravely injured. He's . . .' The reverend paused, as if collecting himself. 'The letter you sent him the other day cheered him greatly, you can't imagine how much. I know it's a huge imposition, but could you come? It would help him so much, and if his time is to be short, then I know he would long to see you just one more time.'

'Oh, Reverend Osborne, I am so sorry. And poor Mrs Osborne. Of course I will come.' She was sobbing again. Her childhood friend, her dearest companion from her youth. How she had loved him when they were younger. And how she loved him still. She couldn't believe that he might be gone soon.

'Calm yourself, dear child. His mother is, as you can understand, quite overcome, but we are trying to accept the will of God. Good friends are with her every hour. And maybe there is still hope. Do you think you could arrange to come immediately? In case God calls him soon. I have spoken to the matron, and she was very sympathetic and accommodating, so she will give you leave.'

'Yes, yes. I'll leave today if I possibly can.' She couldn't see now for the tears streaming down her face. Oh, this war! How she hated it. 'I'd better go and see if I can make arrangements, reverend. I will telegram to say when I will arrive.'

'Thank you, my dear. Even though it's in such circumstances, I will be very happy to see you again.'

The line went dead and for a moment it was as if time had stood still and April was standing outside the burning ruins of her home, trying to face the fact that her father was no more. She wanted to scream with rage. Why Theo? She remembered him as a sweet boy who had done his best to comfort her when her mother died. Then as the handsome young man who had stolen her youthful heart. If only she still felt the same.

Quickly she replaced the receiver and went outside. matron was waiting patiently for her to finish her call.

'I'm so sorry that you have been touched by tragedy once again, Nurse Harvey, and having spoken to the reverend, I can grant you four days' leave on compassionate grounds, starting tomorrow. You weren't due to work this afternoon anyway, were you?'

'No, no I wasn't, but I'm happy to if I'm needed.'

'Don't be silly, child. Get off home and make arrangements and we'll see you in a few days.'

As April rushed away, her mind was in turmoil. I wish I had loved him the way he wanted me to, she thought. But then, if she had, would it not make this news even more unbearable? She wasn't sure that was possible, for now, as well as the grief, she was overcome with guilt. What would she say when she saw him? How could she tell him that there was no future for the two of them, even if he did survive? She determined that, no matter what, she would make him feel loved, and whatever the future held, she would face it as and when it came. It was all she could do for him.

'Oh Theo, I'm so sorry,' she whispered. 'I'm so, so sorry.'

Keeping her head down, she fled down the stairs and as she walked out of the door, a voice stopped her. She'd not noticed anyone or anything around her as she'd left and had hoped that no one would notice her either.

'Hey, April, what's wrong? Are you all right?' It was Bess. The last person she wanted to see right then, but when she saw the concerned look on the other girl's face, the sobs broke out anew.

Bess put her arm around her. 'April? What's happened? Is it Mrs Teague?'

The fact that the only person Bess thought she had to mourn was her landlady made her cry even harder. Because with Theo gone, she was right. Apart from Eunice and her other friends, and now Crawford ... No, she couldn't think of him now when Theo needed her so badly.

'No, no. I have to go to London.'

'To London? But why?'

'It's Theo. He's terribly ill and he might not recover. His parents hope that if he sees me it will help. And, oh, I don't know what I'm going to do! He was my very dearest friend, and now ... what if he doesn't survive?'s

'Your London sweetheart. Of course, you must go.'

'He's not ...' But April stopped. She didn't have the energy to explain it again. 'Yes,' she said. 'Him.'

'You poor thing.' Bess enveloped her in a warm hug and kissed her on the forehead. 'When are you leaving?'

'As soon as I can. Although probably tomorrow now. I've got four days' leave, so I won't see you all for a bit. Give my love to everybody. And thank you, Bess, for being so kind.'

'Oh, April, we might have had our differences, but I would never turn my back on a girl with a broken heart. Go on, now. I'll tell the others.'

Wiping her eyes, April nodded. 'Yes, I better go. Goodbye, Bess.'

Somewhere deep down, April was aware of a niggling feeling of concern. Bess was not to be trusted, she knew that, but right now, she didn't have time to think about it and all she could do was take Bess's uncharacteristic kindness towards her at face value.

∽

Getting back to the house, Mrs Teague was full of sympathy, and though upset, she had clearly decided that April needed practical help.

'Right, you go and pack your things while I go to the station and enquire about trains to London. I will get you on the very first train I can, don't you worry.' She bustled away, leaving April in her bedroom, staring at the walls.

That night April mourned Theo, going over and over their meetings from the days when he made sure she was never left alone after her mother had died, to him playing his cello with such a look of joy on his face. And then she saw him, tall and handsome, wearing his cricket whites, striding out on to the pitch, waving his bat. He'd been so full of life, and so much fun. Those days they'd spent together, cycling through the London parks, going to the pictures, dancing and playing had been wonderful. They'd been children, really, but it hadn't felt like it then. It had felt like true love.

She took out his few letters and read them over again, crying over his words. He really did seem to love her. She saw his face, lit by firelight and tenderness as he'd kissed her that last time. Even though it was not the same as her love for Crawford, she still loved him. Perhaps she always would. For what was it they said? First love never dies. And she felt sure that hers wouldn't either. Even if she had made room for a new love in her life, this one would be with her forever.

∞

Mrs Teague had managed to get her a seat on the six a.m. train to London the following day.

After a restless night, April washed and dressed and went down to the kitchen. There was no way she could eat anything this morning, so she refused the porridge that Mrs Teague had waiting for her.

'I understand, my love, but you need to keep your strength up for the days ahead. At least drink some tea and take this.' She handed April a brown paper parcel. 'I've made you some egg sandwiches, and there's a little cake in there too, plus a couple of apples. Be sure to eat everything. Now, get your coat on and don't worry about letting the Osbornes know, I'll send them a telegram today to tell them you'll be there tonight.' She helped April put her coat on, then gave her a hug. 'Be strong, April. And know that this too shall pass. And don't you worry about Crawford either. I know he's due back any day and if he turns up, I'll let him know what's happened straightaway.'

April swallowed. Oh, heavens, Crawford. She hadn't allowed herself to think of him during the long night. It felt wrong, somehow, when she was grieving for Theo. What on earth would he think about her rushing off to London to visit another man? If he was half the man she thought he was, though, then she knew he'd understand.

Chapter 27

November 1942

It was a long, tedious train journey to London and as usual the train was held up at various points, and so it wasn't until seven o'clock that night that April finally arrived at Paddington. How different it was here. Compared to the verdant green Cornish landscape, London looked tired and grey in the twilight. It suited her mood perfectly. As she sat on the bus to Camberwell, she gazed out at the passing streets, many of them reduced to rubble. Had she really lived here once? She felt no sense of homecoming, and as she drew closer to the Osborne's house, she felt no nostalgia. She didn't belong here any more, she'd found a new home, a new family, and this sad, damaged city seemed alien to her now.

At last she was there, and with a feeling of trepidation, she knocked on the Osborne's door. It was thrown open by Reverend Osborne, who immediately wrapped his arms around her.

'Oh, my dear, thank you for coming so quickly! We've been looking out for you. Now, come in. You look exhausted.' He took her suitcase from her, and she followed him to the kitchen, where Mrs Osborne was seated.

April was shocked when she saw her. Mrs Osborne had always prided herself on her smart appearance, but now she looked years older than when April had last been here: her dress was rumpled and her hair was awry. And when she looked up at April, her eyes were puffy and red-rimmed.

Forgetting all her previous feelings of animosity, April kneeled in front of her chair, taking her hands. 'Oh, Mrs Osborne, I'm so very sorry about what's happened to Theo.'

The woman looked at her wordlessly. It was as if all the life had gone out of her. Then she squeezed her hands briefly and stood up. 'You look tired, April. Let me make you a cup of tea.'

April was surprised. She wasn't sure she'd ever made her tea before, but then, her only child had not been lying gravely injured before.

'Thank you, I'd like that.'

She sat down at the table with Reverend Osborne. 'Where is Theo? And when will I be able to visit?'

'We shall go tomorrow. He's at the Queen Alexandra Hospital. Such wonderful nurses there. We saw him today, didn't we, Bella?'

Mrs Osborne didn't reply, merely continued with her task. 'How is he?'

'He was tired today. We never know how he will be from one day to the next. Sometimes he sleeps a lot. At others, he's more like his old self, but not, if you understand my meaning?'

April didn't really, but she imagined she'd find out soon enough. 'What sort of injuries does he have?'

The reverend shook his head sadly. 'They are extensive, April. But you will know more about that than I so it's probably best if you find out for yourself.'

Mrs Osborne put the tea in front of them, then sat silently, her cup untouched in front of her. Feeling exhausted and unsure of how to comfort the Osbornes, April drank her tea quickly.

'If you don't mind, I think I'll make my way to bed now.'

'Yes, of course. Bella's readied Theo's room for you, haven't you, Bella?'

Mrs Osborne nodded, not meeting April's eye, and it struck her then that Theo had never slept in his old room again once he'd left for war. Because the last time he'd been home, she had been sleeping in it. Did his mother hate her for that, she wondered? She couldn't tell. Aside from the physical signs of grief, Mrs Osborne seemed to show no reaction to anything.

After a brief silence, April bade them both goodnight and wandered up to the room. Once there, she stood with her back against the closed door, taking in the familiar space. All of Theo's trophies and books were still displayed, and the bedspread was the same blue cambric it had been when she was last here. In the corner sat his beloved cello, and, when she opened the wardrobe door, she saw that his clothes still hung there in an orderly row. She touched his white cricket trousers briefly, assailed by bittersweet memories. Would he ever be able to wear these again, she wondered? It seemed unlikely, but she supposed she'd know more when she saw him tomorrow. It was a prospect that filled her with dread.

❦

The following morning, April made her way to the kitchen to find it empty. She wondered where the Belgian refugees had gone. Hopefully they'd managed to find a new home for themselves, perhaps with a kinder host. She made a pot of tea, then dithered over whether it would be rude to make herself something to eat. She'd finished Mrs Teague's food the day before and her appetite had returned. Peeking into the bread bin, she saw half a loaf and cut herself two thin slices. Being used to Mrs Teague's home-made bread, she was dismayed at how grey and mushy this loaf was.

This must be the national loaf that everyone's always complaining about, she mused. And no wonder! But she was so hungry, she decided beggars couldn't be choosers, so she dipped it into her tea to give it some moisture and tried to pretend it was delicious.

When Mrs Osborne hadn't appeared by eleven, April decided to go for a walk, despite the grey, dreary weather. Many of the streets had changed beyond recognition and some had been destroyed altogether. She thought very carefully about whether to visit Guernsey Grove, but decided that it would be too hard. Some things were better left alone, she decided. It would be difficult enough to see Theo, let alone visit the ruins of her home.

She wandered along the road until she came to a post office. She stopped outside and considered sending Crawford a telegram. But then, she expected to be home before he even returned from wherever he was and she'd rather tell him everything in person. Oh, but how she missed him. How she would love to feel his strong, comforting arms around her right now. She hoped and prayed that it wouldn't be long before she was reunited with him again.

Chapter 28

Despite her earlier resolution not to visit Guersey Grove, as she walked back along the street, April found herself drawn there. But when she saw her street ahead of her, she broke out into a cold sweat as the dreadful memories of the air raid started to close in. She stopped and closed her eyes. She should turn back. Nothing but heartache could come of this visit, and she did not want to resurrect her nightmares. When she opened her eyes, she realised that she was outside Charlie's Fruit Bowl. She was astonished to see that the shop had been patched up since the air raid and was once again open for business. She looked inside. Charlie was standing behind his counter looking just as he used to, aside from the fact that his once brown hair was now grey, as was his moustache. Still, she was glad that he'd managed to reopen, although the green-and-white awning had not been replaced. No doubt there was no material for it.

She wandered on, her breath coming in small pants as she drew closer to the spot where her house used to stand in the middle of the terrace, and though the rubble had been cleared, the ruined walls still stood at either end. A stark reminder of what had once been. She looked across the road to Mrs O'Connor's house, which was an empty shell. She supposed Mrs O'Connor would stay in the country for the duration now. The community they'd once had in this small street was all but destroyed, and she couldn't bear to look at it any more. She hurried away, and almost sprinted back to the Osborne's house, where she let herself in and ran upstairs, throwing herself on the bed. Why had she gone there? And just before she was going to see Theo as well. She needed to calm down and collect herself before she went. She could not let Theo see her in this state.

Finally, she heard movement downstairs and went to investigate. Mrs Osborne was in the kitchen making tea and half-heartedly stirring a pot of soup. She looked as weary and dishevelled as she had the previous night, and April guessed that she hadn't slept a wink.

'Is there anything I can do to help, Mrs Osborne?'

'The soup will be ready in five minutes, if you'd care to lay the table, April. And please excuse my lack of conversation. I find I don't know what to say at the moment.'

'I understand completely. But where have the Belgians gone?'

'Got a job in a munitions factory and moved away. Can't say I blame them; I don't think I treated them as well as I could have when they were here. And perhaps I wasn't very fair on you, either. I was a foolish woman with foolish dreams. I realise now that none of them were of any significance. If you can help make Theo feel better, then that's all that matters to me.'

April stared at her in surprise. 'There's no need to apologise, Mrs Osborne. I understand. And I will do my best to help Theo. But you do understand I can't stay? I need to go back in a few days.'

'I know, April, but just having you here now, and knowing that you will be here in the future, will be enough. Once the war is over, then you can move back and we can be a proper family. Theo's happiness is all that counts.'

April felt her stomach sink and she couldn't help thinking that once again Mrs Osborne was manipulating her. Reverend Osborne joined them shortly after, and they ate silently, before setting off for the hospital on the bus.

When they got to the imposing building on Millbank, April took a deep breath before she followed the Osbornes inside. They knew their way and so led April up the stairs to a large room with several beds down each side. The ward sister greeted them as they arrived.

'How has he been today, sister?' the reverend asked a middle-aged woman at the nurses' station.

'He's having a good day today, reverend. He's very much looking forward to seeing his visitor.' She gave April a warm smile.

April smiled back uncertainly. She was pleased that seeing her would cheer Theo, but from the way the sister spoke, it seemed her visit meant a great deal more than even she had imagined.

She glanced along the rows of beds, but could not see Theo. Puzzled, she followed his parents until they stopped at a bed right by the window. Three years of training and nursing and yet she was not prepared for the shock. The beautiful face she had grown up with was scarred and changed beyond recognition, and bandages covered one of his eyes. He looked to be asleep. She took a moment to compose herself and then reached and touched his hand. Immediately his fingers closed around hers. He was surprisingly strong.

'Hello, Theo. What on earth have you been doing to yourself?'

'April!' His smile was lopsided as the left side of his face had been so badly injured; she guessed that the muscles could no longer work. It had clearly been many weeks since it had happened, as there were no bandages, and the scars were pink and raised. 'You came. I knew you would. Don't be put off by my hideous face.' He laughed shortly. 'I'm still the same old Theo underneath it all. Well, almost.'

'Of course you are. And the scars are nothing. I've seen much worse, believe me.'

Mrs Osborne moved towards the bed then and clasped his other hand. 'Didn't I tell you she would come, Theo?' She kissed his unscarred cheek tenderly. 'Now, your father and I are going to leave you two together for a little while. But we'll be back soon.'

'Thank you, Mother. And thank you for bringing April to me.'

'You know we'll do anything for you, darling. We'll be back in half an hour or so.'

Once the Osbornes had gone, April asked gently, 'Oh, Theo. What happened?'

'Took a bullet to the face, but that's all I know, really. I remember lying in the sun for what felt like ages, but then the next thing I knew I woke up in hospital with bandages all over me. I must have looked like a mummy – ironic, don't you think, seeing as I was in Egypt. I expect

I fit right in. But I'm alive, and I'm trying very hard to be grateful for that.'

'How brave you are, Theo. But I always knew you would be.'

'Did you, April? I don't feel very brave. If you want the honest truth, I feel wretched. But in my darkest moments, I would picture your face and it helped pull me through. And now I can see it for real. As radiant and beautiful as you always were. Oh, my darling, how I've missed you all these long months. Has it really been more than a year since I saw you?'

'It really has. And so much has changed. Oh, Theo, I'm so sorry.'

'But you've done nothing wrong, April. I know things will have to change between us. You don't even know the half of it. Have you noticed yet that something's missing on my left side? Apart from my face, that is.' He attempted to smile again.

April looked down the bed and saw that where his left leg should have been the blanket was smooth. She swallowed and blinked back her tears. She must not let him realise how shocked she was to see him like this.

'Tsk, Theo, you have been careless out there in the desert. Fancy losing an eye and a leg at the same time. Still, there are prosthetics to help with the leg, so hopefully you'll be able to get around in no time.'

'Maybe. But my left arm too.' He indicated to the arm that was lying motionless on the bed. 'It no longer works, so that's the end of my cello-playing days, it seems.' He attempted to smile again, but it didn't quite come off this time. April could see how devastated he was. His dreams

297

of being in an orchestra were dead for him now. 'They say I can learn to live without my leg and my arm, but at the moment, all I seem to want to do is sleep.'

'You just need to get stronger. Then you can look to how you will cope.'

He grasped her hand tighter in his. 'Will you help me, my darling girl? I know it's a lot to ask, but with you by my side, I'm sure I could do it.'

April closed her eyes in despair. What on earth could she say to that? Eventually she said, 'You can do this without me. You're brave and strong. You know I have to get back to Cornwall soon. I can't stay.'

'But you can transfer back here, can't you? I mean, you transferred down; you can come back.'

'I don't know, my darling. I have a life down there and I've only just taken my exams, so I need to see if I've passed. I couldn't leave before that.'

He thrust her hand from his. 'Does the sight of me disgust you so much?' He sighed. 'I should understand, I know I should. But, April, I love you.'

'No! Of course it doesn't. But Theo, I have responsibilities in Cornwall that I can't just leave.'

'What responsibilities? You don't have family, so there's nothing to keep you there. Or are you saying that you have another chap? Is that it, April? While I've been telling you how much I love you, have you been walking out with someone else? Please tell me if you have. I need the truth if nothing else. I need to know if I have anything to live for. Because the thought of you is all that's keeping me going at the moment. Who else would want me like this? Who else could love me if not you?'

April's heart was nearly breaking. She felt in an impossible position. How could she let her childhood sweetheart down? But at the same time, how could she give Crawford up? Their relationship was so new, but her feelings already ran deep. It was as A.J. had said to Eunice in his letter – she felt as if she'd been hit by a train, and the thought of anything happening to Crawford . . . well, she didn't think she could live. If it had been him lying here instead of Theo, she would not have hesitated to dedicate her life to caring for him. But if she made that promise to Theo, it would mean giving up a man with whom she thought she wanted to spend the rest of her life. Oh, it was unbearable. Whatever she did, she knew she could not be completely happy.

'I have to go back to Cornwall. But I need you to promise me that you will do everything the doctors tell you and get stronger. I will write all the time, I promise.'

'There's something you're not telling me, I can tell. But if that's what you want, I will do as you ask. And I will be waiting for when you can get back to me. I know I'm only half a man now, and I could probably never be a proper husband to you. But just having you close by would be enough. And if you can still love me, I will be the happiest man on this earth.'

'Always know that I love you, Theo. I always have. But we can't make any decisions while the war is still on and the future is so uncertain.' She comforted herself that she wasn't lying to him. And if it helped him through these next difficult days, then she would tell him what he needed to hear. In the back of her mind, a voice was telling her that misleading him was not fair on either of them, but she just couldn't find the words to tell him the truth right now.

'That's enough for now. And I promise I'll do everything to get better. For you.'

'You do that, Theo. I will come again tomorrow, but I see your parents making their way back to you so I'll leave now.'

He brought her hand clumsily up to his lips and kissed it. 'Thank you so much. You've given me hope.'

Tears streaming down her face, April walked swiftly towards the door. As she passed the Osbornes, she said, 'I think I'll go for a walk before going back. I'll see you later.'

At the nurses' station, she paused. 'Sister, can I ask you something?'

'Of course.'

'How long do you think it will be until he's well enough to go home?'

The nurse sighed. 'He'll be here for quite some time, I'm afraid. If, and it's quite a big if, he gets well enough, he'll then go to a convalescent home and, I'll be frank, unless there's a miracle, I don't see him leaving it. It's the internal damage, you see; he'll always need round-the-clock care.'

April gasped. 'Does he know?'

'Yes, and so does his father. But he's requested we not tell his mother for now. He's a very brave man and wants to spare her any more grief at the moment.'

'But you told me?'

'He told me you were a nurse. And someone very special to him. He also said he wanted you to know the truth if you asked.'

∞

Outside, April didn't notice where she was going. Her mind was full of Theo. What on earth should she do? If his time was limited, maybe she should come back. Surely it was a small thing, to make him happy in his last months. How could she selfishly go back to Cornwall, to Crawford, when she knew that Theo could die at any moment, longing for her? Asking for her.

She thought of Crawford: his beautiful face, those green, green eyes. The way he held her so sweetly. And most of all those kisses. His strong arms around her, his eyes smiling into hers. Oh God! How could she give up the promise of happiness with him? But she must. What sort of person was she that she couldn't provide comfort to the man who'd first captured her young heart? Spotting a bench, she sat down, hugging herself and looking out at the grey, choppy water of the Thames. It was an impossible choice. Her conscience told her she should be with Theo, but her heart didn't agree. It didn't matter that she'd only known Crawford for a few weeks. It didn't matter that his home was thousands of miles away. She would do anything, overcome anything, if only she could be with him. Because, she realised, as she gazed sightlessly at a boat chugging down the river, her heart belonged to Crawford in a way it never had to Theo.

∽

She was cold and dejected by the time she returned to the Osbornes. They were both sitting in the kitchen drinking tea.

Mrs Osborne poured another cup for her. 'Thank you, my dear, for coming to see Theo and comforting him. He told us that you talked about returning to London once you were qualified.'

'Did he?'

'It would mean *so* much to him. And I know it would help him recover more than anything else.'

'Well, no decision was made. My life is in Cornwall right now, and I can't leave it for a while.'

'You know there'll always be a home here for you, if you do return.' Reverend Osborne smiled kindly at her.

April smiled vaguely back. 'Thank you. If you don't mind, I'm going to go to my room. I have much to think about and need a bit of time.'

'Of course. Supper will be at seven.'

April threw herself down on the bed. The thought of living here and looking after Theo filled her with dread. Even if it was for just a few months, she couldn't do it. She loved Theo like a brother, no more than that. And she just couldn't give up her chance of happiness. Because if she left Cornwall, she doubted she'd ever see Crawford again. She'd be betraying him and betraying herself. And she wouldn't do it. The Osbornes expected too much from her.

By the time she came down to supper, April had decided she must harden her heart. So she mentioned nothing of her thoughts, and the Osbornes didn't ask. They seemed to have accepted that she would be going back to Cornwall for now, and they left it at that.

'We'll be leaving at two again tomorrow. You will be coming, won't you, April?'

'Of course I will. But I'm afraid my train leaves the day after, first thing in the morning. I was given only four days leave so I need to get back.'

'So soon? Surely they'd understand if you send a telegram saying you need to stay.' Mrs Osborne's expression was distressed.

'They're terribly short-staffed. So many nurses have left to join the military. I'm needed, and I won't let them down. I'm sorry.'

'Of course you mustn't, my dear, although we shall be sorry to see you go,' the reverend said.

'Thank you. I will be sorry to leave.' It was a small lie and April hoped it didn't give them too much hope. It at least meant that she could escape without causing too much agitation.

The next day at two, they all left for the hospital, and the Osbornes again left April to visit Theo on her own. He was subdued when she arrived beside his bed. She kissed his cheek and sat down beside him, taking his hand.

'How are you today, Theo?'

'Feeling a bit ropey, to be honest. But better now that you're here.'

'Good, I'm glad I've helped. But you must know, this will be my last visit for a while as I have to go back tomorrow.'

'Must you, April?'

'You know I must. But I'll write, like I promised I would. Every day if that helps.'

He sighed. 'It will have to do for now. But tell me about Cornwall. Tell me about your friends.'

So she did, careful to not mention Crawford. But at talk of the dance at the base, his hand tightened on hers.

'Is that why you have to get back? You met some American soldier at the dance?'

'Of course I didn't.' Well, she hadn't met Crawford at the dance, so it wasn't a complete lie.

'You would tell me, April, wouldn't you? If you had somebody else?'

'How would that help you, Theo?'

He didn't say anything for a moment. Just lay with his hand holding tightly to hers. Then, quietly, he said, 'I've known you many years. Loved you for a fair few of those. I know we had that difficult time when I behaved like a cad. And I know you, April. And I think I know when you're lying. If there's someone else, someone with a future who you can love, then you mustn't let me hold you back. I was selfish yesterday, and I'm sorry. But I thought a lot last night, and I realised that if I really do love you, then I would want you to be happy. And how can you be happy looking after a husk of a man like me? Sister said she'd told you the truth, so you know there's no future for us, my darling. And more than anything you deserve a future, a family of your own to love. Something you've never had. Now, promise me something, April. Go back to Cornwall and be happy. Forget about me, my chance has gone, and I will be content knowing that you have a second chance at love. And I will always remember you in the park sitting amongst the bluebells – the exact colour of your eyes – with your hair gleaming golden in the sun. Do you remember that day, my love?'

At his words, April couldn't stop the tears falling. Her heart was squeezing with love and sadness. In that moment, he was the boy she remembered. The little boy

304

with the big heart who'd carried her through her grief. The only person who had changed was her.

'Of course I remember. You picked a bunch for me and pinned one over your heart.'

He smiled his lopsided smile. 'And that's where you will remain. Now, I want you to go.'

'You will always be in my heart too. My first love, I will never forget.' April was crying openly now. She leaned over and kissed his scarred cheek, her tears falling on his face.

'Don't cry. Your life lies before you, and when my time comes, I will watch over you always.'

She lay her head on his chest, weeping while he stroked her hair.

Finally, he pushed her up gently. 'Go now, April. There's only so much selflessness a man can take.'

She nodded. 'Goodbye, my dearest friend.'

Their hands remained joined as she rose. Slowly, she pulled away from him until just the tips of their fingers were touching. She looked at him for what she knew would be the last time, then turned and hurried out of the ward. The Osbornes called to her as she passed, but she couldn't speak. Instead she ran, tears clouding her vision, before she finally collapsed on a bench outside the hospital and wept as if her heart would break.

∽

That night, she did not go down to supper. Instead, she lay on the bed, staring at the ceiling, keeping her mind blank. It was the only way she could hold herself together. Finally, she heard a gentle knock on the door, and Reverend Osborne came in.

'I just wanted to say goodbye in case I didn't see you tomorrow. And to say thank you for coming. I know it's not been easy, but Theo has appreciated it so much.'

She didn't deserve their gratitude, and that thought proved too much for her and once again she burst into tears. The reverend sat on the bed beside her and took her hand in his.

'April, listen to me. I know there is not much more that can be done for Theo.'

She nodded.

'But I can't bring myself to break the news to his mother. She needs to have some hope to hang on to.'

'How can you be so calm about it?'

'It is God's will, my child. And though my heart is breaking, still I must celebrate the years we had with him. He was a gift to us and will always be. I must take comfort in that.'

'Oh, reverend, I am so sorry I could not be the woman he wanted.'

'Now that's silly talk. How could we expect you to give up your life, which is just beginning, to care for him? Dry your eyes and look to the future. Make it a good one, one Theo would be proud of.'

April nodded. 'I'll try. And thank you for being so wonderful. Will you let me know . . . will you let me know if anything happens?'

'I will let you know, child. Have a safe journey. I'll be praying for you every day.'

Chapter 29

April was up early the following morning, and Mrs Osborne was still in bed. Leaving a note of thanks and love for her, she left the house with a heavy heart and made her way to Paddington. She would not reach Truro until later that night, but she didn't mind. She needed the journey to think and as the train made it's slow, stop-start way to Cornwall, she barely noticed the hours passing.

When she finally arrived she walked home, still in a daze. Letting herself in, she realised that Mrs Teague would not have known when she was coming back, but even so, the woman was sitting by the fire, wearing her dressing gown. She jumped up with a glad cry when she saw her.

'April, my love. You look all in. Sit down and I'll get you some food and tea.'

April gratefully dropped on to the sofa, staring into the flames.

Mrs Teague returned with a plate of sandwiches and a pot of tea. 'Was it very bad, lovely?' she asked sympathetically.

April nodded. 'I won't see him again. His injuries are too bad.'

'I'm sorry to hear that. Is there no hope at all?'

'None. I'm sorry, Mrs Teague, I find I can't eat these sandwiches. Will they keep for tomorrow? I think I need to go to bed.'

'Before you go, there's something I need to . . .'

April looked at her expectantly. But then Mrs Teague shook her head, looking uncomfortable.

'Never mind. It can wait. You go on up. I'll have these for my lunch tomorrow.' She kissed her goodnight and left her to go to her room, where, much to her surprise, April slept deeply, waking only when her landlady came in with a cup of tea.

'Time to get up, lovely. You need to be at the hospital soon.' She sat on the bed beside her and stroked the hair from her face. 'Are you all right for work today?'

April sat up. 'Yes. I need it. It will take my mind off the last few days. And when I get back you can tell me what's been going on while I've been away.'

The older woman's eyes flickered briefly and she looked away. 'There's not a lot to say.'

April was surprised at her subdued response. It wasn't like her. But then, maybe, she felt it was inappropriate to chatter about everyday life when she'd been with her dying friend. She let the matter drop and hurried to get ready.

∽

Sister Mulholland welcomed April warmly when she walked into the ward. 'Ah, Nurse Harvey. We've missed you. I hope all's well with your friend?'

'Not really, sister. But work will help. Where shall I start?'

The day was busy as she tended to the patients in the surgical ward. Many needed special care, so she found she didn't have a moment to think of anything else. Finally, it was time for her break and she made her way down to the cafeteria, wondering if any of her friends would be there. It would be good to see them.

She spotted Nancy sitting alone as soon as she got in. Having collected her corn beef hash, which looked extremely unappetising, she made her way over to her.

'I haven't seen you for a while, Nancy. How are you?'

Nancy looked up and a happy smile spread across her face. 'April! How did it go? Was it terribly romantic? Such a shame you couldn't stay and have a honeymoon. Will you be moving back if you pass your exams?'

'What do you mean?'

'The wedding.'

'What wedding?'

'Didn't you go to London to marry your injured child-hood sweetheart?'

'What on earth are you talking about?'

'Bess told us she'd seen you and you were in tears because he's badly injured, so you had to go to him and that you were going to marry . . .' Nancy stopped, noticing the horrified expression on April's face for the first time. 'Oh no. Has he died?'

April felt sick. 'No! He's not dead, and I didn't marry him. I was never going to marry him. Why on earth would she say that? I went because he was asking to see me and he doesn't have long left.'

Nancy frowned, looking puzzled for a moment. 'But Bess told me and Mattie that you'd run off to get married, and it was all terribly romantic. She said we mustn't tell anyone, though, and I haven't, I promise.'

'But it's not true! I don't understand why she'd say this. She knew I'd be back.' The thought that Bess would tell such a lie when the truth was so very different upset her greatly. She knew Bess didn't like her much, but when she'd last seen her she'd been so kind and sympathetic, but she'd known, hadn't she, at the back of her mind, that Bess couldn't be trusted, she just hadn't felt strong enough to think about it at the time. 'Has she told anyone else?'

Nancy went pale. 'Oh dear.'

'What?'

'Oh, April. I have a horrible feeling she's trying to cause trouble for you. We're the only people at the hospital she told, but . . .'

April felt the first flutterings of unease in her stomach. 'Who else did she tell?'

'The other day, I saw her outside with the major. I must say I thought it was strange, especially as she had her arm around him. But when I asked, she explained about the wedding, so it all made sense. I think she must have told him, April.'

'But I was *never* going to marry him and he's *not* my sweetheart. Oh, no! What am I going to do? And why would she do that? After everything with Eunice, and her being so kind that day, I thought that maybe we could at least be civil to each other.'

Nancy shook her head. 'Oh lord! Bess is my friend, but this is going too far even for her. She's always been jealous of you and this whole business with the major has blown it all out of proportion.'

'But why? I've never done anything to her, and she only met Crawford a couple of times.'

Nancy was quiet for a moment, then she said, 'Look, I probably shouldn't tell you this but I think it will help you understand. Bess has had some problems before. She gets fixated with people and just doesn't let go. It happened with this pilot just before you arrived. She gets in too deep too quickly with men and scares them off.'

'But it hasn't happened with Red.'

'She's only seeing him as a way to keep tabs on the major and you. Anyway, this poor pilot was hounded by her. He was stationed at the base in St Merryn, and she used to write to him all the time, sometimes twice a day. And then she started loitering outside the base waiting for him, demanding to know why he hadn't answered her letters. Got to the point when he had to get his commanding officer to have a word with matron. She got such a telling off, was told if she was ever seen there again, she'd be dismissed for bringing the hospital into disrepute. She felt he'd betrayed her. But really, the poor man just wanted to escape.'

April was astonished. She knew Bess was insecure, but she'd never have guessed that it was this bad.

'Then, not long after, you arrived, and everyone seemed to love you. I suppose she was just feeling so hurt and upset that she needed someone to vent her anger on. Then, when you started walking out with the man she thought should have been hers, it got worse. Seems she's transferred all her feelings from the pilot to the major.'

'But I still don't understand. Why is she trying to ruin my life? How could she do this to me? She even told me Eunice didn't want to see anyone, so I stayed away, but Eunice thought I'd abandoned her. I could have lost my friend. Is she trying to take everything away from me?'

311

'Maybe. And I expect she thinks the major is the sort of man who can get her away from everything. Security, you know? I don't think she's really had that before.'

Even though she was distressed, April was surprised at the other girl's sensitivity. People often dismissed Nancy as a good-time girl who was only interested in men and having fun, but April realised they'd all under-estimated her. She'd always known she had a good heart, but there was a lot more to her than that. Homer was a lucky man.

'But what if he believes her? What if he thinks I was playing with him?'

'You need to write to your major and let him know it's not true.'

'Yes, yes. I'll do that as soon as I get home. Surely he won't believe a word of it.'

'Of course he won't. He seems to really like you. And I'll speak to Bess. It's high time she stopped her ridiculous games. Even I'm running out of patience.'

'Thank you for telling me, Nancy. Seems we're all in a bit of a pickle at the moment. Except you. How is Homer, by the way?'

'Oh, he is lovely, April. I think I really am in love. This is the first time in my life that I haven't got bored. I know I can seem like a bit of a flibbertigibbet and I know I can be a bit much sometimes . . . Homer tells me that all the time.' She giggled. 'But he makes me feel calm. My mum is thrilled. I took him home before they went off, and she adored him. Even though . . . you know. She doesn't care, she's just happy I've found such a good man. She knows that if things get really serious and we get married that

Homer will have to stay, so she's even said that we can live with her if we have to.'

'That's wonderful. I wish the same could be said for Eunice. Have you seen her while I've been away?'

Nancy looked grave. 'No. Poor Eunice. I just can't believe it. She's the last person I would have expected to fall in love with someone else. It's as if she's turned into me. Isn't it funny how life surprises you?'

April nodded. 'It certainly is. And not always in a good way.' April wondered if Eunice had told A.J. about the baby yet. She'd said she was going to write to him, but she had no idea whether she had.

Nancy interrupted her thoughts. 'So, what really happened in London? Theo's not really your sweetheart, is he? Having both you *and* Eunice running around with two men is too much. If someone had said this would be me and Bess, I wouldn't have blinked an eye.'

'It's not like that. He isn't my sweetheart, but I care for him deeply. He's more like a brother to me, really. But I probably won't see him again.' She put her face in hands.

Nancy squeezed her arm comfortingly. 'Hey, sorry. I was being insensitive. Don't worry, it'll all work out in the end.'

'Will it?' April shook her head. 'It won't for Theo, and I can't see how it will for me or Eunice. Everything's such a mess.'

Chapter 30

April forced herself to focus on her work for the rest of the shift, resolutely pushing all thoughts of Crawford and Bess from her mind. But it didn't stop her feeling sick with dread.

When she left the hospital late that night, she half hoped to see Crawford waiting for her at the door. Which was foolish considering he thought she was married and in London. She should have written to him to let him know she was going, but she thought she'd be back before he returned so there hadn't been much point. And she never would have thought Bess could be so vindictive.

As always, there was food waiting for her.

'Homity pie tonight: one of your favourites. I thought it might cheer you up.'

April smiled wanly. 'Lovely, thank you.' She washed her hands and sat down at the table.

'Mrs Teague, apparently Crawford is back. Did he come here to see me?'

Mrs Teague, who had been bustling around the kitchen, paused. 'I did see him, yes.' She didn't look at her, so April knew there was something wrong.

'Please tell me what happened.'

'Oh, April, I was hoping to wait until you felt a little better. I'm afraid that I made a hash of it.'

'Please, just tell me what happened.'

'He decided to surprise you at the hospital and bring you home. It was the day you left. But when you didn't show up he went looking for you. And he found Bess. Then he came here to talk to me and the first thing he asked was if you'd gone to London to marry Theo. I was so shocked that I couldn't gather my thoughts, and I think he took my silence as assent. He looked at me with those eyes – so beautiful and so hurt, they were – and before I could say anything, he nodded, wished me all the best and left. Always such a gentleman. I called after him, but he got in his car and drove away.'

April put her head in her hands.

'And then the next day, a letter came for you, with "Please forward" written on the front. I didn't want to give it to you last night, tired as you were, but it's on the mantelpiece.'

April pushed her chair back from the table and rushed into the sitting room. Her name was written on the front, although there was no address so she knew it must have been hand-delivered. She recognised the bold handwriting as Crawford's. With her heart thumping, April walked slowly towards the mantelpiece. She didn't want to open it. She had a suspicion that they might be the last words she'd ever hear from him, and she knew they'd be angry.

She forced herself to pick up the envelope, tearing it open with trembling fingers. Inside, there was just one sheet of paper.

Dear April,

I was shocked when Bess told me that you'd gone to London to marry Theo. The man you'd told me was just an old friend. But then, what we shared was probably too good to be true, so I shouldn't be surprised. I can't pretend to be anything other than devastated. Not just because you have gone, but because you lied to me. That hurts the most. If only you'd told me the truth, I would have understood and left you alone. Instead, I believed you when you said your heart belonged to me; I believed you because I felt the same. But was that a lie too?

Since I met you, I've been wondering whether it's possible to know so soon that you want to spend your life with someone. There was only one answer for me: yes, it is possible, because that is what I felt with you. I am trying very hard not to let my hurt make me bitter. I can't pretend to understand why you have done this, but I do respect your right to do it. Perhaps you didn't want to hurt me, and that's why you led me to believe you felt the same. Or perhaps you just didn't know how to say it, torn as you were between us. So, seeing as I've ended up on the losing side, I have decided I must be gracious in defeat. I wish you every happiness in your new life. Because, despite everything, the thought of you being unhappy hurts me almost more than your lies.

My mother used to tell me that my father is the sort of man who, when he loves someone, he loves them forever. She always said I was just like him. Turns out she was right. It's a blessing and a curse.

Be happy, April,
Crawford

316

April let out a cry and dropped on to a chair, the letter fluttering to the floor. Mrs Teague, who had been hovering anxiously by the door, rushed in and picked it up, scanning the contents.

'Oh no, no, no! How could he believe this of you? Oh, that Bess! I'm not usually a violent person, but I could wring her neck. Well, I am going to make sure he understands what a mistake he's made. The silly, silly man. I thought better of him, really I did. Why wouldn't he let me explain before running away?'

April shook her head. 'There's nothing to be done. He thinks the worst of me, and I can't blame him. I might not have married Theo, but I did leave to be with him. And I lied to him. I told him Theo was just a childhood friend, not that he was once my sweetheart. I'm not sure he could forgive me, even if I did explain.'

'Such nonsense. It's nothing but a misunderstanding that can be cleared up with a conversation. Now, you are going to write back to him this instant explaining everything.'

'Yes. He deserves to know the truth. But he's an honourable man, and I've broken his trust. I know from experience that once trust is broken, it's hard to feel the same.'

Mrs Teague sighed. 'You're tired and upset. Come and have something to eat and then go to bed. Everything will seem brighter in the morning, you'll see.'

∽

The night was a long one for April as she thought of Crawford and wondered what she could say to him to make it better. She sat at the writing table in her room with a blank sheet of paper in front of her, but she could think of nothing at all. Eventually, she decided to sleep on it and write first thing in the morning. But sleep wouldn't come, and the thoughts whirled around and around in her mind. She'd never meant to hurt him, and the fact that she had made tears of guilt and sorrow trickle down her cheeks. Not since her father had died had she felt so battered by emotion. First Theo and now Crawford. It seemed she was destined to hurt the men she loved, however unintentionally.

As dawn broke, April climbed out of bed and sat at her desk. She could not leave it any longer. Crawford deserved to know that Bess had lied, she could at least give him that, and this time, the words flowed.

Dear Crawford,

Words cannot convey how terrible I feel that I have hurt you. But please know that, though I may have lied by omission, I never lied about my feelings for you. I am not married, nor did I go to London to marry. But Bess was right about one thing. I did go to see Theo, and he did used to be my sweetheart, but he hasn't been for a long time, though he has often told me he wishes that wasn't so.

I can't pretend that I didn't think about a future for me and Theo, but then you came into my life and I knew it was impossible. Theo is my childhood friend and the boy I first loved, but I realise now that it was a child's love. Because you came along and showed me just how strong true love can be.

I need to also explain that the reason I left in such a hurry is because he was asking for me. I think I told you he had been injured, but I didn't realise how serious those injuries are. He is desperately ill and may not survive much longer. So, you see, what choice did I have but to see him one last time? I know I should have written or got a message to you, but thought I'd be back before you returned and I was going to tell you all about it when I next saw you. I know you asked for complete honesty, and I was going to give you that.

In answer to your question: Yes, I think it is possible to know you want to spend the rest of your life with someone after knowing them for just a few weeks. Because that is how I feel about you. I understand perfectly that your trust in me has been shattered and things can never be the same again, but I wanted you to know the truth so that perhaps, one day, you can stop hating me.

Please take care of yourself, Crawford. And if ever you change your mind about me, then I will be here, waiting and hoping that one day you can forgive me.

I am, forever,

Your April

Chapter 31

Feeling exhausted from the emotions of the past week, April got ready for work. It was a horrible irony that both the men in her life had said they wanted her to find happiness, and yet it seemed so unlikely now. But life was not at an end. She still had a future, unlike poor Theo. So, for his sake, she would do her best to make amends for her mistakes. She also needed to check on Eunice. She had been consumed by her own problems these past few days, but now it was time to focus on other people.

As for Bess, she supposed she would have to confront her. No matter how futile, she couldn't let her lie about her like this. Was it really about wanting Crawford? Or had she just wanted her to look bad in front of the people she cared about? It made no sense to tell a lie that would be proved false so easily and quickly. From what Nancy had said, there was more to Bess's story, and she couldn't find it in her heart to hate her completely. What good would that do? She thought back to the night of the dance, and how upset Bess had been. It was the only time she had seen her vulnerability, and it had made her think differently about the girl. There was heartbreak there, no doubt. And though she was furious with her, she couldn't let her anger take over. She needed to understand, so she wouldn't spend her life eaten up with bitterness and hate.

∽∞∽

At work, she made a concerted effort to think only of her patients, and it seemed to pay off, as Sister Mulholland called her over to the nurses' station as she was going on her break.

'I have been very impressed with your professionalism over the last few weeks, Nurse Harvey. I know it's not been easy, what with your friend and the bombing, but you have proved yourself to be a dedicated nurse with a calm head, and I have no doubt that you will have passed your exams with flying colours. I would be happy to have you on my ward permanently and hope very much that you will stay with me.'

April liked the sister, and she enjoyed working on the surgical ward, so she was thrilled to hear this. At least one thing was going right in her life.

'I'd be honoured to work with you, sister. You've taught me so much, and it's always a pleasure.'

'Excellent, that's settled then. I will talk to matron.'

April smiled with delight as she left. Yes, if all else failed, she'd always have her work, and as it looked like she might never marry now, maybe she could become a matron one day.

Walking down the stairs, she took in the bomb damage. There was still plaster that needed replacing and the once beautiful, tiled floor in the entrance had been completely ruined and was now covered with a black-and-white linoleum. She glanced up at the ceiling. How they had mended it so fast, she would never know. Even so, the damage was clear to see and the plaster still unpainted. As she passed the reception desk, she waved at Sara on the switchboard, who had her headphones on and was busily talking into her mouthpiece. It was a miracle she'd had the courage to come back after being buried under a ton of masonry. But here she was, as if nothing had ever happened.

The hospital had got back up and running far quicker than anyone had believed possible, and although those who had survived would never forget that ghastly day, the hospital community had drawn even closer together, and April felt blessed to be part of it. War seemed to bring out the best as well as the worst in people, she reflected. And speaking of bringing out the worst, she needed to talk to Bess.

When she didn't spot her in the cafeteria, she asked around. Bess, it seemed, was on nights, so she'd be just getting up now. Steeling herself for what was to come, April marched around to the nurses' home and banged on the door.

Another nurse answered and showed her to Bess's room. She pressed her ear to the door. She could hear her moving around, so she walked straight in.

Bess looked up in surprise when she heard the door open.

'April! What are you doing here? I thought—'

'Don't you dare!' April was furious. How dare she pretend to believe her own lies. 'How could you, Bess? How could you tell everyone I'd left to get married? You must have realised I'd be back soon.'

For a moment, Bess looked guilty, but then the expression was replaced by anger. 'You are a two-timing little *slut*, April Harvey. I may have exaggerated a little about why you left, but I wasn't lying. You left Crawford – the man you stole from me – to be with another man. And guess what? I wasn't at all surprised. Let me see, how many men have you been stringing along?' She held up her fingers and counted them off one at a time. 'One. Crawford. Two. Your chap in London. Three. Red. Four . . . is it A.J? Perhaps you want to take him from Eunice. Or perhaps one of his friends? And God knows who else you've got hidden away. You act so superior but you're nothing but a common little tart.'

April's eyes had gone wide with disbelief. 'But that's a lie! There's only ever been Crawford. Theo was over long ago and you know that very well. So why, Bess? Why have you hurt me like this? And not just me, you've hurt Crawford.'

Bess snorted. 'Believe me, Crawford will get over it. No doubt he'd have dumped you sooner or later, just like he dumped me.'

'And why would you think there was anything between me and Red? I thought you and he . . .'

'Yeah, well, you thought wrong. Red is like all the others: pining after perfect little April.'

April drew a deep breath, reining in her anger with difficulty. She'd promised herself she'd find out why Bess had behaved like this and try very hard to understand. But confronted with the other woman's scorn she was finding it much more difficult than she'd imagined.

'He has never done that and I don't know why you'd think it.'

'Oh, yeah? Why then would he arrange to take Mrs Teague to the film and not me if not to get closer to you?

So, seeing as you'd run off to see another man and poor Crawford was waiting around for you, I decided it was time he knew a few home truths about you.'

April gasped. 'What else did you tell him?'

'Just what I said. You like stringing men along and have been doing it since you've arrived. I'm thinking Crawford might need a bit of comforting now you've betrayed him.'

The thought of Bess and Crawford together made her feel sick. 'Don't flatter yourself, Bess, he wouldn't touch you after what you've done. And I doubt many of the others will either.'

'Oh really? In my experience chaps don't much care who they have on their arm, just as long as they get something out of it at the end of the evening.' Bess turned her back, but April could see that her anger seemed to be turning into something else. Was it her imagination, or had she seen tears in her eyes?

'Is that your experience, Bess? Is that why you're so bitter and angry all the time?'

'Oh, push off, April. You don't know anything. It's all hearts and flowers with you, isn't it? Girls like you make me sick. Men think you're so sweet and innocent, but underneath you're just like the rest of us. And I wanted everyone to know what a hypocrite you are. So now you know, I'd like you to leave.'

April was so stunned by her words that she couldn't move, couldn't even respond. She stood, rooted to the spot, staring at Bess's back.

Suddenly Bess turned back around. 'Haven't you gone yet? I said get out of my room. And next time you see me, do me a favour: don't even look in my direction. I never want to speak to you again.'

April whirled around and left the room. The tears were blinding, but she refused to let them fall. She had tried so hard to get Bess to like her, even just a little bit, but why had she bothered? The woman hated her, and always would. And right now, April returned those feelings a hundred-fold.

As always, when she needed to find peace, she stood taking in the view of the moors. The air was chilly and the moors looked grey under the November sky. Soon it would be Crawford's Thanksgiving dinner, and then Christmas, and the thought of not sharing any of those special times with him made her want to weep. It was appropriate, she thought, that just as nature had shed its bright colours in favour of the more muted browns and reds of autumn, so all the brightness had gone out of her life too. But the world kept turning, and by spring, all being well, Eunice would have her baby, and perhaps some colour would return to both their lives.

∽

For the rest of her shift April worked like an automaton. And as soon as it was time to leave, she slipped out quietly, and looked around in the darkness, hoping, though she knew it was futile, that Crawford might be there. He wouldn't have received her letter yet, though, so she knew there was no chance of that. Would he try to see her when he did receive it, she wondered? She doubted it. She remembered his words to her: 'There's just one thing I ask, and that's complete honesty.' And she hadn't been entirely honest. She sighed. All of this was her own fault. She could blame Bess all she liked, but the fact was that if she'd just written to him or told him, then there would have been no chance of a misunderstanding.

Suddenly, a tall shadow detached itself from a thick hedge and moved towards her. Her heart leaped with hope as she heard a deep American voice say, 'April?'

But then recognition dawned, and she swallowed her disappointment. 'A.J., what a lovely surprise,' she said, and she meant it. 'Is everyone back now, then?'

'Not everyone. A couple of platoons will be gone a bit longer, but me and Homer and the others you met are back.'

'How are you? You know, after everything that happened?'

'That's why I came to see you. I've got so many questions and I've heard some things . . .' He gave her a meaningful look. 'Homer's seen Nancy, and she told him something . . .' A.J.'s voice was choked with emotion.

'What did she tell him?'

'She told him Eunice is having a baby. Is that true?'

April hesitated. There really was only one option, though. She had to be honest. 'Yes.'

A.J. looked stunned. 'Are you telling the truth, or is this another lie?'

'It's the truth, but you really need to speak to Eunice about this.'

He shook his head. 'I don't know what to believe any more. I loved that girl more than I've loved anyone in my life. I would have done anything for her. Even stayed here forever and never seen my family again. Then . . .

turns out she was lying to me all along. And now I hear this. What the hell am I meant to do, April? Is it even mine?'

'Oh, A.J., of course it's yours! And Eunice loves you too, you know. More than you can ever know. She's devastated right now, and her mother hates her. She needs you.'

'So . . . I'm going to be a father.' The enormity of the situation slowly dawned on A.J.'s face. 'But I can't ever look at her the same way again. Not after the way she's deceived me. How *could* she?'

April put her hand on his arm. 'She just didn't know what to do, so she did nothing. I know it was wrong, but can you look at things from her point of view? What if you had a girl at home who you'd grown up with and thought you loved? Someone you thought you would marry. And then you met Eunice. What would *you* have done? Would you have refused to have anything to do with her because of your girl back home, or would you have followed your heart, like she did?'

'I wouldn't have lied! I would have told her there were complications. I would never lie like that. Not if I loved someone.'

'Wouldn't you, A.J.? Are you sure about that?'

'Yes, I'm sure. Hell, I've been taught to tell the truth my whole life, no matter how painful.' He was close to tears and April's heart went out to him.

'You are such a good and honourable man. I really think you would have. But not many people are like you. Some of us are too scared to face the truth. Especially if that truth could lose us the love of our life. Do you understand what I'm saying? Were you not also taught to forgive people? To let go of your foolish pride?'

A.J. rubbed his face. 'You're not playing fair, April. You know very well I was. But so was she.'

'Yes, she was, and believe me, she's paying a heavy price for not being honest. But she still loves you. She just doesn't believe she's worthy of you. She never has.'

'Worthy of me?' He scoffed. 'As if that would enter her head.'

'It was always in her head. Always. She was betraying Norm for you, and it made her sick with guilt, yet she couldn't stop herself. She couldn't stop herself because she loves you. Completely. And not only did she feel guilty because of Norm, she didn't want you to be trapped here, unable to return home because of her. Do you see, A.J.? She's made a terrible hash of it, but none of this was because she didn't love you.'

'I just don't think I can forgive her. But if she's having my baby, what choice do I have? I can't abandon my child.'

'Well, then, you need to talk to her. Decide what to do for the best. And you need to be strong for her, A.J. I'm afraid the neighbours have been so cruel to her, and they will be cruel to you as well. So will her mother.'

'Huh. I'm used to that. And their brand of cruelty is nothing compared to what we face back home, so that don't bother me. But what if there's other stuff she's hiding from me? Will I always be wondering? How can I live my life with someone I can't trust?'

April cringed at the words and wondered if that was what Crawford thought about her. She imagined it was if he believed she'd gone and married someone else after she'd told him she loved him.

'That's something you'll have to work out for yourself. But please go and see her. Talk things through with her. If you love each other enough, you'll find a way; I'm sure you will.'

'You're right. I need to speak to her. But really, if she's having my baby, there's only one thing I can do.'

'If she'll let you.'

'Oh, she'll let me. I'll make sure of that. But it doesn't change the fact that I can't trust her any more.'

'Give her a chance to win back your trust, A.J. She deserves it, I promise you.'

A.J. sighed heavily. 'Seems I've got no choice.'

'No, you don't. And think, A.J. A baby! Such a beautiful miracle. Try and be happy about it.'

'Yeah. I'll try. I am, in one way. But in another . . .' He shook his head again. 'I just don't know if anything can be right again.'

'Course it can. Love will see you through. Trust me.'

A.J. bent and kissed her cheek. 'Thank you, April. You're a true friend, you know? No wonder Crawford is so blown away. Well, I best be off. I've sort of snuck out, so I better sneak back in. You take care, now.'

'You too.' But he didn't seem to hear. He was already striding away to the bicycle he'd left against the hedge.

April stared in the direction he went for a long while, thinking about his words and about how her and Eunice's situations were so similar. If only Crawford was still so blown away by her. She hoped that he would give her one more chance too.

∽

When she got back to Mrs Teague's, April dropped on to a kitchen chair with a sigh of exhaustion.

'Hard day, love?' Mrs Teague asked, putting a cup of tea in front of her.

'It hasn't been easy. I spoke to Bess. She really hates me. I don't think there's much that can be done there.'

'Best to concentrate on putting right what she messed up then, dear. I've had a few thoughts about that myself. How about I try to go and see Crawford and tell him what happened? Or maybe I can speak to Red? Although I'm not sure if he's back yet. I've not heard anything from him.'

'No. I've written my letter to him, so it's up to him if he wants to talk to me. Anyway, I'm lucky, really. I've got you, Eunice, the hospital. And soon there'll be a little baby to care for. Eunice says I can be godmother. Auntie April. I like the sound of that. Like a proper family.'

'Hmph. Well, I have a few home truths for that Bess, but I will respect your wishes for now.' She placed a bowl of fish stew in front of April. 'Get that down you, then I suggest you relax a bit and listen to the *Forces Programme* on the wireless with me. What do you say?'

'If you don't mind, I think I'll turn in early.' She tucked into the fish stew, which, like all of Mrs Teague's food, was delicious, and with a hunk of her home-made bread to mop up the juices, she was soon full.

She stood to help Mrs Teague clear the plates, but the landlady shooed her away. 'Don't you worry about this, lovely, I'll do it. You go and get some well-earned rest and I'll see you in the morning.'

April kissed her gratefully and trailed upstairs. She wondered how Theo was getting on and she decided to write him a cheerful letter before she went to sleep. No matter what challenges she was facing right now, it was nothing compared to poor Theo, so she must remember to count her blessings. And if she never saw Crawford again, she still couldn't regret going to see Theo that one last time.

Chapter 32

It was as well for April that the hospital was so busy over the next week as she had no option but to think only of her patients, but still every time a nurse was called to the phone, or she left the hospital, her heart leapt with hope. But it was futile. She had no visitors, was not called away from the ward to answer a telephone call, and found no one waiting outside, nor were there any letters waiting for her, either from the Osbornes or from Crawford. A week after her return, April was beginning to realise that she would have to accept that Crawford may not ever want to see her again.

Still, she told herself bracingly, as she cycled home one evening, at least things seemed to have taken a turn for the better with the war. The night before, Mrs Teague had been full of excitement at Churchill's announcement that, finally, he thought they were entering the 'end of the beginning'. Whatever that meant. But with victory in Egypt, it seemed that the tide might be turning. Even though the beginning of the war had taken three years, April thought gloomily, that meant there could be another six years left, and the thought made her want to cry.

When she reached the front door, she noticed the tiniest furtive sliding back of a curtain and April smiled to herself. And here was another blessing to count. Mrs Teague, who took such good care of her. With Mrs Teague on her side, she didn't feel quite as alone in the world as she'd used to.

'Your supper's keeping warm in the oven,' she said, as April walked in the door. 'And guess what, I had some visitors today.' She saw the hope in April's eyes and sighed. 'I'm sorry, not your major, dear. It was Red! He's back at last. Bless his dear heart, he brought me some presents. Wait till you see the mountain.'

April went into the pantry and gasped. Two tinned hams, tinned fruits, including pineapple, tinned soups, chocolate bars, American cigarettes, coffee, rice, two bars of perfumed soap and a bottle of brandy.

'Good heavens, how on earth are we going to eat all of that?'

'Well, I was thinking, dear, what do you say I invite your friend Eunice around, and maybe, just on the off-chance, A.J. might pop in? What do you think? And, of course, I'll ask Red. And how about your friend Nancy and her chap? He's a friend of A.J.'s, isn't he? So he can bring him too. Oh, we could have such a wonderful party!' She smiled, but April could see that there was a touch of tension behind her smile. Her landlady was absolutely terrible at keeping her thoughts to herself.

'Mrs Teague, what have you done?'

'What do you mean, dear?' Mrs Teague gave her a wide-eyed look.

'You've already invited everyone, haven't you?'

'How on earth could I have done that?'

'Oh dear, Mrs Teague, you've asked Red to deliver your messages to A.J. and Homer, haven't you? And have you already sent a letter to Eunice?'

'Well, it's about time someone got those two children together.'

'But I told you that A.J. was going to talk to her. We should let them sort it out in peace.'

'Should we? Do you know how that talk has gone, by any chance?'

'No, I was going to cycle over on Sunday.'

'Hmph. However it's gone, they need to have a place to meet with friends. If they're still not in agreement, maybe we can help them along. And if they've decided to marry, then it'll be a celebration. Honestly, April, I have no idea why you're so worried about the whole thing. And if Nancy and Homer are here, surely they can only make everyone feel more relaxed. And, of course, Red is always the most lovely boy, so there's no problems there . . .' She trailed off and looked away.

'Mrs Teague, you've not invited Crawford, have you?'

'Good heavens, whatever gave you that idea?'

'It just seems to me that you've taken it on yourself to play matchmaker to the whole of Truro, so I can't imagine you'd leave me out of it. Don't tell me you've invited Bess too, for Red?'

'I most certainly will *not* invite that little troublemaker. I've had quite enough of her shenanigans. Although, it's like you say, there's got to be a reason for her behaviour, so maybe it wouldn't be such a bad idea.'

'Don't you dare! And if you've invited the major, then I'm afraid I can't be here. He doesn't want to see me, that's very clear, and I don't want him to feel he has to come out of politeness. It would be too awful.'

'Oh, pish, April. How you fuss. You've been wandering around for a week now looking like you've lost a shilling and found a ha'penny, and I'm not going to sit back and watch you waste away with misery. All you do is sit in your room and write letters to your poor dying friend, and of course you have to write to him, but enough's enough; it's time to sort this mess out once and for all.'

April was almost in tears at this. 'No, I'm sorry, I can't be here if he's here too. I couldn't bear to see his face hating me. I love you, Mrs Teague, and I'd do almost anything for you, but please don't interfere in this! And I'm not so sure that it's a good idea to force Eunice and A.J. together. So, please, can you not do this?'

She pushed past her distressed-looking landlady and ran upstairs. Throwing herself on the bed, she buried her face in the pillow and sobbed until she had no tears left. Since her trip to London, she felt very much as she had in those first weeks after her dear father had died, and she didn't know which way to turn for comfort.

Finally, after tossing and turning for what felt like hours, she fell asleep and, for the first time in months, she dreamed again of her father and the air raid. But this time, it was different. This time her mother stood at the window with her father as well. And when April woke, her eyes were heavy with tears and her heart was heavy with grief.

Mrs Teague brought her a cup of tea first thing in the morning. Seeing April's red eyes and puffy face, she sat beside her.

'I'm so sorry, lovely. I never meant to upset you. I'll cancel all the plans, and maybe instead, you can go and see Eunice to see what the situation is. And I will write to all the men and tell them that I'm indisposed and will have to postpone. How's that?'

'It would be lovely to see everyone, but we need to make sure they want to see each other first. I'm sorry if I upset you, it's the last thing I ever want to do. Anyway, I doubt Crawford would have come. Especially as he hasn't even answered my letter. He doesn't want anything more to do with me.'

'I just can't believe that of him. But I will respect your wishes, my dear. Now, are you working today?'

'No. I'm going to go to St Merryn. I want to talk to my mother. Sounds silly, doesn't it? But I dreamed about her last night, and I haven't visited her grave more than once since I came here.'

'Course it doesn't. I visit my Isaac all the time. Particularly when I feel troubled. I'll leave you to get dressed.'

An hour later, April was on the bus to St Merryn. It was a cold, drizzly November day, and the moors were swathed in mist, merging with the sky in the distance, as if the whole world beyond her little patch had had a grey sheet dropped over it. When the sea came into view, it too looked grey and lacklustre, with just the white of the surf providing a contrast to the relentless gloom. April sighed.

Even the countryside couldn't shake her out of her mood today. In fact, she felt very much as if the grey sheet had been dropped on her too.

Once at St Merryn, she stopped and picked some winter honeysuckle from the hedgerows, burying her face in the fragrant flowers and marvelling that even in this cold weather these little flowers bloomed. Almost as if they'd been created especially to remind everyone that life went on, and there was always hope. She must take a lesson from these flowers, she thought, and try to bloom even though the world seemed so hostile. She walked on, buffeted by the wind and the rain, to her mother's grave.

It had been a year since she'd been here. Maybe she should have come more often. But she'd been so busy with her studies and her new life, and then Crawford, of course, that she'd kept putting it off.

She knelt by the grave and placed the flowers carefully on the gravestone. 'Hello, Mum. I expect you've been wondering where I've been for the past year. I'm sorry, I should have come more often. But I see Mrs Villanoweth has been keeping everything beautifully, as usual.

'I dreamed of you last night, Mum. You were standing with Dad at the window, surrounded by flames. I was glad he wasn't alone this time. Were you there, Mum? Keeping him company that night? Were you there to greet him as he died? I hope so. People shouldn't be alone when they die. It's hard enough when you're alive.' A single tear trickled unnoticed down her cheek and merged with the rain drops that were dripping from her hair. Before she knew it, April found she was sobbing out the story of what had happened over the past year and, in particular, her love for Crawford, and what had happened to Theo.

'But then I expect you know all about heartbreak, don't you, Mum? Mrs V told me what happened to your family. You went through much worse than me, and you came out smiling with a family of your own. That gives me hope. Not just for me, Mum, but for everyone. We're all suffering in one way or another. But it's like Dad always said, "This too shall pass." I pray it does.'

When she'd finished speaking, she rose stiffly from her position, suddenly realising how wet she was as the weather worsened. But she didn't mind, because although nothing was resolved, she felt at peace for the first time since she'd received that heart-breaking phone call from Reverend Osborne. She'd also come to a decision. She would try to speak to Crawford. Mrs Teague was right. It was silly to hold on to her stubborn pride when it was causing her so much heartache. She only hoped he'd listen to her. Just once. And give her one final chance.

Chapter 33

April got back to the house at lunchtime. Mrs Teague was out, so she ate the sandwiches that had been left for her, changed out of her wet clothes, then got straight on her bike. It was time to track down Crawford. She couldn't wait around hoping he'd come to her. If she wanted this to be resolved in any way, then it looked like it was up to her to sort it out. She remembered he was stationed at Pencalenick House, so she looked it up in one of Mrs Teague's map books. Satisfied she had some idea where she was headed, she packed a thermos of tea, put her waterproofs on and set out.

It wasn't far, only about thirty minutes or so on the bike, although she was hampered by the wind and the rain blowing into her face. She'd look a fright by the time she got there, but she didn't care. She just wanted to see Crawford.

When she got to the gate, the soldier listened to her request to find Major Dunbar, then politely but firmly turned her away.

'I'm sorry, ma'am, Major Dunbar has left a message that if a woman came to see him, he was not to be disturbed.'

'Did he say that if April Harvey came, he didn't want to be disturbed?'

'No, ma'am, he didn't leave a name. He just asked us not to let any female visitors through, nor to contact him about them.'

'But I'm soaking, and I *have* to see him. Please, could you just see if you could contact him?'

'Those are our orders, ma'am, and this site is high-security, so I'm afraid I'm going to have to ask you to leave now.'

Seeing the man's determination, April turned around, dejected, and cycled down the muddy lane. What did that mean? Was Crawford trying to ensure that she never saw him again? Or was he trying to keep someone else out? Bess, perhaps? Suddenly, the gates opened behind her and a car swished past, drenching her further as it drove through a puddle. She stood, dripping from head to foot and cursing. She looked after the car angrily and saw a face peering out of the back window. It was hard to tell in this weather, but she could have sworn it looked like Crawford. Did he not care that the car had drenched her?

Angry with him and herself for being so foolish, she got back on the bike and started pedalling furiously towards home. She'd thought about cycling over to St Agnes, but she was exhausted and freezing. There was no way she could manage that now. All she wanted was to get home and go to bed. She was back at work tomorrow, so she'd write to Eunice this evening instead.

As for Crawford, well, it was time she put her love for him behind her. She'd only known him for three months; surely it shouldn't take her that long to get over him?

Chapter 34

When she got back to Mrs Teague's, April was shivering uncontrollably, so she made a cup of tea and went to get warm in the sitting room. But the fire was out and she didn't like to start it as they had very little coal or wood, so she wrapped a blanket around herself and switched on the wireless. Suddenly, she noticed an envelope with her name on it sitting on the mantelpiece. Crawford. Leaping up, she snatched the envelope and ripped it open.

Dear April,

Thank you for your letter, and I'm sorry there seems to have been a misunderstanding. I've thought a lot about us, and I understand perfectly that you had to see Theo. What I don't understand is why you felt you couldn't tell me. And A.J.? Do you trust me so little that you couldn't tell me the full truth so I could help him?

I want to see you, April, so that perhaps we can put this behind us, but I don't want you to have any doubts. When you and I get together, honey, I want there to be nothing but love between us. I don't want there to be any anger, and at the moment, I'm still angry and hurt about what Bess told me. I'm trying not to believe her, but Theo was only

one name she mentioned. Was that a lie too? In my heart,
I know that my April is not like that. But my head? Well,
that's where I'm having trouble. But know this, my feelings
haven't changed.

   Until we meet again,
   Crawford xx

The throbbing in April's head increased. So he probably had told the guards not to let her in. How could he be so cruel? Did he want to punish her? She read the letter again; she noticed some of the ink had smudged. Her heart leapt a little at that. Had he been crying when he wrote it? But then a tear dropped on to the page and smudged it a little more. Of course he hadn't. Those were her tears. Oh, she was so sick of crying today. Enough was enough. She needed to lie down and sleep. Maybe then she'd be able to think more clearly.

She climbed the stairs wearily and got under the covers fully clothed. She should really take her wet things off, but she just didn't seem to have the energy, so instead she lay shivering, with the thoughts running around her mind, until eventually she drifted into a restless sleep, during which dreams of Crawford pointing an accusing finger at her and Theo crying for her jumbled up in her mind.

Her eyelids were heavy and her head was thumping when she woke, but she ignored them both and got out of bed, then had to grip the headboard as the room whirled around her and she sat back down abruptly. Goodness, she felt dreadful. Perhaps she'd caught a chill. She washed and dressed, then stumbled downstairs.

Mrs Teague was at her usual spot by the stove, but when she saw April, she gasped. 'Oh, April, are you all right? You don't look well at all. I came in to see you when I got home, but you were dead to the world, so I left you, but I should have checked on you.'

'I'm fine, really. I just need a cup of tea and then I'll be on my way. I'm not too hungry this morning.'

Mrs Teague went over and felt her forehead. 'Hmm. You feel a little feverish to me. Perhaps you should stay home today. I can go to the phone box and call the hospital.'

'I'm fine, honestly. Just a slight chill from getting wet yesterday.'

'Well, all right. You're the nurse. But you must come home if you feel worse, do you hear me?'

April smiled and gave Mrs Teague a hug. 'Course I will. Thank you for caring, but I'll be fine.'

❦

For the rest of the day, April felt terrible, but she tried to focus on her work. Sitting down at the nurses' station after a busy morning, she was reflecting on what to do, when Sister Mulholland's voice broke into her thoughts.

'Nurse Harvey, Mr Steward requires clean sheets and Mr Murphy is calling for water. What on earth is the matter with you, girl? We're short-staffed enough as it is, what with everyone deciding to go off and join the military. So we need all of you to be on top of the work. I cannot run this ward single-handed. Now hop to it, girl. If you're not careful, I might retract my request to have you on my ward permanently.'

April jumped up. 'I'm so sorry. I'll see to it right away, sister. And I'm happy to work extra hours tonight if it helps.'

'Just work properly while you are here, nurse. But I appreciate the offer. It might come to that.'

When she finally went to the cafeteria for a much-needed break, she was alarmed to see Bess sitting with Nancy. She had hoped very much never to see her again and the thought of the trouble she'd caused made her feel sick with anger. With Crawford's letter fresh in her mind, she was on the verge of walking out again, when Bess called to her.

'April, come over here a moment.'

April turned and gave her a scathing look, before carrying on out of the cafeteria. Hearing footsteps behind her, she quickened her pace.

'April, hang on! I just want to apologise.'

April whirled around. 'You're too late, Bess. He never wants to see me again, and frankly, that's exactly how I feel about you. So if you'll excuse me, I'm going to go into town to get a cup of tea. The smell around here is making me nauseous.'

Bess caught her arm. 'Wait. I'm sorry, OK? Nancy says I should apologise, and she's right.'

'Nancy should mind her own business.'

'Look, I've been doing a lot of thinking since you came to see me. Believe it or not, what you said did have an impact on me. Anyway, the fact is, I applied to join the Queen Alexandra nurses, and they've accepted me. I'll be leaving in the next few days.'

'Congratulations. I hope you'll be happy.' April couldn't help feeling relieved that she'd be gone. Crawford or no Crawford, she realised that she'd never been able to fully relax around Bess and had always felt gauche and naïve in her company.

'I decided I needed to put a few things right. I failed, I'm afraid. I went up to where Crawford is stationed and tried to talk to him. I went up several times, as it happens. But I never did manage to see him. So I wrote him a note.'

'It's too late, Bess. I'm not interested. Anyway, I don't believe you for a moment. You've lied far too many times for me to believe anything you say ever again. I wish you well, and hope you stay safe, but I can't forgive you for what you've done.'

Bess nodded. 'Fair enough. Seems you do have a backbone after all. See you around.'

'And it seems that you only apologised to make yourself look good. Have a nice life, Bess.'

April left and went for a bracing walk on the moors before coming back to get her food.

Maybe Crawford hadn't expected her to call at the base. Maybe it was Bess he was trying to stay away from. A small spark of hope started to burn inside her. She tried to douse it, knowing it was stupid, but it was there nonetheless, warming her for the first time that day and enabling her to concentrate more fully on her patients that afternoon.

Despite sister's assertion that she just needed her to concentrate while she was there, April stayed late. The surgical ward had been busy, and many patients needed watching. Finally, two hours after she'd been due to leave, the night sister told her to go. April changed and emerged into a clear, cold night. The stars shone brightly above her and the moon was full. She looked at it in trepidation. She wasn't sure she'd ever look at the moon in the same way again.

As she was cycling down the hill, she heard the ominous roar of plane engines. April looked up to the sky in horror.

'Oh God, not again!' She started pedalling furiously, desperate to reach Mrs Teague and ensure she got into the shelter. But she was too late. In the sky in front of her, she saw two planes release their deadly cargo on the town she'd come to love. She watched, heart in her mouth, as hundreds of bombs dropped and braced herself for the explosions that never came. Instead, as she watched, a huge wall of flames went up and she gasped. It was an incendiary bomb. She'd heard about these on news reports on the wireless; their aim was to cause fire and damage to property. From her vantage point she watched as fires broke out all over Truro. She had to get down there and help.

Tiredness forgotten, April rushed down the hill on her bike towards the nearest fire, which was in a street behind the high street. A scene of chaos greeted her. Shouts, screams and the familiar wail of the air raid siren brought her to an abrupt halt as she closed her eyes and forced the bad memories away. Not here. Not now. When her breathing had calmed, she opened her eyes again. As far as she could make out, the ambulance hadn't arrived yet. Quickly, she rushed to one of the firemen who was holding a hose from which a plume of water sparkled briefly in the flames, before disappearing into the burning houses with a hiss.

'Are there any injuries? I'm a nurse,' she shouted.

'Over there. One of the men just carried out that woman. They've gone back in for the husband. Ambulance is on its way. You think you can look after her till they get here?'

She ran to the woman, noticing that her hair had been completely burned off, and her scalp and face were horribly raw and burned. She'd seen injuries like these many times during the air raids in London, so the sight didn't shock her. A girl of about eighteen was kneeling beside her, crying uncontrollably, and she spoke quickly.

'I need you to go into that pub over there and get some clean towels and a bucket of cool water. Do you hear me?' April pointed at the pub on the opposite side of the street, briefly noting that this was the pub she'd been in that awful night Norm had tried to get A.J. arrested. Pushing the thoughts aside, she started tending to the woman, ripping away her smouldering clothes and talking to her in a calm voice.

'Hello, love, can you hear me? Just you relax, we'll have you safe and sound at the hospital in a jiffy.' She prayed silently that the ambulance would arrive soon. The poor woman had woken up and was groaning and crying in agony.

The girl returned with soaked towels and a bowl of water and April proceeded to wrap them around the poor woman's head. 'Go back. I need more. They're bringing someone else out in a minute,' she ordered. The girl scurried off to do her bidding.

Just then, there was a shout as the firemen emerged carrying another, larger figure. His clothes were smouldering and, like his wife, his hair had been completely burned away. Staggering behind him, April gasped as she noticed

347

a familiar figure. Was that . . . ? Surely not. What was *she* doing here?

She ran over and put her arm around the figure. She was choking and spluttering, and though her face was smudged with dirt, she didn't appear to be burned.

'Bess! Can you hear me? What are you doing here?'

'Was in pub . . .' Bess coughed some more. 'Came to help.' She dropped to her knees, coughing so much she was sick.

'Bess, you've inhaled too much smoke. Soon as the ambulance gets here, you need to get to hospital. All right?'

Bess nodded and sat on the ground. But there was no time to treat her. The man needed her attention much more so she turned back to him, repeating the treatment she'd given his wife, wrapping as much of him as she could in the cool, wet towels.

She went back to check on the woman, who had passed out again, but she wasn't as badly injured as her husband. Ordering the girl to watch her and call her should there be a problem, she returned to the man, who was starting to cough. It must be agony for him, she reflected, with his burned lips. She tried to bathe them in water again, to relieve some of the pain, whispering soothingly all the while.

'All right, sir, you just hang on. You'll be safe in a moment. Help is on its way.'

Suddenly she heard a shout. 'April! Get away from there, the building is going to collapse!'

Looking up in surprise, she saw that whoever had shouted was correct. The fire crews were falling back, and the walls of the terrace were slowly starting to crumble.

'Someone, help me lift this man,' she shouted in panic. She could not leave her patient. A strong pair of arms reached down and lifted the man, carrying him away from the building and placing him gently on the pavement, away from harm. April followed, while another fireman carried his wife over, the sobbing girl following behind them.

'Thank you!' She looked up and saw the last person on earth she expected to see at that very moment. The man she loved more than he would ever know. *Crawford*. But he was already rushing back and she saw him reach Bess's crumpled figure. He bent down and gently lifted her in his arms. She was clearly unconscious, and April felt a stab of guilt at not paying more attention to her. Crawford laid Bess down beside the man, then looked at her anxiously.

'Are you all right? Are you injured at all?'

'I'm fine. But what are you doing here?' She glanced at Bess, lying pale and motionless, then back at Crawford. 'Oh. You were together?'

Crawford nodded and April felt her heart shatter, but she pushed the feelings away. This was no time to fall apart. She was a nurse, and as such she had to keep her cool, no matter what the situation. She bent down to check Bess's vitals.

'April, it's not what you think.' He put a hand on her arm gently.

'It's none of my business. You made that perfectly clear. If you'll excuse me, I need to tend to these people while we wait for the ambulance.'

In the distance she heard the ringing of the ambulance as it made its way towards them. Thank God. She didn't think she could bear to be here much longer.

Once the patients, including Bess, had been loaded into the van, April looked around for her bike. The fire looked like it was under control at long last and with the all-clear sounding, people were emerging from the various shelters and milling around the site of the fire. There was nothing more she could do. She needed to get home before she broke down completely. The fact that Crawford hadn't wanted to see her because of Theo was one thing, but the thought that he had been seeing Bess . . .

'April! Wait up!' Crawford ran up to her and caught her arm, turning her towards him. 'Hey. Are you OK? You sure you're not hurt?'

She shook him off. 'I'm fine, Crawford. Just tired. I need to get back. Mrs Teague will be worried about me.'

'Let me take you. My jeep's just round the corner. Assuming it's not been damaged.'

'No. I can manage, major. I just need to find my bike.'

'April, I—'

'Like I said, there's nothing to explain. Sorry, but I'm very tired. I worked some extra hours, and now I can't think straight.'

'You can't cycle home in this state. Come on, I won't hear any more arguments.'

Feeling too tired to protest any more, April allowed him to lead her back along the ruined street and on to the high street, which was, surprisingly, untouched. Around them, the endless bells of the ambulances and fire engines still rang out, and people were running to and fro, searching for loved ones and examining the damage. Considering the suddenness of the attack, April thought they were remarkably calm. But then they'd all

350

learned to live with this sort of thing over the years. It was amazing what people could get used to.

Crawford opened the door and helped her inside the jeep. She sat down and leaned her head against the window. Relieved, despite the uncomfortable silence, not to be cycling back up the hill in the frosty darkness.

They soon stopped outside Mrs Teague's. The black-out curtains were drawn and the street was in darkness. She couldn't tell whether her landlady was there or not. Fishing out her key, she opened the door.

'Hello? Mrs Teague, I'm back. Are you all right?'

There was no answer – she must have gone to the shelter or she was with Mrs Beetie. At least, she hoped that was where she was; she couldn't imagine that Mrs Teague would have been anywhere near the town.

April took off her coat and made her way to the kitchen. Her throat was dry and her clothes smelled of smoke. She needed some water. To her dismay, Crawford had followed her inside and watched as she hunted out two glasses and turned on the taps.

'I imagine your throat must feel a bit like mine. Here you are.'

Their fingers brushed as she handed the glass to him, and she shivered, remembering the kisses they'd shared and how they'd made her feel. Had he made Bess feel like that too? Could it really be possible that he'd dismissed her from his mind so quickly? Considering what he'd written to her, she'd like to think that wasn't the case, but she couldn't deny the evidence of her own eyes.

Crawford took the glass in silence and drank the water. 'Thank you. I needed that. And, though you may not believe me, I'm so glad to see you, April. I nearly died of fright when I saw your hair shining in the flames.'

'Well, as you can see, I'm quite all right. Although I can't say the same for Bess.'

'She was a real heroine. She refused to go to the shelter in case she was needed, and when the flames came and she heard screaming, she dashed into that house before I could stop her.'

Despite the fact that his words were clearly true, April felt a rush of jealousy course through her. Bloody Bess. Yet again sticking in her nose, causing trouble, and now she was trying to win Crawford. It was unlike her, but she wanted to throttle her. How dare she do this to her. Again.

Trying to keep her thoughts to herself, she forced herself to say something nice. 'Maybe you should get up to the hospital so you can be there when she wakes up?'

Crawford let out a short bark of laughter. 'I doubt she wants to see me, honey. Like I said, it's not what you're clearly thinking. I meant every word of what I wrote in those letters. When Bess told me you'd gone to get married ... Married, April! Can you imagine what that felt like?' He closed his eyes for a moment, as if remembering. When he opened them, there was such a wealth of hurt in his eyes that April felt herself flush with guilt and sorrow.

'I was never going to get married, Crawford.'

'I know that now, but those words hit me like the bomb that dropped on the hospital. The bottom fell out of my world and I was so furious with you. Why couldn't you trust me, honey?'

352

'I'm sorry. I should have explained the whole situation with Theo, but somehow I could never bring myself to do it. I didn't want you to think badly of me. Although, me and Theo, we were just childhood sweethearts. It had been over long before I met you. But he'd decided he wanted me back. That's all it ever was.'

'You told me he was like a brother to you. I wouldn't have minded if you'd told me he was something more. We all have a past. Hell, I had a childhood sweetheart too.'

'I came to see you yesterday, but the guards refused to even contact you. Said you'd told them you weren't to be disturbed under any circumstances.'

'So it was you! I thought I was seeing things. Oh, honey, it wasn't you I was trying to keep out, it was Bess. She'd been coming up so often after she told me you were getting married that I had to do something to keep her away from me.'

'But why? I don't understand. She'd already done the damage; surely she didn't think she could win you over, did she? Hang on, she told me that she'd been going up to see you to tell you the truth.'

'Another lie, I think. She is a very determined woman. Seems she'd set her heart on marrying an officer, and I was the lucky officer she chose. Red told me she was always asking him questions about me and it made him uncomfortable, so he had to drop her.' He shook his head. 'Poor girl. I was harsh on her tonight.'

'What happened?'

'She came into the pub all dolled up, like she knew I'd be there. I have no idea how. She sat beside me and started telling me that if I wanted to kiss her, I'd have to be quick as she was joining the military. Well . . . I wasn't very gentlemanly, I'm afraid. Told her you were worth ten of her. That I wouldn't touch her if she was the last woman on earth. Then the bombs came, and she was off like a flash. I hope she's not badly hurt.'

April's heart stopped for a moment. 'Do you really mean that?'

'What, that I wouldn't touch her if she was the last woman on earth?'

'No. The other bit.'

'Yes, honey, I do. I always knew it. I just needed time to come to terms with a few things. But tonight has forced me to see it quicker. I'm sorry I hurt you.'

'And I'm sorry I hurt you. It's the last thing I ever wanted to do.' She stroked his cheek.

'Oh, April. What you do to me. Even when I was angry with you, my heart refused to hate you. Can you forgive me for being such a boar?'

'Can you forgive me for not telling you about Theo?'

'I'm getting there, honey. I overreacted a bit, I know. But these feelings I have are so strong. It was as if someone had come along and ripped out my heart.'

'Does that mean you still want to see me?'

'Will you have me?'

'I told you in my letter, Crawford. I'll always be here, waiting for you to forgive me.'

'I forgave you long ago. It was my ego that was keeping me from talking to you. Oh, darlin', we can never fall out like this again. Do you promise?'

April wound her arms around his neck. 'I promise, major. Never, ever again will I give you cause to doubt me.'

'Nor I you.' He kissed her then, a long, sweet kiss that left April feeling breathless. She drew in a breath and started to cough.

Swiftly he reached for the water. 'What am I thinking? Look at us! Covered in soot and stinking of smoke. What is it about us being together that sets the world on fire?'

April started to laugh, then she coughed some more, forcing Crawford to slap her on the back. 'Come on, honey, now isn't the time. We've got the rest of our lives to make it up to each other for the past weeks. But you need to wash and get to bed. And so do I. Can I see you tomorrow?'

'Come to the hospital at eight. I'll be finishing then. Can you do that?'

'I wouldn't miss it for the world.' He kissed her again, more deeply this time. Then he pushed her gently away. 'I need to go. Tomorrow, April. That's a promise.'

She walked with him to the door, and as soon as she opened it, the smell of smoke and the noise of sirens came rushing in. She'd almost forgotten it had happened. Being with Crawford always seemed to have that effect on her. It was as if the world disappeared and it was just the two of them again.

Once he was gone, she walked back into the house, her heart full and, despite the terror of the evening, a huge smile on her face. She should wait for Mrs Teague to return; the poor woman would probably be beside herself. But it was long past midnight and she was too tired. Instead, she wrote a note for her and left it on the hall table, where she would hopefully see it when she got back from the shelter.

Then, after washing in cold water, she leaped, shivering, under the covers. How quickly life could change. It was a lesson she'd learned over and over again during this hateful war, and if Crawford truly wanted her, then she would let go of her hurt and grab this love, and pray it wasn't ripped away from her. Ever again.

Chapter 35

For the first time in a very long while, April woke feeling refreshed and happy, she felt completely recovered and she hadn't had any horrible dreams. As she lay there, memories of the night before slowly drifted back into her mind. Crawford still loved her! He forgave her! She hugged her pillow, wishing he was here beside her, no matter how inappropriate that might be.

Jumping up, she rushed to get dressed and ran down to the kitchen, where she could hear Mrs Teague. 'Oh, thank goodness you're all right, Mrs Teague. I was worried when you weren't here last night, but I thought you must be at the shelter. Are you all right?'

'You were worried? Imagine how I was feeling. After the all-clear sounded, I came home and realised you weren't here. I was beside myself, so I went round to the Beeties in tears. When I came back again I found your lovely note. I have never been more relieved in my life. Tell me everything that happened.'

'Oh, it was the most wonderful night.'

Mrs Teague arched her brow sceptically. 'I wouldn't have put it quite that way, dear.'

April couldn't contain herself any longer, and the entire story came pouring out.

'Oh, how romantic! Didn't I tell you to trust in the major? You should listen to your old landlady, she's rarely wrong about matters of the heart. I am *so* happy for you. And once again you're a heroine. So brave, you are, my love. I couldn't be prouder.'

The memory of Bess coughing and spluttering as she came out of the burning building sobered April momentarily. She needed to be at the hospital early so she could check on her.

Leaping up, she kissed Mrs Teague on the cheek and ran to get her coat. 'Got to go. See you later!'

'See you later, my dear. And do say I'll be invited to the wedding.'

April laughed. 'We're not quite there yet! We've only known each other a few months, don't forget.'

'Three weeks! Remember I told you it was only three weeks for me and Isaac. Grasp your chance of happiness while you can, dear. Don't let a silly little thing like time get in your way.'

∽

April found herself grinning all the way to the hospital, even though the weather had turned from clear and cold the day before to drizzly and grey again. She had to walk as her bike had been left somewhere in town. Or rather Mrs Teague's bike. She needed to find that as soon as possible. There was no way she could afford to buy a new one.

'Sara, do you know where Bess was taken last night?' April asked at reception when she got to the hospital.

'Oh, April, wasn't it horrible?' She shivered. 'Brought back the most awful memories of when the hospital was bombed.' She consulted the papers in front of her. 'Ah, here we are. She's in Nightingale Ward. Apparently she's doing well. Just a bit of smoke inhalation.'

April rushed off. When she entered the ward, she greeted the sister with a nod and asked after Bess.

'Go and see for yourself. She's had a bit of breathing difficulty, but no lasting damage, I don't think. Foolish girl. You can see she'll be well-suited to nursing on the front line.'

April murmured her agreement and walked down the rows of beds until she spotted her, lying propped up against the pillows to aid her breathing, with an oxygen mask over her face. She touched her hand gently, and Bess's eyes flew open. Removing the mask, she looked at April sullenly.

'What are *you* doing here?'

'I just came to check you're all right.'

'As if you care.'

'Of course I care, Bess. I was terrified when you came running out of that building. You were so brave! You could have died.'

Bess closed her eyes wearily. 'I wish I had.' April was shocked to see a tear trickle down her cheek.

'Hey, what's wrong? Everyone's calling you a heroine.'

'Really? I don't care.' She coughed and put the mask back in place. When she'd recovered slightly, she took it off again. 'Honestly, I wish you weren't so bloody nice all the time. You do know why I was at the pub, don't you?'

'I have an idea. You went to find Crawford. Why?'

'Why do you think? I *want* that man, but it seems he doesn't want me. They never do. My mother did tell me I'd never find a decent man after . . .' She trailed off.

April's heart squeezed. How could a mother be so cruel? 'After what, Bess?'

Bess sighed. 'My mother's always been a difficult woman, but she threw me out when I was fifteen. I got into trouble with a man. One of the teachers at my school. I thought he loved me and let him do things he shouldn't have . . . How was I to know the man was married already? I thought if I let him, he'd love me. Turns out I was wrong. I sent him letters, so many letters, and one of my classmates found one when she saw me putting it in his desk. She took it to the headmaster, and I was expelled. He didn't have to leave, though, did he? He stayed there and no doubt took advantage of some other poor, naïve fool.'

'Oh, Bess. You were so young. He took advantage of you. That wasn't your fault.'

'Yes, well, I came to live with my nan, God bless her, and my mother hasn't spoken to me since. I always think that if I just let a man know how much I like them, they might like me back. Just a bit. But it never works. Turns out men find me a nuisance once they get what they want. My mum was right. I'm not really good enough for any man.'

'That's nonsense. There'll be the right man for you, you mark my words. You just need to maybe . . .' April paused, wanting to choose her words carefully. 'Take it calmly. Maybe make them wait a bit, make them chase you.'

'That's all right for you to say. You only have to look at someone and they fall at your feet. Girls like me, well, we need to work a bit harder. But your major made sure

I was very certain of one thing: he's not interested in me. No matter what I do or say about you, he still wants you.'

'Oh, Bess.' April squeezed her hand. 'I think, despite everything, you're incredibly brave. Look what you did last night. And look how you managed to rebuild your life after what happened.'

'For God's sake, April. Don't you understand? I tried to seduce Crawford!'

April swallowed. She had known, but she didn't want to think about it. 'Well, that's in the past. You've got a brand new and exciting future ahead of you.'

Bess coughed again. 'Oh, go away, will you? I can't stand your sympathy. Easy for you, isn't it? You've got everything you want. Well, good luck to you, but I don't need to see you again. Once they release me, I'll stay with my nan before I leave. My time here is over, and I can't say I'm sorry. The only people I'll miss are Nancy and Eunice.' She gave a bitter laugh. 'Jesus, even Nancy managed to find a man to love her and her behaviour has been even worse than mine. Just goes to show. Some people deserve it and others don't. Seems I don't.'

'Well, your friends here will miss you.' Despite the fact that her heart went out to her, especially as she was looking so frail and sad, she couldn't quite bring herself to lie and say she'd miss her too.

∽

For the rest of the day, despite the endless congratulations she received from the other staff, April felt preoccupied with what Bess had told her. She felt desperately sorry for the other girl's endless search for love and she wondered if she would ever find someone patient enough to help her. She had so much to give, but despite her fiery nature and her loyalty to her friends, April found it difficult to forgive her for the damage she'd almost caused.

She was mulling things over as she left the hospital that evening when she heard a familiar voice.

'Going my way?'

'Crawford!' She leaped into his arms. 'What are you doing here?'

'Waiting to walk my girl home, just like you asked.'

'How could I have forgotten!'

'Yes, how could you? I never forget a word you say.'

'Not one word?'

'Every utterance that comes out of your mouth is burned on my brain.'

She arched a brow at him. 'Really? What was the first thing I ever said to you?'

'You said, "This way, major".' He grinned, pleased with himself.

'Did I?"

He smirked. 'You think I'm that sappy? I can't remember *that*, but figured because you wouldn't remember either it didn't really matter.'

'Why you . . .' She smacked him on the arm and laughed, then linked her hand with his.

They walked, talking of the night before and what it had meant to them. April told him about her visit to Bess, and Crawford shook his head.

'Poor Bess. I hope she finds someone who can handle her. Though it'll take a pretty strong and patient guy to put up with all her insecurities. Still, she's a brave one,

I'll give her that. But, like you, I find it hard to forgive her for nearly ruining my chances with you and putting me through all that heartache. I tell you, April, I was a boar when I thought you'd betrayed me. The men did their best to stay away from me and the colonel had to take me aside and tell me to pull myself together. It wasn't easy. I couldn't understand how I could have been so stupid as to let a girl treat me like a fool.' He sighed. 'When Bess told me you'd gone to London, I vowed I would never let you do that to me again, so I let my head rule my heart, April. I knew in my heart you weren't like that. I should remember to always listen to my heart.'

'You most certainly should, major. I refuse to let you push me away ever again. I've learned a thing or two about persistence from Bess, and if you do that to me again, I shall sneak on to your base and personally knock some sense into you.'

'Hmm, I like the sound of that. Think I might give it a go.'

April laughed again and hugged his arm. Just being with Crawford made the world seem a better place.

As they neared Mrs Teague's house, April asked, 'Have you heard from A.J. at all? I saw him, you know, and he was devastated. I tried to persuade him to visit Eunice and talk to her, but I've not had the chance to visit. Which, by the way, is your fault. If you hadn't soaked me by driving through a puddle that day, I might have had the energy to think of something other than my broken heart.'

Crawford stopped and pulled her into him, kissing the top of her head. 'Oh, April, please don't remind me. I'm so sorry. But that soaking was not my fault. That was the driver's work, and he was very sorry about it. He wanted to stop, but I wouldn't let him. My stupid pride.'

'I thought you were a gentleman. But now I see it's all an act to get what you want.'

He smiled slyly. 'It's worked, hasn't it?' Then his tone became more serious. 'I haven't seen A.J. You know we're kept very separate. But I can't deny I'm worried. Last time I saw him, he was a broken man.'

'Do you think you could take me to see Eunice one day? In your jeep, if you're allowed?'

'You wanna go now?'

'Now? But how? You don't have your car.'

'Sure I do. I always have one if I want one. It's parked at Mrs Teague's. I figured I'd be leaving from hers.'

'Oh, yes, please. I'm so worried about the whole situation and I feel like I'm partly responsible.'

They reached Mrs Teague's door, and April popped in quickly to let her know she'd be late. Then she was out again in a flash.

'Let's go!'

While they drove, they talked about what was in store for A.J. and Eunice.

'You know, I'm afraid that even if A.J. can forgive Eunice, she won't marry him. She's worried that she'll ruin his life and he'll always resent her.'

'She's right that there are many obstacles in their path. It shows how much Eunice must love him. But she doesn't actually know how the Timpsons will feel. They're good people, who just want the best for A.J. He's the living heart of his family, though, and it's not a decision that he can take lightly. He's already got a place at university.'

'I don't understand, if coloured people can go to the same universities as white people, why can't they marry?'

'No, honey, I'm afraid there are universities that have been set up for coloured people. It's a crazy system and fills me with shame. You know he could leave the US Army when this tour is over . . .' He was quiet for a moment and April filled in the missing words in her head. *If we survive*. 'And maybe he could go to an English college, and get a degree here. Don't think England has crazy rules like we do in the US, so he would be accepted at any university here, I imagine. That would work in his favour. But Eunice is right, he will be stuck here. It's an impossible situation.'

'And not helped by Mrs Granger, who's refusing to accept that Eunice will have a coloured baby. Honestly, Nancy's mother seems completely fine with the idea that she and Homer might settle down, and she can't be the only one. Think about how those people in the pub helped that night. Seems people here don't care as much about colour as people in America. Maybe we can persuade her to accept him.'

'Maybe. I sure have loved seeing the difference in acceptance here. Though clearly some people don't feel the same way, even here.'

They drove the rest of the way in silence. Crawford had to concentrate hard on the dark roads as there were no streetlamps and he wasn't allowed to use his headlights due to the blackout, so it was treacherous, especially down the narrow country lanes. April's heart warmed at the trouble he was taking to help, and if it was possible, it made her love him even more.

∽

When they reached Eunice's house, April walked up to the door nervously. She dreaded the reception she might get from Mrs Granger, and prayed fervently that she'd calmed down since she'd last seen her. Taking a deep breath, she knocked on the door. Mrs Granger answered, and April was pleased to see she looked a little calmer than she had the last time she'd been there. April hoped she was coming to terms with all the blows life had dealt her recently.

'April! Come in. Do you want to see Eunice? She's resting right now, but I'm sure she'd be happy to see you.'

'How are you, Mrs Granger?'

She pursed her lips. 'Bearing up, I suppose. My boy, George, is coming home on leave, so that's helped me. But still no news of Mr Granger.'

April patted her on the arm. 'I really hope you hear something soon.'

'Yes, but what on earth will he think when he gets back? All this scandal and Eunice pregnant and out of a job—' She stopped abruptly, before continuing. 'But I've been taking great comfort in the Bible. In particular Job. If he could bear his troubles, I can bear mine. God only gives us what he thinks we can deal with.' Suddenly she noticed Crawford looming behind April. 'Good heavens, who do we have here?'

Crawford moved into the hallway and Mrs Granger smiled genuinely for the first time. 'Why, it's the handsome major. Welcome to my home.'

'Thank you, ma'am. April has been concerned about your daughter, so I brought her to check up on her.'

Mrs Granger turned and called up the stairs. 'Eunice! More visitors for you.'

'More visitors? Has she been getting many?'

'That Nancy's been by. Apparently she's walking out with a friend of A.J.'s, so at least Eunice isn't alone in that. And A.J.'s visited a few times now. Seems he and Eunice are reaching an understanding, so what can I do?' She sighed dramatically. 'I don't like it, but if the alternative is losing my daughter, then I must accept it. I can't lose her as well as my husband. And what if something happened to George? I'd have no one.'

As a reason for accepting A.J., it left a little to be desired in terms of warmth, but it was certainly a lot more promising than her attitude the last time April had come.

Just then Eunice came down the stairs. She looked a great deal better, and April noticed her stomach was starting to bulge. '

April! Oh, I'm happy to see you. And major! What a wonderful surprise. Come in.'

Once they'd settled in the sitting room, Mrs Granger went to make tea.

'How are you? I hear A.J.'s been to visit?'

'Yes, he's been a few times.'

'And?'

Eunice held out her left hand; on it was a gold ring with a small sapphire.

'Oh, Eunice, I'm so glad!'

Eunice looked sad for a moment. 'Well, it's the only solution. He hasn't forgiven me for what I did yet. But he's trying. For the baby's sake.'

'He'll come round, just give him time. When are you getting married?'

'Around Christmas time, I think. When A.J. can get a moment off.'

'But where will you live?'

'I'll stay here and he will live at the base, as normal. Nothing much will change, you know. And once the war's over, who knows what will happen?'

Crawford interjected then. 'Congratulations, Eunice. I hope you know how lucky you are to have snared a guy like A.J. Not many like him around.'

Mrs Granger came in at that moment. 'You know him well, major?'

'Known him since childhood, ma'am, and I promise you, your daughter will want for nothing.'

She didn't look convinced. 'Hmm. We'll just have to wait and see, won't we? Right, who's for tea?'

After they'd had their drinks, April suggested she and Eunice go upstairs so she could examine her. Once in the bedroom, she felt around Eunice's stomach.

'It all seems fine, Eunice. But tell me, how are you *really*?'

Tears came to her eyes then. 'It's been horrible. Things are calming down, but Mother still doesn't really accept him. And I'm just not sure it's the right thing to do. He doesn't seem to love me any more. Not the way he used to. Remember the letter he wrote to me? Well, it's like being with a different man.'

April hugged her friend tightly. 'Like I said, give him time. It might take a while for him to get over what happened, but once the baby's here, maybe his feelings will soften.'

'I tried very hard to refuse his proposal, but he said I owed him. And I do. How can I deprive him of his child?'

'He's right, Eunice. You do owe him. You've got a lot of making up to do, but it'll be all right in the end. You'll see.'

When they got back to the sitting room, Crawford had worked his magic and Mrs Granger was simpering at him. April rolled her eyes at Eunice, who grinned with delight. It was the first genuine smile she'd seen from her all evening and it filled April with hope that Eunice was strong enough to face what was coming.

Crawford stood when he saw them in the doorway. 'You ready to go, April? I need to get back and you have another early start.'

'So delightful to have you here, major. Please do pop in any time you like.'

Crawford tipped his hat. 'Thank you, ma'am. And please, call me Crawford.'

Mrs Granger fluttered her eyelashes. 'Thank you for coming, Crawford. And shall I pass your good wishes to A.J. when he comes?'

'Please do, ma'am. Tell him not to be a stranger.'

'Fancy A.J. being friends with an officer. Makes me see him in a whole different light.'

'He's a very fine man. You should be proud to call him your son.'

April could see that the magic hadn't gone quite that far, as Mrs Granger suddenly became brisk. 'Yes, well. Good night, you two. Hopefully we'll see you soon.'

Eunice walked them to the door and gave April a hug. Then she turned to Crawford. 'Thank you! I think you've had more influence on helping her accept this marriage than the thought of having an illegitimate grandchild.'

'I hope so. I meant every word. You're a lucky girl.'

Eunice looked down. 'I know. I just hope that one day he can love me again.'

Chapter 36

As the day of the Thanksgiving dinner approached, April found she was in a flurry of excitement, as were some of the other nurses who had also been invited. After being brought so low, she couldn't believe how happy she was now. Crawford tried to meet her after work almost every day, and they spent hours sitting in Mrs Teague's sitting room, kissing and talking. Mrs Teague always tactfully withdrew with a knowing smile when he arrived, which April appreciated.

The day before the dinner, April decided to go into town during her break to see if she could find some lipstick for tomorrow night. She doubted she would, but it was worth a look all the same. She'd be wearing the beautiful green dress that she'd worn for her first dinner with Crawford all those weeks ago, and though she wished she could buy something new, the dress held such happy memories that she thought it was probably exactly the right thing to wear. However, a nice lipstick might make all the difference.

As she walked into town, she noticed a large number of American trucks driving past. Over the past few weeks, there had been a new influx of G.I.s coming into

Truro, speeding through the town, chatting up the girls and generally causing mayhem amongst the local population. Today there seemed to be even more of them, and she wondered where on earth they were all going to stay.

As she drew near Victoria Square, she saw a crowd of people. A lot of them were laughing, others looked alarmed. Curious, she drew closer and saw, to her utter astonishment, what looked to be a truck with a boat attached to the back. Clearly, the driver had taken a wrong turn and the narrow streets of Truro were not built for such an enormous vehicle.

She walked over and joined the crowd. 'What on earth happened?' she asked a man standing beside her.

'Stupid bugger got stuck. Can't go forward, can't go back.' He rolled his eyes. 'And these are the people who are going to help us win the war. God help us! And what do they need with the boat, anyway? Plenty of boats in Cornwall already.' He tutted in disapproval.

Suddenly the crowd gasped in astonishment and April watched as a massive mechanical arm appeared over the rooftops. It was lowered towards the amphibious craft as the G.I.s shouted and gesticulated and finally managed to attach the huge claw to the boat.

'That thing's never gonna lift it!' a voice said, and the crowd gasped as the arm slowly rose, bringing the craft with it and swinging it over the rooftops. A child screamed in terror, and somebody shouted, 'Take cover, everyone! Who needs the Nazis when we've got the Americans!'

April was transfixed. She'd never seen such an enormous crane in her life. Nor a boat like this one: long and flat and grey. What on earth were they going to do with it?

Soon the craft was safely secured to another lorry in the next street and the red-faced driver got back in his cab, amidst a volley of laughter and commentary from the crowd.

'Better than the pictures, any day,' a woman said. 'I don't know, though. These Americans are causing nothing but trouble. Killed all the fish up in Hendra as well. Shampoo.' She shook her head.

'Shampoo?'

'Wash their hair so much all the bubbles killed the fish. I heard some poor bugger got lost in the bubbles on the way back from the pub. Twenty foot high, they were, so they say. Fire brigade had to come out and hose them away.'

April giggled. 'No! I can't believe that.'

'Ask anyone, love. They'll tell you.'

April walked away, smiling to herself. She'd have to ask Crawford when she saw him. She simply couldn't believe a man could get lost in bubbles from the Americans' shampoo. Then again, before today, she'd never have believed that a huge boat could be swung over the rooftops either.

April was full of what she'd seen when she got back, and to her gratification, there were gasps of amazement. It seemed the shampoo incident was true too, and it kept the patients and nurses amused for the rest of the day.

Crawford was not outside the hospital when she left, much to her disappointment, so she walked home alone. She had still not been able to find the bike, and she worried constantly about how she was going to replace it.

Mrs Teague was stirring soup in the kitchen when she got in. 'Touch of frost in the air, my lovely, so I thought a good warming broth would be just the thing. Now, before I forget, there's something for you on the mantelpiece – hand-delivered, it was.'

Curious, April went into the sitting room and picked up the packet. She brought it back to the table, where Mrs Teague was already sitting down and eating her soup. She watched as April carefully opened the parcel, trying to save as much of the wrapping paper as possible. Inside was a small, rectangular cardboard box. She lifted off the lid and gasped.

'Oh, how very lovely. Look.'

Inside the box was a very fine gold chain and suspended from it was a heart-shaped locket. The word 'April', in lovely flowing letters, was etched on the front.

'Open it, open it,' breathed Mrs Teague, who was almost as happy as April.

Inside there was a small folded piece of paper.

I hope you like this little gift. I wanted to do much better but this was all I could find. It's for pictures of your favourite people. If I had a locket, I know who I'd put there. I'll pick you up at 6.30 tomorrow. Be ready.
    I love you, April Harvey.
    Crawford

'Oh, it's so lovely.' April fastened the necklace around her neck excitedly. 'What should I put in here?'

'Well, if you don't know, I'm not going to tell you. Honestly, the way you two have been these past few days,

I'm hearing wedding bells. Oh, it's so romantic.' Mrs Teague clasped her hands.

'Maybe I'll put a photograph of you inside my locket.'

'Don't be silly, love. There's only one person to put in there.'

April smiled. Yes, there was only one person she wanted in her locket. The man who made her heart beat faster and made her feel like the luckiest girl alive.

They washed the dishes together, like mother and daughter, April thought. It was wonderful to enjoy such a simple task. If she went to America with Crawford, she would miss Mrs Teague.

And if my mother had lived, she thought, I would have had to say goodbye to her too.

She touched the necklace around her neck. But she could write to Mrs Teague and maybe she could come and visit. As long as she and Crawford were together, that was all that mattered.

On the day of the Thanksgiving dinner, April had a rare day off. After working for ten days solidly because of the staff shortages, she allowed herself the luxury of lying in bed late, feeling the anticipation fizz in her stomach. She simply couldn't wait for the evening. She didn't care much about the dinner, really. All she wanted was to be with Crawford, to see his smile, hear his voice. But though she was happier than she had ever thought possible, it was tinged with sadness. Theo was still on her mind and she realised she hadn't heard anything from the Osbornes or him since she'd got back; though she had written as often as she could, there'd been no reply. She remembered the dream she'd had about him, when he was crying and looking for her, and her stomach clenched with anxiety. Was that a sign? Surely the Osbornes would have telegraphed her if something had happened to him?

She decided that she would try to telephone the reverend. But not today. If she heard bad news today, it would ruin the evening.

⁓

By six fifteen, April was all spruced up in her green dress and Mrs Teague's gold shoes. Her beautiful locket hung perfectly over the collar, and her hair was rolled to perfection. After all the excitement with the boat in the street, she'd forgotten to look for lipstick, but Mrs Teague had given her some of hers. She was as ready as she'd ever be. She fiddled nervously with the locket as she and Mrs Teague stared out of the window, watching for Crawford. She'd be meeting his colleagues and the colonel this evening and she desperately wanted to make a good impression. She paced away, sat down on the sofa, then stood up once more.

'Well, my lovely, there's a handsome prince at the gate and a carriage on the road. No, you sit until he rings the bell. He's on his way up the path and, my goodness, there's gold braid on his shoulders and medals on his chest. He's in some brownish uniform. Oh, he does look splendid!'

A moment later the bell rang and Mrs Teague hurried to open the door. April followed her out.

'Mrs Teague, a corsage for you.' Crawford handed her a small, clear box containing a purple flower.

'Good gracious, major, is that a real orchid?'

'I hope so, ma'am. And this one is for the belle of the ball.' He turned to April. 'It's a gardenia, honey. They symbolise purity and love. My mom grows them at home and I thought it was just perfect for you.'

'Oh, this is beautiful and such a glorious perfume. Thank you.'

'Then we best go. I'll bring her back safe and sound, Mrs Teague.'

'Happy Thanksgiving, and have a lovely time.'

∽

For once, Crawford hadn't brought a jeep. Instead he'd managed to find a taxi, which April was sure would cost a fortune. Still, she refused to worry about things like that tonight. This was an evening for celebration and happiness.

When they arrived at Pencalenick House, April saw that a huge tent had been erected in the grounds and hung with fairy lights. Crawford took her hand and led her in. April caught her breath. It was undeniably stunning, decorated with real and artificial pumpkins of various sizes; each of the real ones had been carved and there were candles burning inside them. She'd never seen anything like it and was fascinated. Flamboyant paper turkeys seemed to strut across every table.

Crawford led her through the crowd to their designated table and April looked around to see if there was anyone she recognised, but there didn't seem to be. Crawford introduced her to several other officers and their companions, and she was soon in a conversation with Lieutenant Bowyer, a married officer who was happy to talk about his wife, his children and his home in Florida through the first course. April listened politely, barely able to get a word in edgeways – which she was rather relieved about as she still felt a little overwhelmed. He would have continued perfectly happily through the entrée but was nudged by someone and he immediately paid attention to the older woman on his other side.

The food and wine were delicious, and April was sure she'd never eaten so much, and she'd only had the first course! Surely she'd have no room left for the turkey.

Crawford, who was sitting beside her, leaned over and whispered in her ear, 'You OK, honey?'

'Oh, Crawford.' She looked back at him, her eyes shining. 'I've never seen so much food or been any-where this beautiful ever. It's the most glorious night.'

'And I have never sat next to a more beautiful woman than the one I'm with tonight.' He rested his hand on hers and looked deep into her eyes.

April flushed and hit him playfully with her napkin. 'You say such things, but I can't believe that.'

'Believe it, April. I'm the envy of every man in the room.'

She looked at him, lost for words. This man . . . Oh, she didn't even know, but he made her so happy, she could hardly comprehend her luck.

Suddenly, the band, who had been playing all evening, stopped, and there was a drum roll. April looked around, startled, as the turkeys were wheeled in and everyone stood up. Other dishes on the tables were piled high with sea-sonal vegetables from America, for there was corn-on-the cob, fresh lettuce, fresh beans, as well as potatoes prepared in several ways and golden squash, which April had never tasted or even seen before.

'Good grief, Crawford, this could feed the whole of Truro for a week!'

He laughed. 'Relax, enjoy it. Just for one night, let's pretend there's no war on and there is no rationing.'

She smiled and squeezed his hand. 'OK, let's pretend.'

April tucked into her enormous plate of food. It had been years since she'd tasted so many flavours, and she closed her eyes and savoured every mouthful, pretending, just as Crawford had suggested, that life was good and uncomplicated, and out in the world, people weren't being killed.

'Oh, I loved that squash,' she said, as finally, unable to eat anything else, she sat back in her chair.

'I'm never sure whether squash is a member of the pumpkin family or if it's the other way round,' said one of the younger officers, whose date had obviously asked him. 'Major Dunbar, what do you think?'

'I believe they're all gourds, if that helps at all.'

'Boy, am I ever going to write to my seventh-grade teacher,' said another of the younger men. 'She said they were all pumpkins. I forgive her, though, she was from New York. What would she know about farming?'

Everyone laughed and that was the atmosphere of the evening. The men were perfectly well aware of their place in the hierarchy but they were able to laugh, joke and tease one another without fear of offending anyone.

Pumpkin, cranberry and pecan pies followed the main course, but there was also a deep glass bowl of oranges and, for those who wanted, fresh custard or ice cream.

'Enjoy the meal, honey?' Crawford asked as the waiting staff offered coffee, tea and after-dinner drinks. 'There'll be dancing just as soon as the tables are cleared. I'd like something slow and smooth.'

'I was promised the jitterbug,' teased April.

'After all that food?'

'Manners, major.'

'OK, but before I go ask for a jitterbug for you, do you mind if we just walk out for a moment, because if I don't kiss you, Miss Harvey, I will definitely combust.'

'Oh dear, I missed the lecture on dealing with the aftermath of patient combustion.'

He laughed, grabbed her hand and they went out into the cold November evening. Immediately he pulled her into his arms.

'Kissing's the only cure,' he said as he took off his jacket and wrapped it around her shoulders.

'Well, just in case, we better do it a bit more,' she whispered.

By the time they wandered back in, the coffee was finished and the band was playing dreamy dance music. Crawford pulled April into his arms and they joined the others. April's heart was so full, she was sure it would burst, and when the band started playing 'Cheek to Cheek', one of April's favourite songs, she started to sing along.

Crawford bent his head to hers and joined in.

She looked up at him and smiled when she saw the warmth and tenderness in his eyes. It was true, she really had found the happiness she'd been looking for in Crawford's arms. She wasn't sure anything could feel as wonderful again.

But everything good had to end, and to April's dismay, before she knew it, the night was over, and she started to worry about how she would get back.

'Colonel Rivers is lending me a vehicle, April; he knows I'm safe to drive.' Crawford smiled, as if he had understood her concern.

'I wish the night would never end.' April leaned her head on Crawford's shoulder.

'We'll have other nights, just as perfect.'

She sighed. 'I hope so. But nothing is certain, so let's just cherish the memories of this one.'

Crawford brushed her cheek with his finger. 'This has been the very best night of my life, April.' And he kissed her gently on the mouth.

They said goodnight to everyone who was still there and shouts of 'Happy Thanksgiving!' echoed around the huge tent.

Colonel Rivers approached them as they reached the door. 'It was a real pleasure to meet you properly, April. Major Dunbar, you take care of this little lady. She's something special.'

April blushed. 'Thank you for a wonderful evening, colonel. It was a pleasure to meet you too.'

'Excuse me, Crawford,' said the colonel, and kissed April lightly on the cheek. 'And it's Rick, honey.'

'I like Rick, he seems nice,' April said later as they drove leisurely back.

'Yeah. He's a great guy. We'll see him a general one of these days.'

'Do you want to be a general?'

'No way, I'm here because there's a war on.'

They drove in silence for a few minutes more. It was as if they were the only two people in the world right now, and she never wanted the moment to end. She didn't want to go back to her lonely bed; she wanted to be able to stay with Crawford, to wake up with him. Life was too short to waste on doubts, war had taught everyone that, and she wanted to grab this happiness while she had the chance.

They pulled up outside Mrs Teague's house, and as if he'd read her thoughts, Crawford turned to her. 'When the war ends, I'm going back home. Would you think of coming with me, April, far away from everything you know and love?'

April drew in a deep breath. 'I love you, Crawford. I think I'd follow you to the ends of the earth.'

He kissed her deeply, then pulled back. 'I know it seems soon, darlin', but I'm going to ask you anyway. Will you marry me, April, and move home to Carolina with me when all this is over? We can come back to visit, every year, if you want, and Mrs Teague can come visit any time.'

She squealed in delight and stretched up to kiss him tenderly. 'I'll marry you, Crawford Dunbar, and move to wherever you have to be.'

'My mom'll kill me for not waiting, but can we marry soon? I want to make sure you're stuck with me for the rest of my life.'

'Is Christmas too soon?'

'Ah, honey, I want to more than anything, but there's something else I have to tell you. I didn't tell you sooner because I thought it would ruin the evening, but I'm leaving tomorrow, I mean today, and I hope and pray I'll be back before Christmas, and the worst thing is, I may not even be able to send you any letters—'

She put her finger on his lips. 'It doesn't matter, just as long as I know you're coming back to me.'

'Always. So may I tell my folks you said yes?'

'Yes, yes, yes!' she repeated, until after one more kiss he finally tore himself away.

Crawford walked April to the front door, gave her one last long, lingering kiss, then turned and got into the vehicle and drove away. April stood until the sound of the engine had disappeared and then, slowly, she crept into the house.

When she finally lay in bed, memories of the evening came crowding into her mind, and the thought of what she'd just promised Crawford overwhelmed her. What if his family hated her? What if she and Crawford weren't suited after all? Would she be allowed to keep nursing? What if he never came back? How she wished right now that she had a mother to talk to. She adored Mrs Teague and there was no doubt that she was like a mother to her, but she wanted someone who'd known her forever. Who knew all her good points as well as the flaws and loved her anyway. Tears started to fall from her eyes, and turning her head into the pillow, she cried herself to sleep.

Chapter 37

Matrons don't ask if a nurse has had enough sleep when scheduling shifts and April felt absolutely dreadful when she was woken by her alarm clock a few lonely hours later. There was warm water in the bathroom but she washed in the coldest water she could bear and still did not feel ready for a long day ahead.

When she went into the cafeteria for a cup of tea, Nancy was sitting with Mattie and Jean. They all looked up expectantly when April sat down.

'Was it terrific? Describe the food. Describe the men. When are you going to see him again? *Are* you going to see him again?' The questions flew around her tired head like wasps around an open jam jar.

'Later, girls. I had less than four hours' sleep last night.'

'Oh yes? I didn't think you were that sort of girl, April.' Nancy winked at her saucily, and everyone laughed.

April smiled and shook her head at her. She was incorrigible, but she would never forget what a kind heart lay buried beneath the brash exterior.

She managed to avoid a major inquisition on the evening until she got home, where Mrs Teague was waiting for her.

'I've made macaroni and cheese and there are some peaches that Red brought. Now start eating and tell me everything.'

April laughed but did her best. After she'd described everything from the tent, to the food, to the music, she stopped and looked down.

'Is there something you're not telling me?'

April looked up. 'We're going to be married. Crawford wants to marry as soon as possible.'

'Ooooh, my dear. I'm so happy for you! You two are perfect together.'

'And when the war ends he wants us to live in North Carolina.'

'That will be lovely,' she said calmly. 'You'll be able to grow gardenias and possibly even orchids like the ones the major gave me.'

'If we can grow them you'll see them, because you can come and visit any time you like.'

'We'll see, my dear. I'm sure the last thing he'll want is an old woman like me hanging around. Will you move out as soon as you're married?'

April could tell that although she was happy for her, Mrs Teague was holding back tears at the thought of her moving out. She put her hand on her arm. 'Goodness, no. Where would I go? He has to live at the base, and I will carry on nursing. I don't think much will change until the war's over. So I'll be with you a while yet.'

Mrs Teague smiled at that. 'He can stay here any time he likes once you're married. Oh, it will be such fun to have a man in the house again! So when is the happy day going to be? I *must* get a new outfit. And where will you be married?' She chuckled to herself. 'Listen to me. All these questions when you probably don't know yourself yet.'

'Maybe January. He's going away again and he hopes to be back by Christmas. I'd like to get married at St Merryn, so at least I'll be close to my mother. Do you think I should go and talk to the vicar there?'

'I'm sure he'd be delighted. As soon as the major gets back, you two should go up there and ask.'

'It feels so long till I'll see him again. How on earth will I bear all these absences?'

'You'll bear it the way all the other wives and girl-friends and fiancées do. You'll write him lots of lovely letters and, if he should manage to telephone, your voice will smile.'

April thought that over while she ate more macaroni. 'I know what you mean and I do try. I want to be perfect in every way.'

'Oh, April, in all my life I have known many really lovely people but never one, not even my dearest Isaac, who was perfect. We're human – settle for that. Now, when does he leave?'

April's eyes filled with tears. 'I think he's already gone.'

'If you've had enough macaroni, put the plates in the basin while I serve the peaches. Do they grow peaches in North Carolina? I bet they do; there'll be lots of sun there.'

'Yes, I shall be in the garden wearing one of those big, floppy sun hats, tending my gardenias and eating peaches. And you, Mrs Teague, will be sipping lemonade, doing nothing at all except sitting in a comfortable chair, waving a fan and watching me work.'

Mrs Teague laughed delightedly at the thought. 'You'll be like a film star, April. Swanning around, eating whatever you like and never having to worry about bombs again. Oh, life will be wonderful. I'm so happy for you.'

April smiled. She couldn't wait. But for now, she must content herself with whatever time she could get with Crawford and pray he stayed safe.

∞

The weeks after Crawford had left dragged for April. She didn't hear anything from him and she tried not to worry. She did, however, receive a letter from Reverend Osborne, who told her that, all things considered, Theo was as well as could be expected. He told her not to worry about him, and he would send her news if anything changed.

Why won't he write to me himself, April wondered? They were still friends, weren't they? But then, she supposed, if Crawford left for another woman, she would never be able to speak to him again; it would be too painful.

April had elected to work on Christmas Day, but she had Christmas Eve off, as Eunice had written and asked her to come to church with her and her mother. The service was set for 3 p.m., which seemed a strange time to April, but it was Christmas Eve so she imagined that the times were different. Borrowing Mrs Beetie's bicycle, as she still hadn't managed to replace Mrs Teague's, she cycled through the crisp, clear afternoon, anxious to see her friend, who had given nothing away in her letter about how things stood with A.J. and her mother. She also wanted to give her a thorough check-up. Having asked the advice of one of the midwives at the hospital, she'd borrowed a Pinard horn so she could listen to the baby's heartbeat.

She arrived at the church early and went inside, relishing the peace and quiet. It was beautifully decorated with holly and mistletoe, and April sat in quiet contemplation as the organist practised, thinking about the changes this year had brought.

Finally, a few people started to trickle in, and she was surprised when Nancy sat down next to her and gave her a nudge. 'What on earth are you doing here?' She hadn't properly caught up with Nancy for a while, so she was delighted to see her.

'I came with Homer. He's outside with A.J.'

'A.J.'s here? Oh, how wonderful. Does that mean everything's fine between them?'

Nancy winked. 'Apparently. Let's see, shall we?'

April turned and looked to the back of the church. Mrs Granger suddenly appeared, wearing a large hat with a Christmas rose pinned to it. She hurried down the aisle without glancing left or right. But no one else seemed to be coming.

She turned to Nancy. 'What's going on?'

Nancy winked again. 'You'll see. Surprised you didn't know.'

Suddenly the organist started playing the Wedding March, and April looked at Nancy wide-eyed. She had a huge grin on her face, and the penny dropped.

'Oh! Why didn't she tell me!'

'She didn't tell anyone. I only know 'cos Homer told me, and he only knew 'cos he's the best man, although Eunice had asked me to come to church with her today,

which was a bit of a surprise. I mean, *me*? In a church?'
She laughed.

April turned to look again and saw Homer and A.J. looking incredibly smart in their ceremonial uniforms, walking
quickly down the aisle. And just a few minutes later, Eunice,
clutching the arm of a tall, red-haired man in a British
Army sergeant's uniform, and wearing a smart blue suit
with a bouquet of Christmas roses clutched in front of her
stomach, moved slowly towards her husband-to-be. April
was delighted to see she was smiling shyly, and when she
glanced at A.J. she noticed the huge grin on his face. He
looked so proud and in love that her heart sang.

The ceremony was quick but heartfelt, and when they
all left the church, April rushed over to her friend.

'Eunice! Why didn't you tell me? I've been so worried
about you.'

Eunice laughed. 'I wanted it to be a surprise. I'm so
glad you could come. We only wanted our closest friends
and family here. And when I heard George would be here
for Christmas, we decided to do it.'

'It's a shame Bess couldn't be here. Does she know?'

Eunice's face clouded for a moment and she sighed.
'Poor Bess came to see me before she left. I know she did
you a terrible wrong, but she has been a good friend to me
and I can't find it in my heart to be angry with her. She'd
even knitted a little matinée jacket for the baby, would you
believe?'

'Bess, knitting? Now I've heard everything!'

Eunice laughed. 'I know. So, you see, she's not a bad
person, just a little . . . sad, I suppose. I so hope she can
find happiness wherever she's going.'

'So do I. I have been so angry with her, and I doubt we could ever be friends, but I wish things had been different between us. Maybe working in the field will change things for her. She's certainly brave. I admire her in a way. I wish I could be as fierce.'

'I can't imagine you ever being fierce, April. I just hope she stays safe and doesn't do anything foolish. She promised me that she had sworn off men for the duration. Says it's too much trouble and she can't trust herself not to mess things up. Maybe, when she stops searching so hard, she'll find the love she's longing for.'

'I hope so.' April looked over to see George and A.J. standing together, laughing. 'Now, why don't you introduce me to your brother?'

They walked over to them and A.J. gave April a hug. 'Good to see you, April. I'll never forget the part you played in getting us back together. I owe you.'

'You owe me nothing except making sure that you and Eunice are happy for the rest of your lives. What a shame Crawford couldn't be here.'

'I wrote and told him, but don't think he got the letter. Never mind, I've got Homer, and my new best buddy George here.' He clapped George on the shoulder.

George grinned at her. 'So you're the famous April my sis has been telling me so much about? Well, well, if I didn't know you were already taken, I'd be very happy to meet you. As it is, I will have to live with my broken heart for the rest of my life.'

April blushed and Eunice hit him on the arm. 'Stop it, George. You are incorrigible.'

Nancy walked over with Homer and gave Eunice a tight hug. 'I'm so jealous you made it up the aisle before me and Homer.'

Eunice's eyes went wide as she glanced between them. Nancy squealed and held out her left hand to show a small diamond solitaire ring. April and Eunice gasped.

'I don't think I can take much more good news today.' April laughed. 'Homer, you are one very lucky man. Nancy is a catch.'

'I'm the lucky one, April. I never thought in a million years I'd meet a man like Homer.'

Homer gazed down at her, love shining in his eyes. 'Nope, April's right, Nance. I'm the lucky one.'

If only Crawford were here, April thought, the day would be complete.

Just then, the vicar came over to congratulate the happy couple. Mrs Granger was with him, looking surprisingly relaxed considering how hard she'd taken the news.

'April, my dear, how lovely to see you. I hope you brought your major with you to add some glamour to the proceedings?'

'Not today, I'm afraid.'

'Oh well, never mind. I'll have to make do with these two fine fellows.' To April's utter astonishment, she patted both A.J. and Homer on the arm.

Eunice leaned over to her. 'George has won the day,' she whispered. 'My mother can never resist him, and the fact that he loves A.J. means she's started to accept him too. I just wish Father could have been here.'

'He'll be back, my dear. You all think I'm foolish for believing it, but I know in my heart he's still alive.'

The wedding breakfast was held at the hotel across the road. Everyone had pooled their rations, and somehow, A.J. had managed to get hold of a turkey, so they all sat down for a wonderful roast dinner with plenty of wedding toasts and laughter. There was even a cake, baked by Mrs Granger, that was utterly delicious.

Suddenly the door swung open, and a tall figure wearing a side cap rushed in. A.J. was the first to spot him and stood up with a huge grin. 'Crawford!'

April's heart leaped. Crawford was back! She jumped up from the table and rushed over to him. He threw his arm around her shoulder. In his other hand, he was brandishing a bottle of champagne. He let go of April, walked over to A.J. and clasped his hand.

'You think I'd miss my old buddy's wedding? No, sir. We drove through the night to get back in time. And I get to see my girl early as well. And I managed to dig this out. Can't have a wedding without champagne.'

Nancy cheered at that and ordered more glasses from the barman.

Mrs Granger bustled over, fluttering her eyelashes. 'Major, how marvellous. I'm sure we can find you some food and there's plenty of cake.'

Crawford sat down beside April and took her hand. 'So, honey, I realised something while I was away. You want to know what that was?'

April nodded.

'Well . . .' He reached into his pocket and pulled out a small box, and April's heart thumped with excitement.

'I realised that I asked you a very important question before I went away, but I didn't ask properly. So I'm going to do it now.' He opened the box to show a beautiful diamond ring sitting in the middle. He removed it from the box and took April's left hand in his. 'April Harvey, I love you with all my heart. Will you please do me the honour of promising to marry me?'

April, overcome with joy, managed somehow to whisper, 'Yes,' and Crawford slipped the ring on her finger. It sparkled in the light and there was rapturous applause around the table. She stared at it for a moment, then looked back at Crawford.

'It's the most beautiful thing I've ever seen in my life.' She threw her arms around his neck and Crawford kissed her tenderly.

The champagne was poured and George shouted, 'Merry Christmas and here's to strong British–American relationships!'

Everyone raised their glasses and repeated, 'To British–American relationships!'

Then Nancy piped up, 'And here's to us three girls, the G.I. Brides!'

Epilogue

May 1943

April stood in front of the mirror and smiled. Crawford's mother had surprised her by sending April her very own wedding dress. She had been going to wear a lilac suit that she'd managed to buy cheap, so when Crawford had delivered the dress two weeks before, she'd cried with joy. It was, quite simply, the most beautiful dress she'd ever worn. Mrs Beetie had rushed to alter it, and it now fit perfectly. It was white with long sleeves and a fitted bodice that cinched in at the waist, and a full skirt with a lace over-skirt embroidered with tiny violets and studded with seed pearls that finished just above her ankles. A headdress with a long, floaty white veil completed the outfit. Mrs Teague's trusty gold shoes were once again on display, and though the dress was clearly a little old-fashioned, it was so romantic and perfect that April felt like a princess.

Mrs Teague bustled over, looking resplendent in a primrose yellow suit, with a matching hat and a small veil. She looked exactly like the mother of the bride should look, April thought fondly.

'You look breathtakingly beautiful, my love. I've never seen a lovelier bride.'

April smiled and kissed her on the cheek. 'Thank you for everything you've done for me, Mrs Teague. I think you are quite possibly the most marvellous woman in the world.'

Mrs Teague's eyes filled with tears. 'Oh, pish, April. See what you've made me do? I've no time for tears. Come on, the car's waiting.'

They walked out to the car. The neighbours who wouldn't be coming to the wedding stood and applauded April as she walked out, holding a posy of violets to match her dress. She blushed and waved, then settled herself in the car that Crawford had arranged for her.

It took about half an hour to drive to the church, during which time, April was lost in her thoughts. Since that wonderful Christmas Eve when Eunice had got married, life had been busy.

Eunice had given birth to a beautiful baby boy just a month before, which April had helped deliver. They'd named him Alex, and April adored him and couldn't wait to stand as his godmother at his christening next month. As for A.J., he seemed to have completely forgiven Eunice and spent as much time as he could with his new family, who he adored. As for Alex's grandma, she wouldn't hear a word said against the little boy. He filled the void in her heart that had opened when confirmation arrived that her husband had died. It had been a terrible time for the family, but little Alex's arrival had helped soothe some of the pain.

When she arrived at the church, April saw a host of friendly faces waiting for her. Nancy and Homer were standing on the steps, and she grinned at them. Eunice stood beside them, holding Alex, who was fast asleep and looked like a little angel. He really was the most delicious baby she'd ever seen. Inside the church, she knew that some of her hospital friends would be waiting – including Mattie and Jean, and even Sister Mulholland had taken a day's leave especially. April had been touched.

The colonel and Red were also in the congregation, and A.J. would be standing at the altar with Crawford. His choice of best man had caused several raised eyebrows amongst his colleagues, but April was delighted. She loved A.J. and knew how important it was for Crawford to have someone from his past with him. She wished she could have had someone too. She had written a letter to Theo to tell him about her impending marriage. He'd not replied, although Reverend Osborne wrote to wish her happiness. Theo, apparently, was growing stronger, and hopefully could be sent to a convalescent home soon. The fact that he may well die in the home was left unsaid. It was a miracle that he'd lived this long.

April shook her head. Today was a happy day, and although thoughts of Theo were inevitable, it was Crawford she needed to concentrate on.

She looked at Mrs Teague. 'Ready?'

Mrs Teague nodded. If Crawford's choice of best man had raised eyebrows, then April's choice of who was to walk down the aisle with her had too. With no close male relatives, she'd asked Mrs Teague if she'd give her away. Her landlady had sobbed with delight and pride, and now she stood, ramrod straight, arm in arm with her surrogate daughter as they prepared to walk down the aisle. They looked at each other, smiled and nodded, then April walked towards

Crawford, who was standing by the altar, resplendent in the same dress uniform he'd worn at the Thanksgiving dinner when he'd proposed to her. His beautiful green eyes were fixed on her, and she was sure she could see a tear sparkling on his cheek. Her heart swelled. Never could April have imagined such love would enter her life. The sun streaming in through the stained-glass window of the Madonna and child shone on the gold braid on his shoulders, and April suddenly remembered her hope when she'd first seen the window, that it was a sign she'd find her family. And now, she realised that maybe it had been.

The ceremony was a simple one, and when the vicar asked, 'Who gives this woman to be married to this man?' Mrs Teague stepped forward and said firmly, 'Her family and I do.' She turned to April, and with tears in her eyes, lifted her veil. Then she kissed her on the cheek and whispered, 'Be happy, my precious daughter.'

April couldn't prevent the tears welling at that. She clasped Mrs Teague's hand and whispered back, 'Thank you, Mother.'

As Mrs Teague held April's hand towards Crawford, her tears were falling so fast she could barely see. Noticing her distress, Crawford took her shoulders and leaned down and whispered, 'I am honoured to have you as a mother-in-law.' At that Mrs Teague started sobbing in earnest, and April realised that she was not the only one to have found a family. She smiled tremulously at Crawford, her heart full of love, and together they turned to the vicar, ready at last to dedicate their lives to one another.

After the ceremony, April stood on the church steps with her incredibly handsome husband, both being showered with rose petals. She laughed with delight, then looked up at Crawford.

He smiled down into her eyes. 'How do you feel, Mrs Dunbar?'

'Never better, Major Dunbar. The happiest I've ever been! But before we leave, can you come and meet my other mother?'

She pulled him down the steps and around the church, out of sight, and stood before her mother's grave.

April crouched down and carefully laid her bouquet on the gravestone.

'It's my wedding day, Mum, and I wish so much that you and Dad could be here. I've brought Crawford to meet you. He's the most amazing man in the world, and I know you'd love him. So would Dad.

'I'm glad I could get married close to you, Mum. I feel your spirit strongly here. Do you think that's strange? I came to Cornwall searching for my family and found instead that you'd had to cope with loss too, yet you'd managed to find love and start your own family. Your story inspired me to stay strong, and now I'm on the way to creating a whole new future for myself. So, thank you, Mum. Thank you for being strong and brave and not giving up hope. I pray that somewhere you can see me, so happy and content, even in the midst of war. I love you always, Mum.' She kissed her fingers and touched the gravestone, wiping the tears away.

Crawford saluted, then helped her to her feet and they returned to their guests. Once they were again standing on the church steps, April looked out at the small throng of well-wishers. This was what she had been searching for all her life, and though she knew there was uncertainty and danger to be faced, with Crawford by her side, at least she wouldn't have to face it alone. Just as her mother had, she had risen from the depths of despair and created her own happiness. And she vowed that no matter what happened, she would always remember that, even when all hope seems lost, you can find your way back to the light.

Suddenly Crawford turned April towards him and, clasping her by the shoulders, he kissed her deeply while cheers and wolf whistles erupted around them.

'Oy oy, you two. Time enough for that later; we're all starving.'

Giggling, April pulled away and looked over. Nancy was standing there with her hands on her hips and a cheeky grin on her face.

Crawford smiled down at April, then turned. 'As always, Nancy, you're right. The sooner we've eaten, the sooner I can be alone with my wife.' And taking April's hand, they ran down the path towards their future.

Acknowledgements

I would like to acknowledge a few very special ladies.

There were many air force wives who were kind to me. A special thank you to Nancy, Jeanette, Margarita Rosa and Mary Lou for many lessons, especially the haircuts, the beauty tips, the plucked eyebrows, the beautifully made gown for my graduation ball, the Thanksgiving and Christmas recipes for genuine eggnog and cranberry bread. After graduation, thanks to your families for the welcomes to Washington D. C. Virginia, Texas, and Mexico.

Con un abrazo
Eileen.

Welcome to the world of *Eileen Ramsay*!

Keep reading for more from Eileen Ramsay and to discover a recipe that features in this novel.

We'd also like to introduce you to Memory Lane, our special community for the very best of saga writing from authors you know and love and new ones we simply can't wait for you to meet. Read on and join our club!

·MEMORY LANE·

www.MemoryLane.club

About the author

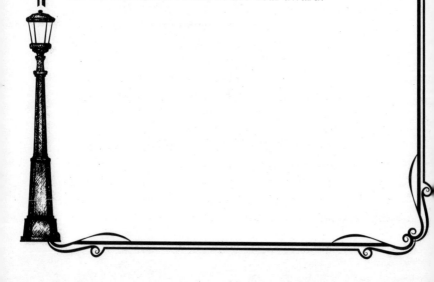

Eileen Ramsay grew up in Dumfriesshire. After graduation she went to Washington D.C., where she taught in private schools for some years, before moving to California with her Scottish husband. There, she raised two sons, finished her Masters Degree, fell in love with Mexico, and published her first short stories and a Regency novel. The family returned to Scotland where Eileen continued to teach and write and to serve – at different times – on the committees of The Society of Authors in Scotland, The Scottish Association of Writers and The Romantic Novelists' Association. In 2004, her novel *Someday, Somewhere* was shortlisted for the Romantic Novel of the Year award.

Dear Reader,

Each book I've written is special to me, but *The G. I. Bride* holds a special place as it's the book that finally allowed me to write about AJ, a real-life inspiration whose mother's support helped me get my first book published.

As many of you know, I have spent a great deal of time in Edinburgh with the U.S. Airforce, and in California with the U.S. marines.

It was in California where we met a marine family who had two children, a nine-year-old boy and a 4-year-old girl. As a mother of two boys, nine and five, we had a lot in common. Their son belonged to a swim club and, strangely enough, our oldest son (a superb swimmer) joined the same club, both of them being trained by the incredible Coach Malone. Every Friday evening our families met at the swimming pool; the two older boys disappeared to the changing rooms, the two moms took the younger children to sit and watch. We became friends. The little girl was called AJ, short for Applejack, and she and our Alistair became inseparable. Little AJ was so kind and gentle, and these became the key characteristics that I wanted my AJ to display in the book. And the friendship between little AJ and our Alistair was the inspiration behind the close friendship between Crawford and AJ in the book. They were the best of friends and nothing could come between them.

The families saw lots of one another as almost every Saturday we travelled all over California to participate in swim meets. And then something happened which was to be extremely important to my future career.

Strolling across the university campus where I was studying, I saw a poster saying that the university was going to host a writing conference with several prominent writers, including Pulitzer Prize winner Michael Shaara and Clive Cussler, the author of *Raise the Titanic*. It also said that wanabee writers could send in a manuscript that would be read and critiqued. I had been trying to write a Regency novel for some time but I didn't own a typewriter and wouldn't have known what to do with it if Santa Claus had dropped it down the chimney. I was definitely a pencil or ballpoint pen writer. At the Friday swim class I must have looked gloomy for Agnes, AJ's mother, asked me what was wrong – I told her. She took my hand as we sat there watching our children and she laughed. 'Honey,' she said. 'I'm a secretary. You come over tomorrow and keep an eye on the kids – (incidentally a word I never use) – and I'll type it up for you.'

I did and she did – and it seemed to take her no time at all. And because of that lovely generous woman I began to think that maybe, just maybe, I could one day be a real writer. I can still remember when she asked me about the story, finishing up with, 'Where did you get that Marquis from, honey?'

'He was in my head,' I said and then her beautiful warm Southern voice floated across to me. 'Well, he's in mine now.' So was created my first novel which I was also allowed to use as part of my Master's Degree.

Thanks to AJ's mother, I signed up for the conference, discovered that Charles Block, a very famous editor, had agreed to read my attempt at a book, and by chance I spent an entire afternoon alone with the incredible Michael Shaara, who told me how he wrote the magnificent Pulitzer prize winning *The Killer Angels*. And then one afternoon, Mr Block was waiting for me outside a classroom. He handed me my manuscript and said, "I think this will go."

It did!

How I wish I knew where the family is now. We moved 6000 miles and AJ's family went where marines had to go. Though the years and miles have separated us, I have never forgotten AJ or her mother, and am delighted to be finally writing a book with a character inspired by that incredible little girl.

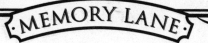

Cheese and Potato Pie

You will need:

1 kg potatoes

2 tablespoons of butter

A dash of milk (optional)

1 white onion

1 garlic clove

125g sweetcorn (canned or frozen and defrosted)

125g frozen peas, defrosted

175g cheddar cheese, grated

4 rashers bacon

A pinch of salt

A pinch of pepper

2 tomatoes, for garnish (optional)

Method:

1. Clean and dice the potatoes, there's no need to peel them, unless you would prefer to. Add to a pan of salted water and boil until soft.
2. Whilst the potatoes are cooking preheat the oven to Gas 5/190 C/Fan 170 C.
3. Peel and dice the onion and crush the garlic. Sauté them both in a little of the butter until softened but not brown.

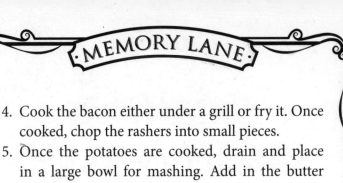

4. Cook the bacon either under a grill or fry it. Once cooked, chop the rashers into small pieces.

5. Once the potatoes are cooked, drain and place in a large bowl for mashing. Add in the butter and the milk (if using), season well with salt and pepper.

6. Stir in the sweetcorn, peas, cooked onion and garlic plus half of the cheese. Spoon this mixture into a large ovenproof dish and, using a fork, smooth the surface.

7. Scatter the bacon and the remaining cheese on top. If using, slice the tomatoes and use to decorate the top.

8. Bake in the oven until the cheese has melted and is a golden-brown colour, approximately 40 minutes.

9. You can try the pie with a variety of different ingredients – try cauliflower, tuna, chopped ham or cream cheese. Share your photos and suggestions at www.facebook.com/MemoryLaneClub

10. Enjoy!

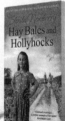